To Jin

Than

support, and friendship

over the years!

Much love,

Bubba

1-18-2010

Finding Alan

by

Jonna Turner

Cover design by Melody Brock

Printed in the United States of America

Scotts Valley, CA

By Jonna Turner

The Desk

New Pictures of an Old Murder, a Highlands Ranch Mystery

The Other Side of Time

Dedicated to the memory of Pauline Lloyd Littler,

Mother and friend.

We all miss you.

Acknowledgments

My heartfelt thanks to all the people who helped to make this book possible. I could not have done it without you!

Editors: Carol Claton, Sharon Frazier, J.D. Hylton, and Diana Yust
Cover design: Melody Brock, Graphic Artist
Format: Tammy Garcia
Legal questions: Scott Atwell, Attorney at Law
Police procedure, U.S.: Sue Kurtz, Sheriff of San Juan County, Colorado
Police procedure, British Columbia: Shannon Renault, Greater Victoria Chamber of Commerce and Kris Kosich, CHRP, Human Resources Manager, Victoria Police Department
Seattle landmarks: Glenn Hampson
LC Smith Tower information: Stephen Willis, Smith Tower Historian
LC Smith Tower lobby tour for J.D. Hylton: Mike Abasi, Security Guard

To all my friends who allowed me to use their names in this book. Thank you! It was fun writing some of you in as 'the bad guy'!

Angela Williams	Anne Barre
Barbara VanNeste	Bill Rathbun
Brent Nelson	Bruce Merrill
Charlie Fore	Christopher Mark Greer
Dave Caldwell	Diana Yust
Dorothea Ellerby	Dylan Conrad
Ed Hickok	Eileen English
Erin Hice	Gaylann Hicks
Judy Huffman	Kathy Sullivan
Keri Kurtz	Lorin Ottonello
Lynette Mulert	Mark Edwards
Marty Martinez	MaryAnne Boruszak
Missy Scruggs	Myra Eldred
Nola Nelson	Patricia Regnier
Ron Ferrari	Sam Tinsley
Samantha Stewart	Sharon Frazier
Shoma Pandit	Sue Coleman
Todd Jones	Tony Eden
Trisha Jorgensen	Wayne Drake

Prologue

Friday, March 11, 1994

Williams returned from the kitchen with a roll of silver duct tape. He ripped off a large piece.

At the tearing sound, Jeagan jumped, raised her head, and watched in numb horror.

He grabbed her hands and jerked them behind her back.

"What are you doing!" She struggled unsuccessfully to free herself from his strong grasp.

"Don't worry about it," he mumbled coldly. "You'll know soon enough." He tore off another piece of the tape and slapped it across her mouth.

She tried to control the rising panic. Her heart pounded in her ears while icy fear spread through her body. Turning, she strained to look out the windows of the family room to see if Madison was still there. He was their only hope. If he didn't help them, no one could. How could she have been so wrong about him and not have seen through him?

While Agnes held Isabel, Williams ripped more tape and bound Isabel's hands.

"No, please!" Isabel cried.

Ignoring her, he pulled another piece of the tape across her mouth.

"Let's get them out to the van," Agnes said.

Williams grabbed the handles of Isabel's wheelchair and rolled it toward the kitchen while Agnes pulled Jeagan from the floor and pushed her after them.

Once outside, Jeagan looked toward Madison, who was bent forward with his head in his hands. "Madison!" Jeagan tried to scream through the tape.

"Don't waste your breath." Agnes jammed the gun in Jeagan's back while she steered her through the breezeway toward the garage. "Madison wouldn't help you even if he could hear you."

In the garage, Williams lifted Isabel's slight body into the rear seat of the van and secured the seat belt around her. Her muffled sobs and tear-filled eyes pleaded for him to let her go. He again disregarded her cries and calmly placed her wheelchair in the rear.

Agnes pushed Jeagan, who kicked and struggled, into the van, slapped her hard across the face, and held her while Williams bound her feet with the duct tape and strapped her in the seat.

The door closed with a *thunk!* Williams moved around the side of the van and climbed behind the wheel.

"I'll follow you," Agnes said through the open window. She walked over to her red Cadillac Eldorado, which was parked next to the van.

After a quick nod, Williams backed out of the garage. Sedately, he drove around the side of the house and down the driveway.

Tears burned Jeagan's eyes. They spilled over onto the raw handprint on her cheek. She tried to blink away the tears so she could see Madison out the window. He hadn't moved; he still sat on the lounge chair with his head in his hands. *He's useless*, she thought. *He cares too much to participate in what they're doing to us but too little to stop it.*

She turned toward Isabel. In shock, Isabel stared straight ahead, her eyes glazed and unfocused.

Jeagan thought about her father. *I'm sorry, Dad! I love you. I wish I had listened to you instead of running off mad at you.* A cold terror gripped her body. When she realized she would never see her father again, especially since they had parted on bad terms, she forced herself to focus on how she could stop Agnes and Williams.

Her mind raced to find some way of escape even as Williams maneuvered the van over the rutted country road behind the estate. Black-and-white cattle grazing in a pasture watched in idle curiosity as the van passed.

After about a mile, the road dead-ended into water. Williams stopped at the water's edge, got out of the van, and walked around to the rear to wait for Agnes, who soon pulled in behind him.

Jeagan searched for something sharp inside the van. She spotted a piece of metal sticking out of the floor that held the seat belt in place. The edge appeared rough enough to eventually tear a hole in the tape if she could reach it. She stretched her bound hands around to the seat belt fastener and pressed the button to unlatch it. When it popped open, she shifted her body toward the floor and angled herself so she could work her wrists against the metal. The tape tightened and dug into her wrists. Heedless, she continued to saw it against the rough edge.

Seconds later, the rear door of the van flew open. Williams reached in, ripped the tape off Jeagan's feet, pulled her out of the van, and shoved her into the front passenger seat. She struck out at him with her elbows and feet, but Agnes grabbed her arms while Williams strapped the seat belt around her. Next, Williams moved Isabel to the driver's seat and strapped the seat belt around her as well.

Jeagan screamed, the sound muffled through the duct tape. *No, this can't be happening!* She struggled wildly against the seat belt and tape. Suddenly, her world went black. The last things she remembered were bright sparkling lights and a sharp pain in the back of her head.

Agnes jerked the tape off Jeagan's hands and mouth and then slammed the door.

Williams waved his hand in front of Isabel's face. She didn't even blink. He pulled the tape off her hands and mouth; she would be no problem.

He reached over Isabel's limp body, started the van, shifted it into drive, backed away quickly, and watched the van coast down the embankment into the cold, rain-swollen lake. Within seconds, the van twisted and bobbed. It slowly sank into the dark, murky water.

Chapter One

Jeagan bolted upright and screamed. "No!" Where was she? Frantically, she scanned the room. *Home. I'm home now. It's all over. I'm safe.*

Tears stung her eyes as she gasped for breath. She really was home and safe. Tension slowly melted away while she sank against the headboard. She closed her eyes and let her breathing and heart rate slow down.

When she felt calmer, she got up, made her way into the bathroom, and leaned on the vanity. Cold water from the tap helped to cool her flushed cheeks. She blotted the water with a hand towel, watching the reflection that stared back at her. To the girl in the mirror, she said, "It's over...done. Those nightmares have got to stop!" She took a deep breath, turned on the cold water again, filled the vanity cup, and drank it all. Maybe a nap hadn't been such a good idea, but she'd been tired after her early morning flight from Memphis to Denver. The idea of an afternoon nap on her own bed in her own townhouse in Highlands Ranch had been irresistible.

She placed her palms on the vanity. "Get a grip!" Standing up straight, she inhaled deeply, and headed for the kitchen. A Coke was what she needed and maybe a few cookies, if she could find any in the pantry. She'd been gone for almost two weeks, so she couldn't remember exactly what she did and didn't have.

Almost afraid to look inside, she pulled on the black refrigerator door. *Hmm!* Thankfully, nothing green or furry jumped out at her, but she spotted several plastic containers, which might need to be discarded *in toto* without being opened. Coke cans lined a shelf on the door. *Ahh!* She took one, popped the top, and took a long drink. The instant charge

4

felt good. She bumped the refrigerator door closed with her hip before turning toward the pantry. A box of stale vanilla wafers sat on a shelf, but she dug into them anyway and stuffed one into her mouth. Box and Coke in hand, she headed outside to the patio.

It was good to be home. Now in her own backyard, it was hard to believe she'd ever been in any danger. Those who had hurt her were securely locked away in a jail near Oxford, Mississippi and would be standing trial soon. She hoped against hope that she wouldn't have to return for the trial, especially since Williams and Agnes had been caught in the act of attempting to drown her and Isabel. And, Madison had confessed to his part in the kidnapping and attempted murder.

She set the can and cookie box on the glass-topped patio table and pulled out a chair. After she sat down, propped her feet on another chair, and leaned back, she felt the warmth of the March sun, set in the cobalt sky, re-energize her chilled body. Unhurriedly, she munched on the cookies and finished her Coke. Then, she got up and roamed around the yard to see what was about to bloom. The lilac bushes wore hundreds of tight red buds, bright green tulip leaves pushed through the layer of bark mulch, and fuzzy caterpillar-like pods dangled from aspen branches, soon to be followed by leaves. Hopefully, a late spring snow wouldn't kill all the early growth.

Her thoughts turned to Roger Sanderlin, the private investigator her father had hired to keep an eye on her while she was in Memphis. The man who, thank God, had ultimately followed her from Memphis to Oxford and rescued Isabel and her from the submerged van. A shiver ran up her spine when she allowed the reality of what had almost happened to come crashing back.

Stop it! She walked back inside and closed the French doors. *It's over!* The empty cookie box and Coke can clunked loudly when she dropped them into the trash can. It was time to unpack.

Returning to her bedroom, she pulled clothes out of the suitcase—sorting by laundry and dry cleaning—and remembered how she had accused Roger of stalking her in Memphis, even had reported him to hotel security and the police. She smiled when she realized how foolish The Peabody Hotel security guard must have felt when Roger whipped out his private investigator's identification and informed the guard that her father had hired him. Well, how was she to know!

After the fact, she was glad her father had thought she was running off on a tangent when she flew to Memphis to investigate a possible murder. A murder she believed had occurred fifty years earlier. But, what else was she supposed to think when she had visions of events surrounding the murder when she sat at the antique desk she had recently bought? It was, she soon found out, the same desk young Isabel had used at The Peabody Hotel at the time her lover was killed all those years ago.

Thank goodness Jeagan's father had had the good sense to send Roger after her. But, she had been right—even if being right had almost gotten her killed.

Her investigation had proved Robert Lloyd, Isabel's father, *had* indeed shot her lover fifty years earlier and dumped his body in the Mississippi River, never to be found. Isabel had never known what happened to Alan. Nearly nine months afterwards, under an assumed name, she had given birth to a baby boy in a hospital outside Memphis.

Robert Lloyd had used his considerable wealth and influence to ensure that Isabel was told her baby was stillborn, when in fact the child was alive and well and sold to a Seattle attorney. The attorney who arranged for the baby boy to be adopted by a family far away from Memphis, so the prominent name of Lloyd would not be sullied.

Though she had almost lost her life doing so, Jeagan had uncovered the truth. Isabel now knew what happened to her fiancé all those years ago and knew that her son had been alive at birth. In her early seventies, Isabel had a son who would now be almost fifty.

After the dust had settled from Jeagan's and Isabel's narrow escape from drowning in runoff from Sardis Lake, Isabel had commissioned Roger to find her long-lost son. Tonight over dinner, Jeagan and Roger would discuss how to begin the search for Alan—the name Isabel would have given him—with the only known clue: a letter from a Seattle attorney addressed to Isabel's father. The letter was dated April of 1945, the month Alan was born, and stated that a check for ten thousand dollars was enclosed.

Almost fifty years had passed. Would Alan, or whatever he was named by his adoptive parents, still be alive? If so, was he living in the Seattle area? Would he even want to know about his birth mother? So many questions—questions for which Jeagan and Roger were determined to find answers.

Jeagan switched mental gears. She found it ironic that Roger wanted to have dinner at Pappadeaux, the restaurant where she had ended her engagement to Brandon two weeks earlier. But, it was one of her favorite restaurants, so she didn't object when Roger suggested it. This time, she felt she could eat and enjoy herself while they talked about 'the case.'

She glanced at the clock on her nightstand. It was still early, so she continued to unpack and put away shoes and toiletries while her mind raced. Lots to do. Her boss, Lorin Ottonello. She had to call him to explain the situation. Her job as a technical writer was important to her, but working with Roger to find Alan for Isabel took precedence over her job at Caldwell & Ottonello Engineering.

The suitcases soon were empty. *Stop procrastinating! Call him and get it over with.* After all, Lorin had been very understanding when she had called him from the Oxford Mississippi Community General Hospital and told him about almost drowning and her concussion. But, she'd been gone almost a week longer than planned. He'd expected her at work on Monday, even if only part-time for a while.

She wondered if he would be there today, a Saturday. A glance at the small calendar on the nightstand told her that he would be there, considering the office was open on the first and third Saturdays of the month during their busy season. She sat on the edge of her bed, gathered her resolve, and reached for the phone. *Brrng!* Startled, she jumped like she'd touched something hot. No chance to say hello after she picked up the receiver.

"Jeagan! I just found out what happened to you. Are you okay?"

Brandon! Jeagan's blood pressure shot up ten points. "Hello, Brandon," she said as politely as she could manage. "I'm fine. I just got home as a matter of fact."

"I'm sure glad to hear that. I ran into your dad at the bank a few minutes ago, and he told me what happened. I'm really sorry you got involved with those people down there and almost got yourself killed. I mean, if you'd listened to me in the first place and returned that blasted desk, none of this would've happened. You'd still be wearing my ring, and things would be the way they were before."

Jeagan was flabbergasted. How dare he? The way they were before! "Brandon, I did what I needed to do. I was right about the desk and the fifty-year-old murder."

"Yes." Brandon hesitated as if thinking. "I'll give you that. You...you were right about the murder, but still you should've listened to me and stayed out of someone else's drama."

How could I have ever thought I loved this man? Jeagan wondered. "Brandon, you're unbelievable, you know that?"

"Well, ignoring your tone of voice, I'm taking that as a compliment. I'd like to see you. I've really missed you. How about dinner tonight? I'll even cook for you."

"No, thanks, Brandon," Jeagan said, although it had always been hard for her to resist him when he was trying to be sweet, even when she knew he was self-centered and egotistical. "I...I already have a date for tonight."

"Oh, it's like that," he said, a hard edge to his voice.

"Brandon, it's not *like* anything." It struck her again why she had broken their engagement. "I believe I returned your ring before I left for Memphis, so it's not like anything. We're not engaged anymore, and I don't owe you an explanation."

"Nevermind! Just forget it! I'll talk to you later." With that, Brandon slammed down the phone.

Jeagan jerked the phone away from her ear and returned it to the charger. *How could I ever have been stupid enough to think I had a future with him?* She reached for the phone again. Once again, it rang before she could pick it up. Grand Central Station!

"Hello?" Jeagan said warily, afraid it was Brandon calling again.

"Hey you!" Jeagan recognized Keri Kurtz's voice, a fellow technical writer and close friend from C&O.

"Hi, Keri. I was just going to call Lorin. How's it going?"

"It's wild over here! Lucie's quit and Sharon's taken some time off and gone to Alaska to be with Bruce. He got hurt in a plane crash."

"Good grief, Keri! What happened?"

"He went on one of those week-long fishing/camping trips with Bill and Charlie. The ones where outfitters fly you in by one of those planes that lands on water—"

"You mean a seaplane?"

"Yeah. Anyway, the guys flew into the wilderness area okay, but when they were picked up at the end of the week, the pilot clipped the tops of some trees trying to fly out. The plane crashed."

"You're kidding!"

"Nope. The guys were pretty banged up, but I don't think any of them was hurt badly enough to keep them from going again next year."

"I leave for two weeks, and the place falls apart."

Keri laughed. "You're right about that. And, I hear you almost got yourself killed!"

"Not on purpose. Fortunately, I was unconscious when they tried to drown me, so I don't remember much about it."

Keri let out a dry laugh. "You call that fortunate?"

"Considering the alternative, I guess I do." Jeagan shivered. "So... with Lucie gone and Sharon out, who's helping you hold down the fort?"

"Just Erin and me for now. Hope you're going to tell me you'll be back here soon."

"Well, like I said, I was about to phone Lorin when Brandon called and then you called."

"Brandon? I thought he was past history... bad Karma... yesterday's old news."

Jeagan chuckled. It felt good to laugh. "He is. Believe me."

"That's good. He's...well, you know how I feel about him."

"I know *exactly* how you feel about him, Keri. Shyness isn't one of your virtues. Anyway, getting back to the workload, I'm afraid I won't be able to help you out."

"What!"

"I'm sorry, Keri. I'll be out a little longer."

"No, don't tell me that, Jeagan!" Keri whined. "I'm working ten to twelve hours a day and still can't get it all done. We're expecting a Request for Proposals from the Department of Energy this week. The proposal will be six to ten volumes. We need you, Jeag!"

Jeagan didn't want to let her co-workers down when they were in a pinch, but wasn't finding Alan more important than a proposal? "Well, let me talk to Lorin, if he's there."

"Okay, but I better see your pretty face around here soon, or I'm coming after you."

"You're the greatest, Keri!" Jeagan laughed. "I'll see you soon."

Keri switched Jeagan over to the operator who placed Jeagan on hold while she tried to locate Lorin.

"He didn't answer the page, Jeagan," the operator told her when she came back on the line a couple of minutes later. "He must be in a meeting. I'll grab him as soon as he comes out and have him call you."

Jeagan thanked the woman, hung up the phone, and went into the bathroom where she turned on the bathtub faucet full blast. A long, leisurely, hot bath was what she needed. She'd missed soaking in a tub while she was in the hospital with only a shower in her room.

Adding a sprinkle of lavender essential oil, Jeagan peeled off her clothes, stepped into the tub, and lay back. She closed her eyes and breathed in the pungent scent of lavender. *What I need is a massage,* she thought. *Wonder if I can get an appointment in the next few days at Shear Art?* Just thinking about how Judy could work her magic on knotted muscles with hot stones and scented oils and soft music helped Jeagan to relax.

* * *

At seven o'clock, she answered the door. Roger stood on the porch grinning. Dressed in an olive silk shirt and khakis with his sandy hair falling over his forehead, he reminded her of someone□a young Robert Redford? Well, maybe a cross between him and Matthew McConaughey. She smiled to herself. *Brandon who?*

"Look at you!" Roger stepped inside.

Pleased, Jeagan smiled and closed the door. "At least I look better than I did the last time you saw me."

"Well," Roger teased. "I was kinda getting used to that white bandage on your head and the hospital gown with the seven dwarfs on it."

"Ha! Ha!" Jeagan frowned. "Not funny." She picked up her handbag and checked her hair in the mirror over the entrance hall table.

Roger helped her on with her black wool coat and opened the door. "Seafood okay with you?"

"My favorite." Jeagan buttoned her light-weight coat over her 'little black dress'—the same one, she realized, she'd worn the night she broke up with Brandon. *Well,* she thought, *Roger isn't Brandon, and I'm not engaged to him.* No worries about a breakup tonight.

After closing the door, Roger said, "I just had an interesting phone call from a buddy of mine. He's retired from the Seattle Police Department."

"Think he can help us find Alan?" Jeagan walked with Roger along the sidewalk to his black Range Rover.

Roger opened the SUV door. "Don't know, but he's interested in trying." He closed the door after Jeagan slid inside. When he went around to the driver's side and got in, he continued. "His name's Will Thompson. He was with the force for more than twenty years, so he knows a lot of the legal eagles and politicos in Seattle. He might be able to dig up some information for us."

"That's great!" Jeagan fastened her seat belt. "I sure hope we can find Alan. Isabel's had enough heartache and pain in her life. She's due a little happiness before… ."

Roger started the car and turned his head to back out of the parking space. "You mean before she dies?" He chuckled. "Don't think she's going anywhere for a while. She's a tough ol' gal."

"I hope you're right." Jeagan remembered when she had first seen Isabel in the lobby of the Orpheum Theater in Memphis. Had that only been eleven days ago? It seemed like a lifetime ago. Isabel had been sitting in a wheelchair looking content, confident, and for all the world— well, regal. That was before Jeagan had turned Isabel's life upside down by telling her that her father had murdered her fiancé.

"Did you talk to your boss?" Roger asked. He checked the side mirror before he pulled into traffic on Highlands Ranch Parkway going east.

"Finally. I didn't think Lorin was ever going to call back, but he did around four-thirty."

"How'd he take the news that you weren't coming back for a while?"

"He wasn't very happy about it, especially since they're so short-handed right now with Sharon out. I really hated to ask for more time off."

"But he was okay with you taking the time?"

In the side mirror, Jeagan watched behind her as the last of the sunset edged the purple mountain tops in orange. It was good to see a Colorado sunset again.

Roger glanced at Jeagan. "Are you with me?"

"Oh, sorry," she said. "I'm still a little spacey. Uh…after I told Lorin how important this is to Isabel, he gave me another week off."

"A week? Is that all?"

"Afraid so. I need to be at work a week from Monday. That's all the time he said he could spare me. They have some really big proposals coming up, and they need me before the first of April."

"So…that gives us about eight days to find Alan."

"Something like that," Jeagan confirmed. "Think we can do it?"

Roger crossed University and continued on Colorado Boulevard toward County Line Road. "We'll give it our best shot." He checked the clock on the dash. "Our dinner reservation's for seven. Looks like we'll be a little early."

"We could sit on the patio and have a drink since it's such a beautiful evening," Jeagan commented. March could be one of the snowiest months in Denver, but today had been an exceptionally balmy day. Crabapple trees were covered in red buds about to open and the forsythia would soon be covered in bright, yellow flowers. Spring was slow coming to Colorado, at least compared to Memphis, Jeagan realized, but when it finally made its appearance, she knew how beautiful it was going to be.

"That works," Roger agreed.

When they arrived at the restaurant, Roger seated Jeagan on the patio at a black wrought-iron table before he went to check in with the hostess. "If a waiter comes by," he said, "order a glass of merlot for me."

"Okay." She listened to the quiet splashing of the waterfall in the center of the patio area while she looked around at the other couples seated on benches or at tables enjoying cocktails. Had it been less than two weeks since she'd met her dad and Brandon here for dinner and had made a fool of herself by stomping out like a bratty teenager? She sat up straighter. Well, yes, she had, but she'd been provoked by her patronizing ex-fiancé and her father. *Stop thinking about it*, she thought. *That's past history.*

"What can I get for you?" a short, dark-haired waiter asked.

"Oh," Jeagan said, startled. "I'll have a glass of Asti Spumante."

"Martini & Rossi okay?"

"That's fine."

Roger returned to the table before the waiter left. He ordered his favorite merlot. "Our table will be ready in a few minutes," he told Jeagan while he pulled out a chair and sat down.

"Why the long face?" Roger asked after the waiter left.

Jeagan shook her head. "Just remembering the last time I was here."

"When you returned good ol' Brandon's engagement ring?"

Jeagan nodded. "That was a particularly black night for me." She tried to put it out of her mind. "But, let's not talk about Brandon. When do we leave for Seattle?"

Roger leaned back in his chair. "Is tomorrow soon enough?"

Chapter Two

"Wow! That was quick. Hope you booked an afternoon flight. I've got ironing to do."

"You'll just have to go wrinkled. The flight's at 7:45 AM."

Jeagan grimaced. "Not much time to get ready." Well, she could sleep on the plane.

"Thought you wanted to find Alan?" Roger teased.

"I do, but I'm—" Jeagan looked at him to see the smile that lit his face and the way the dimple on his right cheek showed when he laughed. *Oh no!* she thought. *You just broke off an engagement to someone you thought was perfect until you got to know him. Don't get yourself involved with someone else, even if he is a Robert Redford look-alike.*

Before Jeagan could say anything else, the waiter appeared with their wine. She thanked him and reached for her glass. "Mmm. That's good," she commented after a sip.

After Roger tasted his wine, he said, "I'll be by about a quarter to six in the morning."

Jeagan groaned, figuring out how early she would have to get up.

"No whining. All you have to do is throw some jeans in a suitcase. Maybe an umbrella since we'll be in Seattle. Oh, and maybe a sexy nightgown or two."

Jeagan laughed and raised her hand defensively. "All right, you! Stop right there. There will be no sexy nightgowns. Besides, I sleep in a big Broncos jersey, number 84 to be exact. And, that brings up hotel rooms. I assume you have booked us into a respectable hotel, in separate rooms."

"Naturally, but I asked for adjoining rooms." Roger's eyes twinkled. "Just in case you get scared during the night or need to borrow a toothbrush," he waved his hands for emphasis, "or something."

It was good to see the smile on Roger's face and to feel lighthearted. "As long as there's a lock on my side of the adjoining door."

The hostess walked up. "Your table is ready."

"Thanks." Roger stood and pulled Jeagan's chair out for her. "You're no fun," he whispered against her hair.

"I can be when I want to be," she whispered back.

When they were seated inside by a window, which faced west toward the Rockies, Jeagan took the offered menu and scanned it.

"How about an appetizer to start?" asked the waiter, freckle-faced with bright copper-colored hair.

"Oysters sound good." Roger looked at Jeagan with a question in his eyes. "Tell me you like oysters."

"Absolutely," Jeagan answered.

"Thank goodness," Roger said trying to look serious. "I could never travel thirteen hundred miles with someone who didn't like oysters."

"Jeagan?" a voice said behind her.

Startled, Jeagan turned around. "Brandon." *Oh, no!* "What are you doing here? Are you following me?"

Brandon, dressed impeccably as usual in a starched white shirt, navy wool suit, and colorful silk tie, shrugged. "How could I be following you when I've been here for an hour sitting at the bar with some of the guys from the office?" He pointed toward the bar.

Jeagan turned her head and noticed about five pairs of eyes looking their way from the bar.

"Aren't you going to introduce me to your date?" Brandon asked. He rested his hand possessively on Jeagan's shoulder.

"Uh," Jeagan stammered, flustered and angry. She shrugged his hand off her shoulder.

Roger stood and offered his hand. "Roger Sanderlin."

"Brandon Montgomery, Jeagan's fiancé." He reached around Jeagan to shake hands.

Jeagan jerked her head to look up at him. "Ex, Brandon. You left off the 'ex.' "

Brandon dismissed her comment. "Only a matter of time before you'll be wearing this again." He pulled out the engagement ring Jeagan had worn only a few weeks before.

Incredulous, she said, "I can't believe you're carrying that ring around with you."

Roger cleared his throat. "If you'll excuse us, Brandon, I believe our oysters have arrived."

A waiter set a platter on the table and asked if Brandon would be joining them.

"No," Jeagan retrieved her napkin, which had slid off her lap to the floor, snapped it, and spread it across her lap.

Brandon patted her on the shoulder. "Well, I'll let you two get on with your dinner. I'll see you later, Jeagan." He made to leave and then turned around, a sly grin on his face. "Nice meeting you, Roger."

"Same here." Roger sat down again. "Good-looking guy."

"Don't let his looks fool you. Under that expensive suit lies a heart of black coal."

Nonchalantly, Roger said, "Seems determined to get you back. Can't blame him for that." He dipped an oyster into cocktail sauce.

Jeagan picked up a fork and jabbed at an oyster. The shell spun, clattered against the tray, and sailed off the table, barely missing a passing waiter who ducked just in time. Jeagan, her face a brilliant shade of red, apologized to the waiter. She mumbled something unintelligible to vent her frustration and got up to retrieve the shell with her napkin.

Roger calmly dipped another oyster. When Jeagan sat down again and placed the napkin on the table, he said, "So, eat out in public often?"

Jeagan's face broke into a smile, and then a laugh finished off the remaining anger. Flashes of Julia Roberts in *Pretty Woman*—when she tried to open a clam (or was it a snail?) shell that flew across the room—ran through her mind. "Slippery little devil," she said, mimicking Julia Roberts, between giggles.

Roger stopped a passing waitress. "Excuse me, could this lady have a clean napkin, please?"

"Of course," the waitress replied. She removed Jeagan's napkin and returned momentarily with a fresh one.

"Now," Roger said, "Where were we?"

Jeagan took a long drink from her wine glass and settled in her chair, determined to relax and not let Brandon spoil her evening. Movement at the bar caught her attention. She glanced up. Brandon looked their way and saluted her as he left the restaurant with his co-workers.

Good! She ignored him, thankful she could now eat in peace.

"I believe we were talking about our trip to Seattle." She squeezed fresh lemon onto an oyster and dipped it. When she swallowed, she continued. "I can't believe him."

"Forget him." Roger dipped another oyster and added extra horseradish. "He'll get the message eventually that you're done with him. Just say 'no' when he calls."

"Ahh. The old 'just say no' trick." Jeagan nodded.

"Yep. If a guy hears it enough, he finally gets the message."

"I'll bet you haven't heard it too many times," Jeagan teased.

"I've had my share of being turned down."

Curious, Jeagan asked, "Have you ever been engaged?"

"Once," Roger said. Jeagan watched a shadow pass over his face.

She placed her fork on her plate. "What happened?"

Roger downed the remainder of his wine as if to fortify himself. He set the glass on the table and looked at Jeagan, anger sparking in his eyes. "Angela was killed in a crosswalk downtown on her way to work. Some guy in a black SUV ran a red light and hit her."

"Oh, Roger, I'm sorry." Jeagan reached out to touch his hand.

"The guy didn't stop. Just kept on going. The police never found him."

"When did it happen?"

"Three years ago." He continued, his green eyes misty with hurt. "I'd still like to find the guy."

"Didn't anyone get a license number?"

Roger shook his head. "It was early in the morning, about seven. Angela was on her way to work at *The Post*. She'd interviewed one of the top executives at U.S. West the day before, after she'd got wind of a possible buyout. She was anxious to dig into the story and scoop *The News*. I remember how excited she was." Memory glazed Roger's eyes.

Not knowing what to say, Jeagan sat still. She remembered how it hurt losing her mother. Not the same but still a deep loss.

"Excuse me a minute." Roger got up from the table.

Jeagan watched him stride toward the restrooms at the rear of the restaurant. *Another reason*, she thought, *not to become involved with him.* He was still mourning the loss of his fiancée.

"I'm sorry, Jeagan," Roger said when he returned after a few minutes. His face was damp. He'd obviously splashed cold water on it. "I get mad all over again when I think about the fact that someone ran her down and just kept going."

"Don't apologize. You have every right to be angry."

"If I could only find the guy and get my hands on him."

"You'll find him, Roger." Again, Jeagan touched his hand reassuringly. "I know you will."

Roger visibly settled down as if by effort. "Yes. I'll find him someday. Then, I'll have closure, and he'll be behind bars where he belongs."

For the next few minutes, Jeagan and Roger worked on the salads, which the waiter brought after he cleared away the oyster shells. Neither spoke until a slim, thirtyish, dark-haired woman stopped by the table.

"Hi, Roger," she said, a wide grin on her face.

Roger, his fork in mid-air, looked up. He smiled and laid his fork on his plate. "Shelley? What're you doing here?" He pushed his chair back and stood. Shelley wrapped her arms around Roger's neck and kissed him on the lips. Roger, obviously caught by surprise, placed his hands on her arms and gently pushed her away.

She laughed. "I came in from Dallas this morning to see Mom and Dad and to get in some skiing. Imagine seeing you here. How *are* you?" Shelley cut her coffee-colored eyes at Jeagan.

"Good." Roger noted the cold look Shelley aimed at Jeagan. "Uh...Jeagan, this is Shelley Boswick, Angela's sister. Shelley, this is Jeagan Christensen."

"Nice to meet you, Shelley. Roger told me about your sister. I'm so sorry about what happened."

"Yes, I'm sure you are," Shelley said, her tone flat and icy. "I see you are moving on, Roger," she added bluntly.

"I—" Roger started.

"No. It's not like that," Jeagan said quickly. "Roger and I are working on a missing person's case. We're leaving in the morning for Seattle to search for a man who was taken from his mother and given up for adoption after she was told he was stillborn." She stopped, her face reddening. "I'm sorry. I'm babbling."

"How touching," Shelley commented—her voice still like liquid ice—and slid her hand up Roger's arm and onto his shoulder. "Call me when you get back in town. I'll be here for a week or two. You've still got my number, don't you?" she crooned.

Roger, embarrassment flushing his tanned face, nodded. "Yes, I've still got your number, Shelley."

So have I, Jeagan thought.

After Shelley detached herself from Roger and walked away, Jeagan said, "Which sister were you engaged to?"

Roger laughed. "She's a real nut case. She was always jealous of anything, or anyone, her sister had. When she found out Angela and I were engaged, she started calling me and telling me Angela was seeing someone else and had never been faithful to anybody and would never be faithful to me."

"Did you ever go out with Shelley?"

"Are you kidding? She's a vampire. I'd be afraid to be alone with her for more than five minutes."

Jeagan laughed. She couldn't imagine Roger being afraid of anyone or anything. She watched him dig into his salad.

He took a few more bites, wiped his mouth, and pushed his plate away. After he rested his forearms on the table, he said, "Enough of my past and yours."

"You're right," Jeagan said, thoughtful. "But maybe we could get Brandon and Shelley together. They'd be a great match. Egotistical jerk and vampiress."

Roger laughed. "Match made in heaven. All you'd need to do is tell Shelley you're still engaged to Brandon, and she'd be after him in a flash." He reached over and covered Jeagan's hand with his. "But, let's forget them. We have a job to do with a short time to do it. I've got us booked at the... ." He pulled a folded piece of paper out of his shirt pocket and opened at it. "We're at the Waterfront Marriott."

Jeagan's eyebrows rose. "Marriott? Isn't that going to be pricey?"

"I've got a nice expense account for this job, so don't worry about the money. Isabel will get her money's worth out of us."

"Okay." Jeagan watched while the waitress placed their entrees on the table. She couldn't wait to bite into her shrimp and loaded baked potato. *Real food!* She tried to forget the pain and the hospital food she'd had at the Oxford hospital. Although not bad, it was generally tasteless. But, then, she'd been lucky to be alive; therefore, any food was good food.

"Still with me?" Roger studied Jeagan's face.

"Oh. Yeah, sure. Just enjoying this heavenly food."

"Well," Roger cut into his ahi tuna, "if you like seafood, Seattle ought to be right up your alley."

After dinner, Roger drove Jeagan home. Both were silent, full from dinner and thinking about the coming trip.

"Have you been to Seattle before?" he asked Jeagan while he walked her to her door.

"No. But, I hear it's beautiful. Dad has told me about his business trips up there."

"It can be beautiful when it's not raining. I checked the forecast earlier today. We might get lucky with the weather."

"Well, thanks for dinner." Jeagan unlocked her door. Uncomfortable, not knowing what to do when she didn't feel like this was a date, but maybe more of a business dinner, she stuck out her hand.

Roger grinned and took her hand. He pulled her to him and kissed her on the cheek. "See you in the morning—early." He released her and stuffed his hands in his pockets as he skipped down the steps and loped across the sidewalk.

"'Night," Jeagan called.

Roger waved before he got into his Range Rover. She watched him drive away.

The door closed and locked behind her, she kicked off her shoes, grabbed them by the sling straps, and headed for her bedroom. When she dropped them in the closet and her handbag on the vanity, she turned toward her room. The message light on the phone blinked red.

She frowned. "That better not be Brandon again," she muttered while she crossed the room. After pressing the message recall button, she heard the mature, cultured, southern male voice of someone who identified himself as Mark Edwards, Isabel Lloyd's attorney.

"Isabel," he informed Jeagan, "has had a heart attack. She has spoken of you often recently while we've been working on her new will, so I thought you'd want to know. She's at Methodist Hospital Central in the Intensive Care Unit. Please call me on my cellphone when you get this message. If I'm not available, you can call the ICU."

Chapter Three

Jeagan sat down on the bed as the message ended with the attorney's phone number and the phone number for ICU. *Poor Isabel. The strain of the last two weeks must have been too much for her. We've got to find Alan before it's too late.* She dialed the number for the hospital.

"ICU. Kathy Sullivan speaking," a soft southern voice said.

"Yes. I'm calling from Denver to check on a friend of mine, Isabel Lloyd. Can you tell me how she is?"

"I'm sorry. I can't give out patient information except to authorized family members," the nurse said.

"But, my name is Jeagan Christensen. I'm a friend of hers, and I'm sure—"

"I wish I could help you, ma'am, but legally I can't." She paused. "Can you hold on for a minute?"

"Of course." While waiting, Jeagan heard sounds of papers being shuffled and a doctor being paged over the PA. She also heard the nurse talking to someone.

Momentarily, the nurse came back on the line. "Sorry to keep you waiting, Ms. Christensen. There's someone here who can help you. I'll put him on."

"Thank you," Jeagan said.

"Miss Christensen?" a male voice said. Jeagan recognized the voice of the attorney who had called earlier.

"Yes. Is this Mr. Edwards?"

"Yes," he replied. "Thank you for calling. I thought you'd want to know about Isabel."

"Yes, I do. How is she?" Jeagan asked.

"She's in surgery right now. It will be a while before we know anything."

"What happened?" Jeagan asked.

"She was at her church practicing a piano solo she was supposed to play on Sunday when she started having chest pains. Luckily, her friend, Barbara VanNeste, was with her at the time. Barbara's the church secretary. She called an ambulance."

"Thank God someone was with her," Jeagan commented.

"Yes," Mark Edwards added. "That certainly helped. If her friend hadn't been with her, we might have lost Isabel."

Jeagan ended the call after she made Mr. Edwards promise to call her as soon as he had any news. She'd become very fond of Isabel and didn't want to lose her. And, Jeagan had to admit, she felt guilty because of all the emotional and physical pain Isabel had suffered after finding out what had happened to her fiancé in 1944.

No wonder Isabel was now in the hospital with heart problems. Over the course of a few days, she'd found out, from Jeagan, that her father had betrayed her in the worst possible way.

Jeagan had no idea why she'd had flashes of the fifty-year-old murder of Alan McCarter when she sat at the antique desk, when obviously many people had sat at the desk over the years. But, for whatever reason, the images from the past had been shown to her and she had felt compelled to find out if what she had seen was real or if she was losing her mind. Her discoveries had definitely stirred up a hornet's nest.

While Isabel was thrilled to know her son had not died at birth, Isabel's older sister, Agnes, was not.

Agnes knew the truth. She'd known for many years what her father had done to her sister and resented the fact that he'd left his entire estate to Isabel to make amends, in part, for ruining her life. Agnes had waited all these years to inherit what she felt was rightfully hers, if not for herself, then for her children. Now, Jeagan had spoiled her plan with her determination to find Isabel's son, the missing heir.

So now, Isabel deserved some happiness, and Jeagan intended to make that happen. Finding Alan was Jeagan's and Roger's job—right now.

Jeagan hopped up from the bed. The clock on her nightstand read nine-fifteen. She set it for four-thirty to give herself time to grab a quick shower and coffee before she left in the morning. Not much time for sleep so she knew she'd better get busy. She turned on the television and checked the Weather Channel hoping to catch Seattle weather.

Thirty minutes later, after she'd packed casual clothes, one just-in-case-she-needed-to-dress-up dress, a leather jacket, and an umbrella—yes, it was raining in Seattle—she cleaned her face, brushed her teeth, and climbed into bed. Tired, she let thoughts of Brandon harassing her float out of her mind. She prayed God would watch over Isabel and heal her body.

Sunday, March 20th

At five-forty the next morning, Jeagan limped to the door, one boot on and one in her hand.

"Good morning," Roger said, after she opened the door, a cheery smile on his face.

"Hmph!" Jeagan hopped over to the couch in the family room and sat down. She pulled on her boot and zipped it.

"It's a beautiful morning in the neighborhood!"

"Not at this time of morning it isn't, Mister Rogers," Jeagan grumbled on the way to her bedroom. "There's coffee in the kitchen if you want it."

"I've got Starbucks in the car for us," he called out. "Is this suitcase ready to go?"

"Yes," she called back. A final glance around her bedroom. The bed was made, well sort of, but it was good enough. She grabbed her trench coat and handbag.

"Why the trench coat?" Roger asked when she returned to the family room.

"Seattle. You know, rain!" She waved her hands to indicate rain while she walked into the kitchen.

"You're a real bundle of joy in the morning, aren't you?" Roger commented.

Jeagan shut off the coffee maker and rinsed the pot. She wished she could sit down, enjoy her coffee, maybe have a nice breakfast. Or better yet, go back to bed.

"Let's go," Roger said.

She rolled her eyes. "I'm coming! A little bossy, aren't we this morning?"

Roger pulled up the handle on her suitcase, a smirk on his face. "A little grumpy, are we, this morning?"

In spite of herself, a smile threatened to break out when she looked at him. "I'm tired. My head hurts. And—"

Roger walked out the door. "Oh, I can see this is going to be a fun trip."

Jeagan followed. She pulled the door closed and locked it. "Well, if you hadn't made the reservations for O'Dark-Thirty." She shivered in the early morning air and pushed her arms into the flannel-lined trench coat.

"Stop your whining and get in." He opened the rear hatch and tossed her suitcase inside.

Unable to think of another retort, she opened the passenger door and got in. The smell of Starbucks coffee greeted her. She tasted hers. Mmm! A small white bag lay on the seat. When she opened it to see pecan rolls, a grin eased across her face.

"Okay. You're forgiven. How did you know I like café mocha and pecan rolls?"

Roger got in and started the Range Rover. "Lucky guess." He backed out of his parking place. "Eat and un-grump."

"Okay, okay." She took another sip of the coffee. "Now this is worth getting up this early for."

Roger laughed. "Maybe the trip's not going to be so bad after all." He looked both ways and drove out onto Tuppence Lane.

"You want part of a roll?"

"No, thanks. I had one on the way over."

"More for me." Jeagan reached over and patted Roger's arm. "Sorry to be grumpy, and I really do appreciate your thinking about me this morning. I just got some bad news last night."

Roger pulled out onto Highlands Ranch Parkway. "What—"
Wham!

Chapter Four

The next thing Jeagan knew, she was lying on the grass and a dark-haired paramedic was bending over her.

"Are you all right?"

"What happened?" she asked, confused. She coughed. It hurt to talk. Her chest hurt.

"Just lie still. We're going to get you to the hospital."

"Hospital?" Jeagan pushed herself up on her elbows and looked around. Bright red lights flashed from an ambulance and a fire engine. Radios crackled. Uniformed men stood in the road around Roger's Range Rover—or what was once a Range Rover. The driver's side of the SUV lay collapsed in like the entrance to a cave; shattered glass sparkled like diamonds around the cave entrance. Diamonds mined in a cave? She shook herself to try to clear her head. *You're losing your mind!*

"Where's Roger?" Frantic, she looked around and spotted him on a stretcher being wheeled to a waiting ambulance.

"Roger!" She grabbed the arm of the paramedic to pull herself up.

"Hey. You need to lie still." The man tried to stop her from standing.

"Let me go! I'm all right." She pulled herself to her feet but held onto the paramedic for a moment until a wave of dizziness passed. In spite of protests from the man, she hurried over to Roger.

Followed by the paramedic, she reached the ambulance before the attendants lifted the stretcher into the back. "Are you all right?" She could see that Roger had cuts on his face. His neck and left leg were immobilized; his clothes were torn and blood spattered.

Roger looked up at her, his eyes bleary. "Hey, you," he drawled. "You look awful."

Jeagan laughed as tears spilled over onto her cheeks. "I look a whole lot better than you." She reached down and touched his face. "Are you hurting?"

"My leg. I think it's going to slow me down for a bit."

"We need to get going, Miss," one of the attendants said and rolled the stretcher into the ambulance.

"I want to go with him," Jeagan insisted.

The paramedic standing beside her said, "You can ride in front with me."

"Thanks." Jeagan moved around to the front of the ambulance.

The man opened the door for her. "We need to get you checked out."

"I'm okay, I told you."

"Is this yours?" someone said behind her.

Jeagan turned to see a gray-uniformed policeman holding her handbag, or the remnants of it. The strap was broken and the bag was ripped.

"Thank you," she said, still not believing any of this was real. She took the bag and stepped up into the ambulance, but winced when pain shot up her back.

"Are you all right?" The policeman helped her into the vehicle.

"I'm fine. What happened to us?"

"Hit and run. No witnesses unless you or your friend can remember seeing who hit you."

"No," Jeagan answered. "I didn't see anything. I was drinking coffee and—"

"Uh...I believe you're wearing it now." He closed the door.

Jeagan looked down at her trench coat. Coffee spatters in creative Rorschach patterns covered her. She grimaced and opened the trench coat. Somehow, her navy slacks and striped shirt were still clean. Had to be a miracle.

The officer closed the rear doors and slapped the ambulance. "You're good to go!"

"Is Roger going to be okay?" Jeagan asked the driver after he turned on the siren and pulled away from the curb.

"Won't know 'til the doc checks him out. His left femur may be broken. Could have internal injuries from the looks of his SUV. A Range Rover?"

"Yes."

He glanced over at her. "You need the doc to check you out, too."

Jeagan didn't respond. The clock on the dash showed almost seven-thirty. She realized their flight would take off in about fifteen minutes. "I hope our tickets are refundable," she mumbled.

"What's that?" the driver asked.

"We were going to the airport to catch a 7:45 flight to Seattle."

Jeagan pulled her cellphone out of her handbag, praying that it still worked. She listened after punching in her dad's number and was relieved to hear the phone ringing. It was answered on the third ring.

"Hello?" Her dad answered, huffing and puffing.

"Dad? It's me. I need you to do something for me."

"Hey, honey. Hold on a minute while I catch my breath. Just came in the door from a run." Jeagan heard the door close and her dad walk across the room. "Okay, what's up?"

"I need you to cancel my reservation and Roger's. We're booked on a Continental flight to Seattle this morning. It's scheduled to leave in a few minutes. And, I need you to cancel our hotel reservations at the Marriott Waterfront."

"Uh, sure, but why do you want to cancel at the last minute? Is something wrong?"

"There's been an accident. Roger and I were on our way to Stapleton when we got hit. Now we're on our way to the hospital."

"Hospital! Are you all right? Where are you? What hospital? I'm on my way!"

"Just calm down, Dad. I'm fine. Roger's the one who's hurt. I think his left leg is broken, and the paramedic said he may have some other injuries. They're taking us to Littleton Hospital."

"Are you sure you're okay, honey?" Geoff sounded somewhat calmer.

"Yes, I'm fine, Dad. Don't worry about me."

Geoff let out a humorless laugh. "That's almost funny coming from you."

"I know...I know. I've been in and out of trouble and hospitals a lot lately."

"Something like that. I'll cancel your flight and meet you at Littleton. You're going to need a ride home anyway."

Jeagan reasoned that he was right, that she had no way to get home. "Okay, Dad. And...thanks. I really appreciate you."

"Hey," Jeagan could hear the catch in her dad's voice, "what are dads for?"

When the ambulance reached the hospital, Jeagan got out and waited for the attendants to unload the stretcher. She walked beside Roger while they wheeled him inside.

"How're you doing?" she asked.

"Hangin' in there." With his right arm, he dug into his back pocket and pulled out his wallet. "Here. You'll need this to check me into this swanky resort."

Jeagan gave him a wry grin. "Glad to see you haven't lost your sense of humor. Where's your insurance card?"

"Next to my driver's license."

"See you in a minute."

While she was still waiting twenty minutes later to get Roger checked in, she turned to see her father walk in the Emergency Room entrance.

"Dad!" she ran over and threw her arms around him. "I'm so glad you're here."

"Another day, another hospital." He hugged her, not showing how relieved he was that she was okay.

"Not funny!" She released him.

"Sorry. How's Roger?"

"Don't know." She shrugged. "I haven't gotten past the registration desk to go check on him."

"Here." Geoff stuck out his hand. "Give me that. I'll give them the information. Have you been checked out by a doctor?"

"I'm fine, Dad." Jeagan handed over the wallet and pushed open the double doors to the ER area. She looked around and then checked the patient board on the wall that showed the room number where they had taken Roger. When she found the room, it was empty.

A slim, young nurse with a ponytail approached Jeagan. "Are you Mr. Sanderlin's wife?"

Jeagan chuckled. "No. I'm just a friend. We were on our way to the airport when we got hit by some maniac." She looked around. "Where's Roger?"

"They've taken him to X-ray. He'll be back in a few minutes if you want to wait in his room."

"Thanks. Is there a restroom back here, Miss…?"

"English, but call me Eileen. And, yes, there's a restroom around the corner on your left."

"Thanks, Eileen. I need to get some of this coffee off."

The nurse gave Jeagan the once-over. "Guess you were drinking it, huh? Your face and hair look kind of sticky."

"Great!" Jeagan grimaced. She headed for the restroom where she washed her face and hands and got as much coffee as she could out of her hair and off her coat.

By the time she returned to Roger's assigned room, he'd returned from X-ray. She knocked on the door.

"Come in," a male voice said.

She entered the room to see a doctor standing beside Roger. "Is he going to live, Doctor?"

"Are you his wife?" the fortyish, bald doctor asked.

"No. Thankfully, I'm not. I'm Jeagan Christensen. I was with him when we got hit." It seemed everyone assumed she was his wife!

"Todd Jones," the doctor said. "Well, it's good to know you're not his wife. Now you won't have to wait on him hand and foot while he recovers from a fractured femur."

"Ow!" Jeagan said. "Is he going to have to have surgery?"

"No, but we're going to put him in a cast. You might want to wait out front so you won't have to listen to him scream," he said with a twinkle in his eyes.

"Hey! Stop talking about me like I'm not here." Roger tried to sit up. "I'm the one who's in pain here while you two are making jokes."

The doctor turned back to Roger. "You won't be in pain much longer." He injected something into Roger's IV.

Jeagan watched and within seconds Roger settled back against the pillows. "That's the quietest I've ever seen him," she commented. "Seriously, Doctor, is he going to be okay?"

"He doesn't seem to have any other injuries according to the CAT scan, but we're running some other tests just to be sure. His left shoulder is bruised, and he'll feel pretty rotten for a few days, but he'll be able to get around with crutches."

Jeagan nodded. She looked over at Roger, lying there with his eyes closed. His face had been cleaned and some of the cuts bandaged.

"Well, guess our trip to Seattle is off."

"Go ahead without me." Roger's words slurred. "You can do it."

"You just rest." She patted Roger's good leg. "I'll see you later."

"Thanks, Doctor." She walked out into the hall.

"We'll take good care of him," Dr. Jones said. He pushed the door closed behind her.

* * *

"How's he doing?" Geoff asked when Jeagan returned to the waiting room and dropped into the chair beside him.

"They're putting his leg in a cast now. He's got a broken femur."

"I need to stay away from you two," Geoff said. "You're not safe to be around."

Jeagan pushed her hair away from her face. She could feel the stickiness of coffee still in her hair. Had it only been this morning when she'd felt good about going to Seattle to begin their search for Alan? Now, here she was in a hospital again, not sure what to do next.

She turned to her dad. "What should I do, Dad? Roger's going to be out of commission for a while. Isabel had a heart attack, and she's in ICU in Memphis."

"I'm sorry, honey." Geoff placed his hand over his daughter's hand that rested on the arm of the gaily upholstered chair. "You've had a lot of tough things happen in the last two weeks. If you still want to go to Seattle, I'll go with you."

"Thanks, Dad. I may take you up on that." She stood. "Right now, I want some coffee and something to eat, and as soon as Roger is okay and settled, I want to go home and change clothes."

"First, I think you're going to have to talk to those police officers." Geoff indicated two men who were walking in their direction.

"If they want to talk to me, they'll have to follow us to the cafeteria." She pulled off her coat and rolled it into a ball. At least she felt like she looked somewhat cleaner.

"Here's Roger's wallet." Geoff handed it to Jeagan and walked over to intercept the officers.

* * *

Ten minutes later, Jeagan and her father, along with Officers Canfield and Losier, were seated in the cafeteria. The three men drank coffee and watched Jeagan while she ate scrambled eggs, bacon, toast, and drank a large orange juice and coffee.

"Feel better?" Officer Canfield asked after she'd had a few bites, his voice heavy with sarcasm.

Geoff, Jeagan noticed, shot him a dark look, and the officer backed off. "Okay. I'm sorry, Miss Christensen. Are you ready to tell us what happened?"

"I wish I knew," Jeagan said. "One minute we were pulling out onto Highlands Ranch Parkway, and the next minute I was lying on the ground looking up into the face of a paramedic."

"Have you been checked out by a doctor?" Officer Losier asked.

"Same thing I asked her," Geoff commented.

"I'm fine." Jeagan ran her fingers through her hair again. "I just need to get rid of this café mocha in my hair."

"So, you don't remember seeing another car before you were hit?" Canfield asked.

"No. I wish I had, but I don't remember seeing *any* cars. We were on our way to the airport, and it was about a quarter to six and still dark."

"Okay." Canfield pulled a white card out of his wallet and handed it to her. "If you remember anything else, give me a call."

"I will." Jeagan took the card and stuffed it in what was left of her handbag after the officers walked away. She turned up the last of her orange juice.

"Feel better now?" Geoff asked. Jeagan noticed the concern that wrinkled his forehead.

"I'm okay, Dad." She stood and groaned. "Really." She not only felt like it but literally had been hit by a truck…or something. Maybe she *should* get checked out.

Geoff picked up her tray along with the other coffee cups from the table and took them to the trash container. He dumped everything and set the tray on top.

"I'm sorry I've put you through so much lately." Jeagan followed him out of the cafeteria.

"Don't worry about me, honey." Geoff placed an arm around her shoulders. "I just want you to be safe and get back to normal."

Jeagan looked up at her dad. "I'll be okay. I promise. I just need to find Alan. I owe Isabel that after what I did to her life."

"You really don't owe her anything, you know. You gave her the truth. That should be enough. Her attorneys can cut through all the legal problems of finding her lost son."

Jeagan walked with her dad to the ER. "I know that, but she hired Roger to find Alan and Roger asked me to help him, so I feel like

30

this is what I need to do. Besides, there are no records of Alan's adoption except for a letter from an attorney in Seattle with a check for ten thousand dollars made out to Robert Lloyd."

"So, Isabel's father sold the baby?" Geoff asked.

"Looks that way." When they reached the ER, she stopped. "I want to check on Roger."

"I'll wait out here." Geoff located a seat in the waiting room in front of a television with CNN showing the latest news.

Jeagan passed through the double doors toward the room where Roger had been earlier. When she checked inside, no one was there.

"Mr. Sanderlin's been moved to a private room," someone said behind her.

Jeagan turned to see a petite, dark-haired woman wearing a white coat. She glanced at her badge.

"Do you know what room he's in, Dr. Pandit?"

"No." The doctor shook her head, dark curls dancing. "Let me check." She walked over to the nurse's station and sat at a computer.

Following her, Jeagan waited while Dr. Pandit checked the computer. "He's been taken to room 312. You can use the elevators around the corner."

"Thanks." Jeagan made her way to the elevator. She rode the car up alone and searched along the hallway for 312. A nurse stopped her to ask if she could help and pointed out Roger's room.

When Jeagan found the room, she knocked. No answer. Quietly, she pushed open the door and saw that the room was dimly lit. Roger was snoring. Good! Let him sleep.

* * *

Jeagan scanned the ER for her father when she returned. He saw her and stood.

"How's he doing?" Geoff asked.

"They took him to a private room. He was asleep when I got there, so I didn't stay."

Together they walked outside to the parking lot. Jeagan breathed in the fresh spring air and raised her face to the sun. "Oooh!" She reached up and rubbed her neck.

Her father studied her over the top of his Volvo, which he had parked close to the ER entrance. "You need to go back in there and have someone check your neck, Jeagan. You might have whiplash."

"I'm fine, Dad, really. Just stiff. I want to go home, clean off some of this coffee, and check on Isabel. I can decide what I'm going to do after that."

Geoff mumbled something about stubbornness and women while he got into his car. He turned on the ignition, shifted into reverse, but stopped when he saw Officer Losier running toward them waving his hand.

"Now what!" Jeagan said.

Chapter Five

She opened the door and got out. The officer carried something battered and black.

"Glad I caught you," Officer Tyson said. "Thought you might want your suitcase, or what's left of it. I assume it's yours. These are women's clothes spilling out of it. "

"Thanks," Jeagan said, relieved she wasn't receiving more bad news. Clothes and suitcases could be replaced.

The officer opened the rear door and placed the suitcase inside.

"Thanks, Officer."

"No problem." The policeman walked back toward the hospital.

Geoff looked over at his daughter when she was inside the car again. Noting her pale face and glassy eyes, he said, "Why don't you come home with me for a few days? Sleep in your old room, take it easy. Let Maria fatten you up with some of her Mexican cooking."

Maria, Dad's housekeeper and cook since his wife's death, wasn't the greatest housekeeper in the world, but who could keep up with the dog hair from two black labs running in and out of the house all day. Maria was an excellent cook though. Jeagan was tempted.

"No, thanks, Dad. I need to pull myself together and make some plans."

Geoff again put the car in reverse and backed out of the parking place. When he pulled out onto Broadway Avenue heading south, he added. "Okay, at least come for dinner. I'll get Maria to make your favorite."

"Beef enchiladas, Mexican rice, and that shrimp dish?" Jeagan asked.

Geoff noted the light in her eyes. "And I'll whip up some piña coladas."

Jeagan laughed. "Okay. Sold. What time?"

"Around six."

* * *

"I can get my suitcase," Jeagan said when her Dad started to get out of the car at her townhouse. She reached over and kissed him on the cheek. "Thanks, Dad. I'll see you tonight."

"Okay, but get some rest this afternoon."

"I will," she promised as she got out and retrieved her suitcase. "Bye." She closed the door. Her Dad waved and pulled away from the curb.

The suitcase was grimy with street dirt, but it might still be usable with a little cleaning, she realized, while she stuffed clothes back inside in order to carry it without dropping her underwear all over the sidewalk. When she opened the door of her townhouse, her phone was ringing. Out of habit, recent habit, she stiffened. *Would it be Brandon harassing her or Isabel's attorney in Memphis calling with more bad news?* Hesitant, she walked into the kitchen, dropped the suitcase on the floor, slung her handbag onto the counter, and reached for the receiver.

"Hello?"

"Hey, Jeagan," Roger said, his words slurring.

Relieved at hearing her friend's voice, Jeagan said, "Hey yourself. How're you feeling? I stopped by your room after I talked to the police, but you were asleep."

"I don't feel too bad actually, other than having this cast on my leg."

"Guess they're giving you some good drugs if you're feeling okay."

"Yeah." His words floated over the phone. "It's like.... It's like I know the pain's there, but it's so far away that I can't touch it."

That probably made some kind of sense, but Jeagan wasn't sure what kind.

"Did the police talk to you about our accident?"

"Yes." She started to remind him that she'd already told him that but decided to let it go. "They came to the hospital cafeteria with Dad and me and asked what I saw before the accident. I told them I didn't see anything. I don't even remember what happened. I just remember opening my eyes with a guy standing over me."

"Hmm," Roger said.

"What? Did you see anything before we got hit?"

"Yeah," he mumbled. "I think I saw the truck that hit us. When I turned off Highlands Ranch Parkway on the way to your place, I noticed an old, dirty, black truck parked on the side of the road. Thought it was kind of strange at that time of the morning, but figured the driver was waiting for somebody. And, then when we pulled out onto the Parkway, this truck seemed to come out of nowhere."

"Do you think it was the same truck?"

"It sure looked like it. I just caught a glimpse of it out of the corner of my eye before it smacked us. Don't think the headlights were on."

"I can't imagine why anyone would hit us deliberately. And, considering the damage to your Range Rover, they could have easily been hurt."

"Maybe not," he paused for a moment, "not if they knew what they were doing."

"That makes no sense, Roger." Jeagan pulled out a bar stool and sat on it. "Who would want to hurt us that badly?"

Roger yawned. "Sorry," he mumbled. "I can think of a jealous ex-fiancé for one. You notice we were hit on my side of the car. Maybe he was aiming for me."

"You've got to be kidding! Brandon's egotistical," she couldn't readily think of another adjective to describe him, "but he wouldn't go so far as trying to hurt us."

"No? Then, do you have a better explanation for someone hitting us deliberately? Does he have an old pickup?"

"No," Jeagan said. "At least, I don't think so. His family might, though. They have a ranch in Sedalia. I think I might have seen an old truck there at some point, but I can't believe Brandon would go this far for revenge."

"You never know what people will do, Jeagan. For now, try not to worry about it. I'll do some checking as soon as I get out of this place. So, when do you want to reschedule our trip?"

"Our trip? I don't think you're going anywhere. Not with that cast."

"Hey, it's a walking cast."

"You'd better talk to the doctor before you think about going anywhere."

"Yeah, I guess you're right. But—"

"No 'buts.' Talk to him, and let me know what he says. Right now, I'm going to check on Isabel and get cleaned up. This coffee in my hair is fermenting."

After she disconnected and went to her bedroom, Jeagan noticed the blinking message light on the phone. She pressed the play button.

"Hello, Jeagan. This is Isabel." Her voice was weak. "I wanted to tell you I'm doing some better and hope they will put me in a private room soon. I hate being in this ICU fishbowl. Anyway, please call me when you get this message. There are some things I need to talk to you about."

Jeagan let out her breath, which she hadn't realized she was holding. *Thank goodness. Isabel's doing better, and Roger's going to be okay. This has got to stop! We all need a break.* She headed into the bathroom and turned on the shower.

* * *

Later, while she was removing a section of her shoulder-length hair from her curling brush, she realized she needed to add a visit to Skye Salon to her To Do list. Hopefully, Marty could work her in soon for a good haircut.

Thinking she heard the doorbell, she turned off the hot-air brush and listened. It rang again. She wrapped her white terry robe more tightly around her and padded barefoot to the front door. A smile lit her face when she looked out a window before opening the door.

"Delivery for Jeagan Christensen," the gray-haired man said.

"Thank you." Jeagan accepted the glass vase of dark red roses. After she closed the door, she carried the vase into the kitchen and set it on the counter. Smiling, she sniffed the roses, enjoying the fresh, sweet scent. She pulled the card from the holder and opened it, expecting the flowers to be from her dad or maybe, heaven forbid, Brandon. She let out a cry when she read the message: "That was a warning!"

Chapter Six

Shocked, Jeagan dropped the card as if it had burned her fingers. This was too much! If the flowers were from Brandon, he was going too far, and he'd never get her back with threats! She grabbed the vase, dumped the water in the kitchen sink, marched to the garage door, jerked it open, and carried the flowers directly to the garbage can where she threw them inside. Back in the house, she picked up the small envelope to find the name and phone number of the florist.

"Chan's Florist," a friendly female, oriental-accented voice said when the phone was answered.

"Yes, this is Jeagan Christensen. Someone from your florist just delivered a dozen roses to me."

"Was there a problem with the flowers?" the woman asked, a concerned note in her voice.

"No. The roses were beautiful, but no one signed the card. Can you tell me who sent them?"

"I happy to check for you." The woman asked Jeagan to spell her name, give her address, and to hold on while she checked the order.

"I'm sorry, I don't have name for you," the woman said when she came back on the line. "It was walk-in order this morning. The customer pay in cash."

With a grimace, Jeagan asked, "Was it a man or a woman?"

"Ticket say my nephew take order. Hold on. I check with him."

Placed on hold again, Jeagan pulled a glass out of the cabinet and filled it with ice and water from the dispenser on the refrigerator door. She downed half the glass.

"Miss Christensen?" the woman said when she came on to the line again.

"Yes. I'm still here."

"My nephew say a woman maybe twenty-five year old place order this morning."

That wasn't much help, Jeagan thought. "What did she look like?"

"All he say is she have red hair, curly red hair."

Jeagan thanked the woman and disconnected. Who did she know with curly red hair? Nobody. While she padded across the family room and down the hall to her bedroom, she tried to remember if anyone who worked at Brandon's brokerage firm had curly red hair.

The card lay on the vanity while Jeagan finished her hair. Who was warning her about what? Was Brandon sending her a warning, thinking she was now dating Roger? Or, a new thought struck her! Could Angela's sister, Shelley, who gave Jeagan a cold stare at the restaurant the night before, be warning her to stay away from Roger? Shelley had appeared none too pleased to see Jeagan and Roger together. Either Brandon or Shelley could have sent someone to the florist.

When she was dressed in jeans, low-rise boots, and a butter-colored sweater, Jeagan stuffed the card in the envelope and tucked it into her handbag. She would show it to her dad.

* * *

The cleaners were her first destination where she dropped off clothes from her trip to Memphis and the coffee-stained trench coat. Now she wanted to get to her dad's house in Parker and forget all her problems for a while. Maybe she should have gone back to work and stayed away from Roger, just let him do his job. If she had, they would not have been seen together the night before by Brandon or Shelley, and maybe no one would have rammed them this morning. Was it only this morning? If so, how could one day last for a week?

She felt the tension easing away by the time she reached Parker and the partially treed horse properties along Flintwood Road. Peace and tranquility emanated from the rolling hills and ponderosa pines. Magnificent chestnut, black, and white horses grazed peacefully in meadows that were starting to turn green, while cedar, stone, or stucco homes and barns gleamed in the late afternoon sun. Soon, she turned up the long gravel drive, which wound through tall pines and scrub oak, their tiny buds waiting for warmer weather before opening.

Bob and Hope, her dad's three-year-old black labs, barked when she drove up behind the two-story cedar-and-stone house and parked by the garage. She got out and greeted the two dogs, who whined and nuzzled her happily. *Were labs eternally cheerful?*

"Hey, guys." She knelt down to hug them. Bob offered her a tennis ball to throw. Jeagan accepted the slimy ball and launched it toward the rear of the property. Both dogs shot after it while Jeagan walked around to the back deck.

"Hi, Jeag." She looked up to see her dad leaning on the railing, comfortably dressed in jeans, cowboy boots, and a khaki-colored golf shirt with the insignia of Pebble Beach, his favorite place to golf. "I thought that was probably you when I heard the dogs. Feeling any better, honey?"

"A little." She walked up the steps from the basement level to the redwood deck. "At least my hair's clean."

"Oh, I don't know," Geoff said. "I kinda liked you with the wet-head look."

"Not funny, Dad." Jeagan narrowed her eyes at him. She walked into his open arms and let him envelope her in a hug. Safe. Secure. That was the feeling she had with her dad, but she wasn't a kid anymore and could—should—take care of herself. She stepped back when she heard the patio door open to see a short, plump, dark-haired woman holding out her arms.

"Jeagan!" Maria cried. Jeagan smiled and let the short Mexican woman wrap her chubby arms around her. Then, Maria released her hold and held Jeagan away from her to look at her. "I'm sorry for the troubles your papa told me about. But, I make you feel better with good food to fill your stomach."

Jeagan sniffed the air as the spicy aromas of Mexican cooking wafted through the open doorway. "Smells wonderful."

"Your papa make you piña coladas. You sit. When ready I bring for you," Maria said with a smile.

"Thanks, Maria." Jeagan walked over to the railing to gaze out over the back of the property. Above the ponderosas and aspens she could see the whole front range of the Rockies, darkening to purple in the waning afternoon light.

"Are you sure you're okay?" her dad asked. "You look like you could use about a week's sleep."

"I thought I was okay until I got a dozen roses this afternoon."

"Roses?" He grinned. "That should have brightened your day a little."

"They would have if this card hadn't been attached to them." Jeagan pulled the card out of her handbag and handed it to her dad.

Geoff read the card. His face losing all color, he said, "Who in the world would do something like this!" He returned the card to his daughter.

"I wish I knew." Jeagan stuffed the card back in her handbag and then leaned against the railing. "I can't imagine who would send them unless it was Brandon being spiteful."

"Brandon wouldn't stoop to doing something like that," Geoff said defensively.

Jeagan shrugged. "I just don't know, Dad." She walked over and dropped wearily into a striped fabric deck chair.

"Have you heard anything from Roger?" Geoff eased back into his chair.

"I talked to him a little while ago. He said he was feeling okay except for his broken leg. But they're giving him good drugs." She smiled, remembering. "He also said he saw the truck that hit us."

Geoff's eyebrows rose. "He did? Did he get a look at the driver or get a license plate number?"

"No. Nothing like that. It was still dark out. He said he saw a truck parked on the side of the road when he turned off Highlands Ranch Parkway, and after he picked me up and turned back onto the Parkway, he said this truck came from out of nowhere and rammed us. He got a flash of it before it hit us. He's almost positive it was the same truck."

"That doesn't make any sense." Geoff got up from his chair. "Why would someone ram his Range Rover deliberately?"

Jeagan shrugged. "Wish I knew."

Leaning with his back against the railing and his arms folded across his chest, Geoff mused. "And, who would send you a warning? About what? Finding Isabel's son?"

Bob and Hope raced up the stairs and sprinted across the deck. Geoff rubbed Bob's ears. Hope moved over to Jeagan to have her ears scratched.

"Does Isabel have any other family?" Geoff continued. "Maybe someone who doesn't want you to find her son?"

"I don't know." Jeagan cuddled the panting lab with the happy eyes. "I don't know of any family other than her sister, who is now in jail for trying to kill us." *Had Isabel mentioned any other family?* Jeagan wondered. *Isabel!*

"Isabel called earlier and left a message, but after I got the flowers—which by the way went straight into the trash—I forgot to call her back." Jeagan dug in her handbag for her cellphone.

"After you talk to her, we need to have a little father-daughter chat. I think you need to forget this detecting business and go back to your regular job...where you'll be safe." He turned to go inside.

"You're probably right," Jeagan agreed. "Every time I turn around, something else happens. My old job is looking better and better."

When Jeagan got through to Isabel, she was having her dinner. "I'm so glad you called." Her voice weak, Isabel paused as if out of breath. "It feels awfully lonely since you left Memphis."

"I know. I miss you too," Jeagan said. "How're you feeling?"

"Like all my energy has been drained out of me. I'm trying to eat a little, but it all tastes the same."

To lighten the conversation, Jeagan said, "Is it better than the hospital food in Oxford?"

Isabel chuckled. "I don't think it's any worse, if that's an answer."

"Well, that's something. When are they going to let you out of there?"

"Not for a while. Dr. Gronauer said they put stents in two of my arteries to keep them open. He said I could probably go into a private room soon, but what I wanted to talk to you about is my new will."

"Your will?"

"Yes. I wanted you to know if anything happens to me, everything goes to Alan, that is, if Roger and my attorney can find him. If they can't, I want everything to go to you."

Jeagan gasped. "Isabel, you can't do that! Don't you have some other family? In fact, that's one of the reasons I called you."

"Not really. The only family left would be my sister's children, and I haven't seen them in several years. They never came to see me and never bothered with their mother unless they wanted money."

Standing to look toward the mountains, barely visible now that the sun had set, Jeagan asked, "Do they know their mother's in jail and charged with attempted murder?"

"I don't have any idea." Isabel added, a deep sadness in her voice. "I haven't heard a word from them. I assume Agnes contacted them, but I was never close to them. Considering what their mother tried to do to me, and you, I don't really expect to hear from them."

"Does Agnes have a daughter, better yet maybe a granddaughter with curly red hair?"

"No. Agnes's son and daughter take after their father. They both have dark hair and olive skin."

"What about Agnes's grandchildren?"

"No. No red hair that I can recall. Why? Is it important?"

"Well," Jeagan said, dissatisfied and disappointed, "Roger and I were involved in a hit-and-run this morning and—"

"What! Are you okay?" Jeagan heard the alarm in Isabel's voice. "Is Roger all right?"

"I'm fine." Jeagan too late realized she probably shouldn't have told Isabel. "And Roger's going to be okay, but he does have a broken leg."

"Good Lord! That poor man! Bless his heart."

"Anyway." Jeagan decided she might as well tell her the rest of what had happened. "Today someone sent me roses with a card attached that said I had been warned."

"Warned about what?" Isabel asked.

"That's just it. I don't know what. The only logical thing I can think of is someone knows Roger asked me to help him find Alan."

"Oh. I'm glad to hear you're going to help Roger, but please be careful. I don't want you getting hurt again." Jeagan heard the concern in her friend's voice. "I *do* think you two will make a good team though."

"Well, maybe someone else doesn't agree with you and is trying to stop me."

"How would anyone out in Colorado know what you two are planning to do?"

"That's what I don't understand." Jeagan turned around to see Maria walking out the door with a frosty glass for her. "Thank you," she mouthed and sipped the piña colada. *Mmm!* It went down smooth.

"Well, maybe, on second thought, you'd better let Roger search for Alan and not get yourself involved in anything else. You've been through enough."

Jeagan took another sip of her drink. "No. I want to finish this, Isabel, that is, unless your attorney finds out something first."

"As of this morning, Mark hasn't found out anything. He said there are no real leads, especially now that the attorney in Seattle is deceased.

"But, he *did* say that he talked to the attorney's son. He's apparently taken over the practice and searched for some kind of record on the adoption, but he didn't find anything."

"Does he still have his father's old files?"

"I guess he doesn't," Isabel said, "since he said he couldn't find anything."

"What's the son's name?" Jeagan pulled out a leatherbound notepad and pen.

"Let me see." Isabel paused, thinking. Jeagan could hear a television in the background. Sounded like the evening news.

"It was McMillan or McFarland. McFarland, that's it, John McFarland. That was the father. The son is Charles, I think."

"Thanks, Isabel." Jeagan jotted the name on the pad. "Just try to get some rest and get your strength back."

"I will," Isabel promised. "Give my love to Roger when you talk to him. And, tell him to let his leg heal before he tries going up to Seattle." Isabel coughed. "I think I'm a little tired now. Thanks for calling, dear."

Relieved Isabel had sounded as well as she did, Jeagan disconnected with a promise to call her the next day to check on her and update her on Roger.

Maria stuck her head out the door. "Dinner's ready."

"Yum!" Jeagan dropped her cellphone in her handbag.

Somewhere behind Maria in the kitchen, she heard her dad say, "I could eat a horse."

"I made enough to feed *dos caballos*, two horses," Maria called back. "You might have to take home leftovers," she told Jeagan.

Jeagan followed Maria inside. Every time she walked into her father's kitchen, she was reminded of her mother—sitting with her at the bar or at the kitchen table, either drinking tea or hot chocolate, and talking. A wall of windows in the breakfast room surrounded the glass-topped table. Many happy family meals had been eaten at that table.

Geoff pulled out a chair for his daughter and then sat across from her. Maria set the hot dishes on trivets and sat down also. A live-in housekeeper and cook, Maria was family.

Jeagan finished her piña colada and drank ice water with her meal, which she needed to dampen the fire of the Mexican chilis. While they ate, she filled her father in on what she'd found out from Isabel.

"So," he said when she finished, "you don't have any real leads to go on. Looks like Alan may be lost to his mother for good."

"That's about it," Jeagan agreed. "Except she's changed her will leaving everything she has to me if Alan isn't found before she dies."

"Good. You deserve it," Geoff said between bites.

"No, I don't."

Her dad, she realized, had more gray in his hair than he had a month ago. She hated to see him growing older by himself. Then, she remembered Candice, the woman she had met on the plane to Memphis two weeks ago. Her business card was still under the lamp on Jeagan's nightstand.

"Changing the subject, Dad. Uh…there's someone I want you to meet."

Geoff looked over at her in surprise. "By that expression on your face, I'd say you mean you want to fix me up with somebody." He laughed. "I haven't had a blind date since college."

"Well," Jeagan admitted, "I met this attractive woman on the plane to Memphis. I think you two would hit it off."

Geoff frowned. "Uh-uh. Not interested, honey, but thank you for the thought."

"You need a good woman to take care of you," Maria said. "Maybe make you not be so grumpy all the time."

"Me, grumpy?" Geoff feigned shock. "I'm never grumpy."

Maria nodded her head enthusiastically. "Grumpy."

"Definitely grumpy," Jeagan echoed, "and bossy," she added.

"And needs good haircut," Maria continued.

"All right, you two. Enough! I'm fine just the way I am."

* * *

After coffee and Mexican flan, Jeagan started for home with a 'care package' consisting of two enchiladas and a small container of the dessert. But, instead of turning west off University onto Highlands Ranch Parkway, she continued north to Dry Creek and turned left. She decided to stop by the hospital to see Roger. Together they could try to figure out what to do next.

A shudder ran through Jeagan's body when she walked in the hospital entrance. Too many hospitals. When she reached Roger's room on the third floor, she tapped on the partially closed door.

"Come in," Roger called from inside.

"Hey, you," Jeagan said when she walked into the room. "I brought you food, and dessert."

Roger looked her up and down. A big grin spread across his face, and his green eyes lit up.

Jeagan felt her face burn. "Forget it, cowboy." She held out the container. "I brought you enchiladas and some Mexican flan. Dad's housekeeper makes the best I've ever tasted."

"Oh, okay. I can handle that."

Jeagan laid the containers on the tray table. She took a good look at Roger. His face was pale, and he had dark smudges under his eyes. "How're you doing?"

"I'm okay. Just sore all over, and my leg hurts, but not too bad."

Jeagan walked over to the window and sat in the lounge chair. "I'm going ahead with our plan to go to Seattle. I talked to Isabel. She said her attorney hasn't had any luck finding a single record of Alan's existence."

"Just wait a couple of days, and I'll go with you." Roger opened the dessert container and stuck his finger in. "Tasty," he said when he licked his finger.

Jeagan grimaced and scanned the room. *Men!* She spotted a spoon on a tray that was ready to go back to the kitchen and got up from her seat. "You might get better results with this." She handed the spoon over.

"Thanks," Roger said with a sheepish grin.

"Anyway," she continued. "I can't sit around and wait. I'll go stark raving nuts if I do." She walked to the door and back, pacing. "I need to be doing something. And," she looked at Roger, "truth be known, I'm ready to get out of town again." She told Roger about the flowers and accompanying card.

Roger stopped with the spoon in midair. "You're done! Off the case! Consider yourself fired!"

Jeagan stopped pacing and stared at Roger. "What? You can't fire me!"

Roger set the plastic container and spoon on the tray table, no longer smiling. "I can and just did. Finding Alan is not worth putting you in more danger. This morning was bad enough. Deliberate. Calculated. Now this! I want you to go out to your dad's where you'll be safe and stay there for the rest of the week."

"Who made you my boss?" she demanded, hands on her hips.

"You need someone to boss you around to keep you out of trouble."

"Oh! Oh! Like you kept me out of trouble in Memphis?" Jeagan felt her temper flaring.

Roger pulled himself up straighter in bed. "Well, if you hadn't been so stubborn and let me help you, you might not have ended up unconscious...in a van...in the middle of a river!"

"Lake!"

"What?"

"For your information, it was a lake!" Jeagan grabbed her handbag. "I had to be out of my mind to think we could work together. You're right. I quit! I wouldn't work with you if—" She couldn't think of anything to follow the 'if,' so she stomped out of the room.

Steamed, she marched down the hall and dug in her handbag for her car keys. Her hand struck Roger's wallet. She stopped, realizing she should take it to him. Instead, she approached a nurse walking along the hall. "Excuse me," she said.

The stout black nurse stopped. "Can I help you?"

"Yes. Would you give this to that...that jerk in room 312."

The nurse chuckled. "You mean that cute Mr. Sanderlin?"

"Cute? I know a few other adjectives that describe him better, but my mama told me not to use them."

The nurse threw her head back and laughed out loud. "I'll be glad to give him his wallet. Don't want you to go stuffing it down his throat."

"Thank you." Jeagan did an about face. She'd like to stuff it all right! She fumed on the elevator ride to the lobby and stalked out the front door toward the parking lot. Several moments later, she reached her car and unlocked it.

Footsteps behind her froze her to the spot.

Chapter Seven

"You okay, ma'am?" a male voice asked.

Jeagan whipped around to see a uniformed security guard. She grabbed her chest and let out her breath. "Yes, I'm fine," she said. I will be, she thought, when my heart starts beating again.

"Drive careful now." He strolled off toward the hospital entrance.

After she checked the rear seat, she got in her car, locked the doors, and backed out of the parking place. The first thing she'd do when she got home was re-book her flight to Seattle. She'd find Alan on her own. She didn't need Roger's help.

The drive home helped to settle her down. Things she needed to get done before the trip ran through her mind. First and foremost was establishing some kind of contact. John McFarland's son. He was the person she needed to talk to.

As soon as she arrived home, she dropped her handbag on the kitchen counter and hurried to her spare bedroom where her computer was set up. While it went through the gyrations of coming to life, she slipped off her boots. The grinding noise from the CPU sounded like it was on its last leg. Someday soon, a new computer.

Finally, the home page appeared and Jeagan typed in 'Charles McFarland' to see if she'd get lucky. Too many names, she realized, when hundreds popped up. She narrowed the search by adding 'Seattle.' That didn't help much so she added 'attorney' to the search. McFarland and McFarland, Attorneys-at-Law. There it was! The address was on Second Avenue with a phone number listed. Jeagan checked her watch. It was almost ten o'clock, so that would make it an hour earlier in Seattle. Why not give it a try? Some attorneys worked late. If no one was there, she could always leave a message.

The phone rang four times, and then an answering machine clicked on. Jeagan opened her mouth to speak when someone answered.

"Charles McFarland," the male voice said.

"Oh," Jeagan said, startled, "I was just going to leave a message for you."

"Still here as you can tell. Everyone else has departed, deserted. No rest for the weary and all that." Jeagan detected a British accent and a smile in the voice. A good sign.

"I understand working late," Jeagan commiserated. "My name is Jeagan Christensen. I'm calling from Denver, well, Highlands Ranch actually."

"Lovely state, Colorado: cowboys, Rocky Mountains, not much oxygen to speak of." His voice trailed off with a chuckle.

"Yes, well," Jeagan continued. "I think you've already been contacted by a Memphis attorney, Mark Edwards, about an adoption, which took place in 1945?"

"Oh, yes. Child named Alan, I believe it was."

"Yes," Jeagan said, her hopes rising. "That's the child. His mother recently found out that he was taken from her at birth and given up for adoption. Well, the truth is he was sold by his grandfather. She was told he was stillborn."

"Yes, yes. Rotten luck that."

"So," Jeagan continued. This was like pulling teeth. "Do you have any information that might help us find Alan?"

"No, actually. Sorry, Miss?"

"Just Jeagan."

"Jeagan it is. No, Sorry. Had my assistant check what's left of my father's files. The senior McFarland, that is. I'm the junior, Charles John McFarland. Long line of McFarlands. All from England, not Scotland. No, most people think—"

Give him an inch, Jeagan thought. "Excuse me, Mr. McFarland."

"Charles. Well, Chuck actually. Never liked the name Charles."

"Thank you, *Chuck*. But, don't you have files somewhere that might have information about the adoption? Surely there are permanent records."

"No. None here in our office. Records only go back to 1960. Don't really know what happened to the earlier records. Before my time that. Was only a toddler then as it were."

"Would earlier records be boxed up, maybe stored somewhere else or on microfiche?"

"Don't know." He paused. Jeagan hoped he was considering possibilities. "Edwards asked me the same question. Told him we moved into this office before my father died. That was the summer of '86, I believe. Hot summer it was. At least hot for me. Just home from Oxford…England, that is. University and all. I remember—"

Jeagan cut in before he went off on another tangent. "So, obviously, all the old records weren't brought to your new office when you moved." She thought for a moment. "Is there some employee who has been with you for a long time who might remember what happened to the old records?"

"Hmm. Good question that. Don't think Edwards asked me that one. Told him I thought the records were misplaced, lost, probably sometime after father passed, since I haven't seen them in the last eight years. But, I remember one old dear who worked for my father."

"Yes? Who was she?" Jeagan asked, hopeful. "What was her job?"

"She was the pater's secretary. Call them administrative assistants now, don't they? Same really, just a new fancy name. 'A rose by any other name,' you know. Shakespeare was spot on."

"Yes, I know what you mean," Jeagan agreed, stifling an exasperated sigh. "What's the woman's name? Can you remember her name? Is she still alive?"

"Alive? Oh, she's still alive all right. Yes. Think I ran into her at the Pike Market a few months ago. Lovely old dear, still active, walks two miles every day, she said."

"What's her name, Chuck? Have you got a phone number for her?"

"Name. Oh, yes, her name's Susan Coleman. Everyone calls her Sue though. Well, that is, except for me. I always called her Lady Coleman. Always got a laugh out of her when I called her that."

"Susan Coleman. All right. Now, Chuck, do you have a phone number for her?"

Jeagan could hear paper shuffling. "Card file. I know it's somewhere on my desk. Ah. Yes, here's the little blighter." Jeagan heard cards flipping. "C… Coleman. Yes. I have it." Chuck read off the number.

"Thank you, Chuck. I appreciate your help."

"Right. Anytime. Anytime. Always glad to help. Edwards might want to talk to her. Might want to pass along the number to him."

"Yes. Thank you," Jeagan said again. Edwards could get his own information. She disconnected. Before she could dial again, the phone rang. Annoyed, she answered it.

"Jeagan?" a male voice said when she answered.

"Yes," she said. The voice sounded familiar.

"This is Madison."

Chapter Eight

Shocked speechless for a moment, Jeagan then found her voice. "Madison? I thought you were—"

"In jail? No, I'm out on bond."

Rallying from the shock, the reality started to sink in along with anger. "You set me up, Madison! You almost got me killed! How could you do that to me?"

"I know, Jeagan. I know I have no right to call you, and I won't bother you again. I just wanted you to know how sorry I am for what I did. I never meant for you to get hurt. I was only supposed to watch you. Agnes asked me to keep an eye on you, to try to steer you away—"

"Away from Isabel and finding out about her son? Then, you could find another way to get rid of Isabel so Agnes could inherit her estate when she died."

"Yes. I admit it, and I'm sorry. There's no defense for what I did. I was blinded by the thought of easy money."

"And you…an attorney!" Jeagan said angrily.

"And me, an attorney." His laugh was hollow. "Ironic, isn't it?"

"That's one way of describing it." Jeagan felt her anger building. "I trusted you. I thought you were becoming a friend."

"I know. I wanted to be your friend. All I can say is I'm sorry. You won't have to ever see me again, except maybe in court. I wanted to apologize, at least, for what I did."

"And, what about what Agnes did, or tried to do to me and her own sister?"

"I can't speak for Agnes. She's never cared about anybody but herself." Jeagan could hear his contempt. "I don't think she's sorry for anything she's ever done."

"Well, she won't get her hands on any of Isabel's money now. Isabel's changed her will."

51

"Which is as it should be, but knowing Agnes, she'll try to find a way to get back in Isabel's good graces and try to get her to change her will again."

Jeagan laughed. "After what she did?"

"Don't laugh. I've seen her in action. She's a real Dr. Jekyl and Mr. Hyde. She's out on bail also, so who knows."

"You can't be serious! Some judge let her post bail after she was caught in the act of trying to drown Isabel and me?"

"I told you she was good," Madison said bitterly.

"Listen, I have to go. I have to pack, and…and I shouldn't even be talking to you."

"Well, enjoy your trip and thank you for at least listening to me."

"It's not a pleasure trip. I'm going to Seattle to—" Jeagan stopped. She shouldn't have said that. "Good-bye, Madison."

"Take care of yourself." Madison disconnected.

Shaken more than she wanted to be, Jeagan hung up. Madison had befriended her while she was in Memphis and then betrayed her, and Isabel. He had no right to call her now, and as a condition of his bond, he'd probably been instructed not to contact her.

* * *

She remembered when she first met him in Café Espresso at The Peabody Hotel in Memphis two weeks earlier. She had only been in Memphis two days and had had no luck in contacting Isabel. When she walked into the noisy, crowded Café Expresso for breakfast that morning, the hostess had told her there would be a short wait for a table.

Before she could sit in the waiting area, Madison had spoken up and asked her to join him at his table. An attractive, well-dressed black man reading the *Wall Street Journal*, Jeagan had felt safe sharing a table with him, especially in a busy restaurant.

An attorney, he'd introduced himself as Darrell Hannah, but said people called him Madison because of the movie *Splash*. She'd laughed. A black, male 'Daryl' Hannah.

Foolishly, she'd thought having a local attorney for a friend might help in her search for the truth about what happened to Isabel's fiancé in 1944, and after his death, what happened to Isabel and their child.

But, in the end, she'd found out too late that the accidental meeting with Madison had been a setup. He'd only befriended her to mislead her. He'd guided her straight into the hands of Isabel's sister,

Agnes, who had tried to kill both Isabel and Jeagan to make sure the missing heir was never found.

Well, that was all over. Jeagan had to face the fact that she would probably have to testify whenever the court date was set, and afterwards Madison, Agnes, and her butler and partner in crime, Thomas Williams, would spend some well-earned time in a Mississippi prison.

* * *

Jeagan chided herself. Getting lost in memories, mostly bad, was becoming a habit. Sue Coleman was her next priority. She dialed the number Chuck had given her.

After three rings, the phone was answered. "Hello?" a soft voice said.

"Yes. Is this the Sue Coleman who used to work for John McFarland?"

"Yes," the woman said, a note of suspicion in her voice. "Who is this?"

"My name is Jeagan Christensen. I'm calling from Denver."

Silence on the other end.

"And," Jeagan continued hurriedly before the woman could hang up on her. "I'm trying to help a friend, an older friend, to find a son who was given up for adoption in 1945."

Still no sound on the other end.

"And, Mr. McFarland handled the adoption. We are trying to find a record of the adoption and—"

"I'm sorry," the woman said quickly. "I can't help you."

"But," Jeagan said, "you worked for Mr. McFarland back then, and his son Chuck said you might know something about the files from before 1960 since they were not with the other files when the office was moved in 1986."

"I don't know anything about the files," the woman said. "I'm sorry I can't help you. Good-bye." The woman hung up.

Jeagan held the phone and stared at it. Sue Coleman had sounded sad or tired or maybe scared. That was the note in her voice. Fear. What could the woman possibly be afraid of? Now, more than ever, Jeagan was convinced she needed to go to Seattle.

* * *

After she had re-booked her flight and hotel reservations, she dumped everything out of her suitcase, carried it into the laundry room, and cleaned off most of the dirt. Fortunately, the inside was still clean and the zippers all worked. The phone rang as she passed through the kitchen.

"Jeagan?" Roger said when she answered.

"What do you want?" she asked, her voice sharp, but she didn't care.

"I wanted to apologize. I know I came on strong, but I don't want you going off anywhere by yourself after the accident and those flowers."

"That's just it, Roger," she replied. "I want to get out of Colorado before I *do* get hurt." She thought for a second. "And, I think I know who feels threatened by me."

"What? What do you know?"

She set the suitcase on the floor, pulled out a bar stool, and sat down. "I just got a call from Madison, rather, Darrel Hannah."

"Hannah? He's supposed to be in jail waiting to stand trial."

"Well, he's out on bail, bond, or whatever you call it. Agnes is too."

"You think they're responsible for what happened today?"

"Possibly Agnes, but I don't think it was Madison." But, she realized she'd been wrong about him before. "He said he called to apologize for what he did to me and Isabel."

"Or," Roger added, "he may have called to check on you, see if you were hurt in the accident. See if the threat worked. Maybe to see if you'll go easy in testifying against him now." Roger paused as if waiting for a response. "I hope you told him you've given up your detective career and are going back to tech writing."

"No," Jeagan said. "I didn't." She should probably tell Roger that Madison now knew she was going to Seattle, but she couldn't admit it to him. Couldn't admit she'd been stupid letting that slip. And, it probably wasn't important anyway. Hopefully.

"But, you *are* going back to your old job, aren't you?"

"As a matter of fact, I'm not, Roger. I've booked my reservations for tomorrow. I'm going to Seattle."

"If I remember correctly, I fired you earlier tonight." Jeagan could hear the anger in his voice.

"Fired or not, I'm going. Don't try to stop me. I'm going tomorrow. Period. And, I've got a lead."

"What kind of lead?" Roger asked, sounding interested despite his anger.

"I talked to John McFarland's son. His name is Charles—Chuck—and he's also an attorney. He said they only have files that go back as far as 1960 in their office."

"Which is no help to us," Roger interjected.

"If you'll let me finish!" Jeagan snapped.

"Okay," Roger said, "so finish."

"He told me his father's former secretary might know what happened to the files."

Excitement in his voice, Roger asked, "So, did you talk to her?"

"I did, but she said she didn't know anything about them," Jeagan admitted.

"So...that's another dead end."

"I don't think so at all." Jeagan got up from the bar stool and pulled a glass from a cabinet. She filled it with ice water from the refrigerator door. "In fact, I think she knows exactly what happened to them, and she may know what happened to Alan."

"And you think that because...?" Roger waited.

"*Because* if Mr. McFarland was buying a baby or babies, his secretary would probably know something about it, might even have handled the paperwork. And, she would probably know where the files are stashed, or she may have destroyed them."

"That makes sense." Roger thought for a moment. "Destroying the files would've been her best bet if she wanted to stay out of jail."

"Exactly. Ms. Coleman sounded nervous or maybe afraid when I talked to her. Hopefully the files haven't been destroyed, and she knows where they are." Jeagan drank from her glass. She walked over to look out the window in the breakfast nook. In the light from the window, she watched a rabbit munching on tender spring grass.

"Or maybe she's just getting old. She's got to be in her seventies or eighties by now. Maybe she doesn't want to be bothered."

"No," Jeagan said, thoughtful. "I think she doesn't want anyone digging up what her boss did fifty years ago."

"So, you're going to go to Seattle to try to convince her to give you information about an illegal adoption that might implicate her as an accessory?"

"Well...when you put it that way... ." Jeagan said nothing for a moment, feeling a little deflated. "But, wouldn't the statute of limitation have been up years ago? Surely by now she wouldn't get into any trouble telling me what she knows, would she?"

"There's no statute of limitation on kidnapping." He added, a smile in his voice. "See, I told you we would make a good team."

Jeagan laughed, not able to stay mad at Roger. "I guess that means I'm not fired."

"I didn't say that," Roger said hesitantly.

"Well, I'm rehiring myself. I won't be in any danger going to Seattle and talking to Mrs. Coleman. I'll be back in a couple of days if I don't find anything."

"All right," Roger said, obviously realizing he couldn't stop her. "Keep in touch while you're there. I want to know exactly what's happening. Remember, Isabel hired me so I need to know what's going on."

"Yes, boss."

"And, Miss Smarty Pants, you can come and bail me out of this place when you get back if I'm still here. But, I'm hoping I'll get to go home tomorrow after the doctor gets the lab results."

"Okay. Fine. My flight arrives around noon on Thursday. I'll stop by and spring you out of that joint, if you're still there."

"Okay, Watson. Go get 'em, but be careful. Your dad will kill me if anything else happens to you!"

"Goodnight, Sherlock." She disconnected with a wry smile on her face. "That man's going to drive me crazy!"

She retrieved her suitcase and walked through the family room toward her bedroom. Suddenly, she felt a cold chill. It felt like someone was watching her. When she turned around and looked out the family room windows, she saw no one in the light from the windows or the street lights, but she walked over and closed the drapes, rechecked the doors to make sure they were all locked, set the alarm, and headed toward her bedroom. Twenty minutes afterwards, she crawled in bed, too tired to worry about anyone or anything.

Monday, March 21st

The next morning, Jeagan's alarm went off at seven. She punched the button to turn it off and pulled herself out of bed aching all over. She pulled off her navy Broncos nightshirt and stepped into a hot shower. The pulsating hot water felt wonderful on her sore muscles. When she got out and dried off, she felt much better. Coffee would make her feel even better. She blew her hair dry and dressed. The aroma of fresh coffee wafted through the townhouse, and soon—dressed in a black wool-and-silk pantsuit, white silk sweater, and black heels—she headed for the kitchen. She thought about the coffee she'd started to drink the day before. Hopefully, this cup wouldn't end up all over her and her trench coat. Trench coat. Seattle. Rain. The three were synonymous. Oh, well, her trench coat was at the cleaners. But, she still had her umbrella.

After pouring a cup of coffee, adding cream and sweetener, she took a long sip. Mmm! Two slices of raisin toast and she would be good to go. She watered the ficus tree in the family room while her raisin bread toasted. The tree drooped from neglect for two weeks but should quickly revive. A little sunlight would help. She walked over to open the drapes. When she did, she glanced out the window, only to see a small black car drive slowly past her townhouse. The driver, a woman, had curly red hair!

Jeagan ran to the door, pulled it open, and bolted down the sidewalk. By the time she got to the curb, the car was gone. If she could only have gotten a license plate number! Back inside, she slammed the door. Who was spying on her and why? Had Agnes sent someone to threaten her? If so, now that Jeagan had let it slip to Madison that she was going to Seattle, would he tell Agnes? Would someone follow her to Seattle? Too many unanswered questions, but she wasn't going to let anyone stop her from searching for Alan.

She locked the door. In the kitchen, she shoved the water pitcher under the sink and poured her coffee into a go-cup. The toast she pulled from the toaster was the same color as her coffee, so she dropped it in the trash. Her morning was off to a roaring start! Getting out of town. That had to be a good thing.

Chapter Nine

As soon as she was on the road to the airport, she felt better. The sky was a clear baby blue with a few white wisps of cloud riding high. Golden sunshine wiped away all traces of the problems from the day before. And, the red-headed woman driving by her townhouse was probably just a coincidence. This was going to be a good day; she was determined that it be so.

The sooner she could find out what happened to Alan, the sooner she could return to Colorado, go back to her job, find out if and when she had to go to Oxford, Mississippi to testify in court, and get her life under control. And, hopefully, Isabel's as well. Maybe in the next few days, she'd have some good news for Isabel. *Please God!*

Driving to Stapleton Airport took all her attention in morning traffic, even if it was past rush hour. She parked in the economy lot and rode a shuttle to the terminal. The curb agent there checked her bag, which freed her to go straight to the Continental gate. With plenty of time before her ten o'clock flight, she strolled along glancing in interesting shops, which displayed everything from books and magazines to designer coffee to colorful fringy western wear to orange Denver Broncos caps and jerseys.

She checked the gates she passed to see where the planes were going: London, San Francisco, New York, St. Thomas. Places she hadn't visited, but hoped to one day.

The agent was announcing general boarding when she arrived at the gate. She joined the remaining people in line, pulled her boarding pass out of her handbag, and waited her turn. While the line inched forward, she looked out the wall of windows and watched while the ground crew loaded luggage onto the big jet.

Only a few people remained in the line in front of Jeagan when she turned around to see if anyone was still seated in the gate area. She knew many people flew stand-by, a nerve-wracking way to travel. As she turned her head, she noticed a young woman standing by a column talking on her cellphone. The woman had curly red hair! Could it be the same woman who had ordered the flowers and had driven by her townhouse earlier?

"Your boarding pass, please."

Jeagan turned to the gate agent who held out her hand.

"Oh, sorry." Jeagan handed over the pass.

Immediately, she looked behind her to see if the red-headed woman was still there, but she was gone. *Don't!* Jeagan thought as she turned to walk along the Jetway. *There are thousands of women with red hair.* But, she realized, if it *was* the same woman, at least she wasn't on the same flight.

While Jeagan walked down the Jetway to the plane and, once inside, along the aisle to her seat, she checked to see if any women fit that description or if she recognized anyone. Her seat was toward the rear of the plane, and she was one of the last to board. So, by the time she reached her seat, she felt confident she'd seen nearly everyone on the plane and that no one was following her—at least no one with curly red hair.

Within minutes, the flight attendant went through safety instructions and the plane backed away from the gate. Jeagan shifted in her window seat to get comfortable so she could watch the ramp activity. Slowly, the plane turned toward the runway. After waiting in line a few minutes for takeoff, the plane thrust forward and lifted into the air. Jeagan watched the familiar places of Denver grow smaller while the plane banked and turned northwest to cross the Rocky Mountains.

She leaned her head back and closed her eyes, planning to rest for a few minutes before the flight attendants came by with coffee. When she did open her eyes, it was not for coffee.

"Miss? Miss?" Someone gently shook Jeagan.

"What?" Jeagan said, popping up like a jack-in-the-box.

"We've landed in Seattle," the flight attendant said.

Jeagan looked around in disbelief. The plane was nearly empty. She stretched, realizing she must have really been tired to sleep through the entire flight. "Thanks," she said to the slim, dark-haired flight attendant. "Short flight."

The middle-aged woman smiled, understanding, and continued toward the rear of the plane.

Jeagan unfastened her seat belt and reached under the seat in front of her to dig out her handbag. She stood, bending over somewhat as she made her way to the aisle, now empty except for her.

At the front of the plane, a flight attendant with one of the pilots beside her waited until Jeagan made her way forward.

"Nice flight. Thank you," Jeagan said.

A blast of cold, moist air hit her when she entered the Jetway. "Oh, no!" she said to no one in particular.

"It's supposed to stop raining this afternoon." Jeagan turned to see a man standing to her left. He was pulling up the handle of a rollaboard and hooking a briefcase over it. "Supposed to be in the sixties by midafternoon."

"That's good news. I didn't bring anything heavier than a leather jacket."

"You should be fine with that," he said.

She liked his casual look: khakis, black sweater, loafers, and a black leather jacket. Neat. He wore black well with his curly light-brown hair and light tan. Indigo eyes smiled down at her.

"Thanks." She started up the Jetway. "I don't want to have to go out and buy a heavy raincoat."

The man walked along beside her. "I live here. These March showers don't last too long."

"That's good to know. I'll only be here for three days, so I hope the weather will be decent."

"You live in Denver?" the man asked as they walked out into the gate area.

"Highlands Ranch. It's a suburb south of Denver."

"Ah." He nodded. "I've heard of it. Supposed to be one of the fastest growing areas in the country."

Jeagan laughed. "Seems like it. Sometimes I think I can actually see it growing as the Californians sweep in from the west and the Texans from the south."

"Trying to get away from high taxes and all that," he commented.

"So I hear." She looked for a sign to show her the way to Baggage Claim.

"Baggage Claim is that way," the man said pointing.

"Thanks. Nice talking to you."

"Same here," he said. "Enjoy your trip."

Jeagan followed the signs to retrieve her luggage. *Nice man*, she thought, *and good looking. Wonder if he's married?* Then she laughed at herself. *You're not here looking for a man.* She strolled along, taking her time and watching people who came in all shapes and sizes, most in a hurry.

Fortunately, her suitcase had made the trip with her and awaited her in Baggage Claim. She retrieved it and wove her way through the travelers to the door and the sidewalk. Again, cold, moist air hit her in the face. She looked around, spotted the Marriott Waterfront shuttle and moved quickly toward it. The driver grabbed her suitcase when she reached the van.

"Good afternoon." He hauled the suitcase on board.

"Thanks." Jeagan stepped up into the van. The heat was on. "Feels good in here," she commented when she found a seat and settled into it.

"Chilly today," the man said, although he wore only a white short-sleeved shirt with a Marriott emblem on it.

Other travelers boarded the van over the next few minutes. When the van was full, the driver pulled away from the curb and drove toward the airport exit. Jeagan watched in delight as a panorama of green unfolded before her, even greener than it had been in Memphis two weeks earlier. Cherry, ornamental plum, and pear were a few of the trees she recognized that graced the airport grounds and could be seen on the rolling hills beyond when they reached the expressway.

Traffic sloshed and splashed through the rain during the ride, but within ten minutes the sun peeped out from shredding gray clouds. By the time the van reached the hotel on Alaskan Way, Jeagan was happy to see the sun was shining brightly. She watched fresh rainwater drip from the new red blooms on the crabapple trees and snowy-white flowers on the pear trees. Artistic plantings of sunny jonquils and pink tulips decorated the hotel entrance. Spring, it seemed, was a collage of color in Seattle. Denver was far behind, with snowfall due again at any minute to hold spring off for a month or so longer.

Jeagan exited the van with a few other passengers, tipped the driver when he handed down her bag, and entered the modern, yet elegant, hotel lobby decorated in blues, black, and gold. She gazed up into a round lighted dome. While she waited in line at the front desk, she looked around the bright, cheerful lobby with colorful artwork on display. She checked in within a few minutes and rode the elevator to her room on the sixth floor. The spacious room, decorated in sea-green, blue, and sand colors overlooked Elliott Bay and Puget Sound. Anxious to check the view outside, she crossed the room to the balcony and opened the sliding glass door. The tangy smell of saltwater met her, when she stepped outside, along with the view of the marina and the grand Mount Rainier in the distance, now wreathed in a fleecy white cloud necklace.

Here, she felt safe. No harm could come to her in Seattle. No one knew she was here except for her father and Roger and Isabel. Well, she'd slipped and told Madison, but what could he do? He couldn't leave the state. Besides he'd called to apologize for his part in what had happened to her in Oxford, Mississippi.

A small voice inside her told her all her Pollyanna-ish thinking was only that. She'd also thought she was safe when she left Memphis and returned to Denver. At the time, she'd thought that the trauma and drama she'd experienced in Memphis and Oxford were behind her. But, after the wreck she and Roger had been involved in, the flowers with the threatening note, and the fact that someone might be following her again, she knew someone was still out there trying to stop her from finding Alan.

And Isabel changing her will was a double reason for someone to try to stop her and maybe get rid of her. That someone would have to be Agnes. But how could Agnes know Isabel had changed her will? Surely Isabel wouldn't have told her. It didn't matter. Agnes was out on bail and could find out somehow. Jeagan needed to get her name off Isabel's will, and soon.

Before she went inside, she rested her arms against the metal railing and let her problems go for a moment, wishing, as she'd done at The Peabody Hotel in Memphis earlier in the month, that she had someone to share the beautiful room and fantastic view. *Brandon, no way! Roger, maybe. That good-looking man she had met in the airport?* She laughed. What in the world made her think of him? Besides, she'd never see him again. No reason to even wonder.

She pushed away from the railing. Once inside, she closed and locked the glass door behind her. Her first priority was to contact Isabel's attorney and get her name off that will. She searched through her handbag for her notepad with the attorney's cellphone number. When she found it, she punched in the number. No answer after four rings, so she left a message with her cell number.

That done, she pulled out the Seattle telephone directory and searched for Susan Coleman. Having her phone number made finding the address easy. Jeagan jotted it on her notepad. Her next order of business was lunch. The strap of her handbag hooked over her shoulder, she left the room. The concierge could probably direct her to a good place for a late lunch, she thought, while she walked along the softly lighted, quiet hallway toward the elevators. She rode to the lobby with two Asian women who were obviously tourists. They said hello to Jeagan and resumed their conversation about the sites they wanted to see today, which included the Space Needle and the Ghirardelli Chocolate Company. The thought of the famous chocolate made Jeagan's mouth water.

She got off in the lobby and looked around for the concierge. A tall, young black man sat at the concierge's desk. He was on the phone when Jeagan approached. He held up a finger indicating he would be with her shortly.

"Good afternoon," he said with a bright friendly smile when his call was finished. "Can I help you?"

"Yes," she said. "I'd like to find a good place for lunch, preferably within walking distance."

"We're close to a lot of good restaurants here. How about the Pike Place Market area? It's the most popular."

"That would be fun. What would you suggest?"

"Let's see. You might try Maximilien, in the Market. French, but not too French."

"Hmm," Jeagan said. "Does it have a view?"

He nodded. "It's right on the Sound. Great views."

"That works for me. Thanks," she checked the nameplate on his desk, "Jerome."

"You're very welcome," he said. "Enjoy."

Jeagan turned to walk away. "Oh," she said turning back. "Which way and how far?"

"It's about half a mile southeast of here. Here," he said. "I'll mark it on this map." He pulled out a Seattle map and marked the route with a red marker.

"Thanks. This will help." Jeagan strode out the front entrance and turned south on Alaskan Way, enjoying the walk along the water. Other tourists carrying cameras and maps nodded to her when they passed on the sidewalk, which was shaded by mature trees showing off new spring-green leaves that gently rustled in the afternoon breeze. The fresh, brisk sea air energized her as she walked along.

* * *

The Market area bustled with activity in the early afternoon. Dodging strollers and baskets, she made her way through the shoppers to the restaurant where she was soon seated at a window table with a view of the Sound. It was good to be in Seattle even if she was alone and on a mission. She planned to enjoy herself, at least for a little while.

A young auburn-haired waitress momentarily brought her a menu and glass of ice water.

"Can I get you something else to drink?" the girl asked.

"Let's see." Jeagan scanned the menu. "How about a glass of your Duval-Leroy?"

The waitress wrote on her pad. "I'll give you a minute to look over the menu."

"Any suggestions?" Jeagan asked.

The waitress smiled, showing a hint of a dimple. "Everything is good, but my favorite is the Croque-Monsieur."

Jeagan checked the menu to see what that was. Black Forest ham and béchamel sauce. "I'll try that."

"With eggs?" The waitress asked.

"Yes. Eggs would be good. Thanks."

The view from the restaurant was spectacular, she noticed, pleased. She could see the Olympic Mountains in the distance partly obscured by clouds. When her wine arrived a few minutes later, she sipped it, leaned back in her chair, and sighed. The atmosphere of the restaurant was busy but casual. Silverware and glasses clinked, diners chatted, waiters passed carrying loaded trays, and aromas from the kitchen whetted her appetite.

She ate leisurely, when her lunch arrived, enjoying herself immensely yet feeling guilty about wasting time. *Well, a girl has to eat. Might as well enjoy it.* A glance at her watch told her it was almost two o'clock. She finished eating, declining a decadent dessert. Maybe another time.

Outside the restaurant, she walked through the Market watching people buying fresh vegetables, plants, knickknacks, and spices. Farther along, she saw a sign which read, World Famous Pike Place Fish Market, Home of the Flying Fish. *What*, she wondered, *are flying fish?*

She soon found out when an aproned young man held up a large red fish. Salmon? A customer nodded approval. The young man yelled something that sounded like he was going to deliver a karate chop, and then the fish went sailing through the air to another aproned man behind the counter. Customers standing around laughed and applauded. *Ahh, that's what they mean by flying fish!* She applauded with the others and then worked her way through the crowd out to the street.

Not far away, she saw a taxi stopped to let out a middle-aged couple. Spotting her, the man held the taxi door open. She thanked him as she stepped inside.

Middle Eastern and turbaned, the driver looked over his shoulder at her. "Where to?"

"Just a second." Jeagan pulled out her notepad. She read off Sue Coleman's address on 57th Avenue Northeast.

"Okay." The driver shifted the taxi into drive.

"How long will it take to get there?" Jeagan asked.

The driver shrugged. "Twenty minutes, maybe thirty, depending on traffic."

Jeagan watched the busy city pass by the window. Soon, they were on Interstate Five and then on a bridge crossing over Lake Washington. They drove past the University of Washington with its groomed lawns, stately brick-and-stone buildings, and towering trees.

"What are all those trees?" Jeagan asked noticing the mass of white flowering trees on the campus.

"Those are the famous Yoshino Cherry Trees," he replied.

"Beautiful," Jeagan commented.

Soon, the driver pulled into an older subdivision and stopped before a small, neat brick home, painted white with dark-green shutters. Jeagan would call it a charming bungalow. Rhododendron bushes bursting with deep pink blooms ran across the front of the house, interrupted only by wide front steps.

"Can you wait for me?" she asked the driver.

"No problem. Take your time." He leaned his head back against the seat and pulled a baseball cap over his eyes.

Jeagan got out and started up the sidewalk. She should have phoned first, but the woman would probably have refused to see her, might not see her now, might not even answer the door. A drape in a front window moved. Well, at least someone was home…and watching her.

"Here goes." Jeagan stepped up onto the porch and rang the doorbell beside the oak front door.

A few seconds passed before the door was opened. Then, a tall, slender, gray-haired woman said, "Yes?" Wary chocolate-brown eyes stared at Jeagan out of a mature yet elegant face, marked by only a few wrinkles.

"I'm Jeagan Christensen, Ms. Coleman. I spoke to you on the phone last night."

The woman frowned. "I thought that might be you. I told you last night that I can't help you. I'm sorry." She started to close the door.

Jeagan held out her hand. "If you'll give me a few minutes of your time, I won't bother you again."

The woman stood straighter. "Young lady, do you want me to call the police?"

Chapter Ten

Jeagan thought quickly. "Yes. Yes, that might be a good idea considering the man you worked for was buying stolen babies."

The woman's eyes widened. She gasped and grabbed her chest. "What do you want from me?" she said, her voice almost pleading. "Mr. McFarland is dead. I don't know where the records are. Can't you leave me alone?"

"No," Jeagan said, gathering her nerve. "I can't. If you know something that will help me find a child who was bought by your former employer, then no, I won't leave you alone. There's a mother in Memphis whose child was stolen from her at birth. She was told the baby was stillborn. Only recently did she find out that the child was alive at birth, and I know your boss paid her father ten thousand dollars for the baby. Ten thousand dollars was a lot of money in 1945." *It still is*, Jeagan thought.

She could see the woman struggling with herself. "May I come in and talk to you for a few minutes," Jeagan said, softening her tone. "I won't stay long. You can see I have a taxi waiting."

"All right." The woman looked past Jeagan to the taxi. "But only for a minute." Sue opened the door wider to let Jeagan into a small entry hall with an apple green oriental carpet covering oak flooring, and ushered her into a living room furnished with a skirted yellow sofa and chairs in a yellow-and-green chintz. A fire burned in the brick fireplace, making the room too warm for Jeagan.

"Have a seat," the woman said.

"Thank you." Jeagan sank into one of the armchairs. "If you'll tell me what you know, I'll go away. I just need to find out if Mr. McFarland's records still exist, and, if so, where they are."

"I told you." Sue Coleman perched on the edge of the sofa as if ready to bolt. "I don't know where Mr. McFarland kept his records."

"You were his secretary. Weren't you the person who filed his correspondence, typed his documents, kept track of all his files?"

"I didn't type all his correspondence, and I didn't have access to all his files." The woman turned to look out the front and then the side windows.

Jeagan's blood pressure jumped a notch. She sat forward. "Are you saying he had files you didn't keep track of?"

Sue turned and stared at Jeagan. After a brief pause, she seemed to come to a decision. "Mr. McFarland kept a four-drawer filing cabinet in a small closet off his office. He had the only key."

"What was in the file cabinet?"

Sue shook her head. "I don't know. I saw the cabinet only when I went into his office and the door to the closet happened to be open. I saw him put files and documents into the cabinet many times. I never asked what was in it, and he never offered to tell me."

Jeagan pressed. "But you suspected, didn't you?"

The woman stood, as the color rose in her cheeks. She waved her hands in exasperation. "I didn't suspect anything! I had a good job. I was raising two small boys, alone. My husband was killed in the war, so I needed to keep my job. I might have been curious about what Mr. McFarland kept in the cabinet, but I didn't ask."

"Did Mr. McFarland do or say anything to make you think he was involved in something illegal?"

"Not really. It's just…well, two or three times a year he would go out of town, he and his wife, and they would make the arrangements themselves."

"Was that unusual?"

"Yes. It was." Sue eased down onto an arm of the sofa. "I always made their travel arrangements, except for these particular times. During the week before they left, there would be a flurry of phone calls from one of three attorneys."

"Who were the attorneys?"

"I…I don't remember their names." Sue cast her eyes down.

Jeagan knew Sue remembered the names of the attorneys. To be this upset over the questions that were being asked her, she had to know something more. Something that had bothered her for many years. Maybe a different approach would help. "How long did you work for Mr. McFarland?"

"For almost forty years, until he passed away eight years ago."

"So, he died after the office moved in the summer of 1986?"

Sue nodded. "Yes. He had heart trouble. He had a couple of heart attacks before he had the massive one a few days before Christmas in 1986."

"Then, after his death, you retired?"

"Yes. Young Mr. McFarland—"

"Chuck?"

Sue smiled, a tiny smile. "Yes. Young Charles, we called him. He took over the office. He asked me to stay, but I couldn't work for anyone but his father. So, I retired."

"Do you have any idea what happened to the file cabinet? That is, after you moved into the new office."

Sue looked thoughtful. "Mr. McFarland brought it with him. I remember the heated discussions he had with his son over having a room set aside for his private closet."

The hair bristled on the back of Jeagan's neck. "But Chuck said the files in his office only date back to 1960."

"That's probably true." Sue got up and walked over to the front windows where she stared out. "I'm sure he had no idea what was in his father's private filing cabinet."

"What happened to the cabinet?"

"I don't know." Sue turned around to look at Jeagan. Tears shimmered in her eyes. "I stayed on for a week after Mr. McFarland died. He died on a Friday. When I came into the office on the following Monday, I went into his private office to get things organized. I noticed the door to his closet was open. I checked inside, and the filing cabinet was gone."

Jeagan sat forward in her seat. "And you don't know who moved it?"

Sue shook her head. "No, and I didn't ask. I'm sure Charles knew who took it, but he never mentioned it." She folded her arms across her chest as if to block Jeagan out and hold further information inside. "If that's all your questions, I need for you to go. There's nothing else I can tell you."

"Just one more question and I'll go." Jeagan rose from the chair. "I think you know the names of the three attorneys who called your boss before he made his mysterious trips, don't you? Please tell me."

Sue flushed again and turned away from Jeagan. "I told you I don't remember. I need for you to leave now. Please!"

She definitely knew the names of the attorneys, but she wasn't going to reveal them. "Just tell me if one of the attorneys lived in Memphis."

"No! I don't know!" the woman said. "Now, please go!" She moved into the front hall and opened the door.

"Thank you for your help, Ms. Coleman." Jeagan followed her into the hall. "I'm sorry I've upset you." She quickly pulled a business card from her billfold and dropped it on a small table. "You can reach me on my cellphone if you remember the names of the attorneys or would like to talk."

The door closed firmly behind Jeagan. The woman was nervous and scared, and she'd only told part of what she knew. Jeagan wasn't sure whom Sue was more afraid of, the authorities finding out she knew something about what her former boss had done or those who were still alive finding out she'd told Jeagan part of what she knew. Sue was definitely in a Catch 22 situation.

* * *

"Thanks for waiting," Jeagan said to the driver when she got back in the taxi.

"No, problem." The man straightened in his seat and started the taxi. "Where to?"

"I need to go to the law office of Charles McFarland. I know he's on Second Avenue. Do you have a phone directory?"

"Sure," the driver said. He reached under his seat, pulled out a large tattered Metropolitan Seattle directory and handed it over the seat.

"Thanks." She flipped through the attorney section until she found McFarland and McFarland, Attorneys at Law. "Here it is." She read off the address to the driver.

The driver nodded. He pulled back onto the street. Forty minutes later, he stopped in front of a skyscraper on Second Avenue.

"Want me to wait?" he asked.

"No, thanks." Jeagan got out. She paid the fare and crossed the sidewalk to the tall, gray stone building. When she looked down, she saw what appeared to be glass blocks in the sidewalk. *Wonder what those are?* She crossed to the entrance. Above the brass-framed glass doors was the name of the building, The Smith Tower, and the date it was erected, 1914.

Jeagan entered the skyscraper and smiled with pleasure at the charm and elegance of the lobby area with mosaic-tiled floors and onyx paneling. Curious, she noticed that carved heads of Indians with colorful headdresses were mounted high on the walls around the lobby area—all the same Indian.

"May I help you?" someone asked.

"Oh." Jeagan turned to see a security guard, neatly dressed in a navy blazer and khaki pants. "Yes. I'm looking for McFarland and McFarland attorneys."

"I believe they're on the eighteenth floor, but let's check the building directory to make sure." Jeagan followed the man along the hall to a brass-framed building directory set in the wall. "Yes, eighteenth floor." He pointed farther down the hallway. "The elevators are over there."

"Thank you." Before moving, she asked, "What are all those Indian heads?"

"They're all the same, as I guess you can tell." She nodded. "They're a composite of the Northwestern Indians."

"I imagine you get asked that question a lot, don't you?"

"All the time," he replied. "And, usually people ask if he's Chief Seattle."

"Is he?"

"No. I don't believe he is."

"This is a lovely building," she commented, noticing the winding marble staircase with the wrought-iron railing.

"It's Seattle's first skyscraper. If you have time, you might want to go up to the observation deck on the thirty-fifth floor. There's a great view of the city and the mountains."

"Thank you, Mr.?"

"Just Mike," he replied.

"Thanks, Mike." She continued toward the elevators. After a few steps, she stopped and turned around. "Can you tell me what those glass blocks in the sidewalk are? They look like some kind of windows."

Mike nodded. "They are. They're skylights into Seattle's Underground."

"Seattle's underground?"

"Yes. Years ago, flooding was a problem in some areas so the City of Seattle raised the streets one story, which left buildings below street level. Some of those were used for the seedier side of Seattle life, but we now own the space under our building and use it for storage."

"That's amazing! Thanks."

"No problem."

To her further amazement, when the elevator doors, complete with a sliding brass and copper grill, opened, she saw a uniformed elevator operator inside. "This is like stepping back in time," she commented as she entered the car.

The gray-haired operator smiled benignly. "Elegance never goes out of style. What floor would you like, Miss?"

After a short ride, Jeagan made her way along a gray-patterned carpet to the attorney's office on the eighteenth floor. She pushed open the glass door and entered a sleek, modern reception area. The gray-patterned carpet carried over from the hallway, but the black leather sofa and black-and-white plaid fabric armchairs complemented it well, especially with polished teak tables and artwork in bold reds, yellows, and blues on silver-gray walls.

Standing beside her desk, the receptionist—dark-haired and sleek like her surroundings and wearing a slim black mini—greeted Jeagan with a dazzling white smile. "May I help you?"

"Yes." Jeagan approached the reception desk. "I don't have an appointment, but I wondered if I might be able to see Mr. McFarland for a few minutes?"

"He's with a client now." The girl traced a perfectly French-manicured nail down her appointment book. "But, he may have a few minutes afterward until his next appointment arrives." She looked over at Jeagan. "Are you a new client?"

"No," Jeagan said. "I'm from Denver. I talked to Mr. McFarland yesterday and wanted to stop in to say hello in person." *Better leave off the fact that I want a chance to 'grill him' in person.*

"Oh," the receptionist said. "I'm sure he'd love to chat with you, if you'd like to have a seat and wait."

"Thank you." *Yes*, Jeagan thought. *If my phone conversation with him is any indication, I believe Chuck would 'chat' with a fencepost.*

"Would you like something to drink? Coffee, juice, or water?" the receptionist asked.

"No, thanks. I'm good." Jeagan sat in a plaid chair. It held her in soft comfort. She reached over and picked up a copy of *Seattle Magazine* from the coffee table. Idly, she flipped through pages filled with pictures of the skyline, the Space Needle, ferries, restaurants, art galleries, real estate agencies, and attorneys' offices.

She stopped when she recognized a familiar face. She studied the page. The attorney. It was a picture of the man she'd met in the Jetway, or at least it looked like him. Posing with three other attorneys, the caption underneath indicated that his name was Scott Singer, Attorney at Law. He appeared younger in the picture by a few years and reminded her of a young Harrison Ford. The tasteful advertisement showed a photo of the offices of Horton, Sweeney, and Singer, located on Fourth Avenue. The cream stone-and-stucco office with black trim appeared to have been converted from a two-story home. The catch phrase for the attorneys read: "Trial Lawyers Committed to Proactive Representation."

Scott Singer, Jeagan mused. *Wonder if he's single?* She quickly stopped herself. *No more attorneys, single or not.*

A door opened in a hallway to Jeagan's right. She heard Chuck speaking to someone while they walked toward the reception area. Momentarily, he came into view with his hand on the shoulder of a salt-and-pepper haired middle-aged man, slightly stooped as if the weight of the world were on his shoulders. When the man raised his head and glanced toward Jeagan, his worried, drawn face confirmed this impression. Jeagan smiled, hoping to reassure him that the sky had not fallen as yet today.

Chuck noticed Jeagan, his eyebrows rising in appreciation of what he saw. Jeagan shuddered. Fair skinned, medium height, round with thinning blond hair, Chuck leered more than looked at her.

"Stiff upper lip now, Dylan." Chuck ushered the troubled man into the hall. "I'll handle everything." Jeagan watched while they spoke for a few moments longer and then shook hands. Chuck pushed open the office door after the elevator doors closed.

He walked over to Jeagan as she stood up. "Good afternoon." He offered his hand and a broad smile. "I'm Charles McFarland. Well, Chuck to my friends...and colleagues...and enemies, come to that." He smiled at his little joke.

Here we go, Jeagan thought. *He's long-winded and a little scattered.* She extended her hand. "I'm Jeagan Christensen." Chuck looked puzzled. "We spoke yesterday on the phone. I called you from Denver."

"Oh!" Chuck said, the light coming on in his eyes. He pumped her hand. She pulled away after he held it a second too long. "Yes. You called regarding my father's files. Adoptions, that sort of thing." He scratched his balding head. "Don't handle adoptions anymore. Too sticky."

"Yes," Jeagan said. "Thought I'd like to see you in person. See if you could spare me a few minutes." She laughed, realizing she was talking like him.

"Oh, right." Chucked glanced at his watch. He turned to the receptionist. "Diana, what time are the O'Reilly's due here."

"You've got ten minutes before they're scheduled," the receptionist replied.

"Good, good. Plenty of time for a chat. Right this way, Jeagan. May I call you Jeagan?"

"Of course," she said, thinking how pseudo-formal he was acting. Pretending or schooling? He held out his hand and placed it on her back while he guided her toward his office.

"Now," he said, ushering her inside his huge office and closing the door. Did she hear the click of a lock? Surely not. "Have a seat." He rounded his ornate mahogany desk.

A little feminine for a man, she thought, but he'd probably brought the desk from jolly ol' England and thought it a reminder of his time at Oxford. She wouldn't comment on it for fear of another litany on the subject of desks or England or what-have-you.

Briefly, she looked around the office with dark cherrywood shelves displaying statues, vases, pictures of a plump woman and similar progeny, framed watercolor landscapes and seascapes on the silver-gray walls, and an antique grandfather clock, which ticked softly in a corner.

She sat in one of the offered black-leather armchairs facing Chuck's desk while he lowered his bulk into his high-backed leather chair. "Now, how can I help you, young lady?" he said cheerily.

"Well," Jeagan began, knowing she had to tactfully get right to the point since she had limited time. "I just came from talking with Sue Coleman."

Chuck sat forward in his chair, resting his forearms on his desk. "Oh?"

"Yes. Sue told me your father had a file cabinet that he moved with him to this office before he died. And she said he kept it in a personal closet to which only he had a key."

"Could have been." Chuck seemed to mull over the possibility. His eyes glazed over. In disinterest or coverup? "Seems he had some sort of private closet with a file cabinet he was keen on keeping a secret.

Think we might have had a row about it at some point, the private closet, that is."

So, he did remember. "Yes. Sue mentioned that. She also said the file cabinet disappeared over the weekend after your father died. She never saw it again."

Chuck rubbed his chin. "Not sure about that, but again it could have been. That was a sad time all round for the lot of us, including Lady Coleman." He chuckled at his name for his father's secretary. "Out of a job, she was," he snapped his fingers, "just like that."

"Yes. She told me."

Lost in memory again, Chuck continued. "Tried to get her to stay on, work for me or the new attorney when we hired one."

"She must have been very devoted to your father," Jeagan offered.

"Yes...yes. Very," Chuck commented.

"So," Jeagan eased him back to the subject of the files. "Do you know what could have happened to the file cabinet with your father's personal files? Any idea where it might have been taken or by whom?"

"No. Barely even remember it. Didn't think anything about it being removed at the time. Too upset by father's sudden death. Afterwards, too much to do. Funeral arrangements. Probate of the will." He looked at Jeagan. "A million details."

"Yes," Jeagan said. "I can empathize with you."

Chuck turned to gaze out the tall windows behind him. The Olympic Mountains lazed in the afternoon sun. "Only one person who might have removed the files."

Hopeful, Jeagan waited for the name.

"After Mum passed on in 1970, the 'pater' married Cruella."

"Cruella?"

"Well, not really her name, is it?" He uttered a dry laugh. "But, my older brother Bob and I referred to her as that. Thrilled she was to pack me off to 'uni' at Oxford and get me out of her hair. Not that I minded. Lovely country and all that England. Except for all the bloody rain."

Although curious about where Brother Bob had been 'packed off' to, Jeagan dared not ask for fear Chuck would be off on another tangent. "What's her name?"

"Patrice. Patrice Bloody Regnier. Had to keep her name when she married my father, didn't she? Proud of her French heritage."

"I'm sorry you didn't get along with her," Jeagan offered in sympathy. "Do you know how I can get in touch with her?"

"Why would anyone with their full faculties want to get in touch with her?" Chuck asked, incredulous. "She's a right witch."

"Well, if she has any information about the missing files, I'd like to talk to her."

A chuckle rumbled from the attorney. "Good luck. She wouldn't give you the right time of day if she was a bloody clock."

Further conversation was interrupted by the intercom. Diana's voice, smooth as silk, informed Chuck that his next appointment had arrived.

"Well," Chuck said standing up from his desk, "don't think I've been much help to you, but I wish you luck in your search for the missing boy, I mean man."

"Thank you." Jeagan stood also. "I appreciate your taking the time to see me. Oh, and one more thing before I go. Can you give me a phone number for your stepmother?"

"Check under Cruella DeVille in the phone directory?" Chuck laughed at his pitiful joke. He rounded the desk. When he saw that Jeagan didn't laugh, he added. "You'll find her listed in the phone directory. Still lives in the family home on Lake Washington. Just around the bend from that Gates fellow, I believe."

Chapter Eleven

Jeagan rode the elevator to the lobby and waved to Mike, who was regaling a group of tourists with the charms of the historic building.

A little past four, her watch showed when she exited the building. "No time like the present," she said aloud and walked out to the edge of the sidewalk to hail a passing taxi. Once inside, she again asked for a telephone directory and thumbed through the pages in search of Patrice Regnier. She found a listing for her on East 37th Avenue in Madison Park. After she provided the address, Jeagan got comfortable for the, according to the driver, twenty-minute drive.

Again, the beauty of Seattle in full spring bloom fed her senses. They drove through the city and past the Washington Park Arboretum with its white flowering cherry trees and bright yellow forsythia. When they arrived at the address, Jeagan gazed up at a large three-story, taupe-colored wood-and-brick home. She asked the driver to wait while she strode through the front white gate and up the brick sidewalk and steps to the front door. Again, calling had not been an option, but what was the worst that could happen?

The doorbell chimed softly when Jeagan pressed it. She heard footsteps and one of the white front doors was opened by a small oriental woman dressed neatly in black slacks and fitted white overblouse. "May I help you?" she asked.

"I'd like to see Mrs. McFarland," Jeagan said.

The woman, probably in her mid-forties, Jeagan guessed, said, "Ms. Patrice. She expect you?"

"Well, no," Jeagan said. "Not really. Uh, I'm doing some research for a friend, and I'd like to talk with her about her late husband."

A wall seemed to come up behind the woman's eyes. "I'm sorry. Ms. Patrice can no see you without appointment. She very busy lady." The woman sharply bowed her head in dismissal.

"But," Jeagan placed her hand on the open door. "I've come all the way from Denver to see her, and it's very important. In fact, it might be a matter of life and death."

Jeagan heard a rustling behind the small woman, who turned her head.

"I'll handle this, Mei Li," Jeagan heard an older woman say behind the oriental maid.

Mei Li bowed slightly and backed away from the door.

An elegant woman, moderately tall with steel-gray hair pulled back in a French twist, opened the door wider. Eyes the color of stormy spring rain clouds focused on Jeagan. "What is it you want?" she said, her tone barely the right side of haughty.

Jeagan took in the expensive cut of the woman's pearl-gray wool suit and freshwater pearls. She didn't know what else to say except the truth. "I'm trying to find a child who was stolen from his mother at birth and sold to your husband for ten thousand dollars in 1945."

The shock of Jeagan's words penetrated the coldness of the woman's stare. Her lips parted as her hand flew to her mouth. She grabbed the edge of the door for support.

"Are you all right?" Jeagan felt like kicking herself for being so blunt, and moved forward to help the woman.

Patrice stepped away. "I'm fine, young woman, but I have no idea what you're talking about, and I cannot help you. Now, if you'll excuse me, I need to leave for an important meeting." She started to close the door.

Again, Jeagan reached out to stop the door from closing. "Please. I need to find information about the adoption of the child. His mother only recently found out he wasn't stillborn, but taken from her and sold. She's now in the Intensive Care Unit in a hospital in Memphis, and I need to find the child for her before something happens to her."

The woman cast her eyes down, hiding her expression. "I'm sorry. I can't help you."

"I know you can help me."

The woman glared at Jeagan. "Excuse me?"

"I've seen a copy of the check from your late husband, and I know he had a filing cabinet that he kept under lock and key. And, I know it disappeared the weekend of his death. So, you must know what happened to it. It may have records in it that will lead me to the—"

Patrice's look hardened. "I've told you I can't help you. Now, I must ask you to leave or I'll call the police." She shut the door with a loud *thud*.

Jeagan stared blankly at the closed door. "Well, that went well," she said aloud.

"So, Cruella slammed the door in your face."

Startled, Jeagan turned to see a tall man with dark, wavy hair. Dressed in tan slacks with a white shirt and light jacket, the smirk on his face reminded her of Roger.

"Oh, I guess you could say that." She watched him walk up the sidewalk to the front porch. "Second time today I've been threatened with the police."

He stepped onto the porch and leaned against a post. "Who are you?" he asked, taking her in from head to toe.

Jeagan stuck out her hand. "I'm Jeagan Christensen. I'm from Denver."

"Denver, huh? Well, pleased to meet you, pardnuh." He wiped his hand on his slacks, like any good cowboy, and stuck it out while giving her a lopsided John Wayne grin. Jeagan giggled, noticing his sky-blue eyes and brilliant white smile. "Name's Sam Tinsley McFarland, at your service."

"Are you—" Jeagan pointed toward the house.

"Afraid so. She's my grandmother."

"You're Chuck's son?"

"No. I'm Bob's son. Bob's Chuck's older brother."

"Oh," Jeagan said. "Well, it's nice to meet you, Sam. Guess I'd better go. I've got a taxi waiting." She started down the sidewalk.

"How long are you staying in Seattle?" Sam asked behind her.

Jeagan turned. "Only a few days. I'm here trying to find out about a child who was," Jeagan didn't want to go into all that with Sam, "a child who was adopted. Your grandfather handled the adoption many years ago."

"Have dinner with me tonight, and we can talk it over. Maybe I can help you get in to see my grandmother. Well, she's really my step-grandmother."

Jeagan hesitated. She *did* have to eat and why not with a handsome man? It wasn't like he was a stranger. She knew who his relatives were. "All right."

"Great!" Sam said. "Where are you staying?"

"Why don't I meet you somewhere?" she suggested.

"Fair enough," he agreed. "Do you like seafood?"

"Absolutely."

"Great! Meet me at Elliott's Oyster House at," he checked his watch, "say eight o'clock?"

"Okay. Where is it?"

"It's on Alaskan Way, Pier 56."

"My hotel's close to there, so I should be able to find it."

On the ride to her hotel, Jeagan realized she hadn't gained much information today, but she felt like she'd advanced a little in her search.

* * *

She opened the door to her room half an hour later, dropped her handbag on the bed, and then sat beside it to search through it for her notepad with the two numbers she needed: Isabel's number in the Memphis hospital and Roger's in the Denver hospital. Too many hospitals! Before she could dial either number, her cellphone rang.

"Mark Edwards, returning your call," the voice said when Jeagan answered.

"Oh, Mr. Edwards. Glad you called. I wanted to ask you to take my name off Isabel's will."

He hesitated before responding. "I'm sorry, Miss Christensen, but I can't do that unless Isabel instructs me to."

"But," insisted Jeagan, "I don't want any of her money. In fact, as long as I'm named as a beneficiary, I believe my life's in danger."

"Have you received a threat of some sort?" he asked disinterestedly, as if they were discussing the weather.

"Yes." Jeagan explained what had happened over the past two days.

"I can't believe anyone in Isabel's family could have been involved in the accident or sending the threatening note with the flowers. After all, Isabel doesn't have any children of her own, and her sister's in a Mississippi jail."

"Correction. Her sister's out on bail."

"How do you know that?" he said, although his tone implied, "How did you find out?"

80

"Madison, I mean, Darrell Hannah called me last night and told me. He's out on bail also."

"Well, that's not good news," the attorney said. He was silent for a moment. "If you really want your name removed from Isabel's will, you'd better talk to her directly. That is, when she feels like talking."

"Has something else happened? I talked to her last night. She sounded a little stronger."

"She had another minor attack today," Edwards continued, "if you can call any heart attack minor."

"Oh, I'm so sorry. Is anyone with her?"

"Don't worry. She's not alone. She has a lot of friends at her church, and there have been people taking turns sitting with her since she came out of surgery yesterday."

"Should I call her or maybe wait until tomorrow?"

"I just left the hospital. She was weak and sleeping. You probably should wait until tomorrow to call."

After disconnecting, Jeagan dialed Roger's cellphone. She'd try that before she tried his hospital room phone. He answered on the first ring.

"Hey, Roger. How're you feeling?"

"Hey, yourself. I'm doing better. In fact, I'm at home now."

"That's great news!" Jeagan said. "Your test results must have come back normal."

"Yep! Dr. Jones said I was good to go home."

"How'd you get home?"

"Umm." Roger was silent for a moment. "Actually, Shelley drove me."

Jeagan heard someone talking in the background. "Oh. Okay. Is she still there?"

"As a matter of fact, she is. Hold on a minute." Roger put his hand over the receiver and said something. He came back on the line in a few seconds. "Can I call you back in a few minutes?"

"Sure," Jeagan said, somewhat annoyed the vampiress was there with Roger. *How had she found out about the accident?* "How did she know you were in the hospital?" Jeagan said, but the phone was dead. Roger had already hung up.

"Well, I guess he likes her a little more than I thought." She got up from the bed and walked over to the balcony, opened the door, and stepped outside. The afternoon sun felt warm, but not too warm with the cool breeze from the water. Feeling deflated or maybe a little jealous that Roger was with Shelley, Jeagan sat on one of the patio chairs. *Don't be silly*, she thought. *Roger doesn't owe me anything. Just because I had dinner with him and planned to come to Seattle with him to search for Alan.... Besides, I'm having dinner tonight with a good-looking guy so I'm not exactly alone myself. Sam's probably a little younger, but that's okay. It's only dinner, and maybe he can help me find those records.*

Jeagan breathed deeply of the fresh, salty air and hopped up from her chair, feeling better after her talk with herself. She returned inside to shower and dress for dinner, glad she'd brought a dressy dress and her black sling-backs.

* * *

At seven-forty-five, the doorman hailed a taxi for her, which put her at Elliott's Oyster House a few minutes before eight. She walked inside the restaurant and gave her name to the hostess. The friendly young woman pointed to Sam, who was waiting in the bar.

A scowl on his face, Sam was talking on his cellphone. When he turned and saw Jeagan, he quickly ended the call. He came toward her smiling.

"Wow!" he said. "You're a knockout in that dress!"

Jeagan laughed, pleased to hear a compliment after the day she'd had. "Thanks."

The waitress showed them to a table overlooking the now-dark Elliott Bay with lights around the dock area that reflected on the gentle ripples of the water. While waiting for their drinks to arrive, they studied the menu. Sam reached for hers. "Let me order for both of us."

Jeagan closed the menu and handed it to him. "All right." She narrowed her eyes. "But if I don't like my dinner, you're in trouble."

"If you like seafood, you'll love it. Trust me."

Right, trust me, she thought. *How many times had she heard those words?*

When the waitress returned with Jeagan's wine and Sam's martini, Sam ordered smoked king salmon on pickled beets, a mussel salad, and poached pears with gingerbread pudding—for two.

"Wow! If that's as good as it sounds... ."

"Believe me. It is," Sam said. "Okay." He picked up his martini. "A toast."

Jeagan picked up her glass. "A toast," she echoed. "What shall we toast?"

"Here's to a lovely Colorado lady. May she find everything she's searching for in Seattle."

"I'll drink to that." Jeagan sipped her wine. "That's really good. I like that."

"So. How can I help you?"

Jeagan set her glass on the table and explained what she was doing in Seattle, leaving out details such as almost being drowned and run down and receiving a threat with a dozen blood-red roses.

When she finished her story, Sam said, "Ouch! I guess I find it hard to believe my grandfather would be involved in anything like buying stolen babies."

"Were you close to him?"

"No, not really. I'm not sure anybody was close to him, except my grandmother. After she died, I didn't see much of him. Then, he met Cruella, and we didn't see him at all. She swept him off his feet."

"I thought it was supposed to be the other way around," Jeagan commented.

Their salads arrived then, so they concentrated on their food for a few minutes.

"What do you think of the salad?" Sam asked after a short silence.

"Not bad," Jeagan said with a smile.

"Not bad! It's excellent!"

"Okay." Jeagan laughed. "Maybe it's a little bit delicious. She soon moved her empty salad plate to the side. "So back to your grandfather."

"Like I said, Cruella breezed in and took over. He fell for her like a rock."

"So, did you ever visit him in his office?" Jeagan asked.

"A few times. I went with my dad, but we didn't stay long. Grandfather didn't seem to want anything to do with us. That hurt Dad a lot."

"Do you remember your grandfather's office layout? I mean do you remember a closet in his office that he kept locked?"

Sam rubbed his chin. "No. Not really. I never stayed in his office long enough to notice much of anything except his indifference to my dad and me and my brother."

"That's too bad, Sam," Jeagan said. "I'm sorry."

After the salmon and while they were eating the pears and pudding, Jeagan asked Sam how he thought he could help her.

"You're here to find records of an adoption that happened how many years ago?"

"About fifty. Your uncle told me your grandfather kept records in his office closet that no one had access to but him. I talked with Sue, your grandfather's secretary, and she said she knew nothing about adoptions, which could mean the records were in those files." Jeagan leaned forward. "If I could find those files, that is, if they still exist, maybe I could find out who adopted Alan and track him down. His mother is very ill. She's never seen him, and I'd like for her to have some time with him before something happens to her."

Roger looked thoughtful. "There may be someone who would know and might talk to you."

"Who?" Jeagan asked, excited.

"Grandfather's former housekeeper."

"Former housekeeper?" Jeagan asked.

"Yes, former. She quit after grandfather died. She was devoted to him, but she couldn't stand Cruella, I mean Patrice. So, after the funeral, she packed up and left."

"Do you really think she'd talk to me, even if it meant betraying the man she worked for all those years?" Jeagan sipped and savored rich, dark coffee.

"All we have to tell her is you're looking for some old files and see what she says? You aren't planning to go public with the information you find, are you?"

"No. Of course not. I only want to find Alan. I don't want to make any trouble for anybody."

"Okay," Sam said. "I'll call her tomorrow first thing. How can I reach you?"

"That's great!" Jeagan gave Sam her cellphone number. "I'll only be here until Thursday morning so I'd like to see her as soon as you can arrange it."

"Doesn't give me much time, but I'll do what I can." Sam straightened in his chair. "Now that that's settled, what's the verdict?"

"Verdict?" Jeagan asked.

"About the dinner. Did you like it?"

"It was okay." Jeagan tried to look serious.

"Only 'okay'?" Sam asked.

"All right." Jeagan lifted her hands in surrender. "It was delicious. You were right. I thoroughly enjoyed it. Thank you very much."

Sam grinned. He signed the credit card receipt and retrieved his card, which he returned to his wallet. "So, where to?"

"I'm ready to call it a night." Jeagan stifled a yawn. "Rich food, good wine, good company, and a little jet lag."

"Hey. The night's young. I know this great little club with the best jazz you've ever heard."

Jeagan couldn't stifle the yawn this time. "Sorry," she said.

"Okay." Sam laughed. "I'll drive you to your hotel and call you in the morning after I talk to Sophia."

* * *

Later, when Jeagan walked into her room, she smiled to herself. She had enjoyed the drive to the hotel in Sam's silver Porsche 911. She'd never been in a Porsche before and had always thought they were the ultimate in cool.

She dropped her handbag on the dresser, then pulled off her shoes and dropped them on the closet floor. When she turned around, she saw a vase of roses, blood-red, on the table in the sitting area.

Her breath caught in her throat. She ran over and pulled the card off the plastic holder. The card read, "This is your last warning!"

Chapter Twelve

This can't be happening, not here! Jeagan grabbed the phone and dialed the front desk. When someone answered, she said, "I need to find out where the roses in my room came from. Can you help me?"

"Just a moment," the young man said. "I'll connect you with the concierge."

After talking to three people, Jeagan was no closer to finding out who had sent the roses. The concierge said they were left on his desk, and he gave them to the bellhop to deliver to her room.

Jeagan dialed her dad. "Dad, I just got back to my room. I found another dozen roses waiting for me."

Geoff Christensen said nothing for a moment. Then, his voice turned hard. "Is there another threatening message on the card?"

"Yes. There is. It says, 'This is your last warning!' "

"Jeagan, honey, I want you to get on the first plane to Denver tomorrow. I'll pick you up at the airport and bring you out here where you'll be safe."

"Thanks, Dad, but I drove my car to the airport."

"Okay, but for once, listen to your ol' dad. I can't protect you there. If I was there, I'd make sure you were safe, but I'm not there."

"I know, Dad." Jeagan let go of some of her fear. "I feel better just talking to you."

"Good. Get your reservation changed. Then, lock your door and try to get some sleep. I assume you talked to hotel security?"

"Yes. I talked to the security guard after I talked to the concierge."

"Okay. Call me in the morning and let me know what flight you're going to be on."

"I will, Dad. Talk to you in the morning. Thanks, Dad. I love you."

"I love you too, little girl. Hang in there."

After Jeagan disconnected, she felt better. Thank goodness for her dad. She checked the lock on her door, got ready for bed, and climbed under the covers.

Tuesday, March 22nd

At eight the next morning, the ringing of her cellphone awakened her. "Hullo," she whispered.

"Jeagan? Is that you?" Sam asked.

"Yes. It's me or at least a reasonable facsimile."

He laughed. "What are you mumbling about? You didn't have that much wine last night, unless you went out again after I dropped you at your hotel."

"Not funny." Jeagan sat up in the bed. "I had a rough night."

"It sure sounds like it. Well, wake up and smell the coffee. I've got good news."

She yawned and stretched. "I could certainly use some good news about now."

"I just got off the phone with Sophia. She's agreed to talk to us, today, for lunch. So, get some breakfast. I'll pick you up at eleven."

"I'll be ready," she said.

"Well, don't get *too* excited," he commented.

Hearing the disappointment and possibly hurt in his voice, she tried to make amends. "Sorry, Sam. I really appreciate your arranging the meeting. I'll explain when I see you."

After she disconnected, she jumped in the shower where the hot water and stinging spray revived her. She ordered room service, dressed in her khaki slacks and a khaki-and-red striped shirt—the outfit she had bought in Memphis two weeks earlier—and dried her hair while she waited for her breakfast.

The hot coffee and orange juice helped to get her going, but she could only manage a few bites of the croissant. The phone rang while she applied her makeup. She hurried to answer it, now almost totally awake. "Hello?"

"Jeagan. I've been waiting for you to call. What time does your flight arrive?"

"Oh, Dad," Jeagan said. "I'm sorry. I haven't booked a flight yet."

"Why not?" Geoff said, alarm ringing in his voice. "Are you all right?"

"I'm fine, Dad. It's just that I've got an appointment to see John McFarland's former housekeeper."

"Jeagan, listen to me. You've been threatened, and your life may really be in danger—again. You need to get on a plane and come home."

"I want to but I can't, Dad. Not yet. I have to talk to this woman and see if she knows anything about where I might find a record of Alan's adoption."

"But, Jeagan—"

"After I talk to her, if she doesn't know anything, I'll change my reservation and come home."

Geoff let out a heavy sigh. "All right. Call me after you talk to her. Promise me."

"I'll call you. And, thank you, Dad. I couldn't have made it through last night without you."

At a few minutes before eleven, Jeagan rode the elevator to the lobby. She spotted Sam across the room on a cushy sofa reading a newspaper. He looked casual but sharp in creased jeans and a light-blue sweater. Seeing him made her feel better, safer. Maybe the next best thing to her dad.

"Hey, Sam." She walked over to him.

"Well." He folded the paper and laid it on a lamp table. "You look pretty good for someone who had a bad night." He stood. "Are you ready to go?"

"I'm ready." She walked with him to his car.

When they were out in traffic, he said, "So what happened to you last night after I left you? You said you'd tell me."

Jeagan leaned her head back on the seat. "It's complicated."

"I'm good at 'complicated.' "

"I think someone is following me and trying to stop me from finding out about Alan."

Sam glanced over at her, a scowl on his face. "Who's following you?"

"I wish I knew. All I know is I was involved in a hit-and-run accident two days ago, and I've received a dozen red roses twice, each time with a note warning me."

"Warning you about what?"

"They don't say, but it has to be about trying to find Alan. That's the only thing I'm doing that should upset anybody. I don't think Isabel's family wants her long-lost son found."

"Well, you're safe while you're with me."

That's what I thought about Madison. But, this is different, isn't it?

"Anyway, back to Sophia. She was glad to get out of the house and wanted to have lunch at the Space Needle. Ever been there?"

Jeagan perked up. "No, but I've wanted to see it."

Sam nodded, obviously pleased that Jeagan liked his choice. "There's a restaurant on the top. I thought we'd have lunch there."

"Does it revolve?" Jeagan asked, suddenly feeling queasy.

"Yes, but you'll never know it or feel it. Just relax."

Jeagan looked at Sam, wondering. "Why are you taking such an interest in me? I'm a total stranger, and you're wining and dining me like I'm...like I'm a client or—"

"Go ahead and say it, like a girlfriend?"

"Well, yes, like a girlfriend."

"I'm not busy right now, and let's just say I liked you the minute I saw you stand up to my step-grandmother."

Curious, Jeagan asked, "If you don't like her, what were you doing there?"

"She had called and asked me to escort her to one of her horticultural meetings at the Volunteer Park Conservatory. She doesn't like me very much, but I make a great escort. I clean up well." Sam grinned, showing his pearly whites.

Jeagan turned in her seat to face Sam, now even more curious, wondering why she hadn't asked him the night before. "What do you do?"

"Well, by trade, I'm a writer, but you've probably never heard of me."

Jeagan thought for a minute. "Sam McFarland. No, I don't think I've heard of you. What do you write?"

"I'm a screenwriter. I've done a few things for TV, one or two movies you've also probably never heard of. Technothriller stuff."

"It sounds like an exciting thing to be involved in," Jeagan commented.

Sam turned into the parking lot for the Space Needle. "Sometimes it can be. The money's good, and I have lots of free time to do whatever I want between scripts. I'm working on a pilot now for CBS. It's a new series about a female president of the United States."

Jeagan laughed. "President Clinton's wife ought to love that. Maybe she'll try out for the lead role."

"Well, at least I made you laugh." He wheeled into a parking place. "Guess we're a little early. Want to go up to the observation deck? You can look out over the city and the Sound."

"Okay. Wish I'd brought my camera."

The elevator ride made Jeagan's iffy stomach turn over, especially since the car was small and confining. But, once she stepped out onto the observation deck, the fresh breeze and the view made her forget her stomach and the blood-red roses. "Oh, this is wonderful! You can see for forever from here!"

"Just about. There's Mt. Rainier to the south and Bainbridge Island over there."

Jeagan rested her arms on the railing and drank in the view. She watched a seaplane touch down lightly on Lake Union and a ferry churn across Elliott Bay.

After a few minutes of pointing out Seattle landmarks, Sam escorted her inside to Sky City Restaurant. They were seated but left word with the hostess to bring Sophia to their table when she arrived.

"Thanks, Sam. This is great even if Sophia doesn't have anything useful to tell me. I appreciate your showing me the sights."

Sam took a sip of his ice water. Then, he reached across and laid his hand on top of Jeagan's. "I figure if I show you a good time, you'll invite me to Colorado and show me around."

Jeagan laughed but self-consciously moved her hand. Didn't Madison say almost the exact words to her before he set her up to be murdered? She liked Sam but was definitely feeling some *déjà vu* here.

Within minutes Sophia arrived. Jeagan watched while the hostess showed her to their table. Sam rose from his chair and hugged the tall, sturdy woman. She looked more like a Hilda than a Sophia. Her graying brown hair was neatly cut in a straight bob. She extended her hand, smooth despite years of hard work, to Jeagan and started to remove her lightweight jacket. Sam helped her and hung it on the back of her chair. Her green sweater complemented bright green eyes set in a face that showed its years but held its youth. Jeagan knew immediately she would like Sophia.

After pleasantries and exclamations over the beautiful day were out of the way, Sophia looked at Jeagan. "Sam tell me you maybe have some questions for me." Strange, her name sounded Greek, she looked to be German, but her accent sounded Asian!

Jeagan took a deep breath. "Yes. I hope you can and will help me because no one else will, and I'm desperate." She briefly explained why she was in Seattle.

"Well." Sophia turned her head and gazed out the window to watch a seaplane soar into the air. "That explain maybe some of strange things that go on in that house."

"Strange?" Sam exclaimed. "After Patrice moved in, everything was strange."

Sophia turned back to Sam and Jeagan. "No, I mean before Her Royal Highness move in. Things were strange already when your grandmother, may God rest her soul, was alive."

The waitress approached their table, delaying further conversation until after their orders were placed. Jeagan ordered a club sandwich and sipped her Coke while she waited for the others to decide what they wanted.

"What was strange at the McFarlands?" Jeagan asked after the waitress walked away.

"The trips they make. They always traveling to exotic places, places I never see, but every year they travel also to big cities in the South. Sometime Atlanta or maybe Charleston or Memphis." Jeagan flinched at the mention of Memphis. "Mr. McFarland always say they going to legal conference. At first, I pay not much attention, but I remember one time your Uncle Charles sick and I need to reach your grandfather. I call the hotel where they say they stay. I think it was in New Orleans. I ask for their room. Tell the operator they with legal conference. She told me there no conference there, but she put me through to the room."

"Why would they lie about something as ridiculous as that?" Sam asked.

"I don't know." Sophia shrugged. "Make no sense to me. But, after one of trips, I find a small container of baby powder in your grandmother's suitcase. I don't understand how it get in there."

Jeagan jumped and knocked over her Coke. "Oh! I'm sorry!" She tried to mop up the liquid with her napkin.

"It's okay. Settle down," Sam said. He and Sophia offered their napkins.

A passing waitress stopped to help. She grabbed a cloth and sopped up the liquid before it spilled over onto Jeagan's lap.

Their sandwiches arrived during the cleanup. Jeagan looked at hers but couldn't make herself pick it up. "Did you ask Mrs. McFarland about the baby powder?"

Sophia took a bite of her corned beef sandwich and chewed for a moment. "Yes. She say she forget to take her favorite bath powder and only baby powder in the pharmacy. But, not true." Sophia shook her head. "Her favorite Chanel No. 5 bath powder in her cosmetic case."

"When was this?" Jeagan asked, her tension level rising. "Do you remember what year?"

Sophia took another bite of her sandwich, looking thoughtful. "Early 1950s, maybe."

"Well, it didn't belong to the baby you're interested in," Sam said. "So relax and eat your sandwich."

Jeagan took a bite of her club sandwich and forced herself to chew and swallow. No, the baby powder had not been for Alan, but it may have been for someone else's baby. Was he or she stolen as well?

"No, the baby obviously wasn't Alan," she said, "but it makes me believe I'm right. I do think your grandfather was involved in buying babies. Whether or not he knew they were stolen is something else, but he obviously wanted to keep the adoptions secret or he wouldn't have kept his files hidden."

"You don't know that the files in his private filing cabinet were records of buying and selling stolen babies," Sam commented.

"Buying babies?" Sophia asked, her eyes wide. "Is that what all those trips about?"

"They may have been," Sam said. "Did you ever hear them mention anything about babies before or after that?"

"No, I don't think so."

Encouraged that she was finally getting some useful information, Jeagan asked, "What I am specifically looking for are records of adoptions. Mr. McFarland had a private filing cabinet, the one Sam just mentioned, in his office that no one had access to but him. It disappeared the weekend after his death. Do you know anything about it?"

Sophia shrugged while munching on her sandwich. "No. I don't remember files except ones he keep in his desk in study. But drawers never locked."

"Do you remember anything that didn't seem right on the weekend my grandfather died?" Sam asked.

"Not really." Sophia again concentrated. "I only want to get the funeral over so I can leave that house. I remember lots of people coming and going. They bring food and flowers."

"Nothing else, like maybe boxes of files from grandfather's office?"

"No, I don't think... . Wait!" Sophia laid her sandwich on her plate. "Strange thing *did* happen that weekend. Something wake me up in middle of night. Loud bang. I sleeping upstairs that night, so I get up and go downstairs. Miss Patrice in the kitchen drinking coffee with a man. A man I never see before. When I ask if everything all right, she tell me everything fine and to go back to bed."

Sam finished his ham-and-Swiss sandwich. "Did you ever see the man again?"

"One time. At funeral. He not like rest of your grandfather's friends. He stand by himself, like he there more to guard than as friend. He kind of like tough guy, if you know what I mean?"

"Do you remember what he looked like?" Jeagan asked.

"Um...I think he was not as tall as Sam, but big shoulders, maybe blond or red-type hair." Sophia took the last bite of her sandwich.

"But you never saw any files or boxes being brought into the house?" Sam asked.

"No. I don't remember boxes."

Jeagan turned to Sam. "But that could have been what that man was doing there in the middle of the night. Maybe he brought the filing cabinet."

"Maybe," Sophia said. "The noise I hear, maybe banging of door to basement."

Jeagan's eyes gleamed. "Did you go down to the basement often?"

"Sure. Lots of times."

"Did you go there after that night?" Sam asked.

"No. Not after that night. I leave in two days."

Jeagan looked at Sam. "I need to get into that basement."

Sam gulped the last of his beer. "You couldn't even get into the house. How do you expect to get into the basement?"

Jeagan gave him a smug look. "You'll just have to help me find a way. Or, you can check for me."

"Oh." Sam folded his arms across his chest and gave Jeagan a wry grin. "So, now you want me to go over to Cruella's and ask if I can check out her basement for files that prove she's involved in buying and selling babies."

Jeagan laughed. "Well, when you put it that way… ." She placed her forearms on the table and leaned toward Sophia. "Did Cruella, I mean Patrice, go with Sam's grandfather on any of those strange trips?"

"No." Sophia looked over at Sam. "Trips stop after Sam's grandmother die. Your grandfather was very sad until he meet Miss Patrice. I never like her, but she make your grandfather happy."

"So," Sam said, "if she had the files brought into the house after my grandfather's death, she must have known what he'd done."

"Maybe she was trying to protect him," Jeagan suggested.

"Maybe," Sam added, "and maybe she has since destroyed the files."

"But, I have to know." Jeagan pushed her unfinished sandwich aside. "It's all I have to go on. If the records are destroyed, I don't have much hope of finding Alan."

"I wish I could help more," Sophia said, "but that all I know. I haven't been in house since that weekend and never want to go there again. Miss Patrice call me maybe a week ago and ask if I help with one of her parties. I say 'no.' "

"Parties!" A grin spread across Sam's face. "Patrice is hosting a fund-raising soirée for the Arboretum."

"That the one she talk about," Sophia nodded.

"When?" Jeagan asked.

"Tomorrow night." He turned to Jeagan. "I'm invited, and you've got to go with me, as my date."

"Are you kidding? After she slammed the door in my face? Besides, my dad will fly up here and literally drag me back to Denver if I'm not on a flight home today or tomorrow."

Sam challenged her. "Are you going to run back to Denver without at least checking out Cruella's basement?"

"Well, thank you very much for lunch, Mr. Sam, but I have to go now." Sophia turned to Jeagan. "I hope maybe I help you?"

"You have, Sophia. Thank you for taking the time to meet us." Jeagan reached over to take the woman's hand.

"It was good to get out of house for while. Babysit my niece's baby for two months. I need a break." Sophia grinned sheepishly.

Sam stood and helped Sophia on with her jacket. He hugged her and thanked her for coming. After she left the restaurant, he turned to Jeagan. "What do you say? Are you brave enough to go to the party with me?"

Chapter Thirteen

Jeagan thought for a few moments. She'd come this far. Going home without making every effort to find Alan was being a quitter. "Okay, I'll go."

Sam grinned. "Good girl! Come on. Let's go call your Dad."

"And I need to call and check on Isabel."

When they were in Sam's car, Jeagan pulled out her cellphone. She called her dad, but got his voicemail. She explained that she was fine and was with a friend and had a lead on the lost files, which she was going to follow up on, and would have to stay another couple of days. "He's probably not going to like that," she said after she switched off the phone.

"Maybe not, but he'll understand."

"Guess he'll have to," Jeagan mumbled. She dug in her handbag for her notepad and punched in the number for the Methodist Hospital. After two rings, someone answered.

"ICU, Anne Barre speaking."

Jeagan told the nurse she was calling to check on Isabel. "Oh, Isabel Lloyd, yes. I was just in her room. Did you say your name was Jeagan?"

"Yes. Jeagan Christensen. I know I'm not a relative or anything, but—"

"The chart here says you have permission to receive information on her. She's weak but stable right now. She did eat a little breakfast this morning and took a few bites of her lunch. Would you like to speak to her?"

"Yes, please," Jeagan said, fighting the tears. Would it never stop for that poor woman? When Isabel came on the line, Jeagan tried to sound cheerful. "Hi Isabel. How are you?"

"Oh, I guess I'm a little better than yesterday. I'm not in any pain, but I feel like a wet dishrag. I can't wait to get out of here and get back in my own bed."

"Well, I hope I have some news that might cheer you up a little."

Expectant, Isabel said, "Have you found my son?"

"No. My news is not that good, but I may know where the files are that could lead to him."

"Oh, I hope so! I'll go through anything if I can see my son before I die." Jeagan could hear the tears in her voice.

Hoping to give her something positive to hold onto, Jeagan said, "I'll do my very best to find him for you, and you'll have lots of good years together before you go anywhere."

"From your lips to God's ears," Isabel quoted with a small laugh.

Jeagan disconnected soon after to allow a more cheerful and hopeful Isabel to rest. "I can't let her down now that I've given her some hope," Jeagan told Sam.

Sam started the car and pulled out of the parking lot. "Is there anything special you'd like to do today while we plot our caper?"

Jeagan smiled in spite of herself. "I'd like to find out who is tormenting me by sending those dreadful blood-red roses. I'll never like red roses again!"

"I'll remember that." Sam merged into the stream of traffic on Broad. "As far as finding out who's sending the flowers, if the concierge or front desk clerks don't remember seeing anyone deliver the roses, I'm not sure how we can find out. But, I do know I'm going to stick to you like glue to keep you safe while you're here."

She looked over at Sam. "Why?"

"Why what?" He turned left turn onto Alaskan Way.

"Why are you doing all this for me? You don't even know me."

"It's simple. I met you; I liked you. I don't have any deadlines, the weather is gorgeous, and I'd like to spend time with you and show you the around. How about a ferry ride over to Bainbridge Island?"

"Ooh, that sounds like fun!" Jeagan's faced beamed like a little kid's. She knew she should be working on 'the case,' but couldn't think of anything else she could do today. Why not take a ferry ride, one with lots of people around?

Sam looked over at her. "How old did you say you were? You look like you're about ten!"

Her lower lip stuck out, Jeagan said, "I'm probably older than you!"

Sam laughed. "I doubt that. I'm thirty-two."

"You *are* not!" Jeagan said, her eyes wide in surprise.

"Almost thirty-three, as a matter of fact," Sam said smugly. "So, how old are you?"

"I'm twenty-eight, not over the hill like you." She laughed when he shot her a dirty look.

He turned into the ferry parking lot and found a spot. "We'll take the ferry and leave the car here, if that's okay with you. We can rent bikes or a motor scooter and ride around the island."

"Sounds great! I've always wanted to see Bainbridge after that movie with Richard Dreyfuss."

"You mean *Stake Out*?" Sam got out of the car and met Jeagan as she opened her door.

"That's it. Everything looked so lush and green in that movie." She fell into step beside him while they headed for the ferry.

"But, in Colorado, you've got those fantastic mountains."

"Which you also have here," she countered.

"And that dry climate. I get really tired of the rain and fog here, especially in the winter."

"Well, that's true. I do prefer the three hundred plus days of sunshine and dry climate that we have in Colorado, which is good for the hairdos, but not for the skin."

"Guess no place is perfect." Sam checked the posted schedule. "Come on. This ferry's about to leave." He grabbed her hand. They got their tickets at a kiosk, ran, and jumped on board seconds before the gate closed.

Laughing and out of breath, Jeagan followed Sam to the front of the ferry and watched while the boat bumped away from the dock. She turned to take in the view of the Seattle skyline basking in the afternoon sunshine. The fresh breeze and light spray felt wonderful. Problems, what problems? She leaned against the railing and let the wind blow away all of her problems, at least for the time being.

Talking was next to impossible over the roar of the engines, which allowed Jeagan to savor the tangy smells and the sun and the view. After a few minutes, she started to feel chilled and ready to get out of the wind. She nudged Sam. "Can we go inside?" she shouted.

"Sure." He turned around and walked with her toward the lounge.

"What a difference," Jeagan commented when they were inside. "Seems awfully quiet in here." She ran her hands through her hair. "I think I need to find a ladies room."

"That way." Sam pointed to a hallway.

"Thanks." Jeagan stumbled across the rocking floor toward the restroom. When she looked in the mirror, she was surprised at the face she saw staring back at her. A happy, smiling face, flushed by the wind, with hair swept back in a new windblown look. *Is that me?* She'd been stressed for too long. It was good to see a smile on her face. She again ran her hands through her hair trying to tame it somewhat.

Minutes later, when she returned to the lounge, she scanned the area for Sam but didn't see him. *He's probably also in the restroom*, she thought. She wandered around the lounge area and rummaged through the sweatshirts and windbreakers with Seattle imprinted on them. A red sweatshirt caught her eye.

"Would you like a bag for that?" the clerk asked while she pulled out her billfold.

"No, thanks. I'm going to put it on. Could you cut the tags for me?" Jeagan asked. After she paid for the sweatshirt and the tags were removed, she pulled it over her head. That felt better. She looked toward the restrooms but still didn't see Sam. A glance around the lounge soon told her he stood at the rear talking on his cellphone. Again, he appeared to be in a heated discussion with someone. What was with him? A girlfriend somewhere? Oh, well.

The sweatshirt helped, but she still felt a little chilled. She looked around and spotted a menu board featuring hot chocolate along with other beverages and snacks. That sounded like it would warm her up. She ordered a cup at the snack counter and carried it over to a chair close to the front of the lounge. By the time she was settled, Sam returned.

"There you are," he said.

"No, there *you* are," Jeagan responded.

Sam squinted at her. Obviously, noticing something was on her mind, he said, "That was my agent. He's negotiating with the TNT big wigs over my contract for the pilot episode."

"Oh," Jeagan said, somewhat relieved that nothing more disturbing than contract details was making Sam angry. From what she'd seen of his two telephone conversations, he had a temper.

"I see you've bought a sweatshirt. Good idea. It can get cool on the ferry and may be windy on the island. What are you drinking?"

"Hot chocolate. Not too bad." Jeagan took a sip and wrapped her hands around the cup.

"Be back in a minute."

She watched Sam as he bought hot chocolate and added cream to it. He looked like he didn't have a care in the world and didn't seem a bit worried about a contract. When he returned and sat in the chair next to her, he said, "Now, about the party tomorrow night... ."

"About the party," Jeagan repeated. "How do you think your grandmother—?"

"Step-grandmother," Sam corrected.

"Okay, step-grandmother. How's she going to feel when you show up with me?"

"She'll be so busy schmoozing with her wealthy guests, trying to squeeze money out of them, that she won't pay any attention to you or me for that matter. She only invited me to escort her around the room or carry instructions to the hired staff or fetch for her."

"Hmm," Jeagan said hopeful. "In all the confusion, do you think we'll be able to sneak into the basement?"

"That's what I'm banking on. And, if you wear your hair in one of those upsweep dos, I'm sure she won't even recognize you."

"I can do that." Jeagan grabbed her hair, twisted it, and pulled it up on top of her head.

"Yep," Sam said. "Just like that."

Jeagan felt the ferry slow and looked outside.

"They're about to dock. Want to go outside?" Sam got up and tossed his empty cup into a trash receptacle.

"Sure." Jeagan finished off her hot chocolate, stood, and tossed her cup also. After Sam opened the door for her, they walked over to the rail along with many other passengers and watched the docking procedure. When it was over, they filed off the ferry and up the walkway with the others.

"Let's find a place to rent a scooter," Sam said, "unless you'd rather get on one of those tour buses or rent a bicycle to see the island."

"I like the scooter idea better," Jeagan said. "Besides, I'd love to find that house they used in *Stake Out*."

"Fat chance of that."

Not long afterward, with a bright yellow scooter and a map in hand from the Visitor Center, they pulled on helmets. "Let's see if we can find a winery."

Jeagan moved close to him and scanned the map also. "Here's one," she said after a few seconds.

"Good," Sam said. "Let's see. We take 305 north until we get to Northeast Laughing Salmon Road."

"What a name for a road," Jeagan commented. After Sam straddled the scooter, she threw her leg over and got on behind him.

He cocked his head around. "Gotta hold on tight."

"Yeah. I bet you say that to all your biker babes."

"Every one," Sam agreed, grinning. "Okay, let's see if I can operate this mama." He turned on the ignition and the scooter roared to life. "Here we go." After a shaky start and a few screams from Jeagan, they were on their way.

Sam turned off the highway ten minutes later.

Holding on tightly, Jeagan enjoyed the exhilarating ride and closeness to Sam. She tried to check out the lush scenery they passed but was too busy watching for the winery. "There it is," she soon yelled over the engine. Sam slowed. He turned onto the gravel drive and under the sign proclaiming Laughing Salmon Winery toward a neat log building set among tall lodgepole pines and spruce. Only one vehicle sat in the parking lot, an old blue pickup truck, vintage 1950s.

"Looks like it's closed," Jeagan commented, a little disappointed.

"Yeah. It does, but somebody's here. Let's go check it out." He shut off the engine.

Jeagan stepped off the scooter and followed Sam to the white front door. He turned the knob, finding the door unlocked, and they entered a paneled wine tasting room. A sandy-brown-haired man, dressed in a plaid shirt and khaki pants, looked up when they walked in.

"Can I help you?" he asked.

"We're on the island for the day and wondered if maybe you were open," Sam said.

"Not yet," the man responded. "We don't reopen until the first of April. I'm only here today to do an inventory."

"Oh, well, thank you, anyway." Jeagan turned to leave.

"But, as long as you're here, and I'm not real busy right now, want to try one of our wines?" He laid his clipboard on the polished tigerwood counter.

"That would be great!" Sam took Jeagan's arm and turned her back into the room.

"Come on over here and have a seat," the man said. "Name's Ed Hickok."

"I'm Sam McFarland and this is Jeagan Christensen. I live in Seattle, and she's visiting from Denver."

"Welcome," Ed said. "My selection is limited right now, but I can offer you two or three good table wines. We've got a Lake Country White, which is our most popular.

Jeagan quoted from the card on the counter, "Its low alcohol and light sweetness make it a favorite for those searching for a refreshing white wine to go with light summer menus."

Ed laughed. "That's right. And we have a Pinot Noir."

Jeagan ran her finger down the card and started to read again. "This wine is produced in the traditional style of exquisite burgundies—"

"I can read for myself," Sam said.

"Or," Ed continued, "I can offer you a Pinot Grigio."

"It highlights the palate-pleasing flavors of—"

"That's enough." Sam placed his hand over the card.

"Okay, fine." Jeagan laughed. "I'd like to try the Lake Country White."

"Make mine the Pinot Noir," Sam said. "That sounds interesting."

"Coming right up." Ed poured two sample glasses for Sam and Jeagan.

Jeagan sipped hers. "Mmm. Sweet but not too sweet." She looked at Sam. "How's yours?"

"Not bad," Sam commented.

They left the winery a short time later with two bottles of wine, which Jeagan secured between herself and Sam. The next hour they spent touring the island, stopping once or twice to ask if anyone knew where the house Jeagan wanted to see was located. No one knew. She finally quit asking and enjoyed the sunny day and the views of the Sound and the lush trees and ferns on the island. On their way back to the dock, they stopped at Little & Lewis Gardens and wandered through their unique plantings set with sculptures and paintings.

By the time they returned the scooter and walked across the dock, the ferry was loading for the three-fifty departure. They joined the crowd flowing onto the ferry after a day of work or a day trip to the island.

"That was fun! Thank you," Jeagan said after they stepped onboard. She couldn't remember when she'd last had any fun.

"That *was* fun," Sam agreed. "Sometimes I forget how beautiful the state is. It's good to see it through a visitor's eyes."

Jeagan looked at the clouds. "Looks like it's going to rain soon."

"Yeah. We'd better go inside." They strolled toward the lounge and found chairs by a window.

Sam placed the wine bottles on the seat next to Jeagan. "Want something to drink or something to snack on?"

"I'd love another cup of hot chocolate," Jeagan said.

"You got it. Be right back."

Jeagan gazed out the window, windblown but content. It had been a break from reality, spending the day with Sam. She knew almost nothing about him, but felt safe with him nevertheless. Besides that, he made her forget her worries. *What would tomorrow bring?* She wondered. *Would they be able to find anything in Patrice McFarland's basement that would help to find Alan?*

Just then, her cellphone rang. "Well, finally," her dad said. "I've been trying to reach you all day." He sounded upset. "Are you all right?"

"Hi Dad. Yes, I'm fine. I've spent the day on Bainbridge Island with the man who's going to help me get into the McFarland house tomorrow."

"So, you're not coming home today?" Her dad sounded none too pleased.

"No, Dad. Didn't you get my message?"

"I haven't checked my messages yet. I just came in the door."

"Well, I'm going to stay at least through tomorrow and see what I can find. I'm safe with Sam."

"How do you know that, Jeagan? You know, for someone who's intelligent, your judgment of who is and isn't 'safe' is not the best in the world."

"But, Dad—"

"Let me finish. I talked to Roger earlier, and he's ready to come up there to help you. Cast and all."

"I'll call him and see what he wants to do. How's that? Will that please you?"

"If you promise me you'll do that."

"I promise. And, Dad, thanks for worrying about me. I'm sorry I got so upset last night and worried you. The security guys at the hotel are keeping an eye out for me and anything that might come in for me, so I think I'm okay now. Only a couple more days, and I'll come home."

Jeagan heard her dad sigh heavily. "All right. I guess I can't make you do anything, but please be careful."

Jeagan ended her call as Sam arrived with their drinks. "My dad," she explained. "He still wants me to come home."

"Doesn't he know you're in good hands now that I'm around?"

Jeagan gave him a wry look. "Oh, are you the Allstate guy?"

The ferry docked forty minutes later. After they exited and found Sam's Porsche, Jeagan thanked him for the day. "I had a really good time, which is something I haven't had in a while."

"How about dinner tonight and maybe hit that jazz club I was telling you about?" Sam suggested. He started the car and entered the slow line of traffic to exit the dock area.

"Not tonight. I need to make some calls and see if Roger is really coming up here."

Sam turned to Jeagan. "Roger? Who's that?"

She wasn't sure exactly who Roger was to her. "He's my boss. He was hired to look for Alan and asked me if I wanted to help. He's currently in a cast from the hit-and-run accident we had on the way to the airport, but my dad said he wants to come to Seattle to take over," she used her fingers for quote marks, "the investigation."

Sam gave her a crooked smile. "Seems like you're doing pretty well on your own, now that you've got me for a sidekick."

"So, sidekick, about tomorrow."

Sam chuckled. He turned onto Alaskan Way in the direction of the Marriott. "About tomorrow. I'll pick you up at your hotel at five-thirty. The party starts at six, but we don't want to be early and give Patrice time to get a good look at you."

"That sounds fine. I may go shopping tomorrow. What's appropriate for one of Patrice's galas?"

"Well, she usually wears something long and sleek, but I'd say you'd look great in the dress you wore last night."

"I'd really like to buy something new. It's been a while since I've had a good excuse to dress up. Maybe a slinky black pantsuit."

"Ooh, I like slinky," Sam commented slyly. Jeagan giggled.

"Well, here you are. Back in one piece all safe and sound. Do you want me to come in with you to make sure your room is rose-free?"

"No, thanks. Hotel security should be checking on that. But, I appreciate the offer."

"Well, if you're sure. Maybe you want to show me your etchings, or something?" He grinned mischievously.

Jeagan laughed. "Tell me you didn't just say that!"

Sam scratched his head. "It used to work, at least on Seattle girls. Guess guys use different lines in Colorado."

Jeagan cut her eyes at him. "Yeah, but I'm not going to tell you what they are."

"Oh, well." Sam reached over the seat, grabbed the bottle of Lake Country White and handed it to Jeagan. "Don't drink the whole bottle by yourself tonight," he teased.

"I won't," Jeagan leaned over and kissed Sam on the cheek. "Thanks again. I had a great day." She stepped out of the car when the door was opened by the hotel doorman.

"You're welcome," Sam called after her. "I'll talk to you tomorrow."

She waved to him and walked into the hotel. Before she went up to her room, she stopped at the concierge's desk. Fortunately, no blood-red roses or any other thing, living or dead, had been delivered to her room while she was gone.

A strange thumping sound seemed to follow her when she crossed the lobby to the elevators. She ignored it until someone behind her said, "Hello, stranger."

Chapter Fourteen

Jeagan whirled around to see Roger in all his leg-cast glory standing there grinning like the Cheshire Cat.

"Roger! What are you doing here? You should be at home resting."

Eyes narrowed in hurt, Roger said. "Thanks for the warm welcome. But, if my memory serves me correctly, this is my gig, not yours," he added, his voice gaining volume with each word. "So, as I see it, I'm the one who should be here, and you should be at home," he waved his crutch-free arm to include their surroundings, "not running around the city with guys in Porsche 911s!"

Crimson-faced, Jeagan said, "Shhh. Be quiet Roger! The whole lobby can hear you."

"I don't care," he said, his voice nonetheless lower. "You act like I'm imposing on you or raining on your parade by being here!"

"Come on up to my room where we can talk." Jeagan pressed the elevator button. While they waited in silence for the door to open, she realized that he was right. She *had* taken over the investigation without regard to his feelings, and she *had* been having fun running around with Sam in his Porsche.

When they reached her room, she inserted her key card and pushed on the door. As she walked inside, someone pushed past her, knocking the bottle of wine out of her hands, and tried to run out the door. She screamed.

Roger, quick on the draw, stuck out his crutch and tripped the person.

Thud! The person fell with a groan, rolled, and quickly regained their feet. Then, he or she sprinted down the hall.

Jeagan bolted out the door after the person.

"Come back here!" Roger yelled. "Are you crazy?"

Jeagan stopped at the end of the hallway when she rounded a corner and saw the door to the stairs close. She couldn't catch him or her on the stairs. Winded, she turned around, headed toward her room, and saw Roger clumping down the hall toward her.

"What were you thinking!" he said when he reached her.

"Just stop it!" She grimaced. "Let's go see if they took anything."

Roger clumped along behind her. When they were inside her room, he grabbed the phone while she retrieved the bottle of wine, fortunately unbroken in the padded bag.

"What are you doing?" she asked as she opened her suitcase to check inside.

"I'm calling Hotel Security. Is anything missing?"

"No," Jeagan answered while she searched through her bag. "Nothing's missing, but my suitcase's a mess. They must have been looking for something, but I can't imagine what unless it was money or jewelry and I'm wearing what little jewelry I have."

"Do you realize what could have happened to you if that guy had turned on you? Or, for that matter, if you'd been alone when you opened your door?"

"Okay," she dropped into a chair. "You're right. I had no business chasing after him. But, I was so scared and mad at the same time that I didn't think. I just reacted." Now that it was over, she began to shake. "I don't even want to think about what would've happened if I'd been alone when I found him in here." Tears stung her eyes. She swiped at the tears, closed her eyes, and rested her head against the chair.

Roger quickly told Security what had happened and disconnected. He went over to the mini bar and pulled out a small bottle of white wine. He opened it and poured it into a glass. "Here, drink this. It'll help."

"Thanks." Jeagan took the glass and drained it. It was a bitter wine, but she didn't care. "When's all this going to stop?" she asked after a minute of silence.

Roger sat in a chair facing Jeagan. "That's why I'm here. To help get this over with. Together, with your tenacity and my brains." Jeagan raised her eyebrows. Roger recanted. "Okay, maybe not brains but at least experience. Surely, we can get this sorted out and find out who's trying to stop us from finding Alan."

Loud knocks sounded at the door before Jeagan could respond.

She started to get up. "Sit still," Roger ordered. For once, she did as she was told.

Roger opened the door to admit the hotel security guard and explained what had happened.

"I'll have her room changed right away." The guard walked over to the phone to call the front desk. Roger followed and spoke to him quietly. After the call, the guard turned to Jeagan. "Someone will be here to move you in a few minutes." He lifted the receiver again. "I'm going to call the police."

"That's not necessary," Roger said. "I've got a friend in the department. I'll call him."

"But, I need to log it in my report," the security guard continued.

"If you need a name, it's Captain Will Thompson. I'll call him after we get Jeagan settled in a new room." The guard grudgingly wrote the name in his report.

Another knock on the door. When opened, a bellman came inside to pack up Jeagan's things and move her. They were soon on their way to the tenth floor.

"Where's your room?" Jeagan asked while the bellman unloaded her things in her new room.

"Right through there," Roger said, indicating the door to an adjoining room.

"Imagine that?" Jeagan commented dryly, hands on her hips.

After her belongings were unpacked, the security guard assured her the hotel records would not show her name in their computer or give out any information about her.

Roger added that he was using one of his alternate identities: Mike Hammer. Both rooms would be registered in that name.

"Mike Hammer!" Jeagan asked. "Couldn't you come up with something more original?"

"What's wrong with that name?" Roger spat back.

Shaking his head, the security guard backed out of the room. He had no intention of getting into that argument.

Jeagan threw herself into a chair. "Now, what, Mr. Hammer?"

"Now, we have some dinner and try to decide where we are and what we should do."

"Well, all right. I could use some comfort food right now."

"Go fix your face and let's go downstairs. I saw a nice restaurant off the lobby, and I don't want you out on the streets tonight."

Jeagan opened her mouth for a retort, but was too frazzled to argue. Instead, she pushed herself up from the chair. Thirty minutes afterward, she knocked on the adjoining door. She had showered and changed into her navy slacks and jacket with a white cotton sweater. Roger approved, she could tell, by the low whistle.

"You look so nice, maybe I ought to change," he said.

"You're fine in your khakis and turtleneck. Besides, you can't dress up much with a cast." He really did look fine, Jeagan realized, with his sandy-blond hair falling in his face and his sexy green eyes. Sexy? Where had that come from?

In the lobby, Roger escorted Jeagan toward Restaurant 2100. They only had to wait a few minutes for a table next to floor-to-ceiling windows with a view of the marina. Jeagan felt her insides start to unwind when she gazed out at the peach-colored evening sky reflecting on the calm waters and the expensive cruisers and sailboats docked in the slips. When it arrived, she sipped her white Chilean wine and sighed. The restaurant, decorated in fresh golds, reds, and blues, was softly lit. She felt herself letting go.

Roger watched her closely. He let her get good and relaxed before he broached the subject of the investigation. After they both ordered Alaskan King Crab, he took a long drink of his Ash Hollow wine. "I talked to Will while you were taking a shower."

"Who?" Jeagan asked.

"My buddy, the guy who's retired from the Seattle Police Department. He offered to send an officer out, but when I explained to him what's been going on, he said he'd come himself. I told him not to rush now that I'm here, but that I would like to meet with him tomorrow." Jeagan squinted at him. "I meant *we* would like to talk to him tomorrow. He said he'd be by around ten tomorrow morning but to let him know if anything else happens, and he'll come right away."

"That's a good idea. Things are getting out of hand." Jeagan set her wine glass on the table. "Every time something happens, I keep thinking that it's the last and nothing else bad will happen."

"It's great to look on the bright side, but that's not very realistic."

"I know," she agreed. "But we can't stop now, can we? Isabel's depending on us."

"You could go home where you'll be safe and let me take it from here."

"No way!"

"Okay, then. Where are we?"

What do you mean *we*? was Jeagan's first reaction, but she held her tongue. She filled Roger in on what had happened since she'd arrived in Seattle. When she mentioned Isabel's second heart attack, she stopped. "I need to call and check on her." She grabbed her handbag and began to dig for her cellphone.

Roger reached across and touched her hand. "It's okay, I called earlier. The nurse said she was feeling better. A friend named Myra was sitting with her, and her lawyer had left a few minutes before."

Jeagan dropped her phone into her handbag. "That's good news."

"And, I talked to your Dad while you were changing. You don't have to call him either."

"Wow!" Irritated, Jeagan added, "You're just Mr. Take Charge, aren't you?"

"Only trying to make life a little simpler for you." Their salads arrived. Between bites, she relaxed and told Roger about the party she was going to the next night. He wanted to know if he could tag along.

"I don't think so," she said. "It would be hard for you to be inconspicuous with that cast. I just hope Patrice doesn't recognize me and throw me out."

"So, okay, what's your big plan?"

"Well," Jeagan's eyes brightened, "Sam thinks there will be so many people at the party that we can sneak down into the basement without being seen, except maybe by some of the catering staff. If anyone asks, he'll tell them he's Patrice's grandson, which he is."

"Why's he helping you?"

Her fork in midair, Jeagan said, "I've been trying to figure that out. I'm not really sure, but we seemed to hit it off the moment he saw Patrice slam her front door in my face."

"I take it he doesn't get along with his grandmother very well?"

"She's his step-grandmother, and, no, he doesn't. The name his dad and uncle tagged her with is Cruella DeVille."

Roger laughed out loud. The diners around them turned to stare.

Jeagan hid her face in her napkin to keep from laughing. "Behave yourself," she whispered. "It's not that funny."

A passing waiter offered to refill Roger's empty wineglass. He declined. "So was good ol' Sam close to his grandfather?"

Choosing to ignore the sarcasm, she took a bite of her salad. After a moment, she continued. "No, Sam said his grandfather treated him, his father, and his uncle like dirt after his wife died. So, no love lost there. I guess Sam feels that by helping me he's getting back at his grandfather and Patrice."

"Well, whatever works. Meanwhile, I'm sure Will can help us. But, I wish I could physically do something instead of sitting around watching you get ready for your big date tomorrow."

"Speaking of dates, what's up with you and Shelley? How'd she find out about your accident?" Jeagan finished the salad, and her plate was whisked away unobtrusively by a passing waiter.

Roger had the good sense to blush, at least a little. "I'm not sure. She said she ran into a mutual friend who told her. But, she never said who."

"That's strange. It's almost like she's stalking you. She just keeps showing up."

"Yeah. Like a really bad penny."

"Well, she *did* drive you home from the hospital, and I'll bet she waited on you hand and cast."

The entrees arrived before Roger could think of a good comeback. So, they concentrated on their delicious crab and potatoes au gratin.

After dinner, Jeagan asked Roger if he felt like a short walk along the dock. He agreed to a very short stroll, only long enough to walk off their dinner. He didn't want to get far away from the hotel grounds.

A glance out the window told him other people were enjoying the evening. They should be safe.

Jeagan folded her arms to keep warm in the cool evening air once they were outside. She enjoyed the tangy sea smells and the cries of the gulls as they dove into the water for their dinner. While they walked along the dock, she listened to the metallic *clink* of rigging in the masts of the sailboats that bobbed in their slips. Several other strollers passed them and nodded as did couples sitting on benches.

"This place is beautiful. I could live here," she commented.

"You haven't been here during the rainy season." Roger clumped along beside her.

"Isn't this supposed to be the rainy season?" she asked.

"Don't really know, but I hope the weather holds. I don't think this cast would be too easy to get around with if it got wet. Ouch!"

Jeagan stopped. "What's wrong?"

"Oh, I stubbed my toe on this uneven dock. Let's go inside."

"All right." Jeagan frowned. "You're sure no fun when you're on the injured reserve list."

"Hmph! You try walking around with a hundred pound cast on your leg. Well, maybe it's not a hundred pounds, but it feels like it! It's painful enough having a broken leg, but having to lug around this cast is adding insult to injury."

"I'm sorry. I'm not being very sympathetic, am I? How long do you have to wear that thing, anyway?"

"Not sure. I go back for the doctor to check it in three weeks. He'll do an X-ray and tell me something more definite then."

Jeagan reached over and took Roger's hand and held it while they walked along. "I really am sorry. What can I do to make things easier for you?"

"Well, did you bring a sexy nightgown?"

Jeagan slung his hand away. "You don't quit, do you?"

"Nope," he said, grinning like a fool.

* * *

Back in her room, Jeagan locked the adjoining door. Next, she checked the lock on the door to the hall. All was secure. "Please, Lord," she prayed before she went to sleep, "help us to find Alan soon, before something really bad, something irreversible does happen to Roger or me."

Chapter Fifteen

At nine-thirty the next morning, following an uneventful night, Roger and Jeagan, dressed in jeans and a pale pink sweater, rode the elevator downstairs for breakfast and to wait for Captain Thompson. They started across the lobby to the restaurant, but Jeagan stopped when she heard a familiar voice at the front desk.

"But, I know she's staying here," she heard someone say. "I dropped her off here yesterday afternoon."

Sam! "Wait a minute, Roger," she said, touching his arm. "There's Sam."

"Oh, great!" Roger grumbled.

"Don't be a grump! Go on in and get a table if you want to."

"No. I think I'd like to meet this Mr. Seattle for myself," Roger said dryly.

"Okay, but try to be nice."

"Hmph!" Roger clumped along beside Jeagan across the lobby to the front desk.

"Sam!" Jeagan came up behind him.

Sam turned to see Jeagan. His face lit up; Roger frowned. Jeagan laughed when Sam pulled her in for a hug. "Hey, you! They told me you weren't registered here."

"Well," she said when Sam released her, "that's a long story." She held out her hands. "But as you can see, I'm still here." She fidgeted awkwardly and turned to Roger. "With my boss."

"Your boss?" Sam looked Roger over.

Roger put on a good-ol'-boy grin and stuck out his hand. "Yep, I'm her boss. Roger Sanderlin. Howdy."

Sam, obviously taken aback by Roger's folksy manner, shook hands. "Sam McFarland. Nice to meet you." He looked questioningly at Jeagan. "I didn't know your boss was with you."

Roger gave Sam a pseudo-smile, showing most of his teeth. "I jetted in yesterday while you two were doing the tourist thing. Thought I'd see how 'the case' is progressing. Make some observations and suggestions." He waved his hand for emphasis. "You know, the sort of things bosses do."

"Stop it," Jeagan whispered to Roger out of the side of her mouth. She looked over at Sam. "How about joining us for breakfast? We were just going in. Maybe we can all sit and talk."

"Sounds like a good idea," Sam said, watching Roger warily.

Roger returned the look. Jeagan laughed and shook her head. "All right, boys, play nice."

They were soon seated at a table for four, once again overlooking the marina, its slate-blue water and white sailboats and cruisers glistening in the early morning sunshine.

"Don't know what it is since you got here, Jeagan, but this weather is unbelievable," Sam commented while the waitress filled his cup with coffee. He added cream. "The week before you came, I think it rained every day."

"Just call her Little Miss Sunshine," Roger added, his sarcasm dripping.

Jeagan had had enough of Roger's sneers and snarls. "Look, Roger. We're both here to do a job, and Sam has volunteered to help. Be grateful and stop acting like a brat."

Sam's eyes widened in shock. Roger grinned at Sam. "She's got a temper, too. Watch out for it. It bites." Jeagan elbowed him.

"Do you two take your show on the road?" Sam asked with a grin.

Jeagan opened her mouth with a ready retort, but stopped when she saw the hostess showing a man to their table. Tall, with thick gray hair and a slight stoop, he reminded Jeagan of one of her favorite actors, Jerry Orbach. "I believe that's your friend heading this way, Roger."

Roger turned and pushed back his chair to stand. He held out his hand when the man reached their table. "Hi, Will. How are you?"

Sam stood also and stretched out his hand. "Sam McFarland." Will shook Sam's hand also.

"And, Jeagan Christensen," Roger added. Jeagan also held out her hand.

When they were seated again, Will looked over at Jeagan, his warm brown eyes crinkling at the corners. He said half-teasing, "So, you're the young lady who stirred up all the business about murdered lovers and stolen babies, got yourself in all kinds of trouble in Memphis, and are starting all over in Seattle."

"Yep." Jeagan felt herself blushing. "I guess that's me, all right. Once I commit myself to something, I can't let go." Roger and Sam looked at her. Both hopeful?

"And, she pulled both of you guys right into the middle of it?" Will looked at Roger and Sam in turn.

"You could say that," Roger admitted. "Actually, her dad got me involved. He hired me to try to keep her out of trouble in Memphis."

"How'd that work out for you?" Sam asked straight-faced.

Roger narrowed his eyes at Sam, opened his mouth to say something sarcastic, but obviously thought better of it. "Not very well, truth be known," he admitted. He nodded his head toward Jeagan.

The interruption of the waitress, pouring coffee and taking breakfast orders, stopped further bantering and bickering. Orders placed, Jeagan asked Will if he could help them.

"I might be able to call in some favors from friends at City Hall. Check into who knew or remembers any talk about John McFarland."

"My grandfather," Sam added.

Elbows on the table, Will nodded at Sam. "McFarland, I should have made the connection. I'm surprised you'd be helping on this."

"Oh, you mean family name and reputation?"

"Something like that. Yes."

Sam shrugged and sipped his coffee. "Not really a problem for me. My grandfather and I weren't close. Anyway, he and my grandmother are gone now. Only person left who could be harmed is my step-grandmother, and there's no love lost there."

"I've questioned everyone I can think of and haven't gotten anywhere," Jeagan said dejectedly. "I talked to John McFarland's former secretary, but she stonewalled me, although I think she knows more than she's telling. She looked scared when I talked to her."

"Scared?" Will and Sam asked at the same time.

"Yes. I don't believe she was involved in the adoptions, but she knew something not-quite-right was going on because of the files her boss kept under lock and key. Roger told you about those?" Will nodded. "Well," Jeagan continued, "Sue mentioned that Mr. McFarland had several phone conversations with at least one of three attorneys during the week before one of his mysterious trips out of town. She said she didn't remember the attorneys' names, but I'm almost positive she does. Is there any way you can coax her to tell us?"

The waitress delivered the breakfast orders and sorted them round the table.

Will dug into his eggs Benedict. "I wish I could," he said after a bite. "But, I don't have any authority to question her. This would be a federal case if you pursued it through the official channels."

"Do they know what we're planning tonight?" Sam asked Jeagan. He took a bite of his English muffin.

"Roger told me," Will said. "I'd advise against it, but because you'll be in your grandmother's house by invitation, Sam, with Jeagan as your guest, legally no one can arrest you for breaking and entering."

"That's good to know," Roger added between bites of his western omelette. "Your dad wouldn't be too pleased to have to come up with bail money."

Jeagan ignored the remark and bit into a piece of crunchy bacon. "What about if we find the files? Can we take them?"

"No. Better not try that." Will shook his head. "But, you could take a camera and photograph them."

"Good idea. I've got a small camera we can use," Sam said.

"If you can get some names for me, I'll help you track down the attorneys and maybe even the babies." Will offered.

"And, hopefully, Alan."

When breakfast was finished, Will said he needed to get to City Hall. He gave all three a business card. "My cellphone number's on there. Call me if you need me. And, now, about the break-in last night."

"Break-in? What break-in?" Sam looked at Jeagan.

"Someone was in my room when I got back yesterday. Fortunately, Roger was waiting for me in the lobby and was with me when I opened the door. The guy pushed past us and took off. I ran after him, but couldn't catch him."

"And, that wasn't a smart thing for you to do," Will commented.

"Got that right!" Sam glared at Jeagan. "What would you've done if you'd caught the guy?"

"S'what I tried to tell her," Roger chimed in.

Jeagan looked around the table, ready to lash out at them, but took a breath and realized that that wasn't fair. They were all trying to help her and keep her safe. "Thanks, guys. I'll try to be more careful."

"Right about that. I'm," Roger cut his eyes over at Sam, "I mean *we* aren't going to let you out of our sight," Sam nodded confirmation."

"Teamwork," Will added and slapped the table. "That's what I like." He stood up. "I'm going to talk to the guys in Hotel Security before I leave."

Roger walked or rather clumped to the front desk with Will while Jeagan walked into the lobby with Sam. "Why did you come by this morning? I wasn't expecting you."

"Well," he explained, "I knew you wanted to go shopping for an outfit for tonight. I thought I'd go with you....to keep you safe, that is." He had the good grace to blush slightly. "And, after hearing about the break-in, I definitely want to go with you. I guess that's why they told me at the front desk that you weren't registered here."

Jeagan touched Sam's arm. Her heart swelled a little. "Thank you. That's a great idea. And, yes, that's why they don't show me registered. They changed my room, which is now adjoining Roger's." Sam grimaced. "There's nothing going on between us," she assured him. "I keep the door locked, but I admit I feel safer knowing he's on the other side."

"I guess there's something in that," Sam admitted. He checked his watch. "How soon can you be ready to go?"

"Give me a few minutes to freshen up and call Isabel."

"Okay. I'll make a few calls myself and wait for you over there." He indicated the seating area.

"Fine. See you in a few minutes." Jeagan strode toward the elevators, a definite spring in her step. After she pressed the button, she turned to watch Sam. He was a definite hunk with that dark wavy hair and bright blue eyes. How did she get lucky enough to have two good-looking guys helping her?

Roger walked up as the elevator door opened. "Is *he* leaving?" He didn't try to hide his feelings about the interloper.

"No." Jeagan stepped into the elevator. "*He* is going shopping with me. I want a new outfit for the party tonight. Something very Seattle-y so I'll fit in with what everyone else is wearing."

"That's probably a good idea." Roger pressed the button for the tenth floor. "After Will and I talk to Hotel Security, we're going to SPD to check out some mug shots."

Surprised, Jeagan said, "I didn't think you got a good look at the guy who broke into my room."

"Only an impression of a face is all I got, but something might jog my memory if the guy—"

"Or girl," Jeagan added.

"Or *girl*, has a record."

When they reached Jeagan's room, Roger took her key card and inserted it in the door and then checked out the room. Satisfied all was well, he opened the connecting door. "You two girls have fun shopping," he said before he quickly closed the door behind him, dodging the pillow that Jeagan threw at him.

Within ten minutes, Jeagan joined Sam in the lobby. "All ready."

"Great!" He took her arm. "I've put the top down since the day's so nice. If you keep hanging around, maybe we'll have better weather."

Jeagan laughed, pleased.

They walked out to Sam's car. "I haven't ridden in a convertible in a long time, not since Brandon's"

"Who's Brandon? An old boyfriend?" Sam opened the door.

"Ex-fiancé," Jeagan said as she got in.

" 'Ex' is good," Sam commented as he got in the driver's seat and started the car. "Now, where to?"

"I don't have a clue," Jeagan replied. "Where's a good place to shop for something that will fit in with all the 'nobs' we'll be 'hobbing' with tonight?"

"Want to try Neiman's or Nordstrom?"

"Probably either would be good."

"Let's go to Nordstrom first, since it's close." Sam turned onto Alaskan Way.

"This is great!" Jeagan said over the traffic noise and wind, which felt good even if it was destroying her hair.

"Is the wind too much for you?"

"No. I love it!"

* * *

After finding a parking spot near Nordstrom on Pine Street, Sam got out and opened the door for Jeagan. He took her hand to help her out of the low car. She smiled up at him, enjoying the gallantry and the little fizz holding his hand brought. How could she feel this good with all that was going on around her? She felt like her life lately was a braided chain, one chain fun and one chain disaster interwoven together to drive her crazy.

Sam continued to hold her hand even after she was on the sidewalk. She didn't complain or pull away. It felt comfortable and safe—with a little frisson— holding onto him. *Roger who?*

"Okay," he said when they were in the store. "I'm not sure where the dress department is."

"It's usually on the second or third floor," she commented.

They passed through the men's department. Jeagan again marveled at the gorgeous men's clothes Nordstrom carried, especially their expensive Façonnable line, which Brandon wore.

Soon, they were in the women's department. Jeagan let go of Sam's hand and started toward the 'After Five' wear. Sam tagged along behind. When she turned around, she saw that he looked uncomfortable. "Don't shop for women's clothes much, do you?"

Sam scratched his head. "Um. Not much. How about if I sit over there while you shop?"

"Fine." Jeagan looked through racks of cocktail dresses, then two-piece dresses. After about ten minutes, she turned around to check on Sam. He was sitting comfortably in a cushy chair, arms folded, watching her. She enjoyed having him with her and continued shopping, moving on to a rack with understated evening wear. Within minutes, she had three outfits she wanted to try on. She took them over to Sam. "What do you think of these?" She held up each one in turn for him to judge.

He rubbed his chin after seeing all three. "I think that bluish color or the black. Both would fit in with what I think the other women will be wearing."

"Okay. I'm going to try them on."

"Come out and let me see what they look like."

"My pleasure." She bowed, pivoted on her right foot, and headed for the dressing room. After she changed into the pale turquoise silk pants and sweater with a beaded v-neck, she admired the fit and look in the mirror. Pleased with the way the color made her skin and hair glow, she walked out to show the outfit to Sam.

Jeagan's stopped in mid-stride when she saw him talking to a young woman—with curly red hair!

Chapter Sixteen

She looked like the same woman Jeagan had seen in front of her townhouse and at the Denver airport. When she started toward Sam, the woman glanced up and moved away.

"Wait!" Jeagan called out. The woman turned around and waved as she stepped on the down escalator. "Who's that woman?" Jeagan wanted to know when she reached Sam.

"Don't know." Sam shrugged. "She just walked up and asked me a question."

"What did she ask you?" Jeagan demanded.

Sam rose from his chair. Clearly, irritated, he said. "Don't get all huffy and jealous. She only wanted to know the name of a good restaurant close by for lunch."

Jeagan, hands on her hips and brows furrowed, countered. "Sam! She looks like the same woman I saw in Denver. I think she's following me!"

Sam reached out and placed his hands on Jeagan's shoulders. "Just calm down. She said she was from Minneapolis and here for a conference that doesn't start until tomorrow and was doing some shopping."

"Oh." Jeagan backed down. Maybe she was getting upset for no reason. "She didn't ask you anything about me?"

"No. Why should she?" Sam looked entirely innocent, but maybe too innocent, making Jeagan wonder. "Um, that outfit looks great on you! Fits you like a glove, in all the right places."

Pleased but not distracted by the compliment, Jeagan hoped Sam was telling the truth, and, after all, the world was full of red-headed women, wasn't it? She took a deep breath and tried to calm down.

"Do you think this would fit in with what the other women will be wearing?"

He grinned. "Who cares what the other gals will be wearing."

"Okay. I'll try on the other two and let you see what you think." She returned to the dressing room, still a little shaken by the incident. *Sam has given you no reason to distrust him. Don't look for trouble!*

After trying on the champagne color and the black outfits, Jeagan—with Sam's input—went with the pale turquoise. She stopped in the shoe department and found a pair of bronze-colored sandals that complemented the outfit and left the store soon after with a beaded shoulder bag to complete the look.

"Need to do any more shopping?" Sam asked when they were out on the sidewalk.

"No," Jeagan said. "Better quit while I'm ahead. This outfit cost me a week's salary."

"The way it looks on you, it's worth every penny," Sam said with a leer.

Jeagan punched him on the arm.

"Any place else you want to go while the day's still young?" he asked when they reached his Porsche. He unlocked the door and opened it for her.

"Not that I can think of." Jeagan stepped into the car, and Sam closed the door. "I should get back to the hotel and see what Roger and his friend have found out."

"Can't you call good ol' Roger? You won't be here long, and you really need to see more of Seattle."

Jeagan gazed up at the clear blue sky with only a few puffy white clouds to the west. It was a gorgeous day, and what else could she do about finding Alan or the person who broke into her room unless Roger and Will found something? She reached into her handbag for her cellphone.

Roger answered on the first ring. "Hey, Jeagan. Having fun with Mr. Seattle?"

"As a matter of fact," Jeagan responded, glancing over at Sam, "I am. I've got a new outfit for tonight that will help me fit in with the crowd."

"If Sam helped you pick it out, I'm sure it's slinky," Roger retorted.

"Would you please just stop, Roger!"

Sam coughed and turned his head to keep from laughing.

"Okay. I'm sorry, Jeagan. It's just that you're out having fun, and I'm sitting in this ancient and dreary police station checking out pictures of criminals."

Ignoring his whining, Jeagan asked, "Do you see anyone who looks familiar?"

"Nope, not a one. I think I've looked at about five hundred pictures. Will's going to drive me back to the hotel so we can check out the security videos to see if I recognize anyone."

"That's a good idea," Jeagan said. "I didn't think of that. We should have looked at the tapes this morning. Maybe one of us would have recognized the guy."

"Will mentioned it earlier, but the Chief of Security was in a meeting this morning and couldn't review the tapes with us for a couple of hours."

"Okay. I'll meet you at the hotel and watch the tapes with you." Jeagan looked over at Sam, who frowned.

"I can handle it myself if there's something else you wanted to do," Roger offered.

Did he really mean that or was he being sarcastic? Jeagan couldn't tell. She felt pulled. Spending the beautiful afternoon with Sam would be fun, but she needed to focus on why she was here even though the temptation to play was hard to resist. "We're on our way to the hotel now. See you when we get there." She disconnected and looked at Sam.

"Well, there goes the afternoon," he said resignedly and started the car. He pulled out onto Pine.

"Wish I had more time, but I'm here for a reason, and the sooner I…I mean *we*, can get a lead on Alan, the sooner I'll feel safe again, and maybe the roses and break-ins and car accidents—"

Screech! Jeagan felt herself fly forward. Her head slammed into the dash.

"You idiot! Watch where you're going!" Sam yelled. He looked over at Jeagan. "Are you all right?"

"I think so," she said sitting back in her seat. She touched her forehead. When she checked her fingers, she saw no blood. She was grateful for that, at least. "What happened?"

"That idiot cut right in front of us, and I nearly hit her!" Blaring horns startled him. "Are you sure you're all right?" He put his foot on the accelerator and moved ahead into traffic.

Jeagan grabbed the seat belt, which she'd been in the process of fastening when Sam jammed on the brakes. She locked it into place. "I think so."

"Let me see," Sam said when he stopped at a red light.

Jeagan turned toward him and pushed her hair away from her forehead.

"You've going to have a lump. I'll get you some ice when we get to your hotel."

The wind on her flushed face helped on the drive to the Marriott. When they arrived, Sam grabbed her packages and insisted on escorting Jeagan to her room. Her head throbbing, she didn't object.

"Lie down and I'll take the bucket and get some ice," he said when they were inside her room. He went to the closet to hang up the plastic draped outfit and set the bag with the shoes and handbag on a table.

"I think I'll feel better sitting up." She sat on the couch and leaned her head back.

"Whatever is comfortable." He walked over to her, reached down and pulled her feet up, pulled off her shoes, and then propped her feet on the coffee table. When he saw that she was set, he grabbed the ice bucket along with her key card and left the room. He returned soon with the bucket full. He found a plastic bag in a drawer of the entertainment center, filled it with ice, and placed it on Jeagan's forehead. "Hold this."

Jeagan held the bag in place. She closed her eyes and tried to relax. "Thanks," she whispered.

"Do you have any aspirin? If you don't, I can go downstairs and get some?"

Jeagan opened her eyes. He really did look concerned. "I think there's some in my cosmetics bag in the bathroom."

Sam went into the bathroom. She heard him rummaging through her bag. "Found some," he called. She heard the tap running, and he returned to the room with aspirin and water. "Here," he said.

She accepted the water glass and aspirin. After she swallowed, she handed the glass back to him.

He sat beside her, lifted the ice bag off her forehead, and bent over to take a look. "Doesn't look too bad," he commented.

A knock sounded on the connecting door.

"That'll be Roger." Jeagan knew what was coming next.

Sam walked over and unlocked the door. When he pulled it open, Roger glared at him. "What're you doing here?"

"He's helping me, Roger," Jeagan said from across the room, impatience ringing in her voice.

A glance told Roger that Jeagan had been hurt again.

Before he could ask, Jeagan said. "We had a slight accident, and I bumped my head."

"I thought you were supposed to be watching out for her?" Roger accused Sam.

Sam ran a hand through his hair. "I was. I mean I did. It was an accident."

"Someone pulled out in front of us, and he had to put on the brakes. That's all," Jeagan said. "I'm fine really. Just a little bump." She pulled off the ice bag to show Roger.

"I'll take it from here," Roger said cutting his eyes at Sam.

"You know what? Fine!" Sam stalked toward the door. He jerked it open and stopped, silent for a moment, as if trying to pull himself together. Then, he turned back to look at Jeagan, fire in his eyes. "I'll pick you up at five-thirty."

"I'll be ready," Jeagan answered, wanting to apologize for Roger's behavior but tired of trying to stop the bickering. "Thanks, Sam."

"Call if you don't feel like going, and I'll search the basement," he added.

"Don't worry, I'll be ready when you get here."

Sam nodded and left the room, letting the door slam behind him.

Jeagan turned a look that could melt stone on Roger.

"Don't say it." Roger held out his hands defensively. "I know I was out of line. I'm sorry." He walked over to check out her head.

"I'm fine." She said coldly, turning away from him, and felt her head. "The lump's almost gone." She slowly stood and carried the ice bag to the bathroom where she emptied it in the sink.

"Do you feel up to watching the security tapes?" Roger called to her.

"Of course. Let's go." She collected her handbag and key card and opened the door. She turned around. Roger still stood there watching her. "Coming?"

"Oh, yeah." He followed her out the door.

When they were on the elevator, Roger jabbed the button for the lobby. "I'm sorry, Jeagan." He kept his face forward. "It's just... ."

"It's just what, Roger?" she responded, her temper rising. "I'm trying to make this work, and you keep acting like a jealous lover...or something."

Roger looked at her, hurt written across his face. "I never said I was. In fact," he stuffed his hands in his pockets, "I'll be glad when this gig is over so I can go back to working solo."

"Well," Jeagan said, feeling like she'd gone too far but not wanting to back down and apologize. "Me, too."

The elevator stopped on the third floor, and a young couple holding hands stepped on. Stars in their eyes, they smiled as if they hadn't a single care and were the only two people in the world.

Newlyweds, Jeagan thought. She pushed the envy and jealousy she felt deep inside her. *Will that ever be me?* Probably not, she realized, unless her attitude changed. Right now, she found both men in her life to be royal pains.

When the elevator stopped again, they followed the couple into the lobby. Jeagan watched them walk toward the entrance.

"Hotel Security's office is down this hall," Roger said, his tone all business now. He pointed to his left. Jeagan walked along beside him. Both were silent until they reached the Security office.

Roger introduced her to Ron Ferrari, the Chief of Security, who looked like a professional football tackle. All three sat in front of a video panel with screens recording happenings in areas inside and outside the hotel.

"Where should we start?" Jeagan asked. "The guy, or woman, could have come in at any time during the day."

"Or, he could be a guest here," Roger added turning to look at her.

Jeagan shivered. She hadn't thought of that possibility.

"That's true." Ron ran his hand across his close-cropped brown hair. "So, if that's the case, we'll need to check several different areas, starting with footage from the camera behind the front desk." He checked the dates on the tapes. "What day did you check in?" he asked Jeagan.

"I checked in Monday afternoon."

"Okay, let's start with noon on Monday the twenty-first." He sorted through the tapes and inserted one into the VCR.

Roger leaned forward, his elbows on the arm rests. He and Jeagan watched closely while the tape rolled forward with time stamps flashing. After a few minutes of slow fast-forwarding through the tape, Jeagan identified herself registering at the front desk. "There I am." She frowned when she saw how wrinkled her pants suit looked.

"Okay," Ron said, "let's see if our guy came in sometime that afternoon."

"Wait! Back up the tape!"

Ron rewound the tape. "What do you see?"

"That woman there," Jeagan pointed to a woman with shoulder-length curly hair. "That could be the red-haired woman who's been following me."

Alarmed, Roger said, "What red-headed woman? Someone's been following you?"

"I think so. I thought I told you. Anyway, I'm not sure, but she looks like the red-headed woman I saw at Stapleton before I left Denver and again at Nordstrom today."

"How can you tell?" Roger asked, skeptical. "The film is black-and-white."

"I know that," Jeagan retorted, "but that still looks like her."

"Are you sure?" Roger asked.

"No." Jeagan sat back in her chair. "I can't be sure, especially since the tape's not in color."

"Well, I don't think that's the person who ran out of your room either," Roger commented coolly.

"Let's keep looking then." Ron restarted the tape. No one on the rest of the tape appeared familiar. He next inserted the tape from the night before of the elevators in the lobby and then the elevators on the sixth floor. No one who either looked familiar or suspicious appeared.

"That's all I have." Ron stopped the VCR and pushed the rewind button. "I wish we could have spotted the guy."

"Thanks for your time, anyway." Roger stood up from his chair. "The guy must have used the stairs after he got inside the hotel. I was hoping we could have noticed him at least coming in the entrance."

"Maybe he came in with some other people so he wouldn't be conspicuous." Jeagan stood and realized how tense she'd been while focusing on the tapes. Her head and neck ached, and her eyes hurt.

"Well, now that you're in a different room and there's no record of you being here, you should be safe from any further intruders," Ron said. "And, we'll continue to keep our eyes open for anyone who acts suspicious…or has curly red hair."

She offered her hand. "Thanks. I appreciate that."

Jeagan and Roger returned to the lobby and rode the elevator to the tenth floor in silence. "I'm going to lie down for a while." She inserted the key card in her door.

"Fine," Roger pushed the door open and walked inside. "Let me check your room first, and then you can do whatever you want."

Jeagan followed him in and laid her handbag on the desk. She knew she should try to smooth things out with him, but at that moment, she was too tired to care. "What are you going to do while I'm gone to the fund raiser?"

"All clear," Roger announced when he finished his search. "To answer your question, I might go to the bar and drink away my frustration and aggravation," he announced coldly and strode toward the connecting door.

"Well, that sounds helpful!" Jeagan bit back.

Roger opened the door. "Have fun on your date." He closed the door behind him with a *thud*.

"Men!" Jeagan walked over and locked the door. Then, she kicked off her boots. She lay across the bed and closed her eyes. They popped open again though when she remembered she should set the alarm. Didn't want to oversleep. The alarm set, she lay across the bed. Within seconds, she was asleep.

Bells rang, music blared! Jeagan popped up, suddenly awake and confused. Where *was* she and what was making that dreadful noise? As she became aware of her surroundings, she realized the alarm on the radio had gone off and the phone was ringing. She grabbed for the phone and punched the button on top of the radio to silence it.

"Hullo?" she said sleepily.

"Hey honey." She heard her dad's voice. "You okay?"

"Hey, Dad. Yeah, I'm fine. I was taking a nap."

"Sorry. Didn't mean to wake you. Resting up for the big night?"

"That's okay. It was time to get up and get ready."

"Are you sure everything's okay? Are Roger and that other fellow watching out for you?"

"Sam. His name's Sam. And, yes, they're watching out for me. Don't worry. I'm fine. I only wish we were having more luck in finding out something about Alan."

"No new information then?"

"Not much. Only a few tiny pieces of information, which haven't helped very much."

"Well, I know how tenacious you are. You won't let go until you get 'your man.' " He chuckled at his own little joke.

"Cute, but true. Thanks for calling. I love you."

"Love you too, little girl. I'll be thinking about you tonight. Good luck."

"Thanks. I need all the luck I can get."

After she disconnected, Jeagan pushed herself up from the bed. She felt tired, but at least her head no longer ached. Her stomach growled, which made her realize she hadn't had any lunch. She walked over to the miniature refrigerator and pulled out a packet of cheese and crackers and a Coke. Something to fortify her before her big night.

A hot shower revived her. She worked with her hair, pulling it up into a French twist, and experimented with eye shadow and makeup to give herself a bit more glamorous look. By the time she put on her new outfit, she felt energized and ready for the next step in the investigation. She hoped the night would not turn into a disaster with her being recognized by Cruella and thrown out of the house.

Chapter Seventeen

A knock on the door at five-thirty sharp told her Sam was punctual, but she hesitated and peered through the peep hole anyway to make sure it was him. It was. She opened the door to see that he was dressed in an expensively cut charcoal-gray suit, crisp white shirt, and black-and-gold silk tie. He looked rather James Bondish.

He gave a low whistle when he saw her. "Wow!"

She laughed, pleased. "You clean up rather well yourself. Come on in while I put on my shoes." She slid her feet into the new sandals and picked up her tiny bag. "Okay. I'm ready."

Sam held the door for her. "You look great! Cruella will never recognize the new and improved version of you." His eyes glittered with mischief.

"Thanks...I think. Anything in particular that I need to know about tonight?"

Sam punched the button for the elevator. "Nothing I can think of offhand, except maybe that there'll be a lot of her friends there who can be a little snobbish. Oh, and she's invited two up-and-coming young actresses, I mean actors."

The elevator stopped and they stepped on. The car was loaded with giggly teenage girls in cheerleading outfits, who checked Sam out and whispered among themselves.

Jeagan glanced over at Sam—who appeared to be slightly uncomfortable—pleased that he was her date.

In the lobby, Sam continued. "Anyway Cruella, I mean Patrice, invited the two ladies to draw in the rich old men who enjoy rubbing elbows with beautiful Hollywood starlets."

"Who are the starlets?" Jeagan glanced around the lobby while they walked toward the front entrance. She thought she might see Roger waiting to watch them leave, but he was nowhere around.

"I believe she said she invited Samantha Stewart, a gal originally from Brentwood, Tennessee, where all the famous country music singers live."

"Is she a singer?"

"Not sure, but I know she's landed a leading role in a new romantic comedy starring opposite Matthew McConaghey."

"Wow! Too bad Patrice didn't invite him."

Sam scowled at her. "Anyway," he said, as he followed her out the front entrance, "the other actor is from Denver. Her name is Dorothea Ellerby. I believe she's been signed for the lead in a time-travel love story."

"Denver? Hmm. Her name sounds familiar."

"How's your head?" He asked when they were in his Porsche, this time with the top up.

"It's fine. I feel much better since I took a nap after we watched the security tapes this afternoon."

"Did you or Roger recognize anybody?" He drove out of the parking lot and turned right onto Alaskan Way.

"Not really." Jeagan watched the lights along the marina coming on as the sun neared the western horizon accompanied by splashes of pink and orange. "But I did see someone who checked into the hotel a few minutes after I did. She looked like that red-headed gal you were talking to in Nordstrom."

"Really?" Sam said. "Now that's strange."

Jeagan watched his reaction. She trusted yet didn't trust him. He was like quicksilver. She couldn't quite grasp him and really knew little about him, only what he told her. *Have you bothered to check him out? Was he lying when he said he didn't know the woman who spoke to him in Nordstrom?* She was committed to the evening now, even if she had minor doubts about Sam. Other than a few secretive phone calls and the conversation with the red-haired woman, Sam had been friendly, helpful, and a great tour guide. *Concentrate on tonight and stop worrying about any ulterior motives that Sam might have. He's not Madison!*

"Anything else I should know before we get there?" she asked after they turned onto Spring Street.

"Not really," Sam replied. "Just smile and be polite, and stay close to me."

"No problem there. I don't want to even speak to Patrice if I don't have to."

"Well, you'll probably have to say 'hello' to her at least and 'good-bye.' " He turned off Spring onto Terry Avenue and then left onto Madison Street.

"Okay, we're here," he said a short time later. They parked in front of the imposing wood-and-brick home. The occupants of the Mercedes in front of them exited their car, which was immediately driven away by a valet. Another valet opened Jeagan's door.

"Good evening." He held out his hand to help her out of the car.

Jeagan smiled. "Thank you." She stepped onto the sidewalk and waited for Sam to give the keys to the young man and come around the car. "I could get used to this," she whispered while they walked up the sidewalk.

Sam whispered back. "It's all show for the rich guests." He knocked on the front door, which was almost immediately opened by a maid in a black-and-white uniform. Jeagan was relieved to see she wasn't the Asian woman she'd encountered two days earlier.

"Good evening," the woman said in a British accent. She opened the door wider to allow Jeagan and Sam to enter a grand white-marble foyer.

A polished round table sat in the center of the entryway. On it sat an enormous oriental vase of spring flowers beneath a dazzling crystal chandelier. Jeagan tried not to gawk at the elegance, but was in awe of the beauty of the grand staircase that wound upward to the floor above with a continuation of the white marble. To her right, pale blue silk graced the walls of the living room above polished wood floors and floral oriental carpets. To her left, she glimpsed a music room with a shining white grand piano set on polished hardwood with overstuffed blue floral chairs set about on another oriental rug.

"This house is gorgeous," Jeagan whispered. They walked along the hall past an enormous two-story paneled library on their left and, on their right, a formal dining room with a long mahogany table and ornately framed landscapes on the walls. The paintings appeared to be the work of Pissarro and Monet. *Surely not originals*, she thought.

Sam squeezed her hand that was holding onto his arm. "Do I know how to show a girl a good time, or what?"

Voices from the rear of the house grew louder before they entered a long room, which seemed to stretch forever across the back of the house. She observed beautifully coiffed women dressed in black or white or gold after-five dresses or pantsuits. Their martini glasses and jewels sparkled while they moved about chatting or sat on groupings of white couches, with large colorful pillows, and green-striped chairs. The men in their dark suits and white shirts, many going gray or balding, were gathered around two beautiful young women. Both women radiated glamour and poise. The actors were certainly doing their jobs.

Jeagan did a double take. The man she had talked to in the Jetway. He was in the crowd of men around the actors and stood out because he was probably thirty years younger than any of the other men. She'd seen his picture in the magazine in Chuck McFarland's office. What was his name? Scott Singer. That was it.

He looked around at that moment and noticed Jeagan staring at him. A quizzical expression on his face, he suddenly smiled and walked toward them.

"Scott!" Sam said when the man walked over and stuck out his hand.

"Hi Sam." Scott Singer turned to Jeagan with a grin. "Didn't know you knew this character."

Jeagan laughed.

Puzzled, Sam asked, "How do you know each other?"

"We met at the airport." Scott took Jeagan's offered hand. "We were on the same flight from Denver. I told her not to be discouraged by the rain in Seattle. But, I didn't get your name."

"Jeagan Christensen," she said.

"Scott Singer."

"I know," Jeagan admitted. "I saw your picture in *Seattle Magazine*. And you were right. It did stop raining by the time I got to my hotel."

"Ah," Sam said. "And it hasn't rained since. I think she brought the sunshine with her from Colorado."

"Looks that way." Scott admired Jeagan from head to toe.

"Buy you a drink?" Sam asked, looking uncomfortable.

"Thanks, but I need to get back to my date."

"Are you with one of the actors?" Jeagan asked.

Scott nodded. "Dorothea. Met her at a party at Wade Phillips's home in Denver."

"Ooh, I'm impressed." Jeagan's eyebrows rose.

"Don't be. My dad went to college with Coach Phillips, so I've seen him a few times over the years." Scott looked back to where the actors were still smiling and talking to their circle of admirers. "Well, nice seeing you again," he said to Jeagan. "Talk to you soon, Sam."

"Good-looking guy," Jeagan commented.

"Yeah," Sam admitted a bit grudgingly. "We went to high school together. He was a popular guy, and I have to admit he has turned into a fine attorney."

"Well," Jeagan whispered, "if we need someone to bail us out of jail after we get caught, maybe we could call him."

Sam squeezed her hand. "If we're careful, we won't get caught."

"Hope you're right." Jeagan gazed out the ceiling-height windows with a view of the terrace, a manicured lawn, a rose garden, and Lake Washington beyond reflecting lights from the homes across the lake in the early evening twilight. "What a view!"

"Oh...yeah. It is," Sam said absentmindedly. "There's a good crowd here." He scanned the room for Patrice and found her standing with the men and starlets. She smiled and waved. Sam did the same.

Jeagan turned her head, pretending to look the other way.

Patrice excused herself and started toward Sam and Jeagan.

"Here she comes," Sam whispered.

Jeagan stiffened.

"Relax," he said out of the side of his mouth.

At the last second, Patrice strode past Sam and Jeagan, giving him a pat on the shoulder and a "how nice to see you" while she hurried to greet two more couples entering the room.

"Whew!" Jeagan let out her breath.

"Let's get something to eat."

"Fine."

Sam guided her to the right end of the room where buffet tables were filled with cold seafood, salads, and fruit along with hot dishes: wild rice, asparagus with hollandaise, and a roast beef being sliced by a waiter.

"This looks delicious," Jeagan whispered. She secured her bag strap over her shoulder and picked up a snowy-white gold-rimmed plate. In the middle of the plate was the logo for the Washington Park Arboretum. "She's serious about this fund-raiser, isn't she?" Jeagan commented. She filled her plate and asked for a ginger ale from a bartender.

"That's no way to keep that girlish figure," Sam teased. He followed Jeagan to a small white-clothed table set against the far wall of windows. He nodded to other couples seated at nearby tables and held a chair for Jeagan.

"I'm starving, but I may not be able to eat."

"Better eat it all," Sam whispered. "It may be your last decent meal if we get caught and arrested."

Jeagan cut her eyes up at him, momentarily startled, but relaxed when she saw his grin.

"Enjoy your food. Patrice does know how to put on a nice party." Sam dipped a forkful of crab into cocktail sauce. When he swallowed, he added, "We'll wait until most of the guests are here and everyone's drinking and not paying any attention to us."

Jeagan nodded and watched the younger of the actors—a tall, slender girl with long, dark hair and a dazzling smile—who talked animatedly with a salt-and-pepper haired man dressed in black, looking much like a Mafia don. The girl's facial expressions and mannerisms reminded Jeagan of a young Cher.

"I think that's Samatha Stewart," Sam said, noticing the direction of Jeagan's gaze.

The other actor, Dorothea Ellerby, was blonde and petite with delicate features and a sparkling smile that made her face light up. The two portly, balding men talking to her seemed to bask in her glow.

"Well, will you look at that!"

"What?" Jeagan turned in the direction Sam indicated. "Isn't that Sophia?"

"It sure is!" Sam confirmed. "I can't believe she's helping out after what she said yesterday about never wanting to set foot in this house again." Sam rose from his chair. "I'll be back in a minute." He walked toward Sophia.

Sophia nodded politely when Sam reached her, but gave no indication of having recently shared lunch with him. After exchanging a few words, she carried a tray of dishes and glassware toward what must be the kitchen area behind the buffet setup.

Moving toward the front of the house, Sam shook hands and spoke to people along the way. He soon disappeared from sight.

Where's he going? Jeagan hated being left alone. Suppose Patrice came over to talk to her and recognized her? She continued to eat, but, out of the corner of her eye, she saw Patrice heading her way. Slowly, Jeagan got up from the table and threaded her way through the crowd to join Scott in the group around the actors.

Scott smiled when Jeagan joined them and introduced her to Dorothea. They discussed Denver, the Broncos, and skiing for a few minutes.

When Jeagan glanced around again, Patrice was busy greeting more new arrivals, which gave her the perfect opportunity to excuse herself from the group. She needed to get out of Patrice's line of sight before she recognized her.

The terrace seemed to be empty. Jeagan opened one of the French doors and stepped outside. She breathed in the fresh smell of the water in the cooling evening. Sam, she saw when she looked to her right, was at the other end of the terrace talking to Sophia. Good! Jeagan walked slowly toward them, not wishing to draw attention from inside the house to her movements.

"Glad you came out here," Sam said when he saw her.

"Hi, Sophia. I thought you said you weren't going to help out at the party."

"I know, but Miss Patrice call me again yesterday and almost beg me to come help. She say the caterer not have enough people. And," Sophia appeared embarrassed. "And, she offer me two time my usual wage."

"Well, glad you're here," Sam said. "It's nice to have a friend in the enemy camp."

"I see someone you talk about yesterday also," Sophia commented.

"Who?"

"Mr. McFarland's secretary, Mrs. Coleman."

"She's here?" Jeagan asked, surprised.

Sophia nodded. "Yes. She come in only a few minutes ago. I see her when I come from kitchen. She was in the dining room talking to Mr. Charles and Mr. Bob."

"My dad's here?"

"Yes," Sophia confirmed.

"Charles, I mean, Chuck is here, too?" Jeagan's eyes widened when Sophia confirmed this with a quick nod. "Oh, no!" She was in big trouble now with both Sue and Chuck being able to recognize her. She felt like making a hasty retreat before she was found out and kicked out of the house.

"Don't get rattled, Jeagan." Sam placed a comforting arm around her shoulder. "Let me think a minute."

Sophia looked behind her. "I need to go to kitchen now."

"Okay. Thanks, Sophia," Sam said. "Let me know if you hear or see anything that will help us."

"If I go in basement, should I check for the cabinet with files?" Sophia asked.

Jeagan looked hopeful. "Do you think there's a chance Patrice will send you to the basement for something?"

"Maybe, since I work here for many years and know where everything stored."

"That would be great," Sam said. "We want to wait a while before we go down there, until everything is busy and noisy. Then, we should be able to slip into the hallway and get to the basement stairs unnoticed."

"That good plan, but maybe I can help. If I go down before you, I check around little bit." Sophia's eyes sparkled with conspiracy.

"Thanks." Sam patted her on the shoulder.

"Now what?" Jeagan said.

Sam checked the time. "We probably need to lose ourselves for a half hour or so. Everyone should be here by then."

A door opened behind them.

"Oh, no," Sam whispered and threw his arms around Jeagan. He pulled her into a full hug while turning her back toward Patrice. "It's Patrice," he whispered. "Play along." Sam bent his head to kiss Jeagan.

Resisting at first, Jeagan felt her insides quiver and her body melt against his, even if he was only kissing her for Patrice's benefit.

"There you are, Sam. I've been looking everywhere for you." Patrice called across the deck, impatience ringing in her voice. "I could use your help inside."

Sam released Jeagan and looked over her shoulder. "Oh...of course. I'll be right there."

The sound of the door opening and closing filled the embarrassed silence.

Jeagan stepped away from Sam and smoothed her hair.

"Sorry about that." Sam pulled out his handkerchief and wiped lipstick off his face.

"No need to apologize." Jeagan looked into Sam's eyes, now shadowed in the lights on the deck. "I know you were only trying to protect me."

He opened his mouth to say something, but didn't. After a look toward the other end of the deck, he suggested they go inside. He took Jeagan's arm and guided her to the door that Patrice had come through.

What am I supposed to do once we're inside? she wondered. With three people there who knew her, the chances of her being able to conceal her identity were slim.

"I'll be back as soon as I can." Sam left her at their table. He grabbed his champagne flute and took it with him. "Maybe I can get Dad to keep Uncle Charles occupied."

With a nod to Sam, Jeagan took a flute of champagne from a passing waiter. She scanned the room. It didn't take her long to spot Chuck McFarland, who was in the group of men surrounding Samantha and Dorothea. He seemed to be immensely enjoying filling his eyes with the gorgeous young women. That, much to her relief, should keep him occupied.

Where was Sue Coleman, and would Sue recognize her if she saw her? Well, she couldn't stand around like a wallflower. Move and mingle. A group of younger women—trophy wives?—stood in a semi-circle around an athletically built and vaguely familiar young man. Jeagan joined them. She smiled and nodded to the women, hoping she fit in with their general age and appearance, minus the jewels, and kept her back to the rest of the room. She soon found out that the attractive man was Rick Mirer, quarterback for the Seattle Seahawks.

The noise level of the background music and crowd behind her escalated while Jeagan listened to the questions and flirtatious banter between the man and his admirers. After a few minutes, she'd had enough and decided to move on. She moved to the far side of the semi-circle.

From there she could see most of the rest of the room. Sam was moving through the crowd with Patrice on his arm. She held onto him possessively like he was her lover. *Poor Sam*, Jeagan thought, but at least he was keeping Patrice occupied.

Chuck seemed to be enjoying himself. She watched him stop a passing waiter to exchange his empty champagne flute for a full one. Jeagan continued to scan the area. Where was Sue Coleman? She didn't appear to be in the room. Maybe this was a good time to move away from the group and out of the room while the noise level was fairly high. Maybe she could even slip downstairs by herself while Sam had Patrice busy and mingling.

Jeagan edged away from the group and out into the hallway. She could see through to the front of the house. All the doors were open, so the door to the basement was obviously not there, but she did notice that the hallway veered off to her right between the music room and the library. She walked past the library and turned. If anyone asked her what she was doing, she could always say she was looking for the powder room. And, sure enough, the powder room was to her left when she made the turn. At the end of the hallway, she spotted an open solarium. The earthy smell of potting soil and foliage drew her as she continued toward it to look inside.

A winding flagstone pathway set in bark was flanked by rows of orchids. Every description and color greeted her, from the palest shades of pink to the brightest shades of orange, green, purple, and red. Weeping fig trees and small palms, along with yellow roses and lacy ferns lined the path. The solarium was alive with color. An inviting area with rattan furniture and tables off to her right at the end of the path tempted her, but she couldn't stay in one place too long.

When she looked more closely, she realized two people were sitting in the floral-cushioned chairs and talking. The man was wide, dwarfing the rattan chair. His ruddy complexion and rust-colored hair stood out against the green foliage. The woman was staring out the windows toward the lighted lawn and lake beyond. All she could see was the woman's profile, but Jeagan recognized Sue Coleman and edged away from the doorway before Sue could turn around and recognize her.

"I say!" Someone grabbed her from behind.

Chapter Eighteen

Jeagan gasped and whirled around, freeing herself.

"Oh, I didn't mean to startle you." Chuck withdrew his hands from Jeagan's arms. "I was trying to keep from running into you."

Her cheeks burning, she glanced up at Chuck's chubby face and leering eyes. "I...I was just leaving. Thank you." She ducked her head. Did he recognize her? To his left, stood the blonde actor, smiling politely.

"Wouldn't want to run you over with all this bulk, would I?" He chuckled and patted his expansive stomach with both hands. "Giving Dorothea a tour, as it were." He beamed at the young woman.

"The solarium is beautiful. I'm sure you'll enjoy it," Jeagan said, her voice low. "Go right in."

Chuck, nodding to Jeagan, took the young woman's arm and guided her onto the path. They were soon swallowed in the greenness of plants and trees.

Enamored of the beautiful woman, Jeagan was grateful no sign of recognition had registered on Chuck's face. The hallway was once again empty. She quickly opened the first door on her left. Without turning on a light, she recognized an artist's studio. Tall windows facing the lake and a large skylight stared at her blankly in the dimness. Silently, she closed the door and tried the one on the other side of the hall. Inside this room was what she would call a lady's morning room— small antique white writing desk with a cushioned chair, small skirted chintz armchairs, and a matching floral rug. Jeagan silently closed this door and checked the main hall again. A woman walked into the hallway and immediately into the powder room without looking toward Jeagan.

While no one was around, she tried the last door on her left. She opened it to find a downward staircase. The basement! Why not go down while everyone else was busy? She quietly closed the door behind her and started down, straining to listen for the presence of anyone else. No sounds from the basement. Silently, she descended the stairs, lit by lights on the risers. When she reached the bottom, she stepped into a softly lit playroom with a large pool table, a poker table, a wall-mounted television, and bar area on her left. To the right of the bar was an open doorway that led to a wine room with shelves of wine bottles on slanted racks. She found a short hallway farther along, which revealed a large workout room with several large pieces of equipment and a draped massage table. A doorway on the other side of the workout room no doubt led to a sauna and shower area. What, no indoor swimming pool?

Two other doors off the hallway revealed small bedrooms with baths. Maybe for the live-in help? And, where was the storage area? There had to be one. Jeagan looked across the game room and spotted another short hallway behind the stairs with several doors off it. She crossed the large room and found that the first door opened onto a half-bath. Another was a coat closet.

Jeagan heard music and laughter from upstairs. Had someone opened the door? Footsteps sounded on the stairs. Her heart raced! Where to hide? She opened the coat closet and ducked inside, pulling the door shut behind her. Moments passed. Then, someone shuffled along the hallway, making very little sound on the carpeting. The door at the end of the hallway opened, squeaking slightly. Jeagan cracked the closet door enough so she could see who was in the basement with her. It was Sophia!

"Sophia!" Jeagan called quietly as she pushed open the door.

The woman stopped in her tracks and visibly stiffened.

"It's me, Jeagan."

Sophia turned and grabbed at her chest. "You scare me," she said, a look of relief on her face.

"I could say the same thing," Jeagan added. "But, I'm glad it was you and not someone else."

"I have a few minutes that I can check for you."

"Let's look together. Maybe with your help we can find out if the filing cabinet is here."

"Okay, this is storeroom down here."

Sophia opened the door and turned on the lights. Unused furniture, shrouded in white sheets like so many resident ghosts, shared the space with metal shelves, which held household cleaning supplies, canned and bottled goods, bird seed, cushions and umbrellas for outdoor furniture, along with gardening supplies and equipment—but no file cabinets.

"Doors down there also." Sophia pointed to another short hallway. "One room is for electrical and heating, I think."

"Haven't you been in those rooms?"

"No."

"Weren't you ever curious?" Jeagan asked. She walked toward the closed doors.

"No time to be curious in this busy house."

The first door Jeagan opened was indeed the electrical room. No file cabinet there. She tried the next door. "Locked," she announced, disappointed. *Of course*, she thought. *What did you expect?*

"I think I know where key kept." Sophia returned to the main storage area and pulled a sheet away to reveal a roll-top desk. She eased out a drawer, reached above it inside the desk, and pressed a lever. With a loud *click*, a compartment above the drawer popped open. Jeagan walked over to peer inside. Inside lay a silver door key.

"Wow! How'd you know about this hiding place?" Jeagan asked as Sophia picked up the key.

Enjoying herself, Sophia smiled conspiratorily. "I was in basement one day when Mr. McFarland still alive. He not see me in room on other side bending down to get bag of flour for the kitchen. I see him through shelf and stay quiet. He pull out drawer, stick hand in, and I hear *pop* sound. He pull his hand out with key. He take key and unlock door, go inside, and close it. I grab flour and hurry upstairs. He never know I in basement."

"Hmm," Jeagan said. "Let's check it out before someone comes down here looking for you...or me."

Rustling somewhat in the quiet basement, the sheet settled back into place when Jeagan tugged on it.

Sophia was right about the key. It did unlock the door. As soon as they were inside, Jeagan closed the door and turned on the light. Inside the room was a small office with an old, scarred oak desk and matching chair. The windows set in the rear wall were heavily draped with blackout curtains. That helped. Then, in front of them, in a corner, she saw it. A gray metal four-drawer file cabinet!

"This could be it!" Jeagan's heart skipped multiple beats. She hurried over to pull on a drawer. Locked! She pushed a lever and pulled on the drawer. It still didn't budge. She turned toward the desk. Maybe—

please God!—someone had left a key in the desk. "Help me look for a key to the cabinet."

They opened drawers and riffled through the few items stored there. Jeagan came across several business cards, now yellowed with age and held together with a paper clip, all for attorneys—attorneys in southern cities!

"Here is key!" Sophia said, holding a small silver key.

"Try it." Jeagan thumbed through the few business cards until she found one with the name and address of a Memphis attorney. Eureka!

Sophia walked around the desk, inserted the key into the lock, and turned it. With a loud *clunk*, the lock popped out.

Hands shaking, Jeagan walked over to the cabinet and eased out the top drawer. A sudden feeling of *déjà vu* overwhelmed her—from two weeks earlier in another basement, the basement of The Peabody Hotel. Although it had taken her a while, she'd been lucky to find what she was searching for there. Would she be that lucky now?

Green hanging folders, topped with hand-printed names in clear plastic tabs, filled the drawer. The same names that were on the business cards? Jeagan went to the desk to check the cards. Before she reached the desk, however, she heard someone in the hall. She and Sophia froze. Their hearts beating wildly, they watched the doorknob slowly turn and the door silently open. A dark head appeared around the door.

"Sam!" Jeagan whispered loudly, grabbing her chest. "You almost gave us a heart attack!"

Sam stepped into the office. "I thought you were going to wait for me to come with you," he said in a loud whisper.

"Well, we didn't. We found an opportunity and took it. Look at this!"

Sam's eyebrows rose. "Is that the file cabinet that used to be in my grandfather's office?"

"I'd be willing to bet it is." Jeagan took the business cards from the desk, shuffled through them, and found the one with the name of a Memphis attorney on it: Christopher Mark Greer, Attorney at Law. The address was on Main Street. "Here's a card for a Memphis attorney. Now, if I can find a file with his name on it, maybe we'll have something."

She moved over to the files and flipped through the folders until she came to one with Greer's name on it. Heart pounding, she pulled the green folder out of the cabinet and carried it over to the desk where she spread it open.

Heavy footsteps clumped down the stairs. Startled, all three stopped moving and listened.

"How about a small wager, Bob? Say twenty a game," they heard a muted masculine voice say. It sounded like Chuck.

"You're on," another male voice answered. After that, they soon heard the sounds of cue balls being racked.

"What're we going to do?" Jeagan whispered to Sam.

"Leave it to me. That's my dad with Uncle Chuck. Just keep quiet." He left the office and closed the door behind him. Jeagan opened the door an inch and watched as Sam moved noiselessly toward the storeroom door. Opening it a crack, he peeked down the hall into the game room. Then, he slipped out the door, and within a minute, the women heard the sound of a toilet flushing followed by water running in a sink. Next, they heard a door, obviously the bathroom, open and close.

"Sam, my boy!" Jeagan heard a masculine voice exclaim. "What're you doing down here?"

"Hi, Uncle Chuck. The loo was occupied upstairs so I came down here."

"More exciting down here than upstairs now that the young ladies have left," Chuck whined.

Jeagan listened at the door. Oh, no! Bad timing. The party might start to wind down quickly now that the actors were gone.

"I need to go upstairs," Sophia said, looking nervous and trapped, "before someone miss me."

"What about the windows?" Jeagan walked across the room. She bumped into the desk chair, which bumped into the file cabinet. *Clang!* She stopped in her tracks, holding her breath. How could she be so clumsy?

"What was that?" Sam asked the question before Chuck or his dad could.

"Probably the sprinklers coming on," Chuck said.

"It's okay," Sophia, listening at the door, whispered to Jeagan when she heard Chuck's voice.

Jeagan walked quietly over to the windows. "Turn out the light." When the light was out, she opened the drapes and unlocked a window. Stiff though it was, she managed to raise it. It opened onto a basement patio, softly lit with torch lights flickering in the breeze. "If we can get this screen off, you can slip out this window," Jeagan whispered in the dim light from the patio. "See if you can find anything in the desk to pry off this screen."

Sophia opened the desk drawer and rummaged around. "I find letter opener. That should work." She took it to Jeagan."

"That should do it." Jeagan easily pried the screen off the window and helped Sophia out.

"Thank you," Sophia whispered and hurried up to the terrace.

Jeagan quickly replaced the screen and closed the window. Next, she pulled the drapes together and held out her hands while she fumbled her way over to the desk. Remembering a brass desk lamp, she slid her hands along the top of the desk until she touched the lamp and switched it on. Then, she searched through the folder on the desk, hoping to find the name of Isabel Lloyd or Alan Lloyd or Isabel's father, Robert Lloyd. Names and dates flashed by as she went back in time.

The earliest date was December of 1985. It was a letter from John McFarland to Christopher Greer regarding MaryAnne Boruszak. Another adopted child? Stolen? Jeagan quickly scanned the page. The word 'adoption' jumped out in the first few sentences. Jeagan involuntarily cried out. She quickly covered her mouth. Could the men hear her out in the other room? Heart thudding, she listened. The billiard balls were clacking and the men were talking loudly. No one was paying any attention to her. *Thank you, Lord.*

She heard a scraping sound behind her. Quickly, she reached over to switch off the light, hoping for no gap in the curtains. Afraid to breathe, she listened for another sound. The seconds ticked by slowly. Shoes scraped on stone. Whoever was out there appeared to be moving away from her. Surely she was safe, but she had no way of knowing if the person had seen the light and might mention it to Patrice.

My luck can't hold out much longer, Jeagan thought after she switched the lamp on again. She thumbed quickly through the papers in the folder. Dates flashed by: 1984, 1980, 1978, 1975, 1963, 1956, 1954, 1948, and finally 1945. Then, she came across a carbon copy of a letter to Christopher Mark Greer in the matter of Baby Lloyd! She gasped and her heart almost stopped completely. The letter was copied to Robert Lloyd. Not taking time to read the letter, Jeagan looked at pages beneath it. Three sheets were attached. No time to read any of them now. She needed to photograph them.

The camera! She'd forgotten to get it from Sam. No choice left but to take the document. Quickly, she pulled the pages out of the folder and returned it to the file cabinet. She listened for a minute until she heard laughter and the sound of the billiard balls being racked again. To block the noise, she covered the file cabinet lock with her body while she pushed it back into place. The key returned to the desk, she folded the four sheets of thin carbon copies and placed them in her bag. It was past time to get out of there.

Quietly, she opened the door and peeped out. The storage area was dark and still. She remembered seeing a penlight in the desk and returned for it. Using it, she made her way over to the roll-top desk, where she lifted the cover and returned the key to its hiding place. She waited until she heard more shots being taken in the game room. Quickly, she relocked the compartment where the key had been hidden, replaced the drawer, and pulled the dust cover in place. She moved noiselessly back to the office where she closed and locked the door. After turning off the light, she carefully felt her way to the window and opened it. The metallic scrape of the screen when she removed it sounded loud, but she had no choice. This was the only way out. The window needed to be locked, she realized when she was on the patio, but she couldn't lock it from outside. Leaving it unlocked shouldn't be a problem if no one knew she'd been in the office. Heart racing, she dashed up the stone steps to the terrace.

At the top, she stopped to catch her breath. Then, she turned and walked slowly across the terrace for one of the French doors. She reached out to open it, but it was pulled open from the inside before she could touch the handle. Jeagan looked up to see Patrice McFarland directly in front of her.

"Oh, excuse me." Jeagan ducked her head and moved out of the way.

"Quite all right." Patrice stepped onto the deck followed by an attractive middle-aged man, his dark hair slicked back into a ponytail. She turned toward Jeagan and studied her for a second. "You're Sam's date, aren't you?"

"Yes," Jeagan said, raising the pitch of her voice.

Patrice stared at her as if she couldn't believe her ears. "Well, where *is* he? I've been trying to find him for the past half hour."

"I don't know. He was talking to Chuck...I mean Charles McFarland the last time I saw him."

As if trying to remember where she'd seen her before, Patrice continued to stare. She opened her mouth to say something else, but instead shrugged and walked out onto the deck followed by the man, who nodded and smiled at Jeagan.

Before she could step inside the house, Jeagan heard Patrice call out to her. "What did you say your name was?"

Jeagan froze. "Uh…Leigh. My name is Leigh," she replied, offering her middle name as she turned around.

"Well, Leigh, please tell my grandson I'd like to see him before he leaves."

With that, Jeagan stepped inside the house and closed the door behind her. She needed to find the 'loo,' and worked her way through the thinning crowd to the powder room. When the door was shut, she leaned against it and closed her eyes for a few moments, willing her heart to slow down. Little attention did she pay to the creamy-marble fixtures and peach silk walls while she splashed cold water on her burning face and looked at herself in the mirror. Though the pink lighting was flattering, it could not disguise the burning eyes that stared at her out of a red-splotched face.

Strands of her hair stuck out from the French twist and fell into her face. She quickly powdered her nose, applied fresh coral lipstick, and tucked her hair back into place. Her reflection now appeared calmer, neater. Time to find Sam and leave before Patrice took a closer look at her and recognized her.

A knock sounded on the door. "Just a minute," Jeagan automatically called out. A silver-haired man stood waiting in the hallway when she opened the door. He nodded to her as she passed him.

The hall was now empty. Sounds from the party were dying down. Where was Sam? She needed to leave—now.

"Good game," she heard Chuck saying in his hearty British accent when he pushed open the door from the basement.

"Guess I'd better go find my date before she takes up with somebody else," Sam said.

"Don't believe I saw her," Chuck replied and turned toward the back of the house.

"Talk to you soon," Sam said when he stepped up into the hallway followed by another man. He turned his head and saw Jeagan. "Oh, there you are." He crossed the hall. "I'd like you to meet my dad,

Bob McFarland. Dad, this is Jeagan Christensen. She's visiting from Denver."

Jeagan looked up at an older and slightly shorter version of Sam with the same sky-blue eyes, only his were stormier. She extended her hand, "Nice to meet you, Mr. McFarland."

Bob McFarland clasped her hand and squeezed. Jeagan winced and withdrew her hand quickly before he broke something. *Why do some men do that?* She wondered. *A need to prove their masculinity or merely inconsideration?*

"Are you enjoying your visit?" Sam's dad asked, polite but clearly not interested.

"Yes, I am," Jeagan responded. "Seattle has it all. It's lush with a view of mountains, and it's on the water."

"Glad you're enjoying yourself. Are you staying long?"

"No, only a few more days," Jeagan said. Out of the corner of her eye, she saw Patrice walking in their direction from the solarium. Slowly she turned her back to her.

Bob spotted Patrice. "Excuse me a minute. I need to talk to our hostess."

"That's okay, Dad. I think we're ready to leave."

"Nice to meet you, Jeagan, and talk you later, son." Bob strode toward the solarium.

"We need to get out of here," Jeagan whispered to Sam. "I ran into Patrice outside. I don't think she recognized me, but I'd like to leave before she does."

"Okay." Sam took Jeagan's arm and guided her toward the front door.

A glance toward the solarium told her Patrice was looking their way. "She's coming this way," Jeagan said.

Sam walked her to the front door and opened it. "You go outside and give this ticket to the valet, and I'll be out in a minute."

"Okay." Jeagan took the ticket and hurried along the sidewalk. Good manners dictated that she should have thanked her hostess and said goodnight, but good manners might have gotten her into real trouble tonight. She shivered in the cool evening air, or was it from nerves? Probably a little of both.

One of the valets took her ticket and sprinted off to find the Porsche. Jeagan hugged herself while she waited. She wanted to get inside the car where she would be hidden if anyone who might recognize her came outside, either Patrice or Sue Coleman. A few long seconds went by before Jeagan heard the distinctive sound of the Porsche engine coming up the street. Behind her, the front door opened. She turned around slowly to see who was leaving. It was Sue Coleman with Chuck.

Hurry, please! Jeagan slowly walked away from the gate to her right where she hoped the valet would see her but no one else would. She reached into her bag and pulled out what she thought would be an appropriate tip. When she looked back, she saw Chuck go inside and close the door. Footsteps behind her told her Sue was walking toward the gate. Just then, the Porsche rounded the corner. The valet drove around the BMW parked in front of the house and stopped in front of Jeagan.

"My date will be out in a minute," she quietly told the valet when he accepted the tip and opened the passenger door for her. She huddled down in the seat as soon as she was inside the cold car. Now she was safe. She breathed a sigh of relief.

Click! Click! Jeagan jumped when she heard what sounded like fingernails tapping on the side window. She looked up and found herself staring into the face of Sue Coleman.

Chapter Nineteen

"Open the window!" Sue ordered. She looked toward the house and then back at Jeagan, who hesitated. "Hurry! We don't have much time!"

Jeagan turned the key in the ignition to be able to lower the window. Finding no words to say, she stared at Sue, noticing she was dressed elegantly in a simple black sheath with several long strands of pearls that glowed in the darkness.

Frowning, Sue said, "You shouldn't be here!"

Well aware of that fact, Jeagan could only say, "Why?"

"Because Patrice can be dangerous. She'll do anything to protect her husband's name and reputation."

"Really?" Jeagan, recovering from the shock of seeing Sue face to face, opened the car door. "Why would she feel she has to protect her husband's name when you told me he wasn't doing anything illegal?"

Sue pushed the door closed before Jeagan could get out. "No. Stay inside. You need to get away from here as quick as you can. You should never have come with Sam McFarland. He's one of 'them.' "

"Them? What do you mean 'them'? Who are 'them'?"

"The McFarland family. The only one of them who was trustworthy was John."

Jeagan smirked. "Do you call buying stolen babies 'trustworthy'?"

"You don't know—" Sue began.

"I now have proof." Jeagan pulled the papers out of her handbag and held them up triumphantly. Immediately, she regretted it.

Sue glanced back toward the house. Jeagan heard the front door open. Fear shone in Sue's eyes when she turned briefly back to Jeagan. "Stop what you're doing and go home. I'm warning you!" Sue hurried along the sidewalk to the valet and handed him her ticket.

Jeagan turned in her seat and watched Patrice and Sam walk out the front door, their heads together in conversation. After a couple of minutes, Patrice hugged Sam, and he strolled down the sidewalk seconds after Sue drove off. He whistled while he walked through the gate, hands jammed in his pockets, looked both ways, and spotted his Porsche. He loped toward the car and hopped in the driver's seat.

"Are you okay?" He started the engine. "You must be cold without a coat."

"I'm fine," Jeagan said tight-lipped.

"So, what did you find?" He looked behind him and pulled away from the curb.

"Nothing," Jeagan lied, no longer sure whom to trust.

"But, I thought you said you found business cards for several southern attorneys in the desk." Sam retraced his route to the hotel.

"I did, but we didn't find anything in the filing cabinet." She hated lying to him, but he had no way of finding out she was lying unless he checked her handbag. "I'm tired and my nerves are strung out. I need to get back to the hotel."

"Well," Sam said when he stopped at a traffic light. He reached over and patted Jeagan's hand, which she pulled away from his touch. He turned to look at her, but she kept her eyes straight ahead. "Did I do something to upset you?"

"No. I just want to go to the hotel. In fact, I'll probably go back to Denver tomorrow."

"You're kidding, right?" Sam sounded incredulous.

Jeagan looked over at him. She could tell that he was hurt and a little angry. "No, I'm not kidding. I've reached a dead end, so I need to go home. Roger can stay on if he wants to. I want to get back to my real job."

Sam hit the steering wheel. "Fine!" He turned onto Madison.

Tension, thick as the fog from the harbor, hung in the air between them during the ride to the Marriott. When Sam stopped at the hotel entrance, a doorman rushed to open the passenger door. Sam stared straight ahead, hands gripping the steering wheel.

Jeagan touched his arm. "Thank you for all you've done for me, Sam. I really do appreciate it."

"No problem," Sam mumbled.

Jeagan stepped out of the car. "Good-bye, Sam."

"See ya!" Sam gunned the engine as soon as the doorman closed the door. Jeagan watched him disappear from view after he screeched out onto Alaskan Way.

She walked slowly into the hotel. Had she done the right thing? Was Sue telling her the truth about Sam and the rest of the McFarlands? He had been nothing but kind and thoughtful to her for the last few days, and this was how she repaid him? Tears of frustration and confusion burned her eyes. Maybe she really should give Roger what she'd found in the filing cabinet and head for home tomorrow. Let Roger deal with the McFarlands.

"Hey, gorgeous!" Roger clumped toward her from the seating area when she entered the lobby. "What did you say to your date?"

"What're you talking about?" she said sniffily.

"Oh, it's like that, is it?" Roger teased. "Lover's spat."

"Grow up, Roger!" Jeagan stomped toward the elevator.

"Hey, I was only joking."

Jeagan pushed the up button and turned to face Roger. "I found the file cabinet."

His eyes lit up like it was Christmas morning. "You did!"

"You can have the documents I found. I'm leaving tomorrow."

"Seriously?" Roger eyed her suspiciously.

"Seriously. I've had enough. I've been warned off one time too many." She focused on Roger's cast. "I don't want to get hurt like you, or worse."

"What happened?"

The elevator doors opened. Roger followed Jeagan inside.

Facing forward, Jeagan said, "Sue Coleman was at the party. After it was over, she told me to go home, that I couldn't trust any of the McFarlands, including Sam."

"Oh, so that's what's bugging you. She knocked your knight in shining armor off his white horse."

Jeagan stepped off the elevator on the tenth floor. "Don't be ridiculous. I'm ready to give you what I found and go home."

"I thought I knew you better than that, Jeagan." Roger walked with her along the hall. He took the key card from her and opened the door. Then, he followed her inside.

"I would've thought you'd want to see this thing through to the end. 'Til we reunite mother and child," he said dramatically.

Jeagan dropped onto the couch. Again, tears burned her eyes. She did want to find Alan and personally escort him to Memphis to see his mother, but she was tired of being threatened and trusting people who turned out to be untrustworthy.

Roger sat in the armchair. "Okay, let's see what you found."

Jeagan reached over and opened her bag. She pulled out the folded papers and smoothed them flat on the coffee table. Upset, yet curious, she bent forward to see exactly what she had found. Curiosity soon took over, and she forgot about what Sue had told her.

"This is a carbon copy of a letter to Christopher Mark Greer, a Memphis attorney, from John McFarland dated April 10, 1945, regarding Baby Lloyd. Robert Lloyd is copied." She pointed to the 'cc' at the bottom of the first page.

Roger got up and moved over to sit beside her on the couch. She moved the papers over so he could read along with her. "It's faded, but you can still read it." They scanned the letter. "It says McFarland has found a couple who want to adopt the child whether it's a girl or boy."

Roger flipped to the next page and read. "This is a contract for the adoption. The price is ten thousand dollars." He looked at Jeagan, his eyes shining. "You did it!"

"I'll only have 'done it' if we can find the name of the people who adopted Alan." She ran her finger down the contract. Partway down the page she found it. "Here it is!" She grabbed Roger's arm. "The couple who adopted Alan: Brent and Nola Nelson! Look!" She said nothing for a few seconds, savoring the victory. "Where's the phone directory?"

"Try the nightstand," Roger offered while he finished reading the document.

Jeagan jumped up from the couch and ran to the nightstand where the phone was located. She jerked open the drawer and pulled out the directory. "Nelson," she repeated while she searched through the pages until she came to the name Nelson. She searched more pages until she came to the *B's* and ran her finger down the page. No Brent Nelson. She tried *N* for Nola. No Nola Nelson.

"Find anything?" Roger asked.

"Not yet." Jeagan flipped back to the *A's*. She knew it was a long shot, but maybe the Nelsons let Alan keep his birth name. No luck there. No Alan Nelson. Maybe they spelled it differently. Maybe Allen. No Allen Nelson either. She slapped the phone directory shut and dumped it in the drawer, which she bumped with her knee to close. "Nothing under Brent, Nola, or Alan." She walked across to the couch and plopped down beside Roger. "We were so close!"

Roger reached over and laid his hand on top of hers. "Don't give up yet. We still have the name of the Memphis attorney."

"That's right! We do!" Jeagan sat forward. "It's too late to call him tonight, but I'll call him tomorrow."

"You can go ahead and check with information to get his number tonight."

"Good idea." Back to the phone. Jeagan dialed Memphis information. After a brief chat with an operator, she was informed they showed no listing for Christopher Mark Greer, Attorney at Law. She disconnected. "I knew it was too good to be true," she said dejectedly. She kicked off her shoes and sat cross-legged on the bed. Her feet ached from wearing the new sandals. Idly, she rubbed the bottoms of her feet.

Roger watched her, a spark kindling in his eyes. "Want me to do that for you?"

She stopped what she was doing and slung a sandal at him.

"I think it's time for you to get some sleep, Ms. Grumpypants." He rose from the couch. "I'm beat too." He walked over to the door to his room. "Let's talk in the morning over breakfast. Don't make any decisions about going home tomorrow until after you've had some sleep."

"I guess you're right," Jeagan said. "I'm too tired to think anymore tonight anyway. Goodnight, and thanks, Roger."

"For what?" Roger asked, doorknob in hand.

"For putting up with me for one thing."

"All part of the job." He chuckled and entered his room, closing the door quickly behind him before she could make a comeback or throw something else at him.

Roger was a prince to put up with her, she realized, especially after she'd excluded him from much of the investigation. She hadn't thought of him much lately while forging ahead alone, well, not alone. Sam had been a tremendous help.

Sam. He'd helped her as much as he could, and she'd dumped him, all because Sue Coleman had said he couldn't be trusted. Why had she believed Sue? She wondered while she creamed makeup off her face. Sue hadn't lifted a finger to help two days earlier. Now Sue was warning her and telling her to go home. Another day, another warning.

Like Miss Scarlet, I'll won't worry about that 'til tomorrow, she thought. Anyway, everything that could be done today had been done. She checked the locks on both doors, slid into bed, turned off the lamp, and pulled up the covers.

* * *

Brrng! Jeagan rolled over and pulled the covers over her head. What was that awful noise? The timer on the microwave? Was her popcorn ready? She reached over to push the button to open the door. In the process, the receiver went flying off the phone.

"Jeagan? Hey, Jeagan?"

"Hmm?" Hearing her name, Jeagan opened her eyes. "What?"

"Jeagan!"

"What!" She looked around the almost dark room and realized where she was and that for some reason the phone receiver was lying in the floor. She reached over the side of the bed, nearly falling out, and grabbed the receiver. "Hullo," she mumbled.

"Jeagan, wake up!"

"Sam? Why're you calling me in the middle of the night?"

"It's not the middle of the night." His voice strained, he continued. "It's nine o'clock, and you need to wake up and listen. Sue Coleman is dead."

Chapter Twenty

Jeagan popped straight up in bed. "Sue's what?"

"She's dead, Jeagan." He was silent for a moment. "Look, I'm sorry about last night. I don't know what I did to make you mad. I've thought and thought about what I could have said or done to—"

"Sue told me not to trust you," Jeagan reluctantly admitted.

"You talked to Sue last night?"

"Yes. She came outside while I was waiting for you in your car and told me not to trust any of the McFarlands, including you. She said your grandfather was the only one she ever trusted."

"That's because she was in love with him," Sam said flatly.

"Sue was in love with your grandfather?"

"Yes. Always was," Sam hesitated. "But, I can't imagine why she told you not to trust me. I haven't deliberately hurt anyone, least of all you."

Jeagan could hear the pain in his voice. "Sam, I'm sorry for what I said last night." She threw off the covers and sat up on the side of the bed. "I let Sue find the right button to push my nerves over the edge. What happened to her?"

"A kid delivering newspapers noticed her car in a ravine not far from where she lived."

"That poor woman." Jeagan remembered how upset Sue had been the night before. "Sue was scared, but I was too afraid of being caught to pay a lot of attention to her. She acted the same way she did when I went to see her. What did she have to be scared about unless—"

"Unless," Sam finished the thought, "she was afraid that if you kept digging around and asking questions that you'd find out something about her that she didn't want found out."

"Do you think she was involved in the baby-buying business with your grandfather?"

"I don't know, but I think we need to talk about it." Sam hesitated. "Will you have breakfast with me?" he asked tentatively.

"Yes." Jeagan knew she didn't deserve it after the way she had treated him the night before, but he was back in her life. "And, Sam—"

"Great!" She could hear the relief in his voice. "I'll meet you downstairs in the lobby in an hour."

"Sam?"

"Do you need more time?"

"Sam? Listen to me." She paused, gathering her nerve. "I didn't tell you everything last night. I did find documents in the file cabinet, and I have them with me."

Sam was silent for a moment. "You lied to me." All the energy had drained out of his voice.

"I'm sorry, Sam. I really am. I was confused and scared after what Sue said to me."

"Well, we can talk about it over breakfast," he said with little enthusiasm. "See you in an hour." He hung up.

Jeagan replaced the receiver. "You've got a real knack for hurting people," she said out loud. "Why in the world did you believe what Sue said?"

"Jeagan?" She heard a knock and Roger's muffled voice on the other side of the connecting door.

"I'm awake!" Jeagan called out.

"I just got a call from Will Thompson. Open the door."

"Wait a minute." Jeagan pulled on the hotel's white terry robe and walked over to the door. She opened it and blinked at the sunshine pouring in from the open sliding glass door.

"So this is what you look like in the morning?" He grinned.

"Grrrr! It's early and I just got up." She noticed he'd already showered and dressed, and he smelled like Old Spice.

"Well, get some clothes on," he said, all business now. "Will called to tell me that the lady you talked to last night is dead."

"I know. Sam just called and told me."

"Sam?" Roger's face registered surprise. "But, I thought you said you dumped him last night?"

"I was rattled." Jeagan ran her hands through her hair. "I let Sue scare me."

Roger leaned on the door frame. "Yes. She did a good job of that, and then somebody killed her."

"Killed her? Sam told me her car was found in a ravine. I assumed it was an accident."

"Nope. Will said the back of her head was bloody. Someone knocked her out and pushed her car into the ravine to try to make it look like an accident."

Shock flashed across Jeagan's face. "Oh, my God! That poor woman!"

"Maybe somebody saw her talking to you and was afraid of what she told you, or might tell you."

"Maybe," Jeagan said. "Chuck came out with her and then Patrice could have seen Sue talking to me when she came outside with Sam before we left." She'd run the idea by Sam at breakfast. Then, she thought about Isabel. "I have to call and check on Isabel."

"Good idea," Roger said. "At least you'll have some positive news for her. After you talk to her, let's go have some breakfast." Roger pulled the door toward him.

"Sam's meeting us for breakfast," Jeagan called out.

"Why am I not surprised?" Roger mumbled. He firmly closed the door.

The brilliant sunshine poured into Jeagan's room when she opened the drapes. Another beautiful day in Seattle. She settled on the bed and dialed Isabel's number.

"How are you?" Jeagan asked when Isabel answered.

"I want to get out of this place." Isabel sounded tired and irritable. "I'm sick to death of hospitals."

Jeagan laughed. "No arguments from me there. But, I may have some good news for you."

"Did you find Alan?" Isabel asked, hope in her voice.

"No, but we did find the names of the people who adopted him."

"That's wonderful!" Isabel cried. "Have you contacted the people?"

"No, not yet. They aren't listed in the phone directory."

"Oh," Isabel's voice deflated.

"We aren't giving up, Isabel, so you shouldn't either." Jeagan hopped up from the bed. "We've come this far, and we won't stop until we find out what happened to Alan."

"Thank you, Jeagan. I know you and Roger will do your best."

"By the way," Jeagan said. "Do you happen to know a Memphis attorney by the name of Christopher Mark Greer?"

* * *

Jeagan knocked on Roger's door when she was ready to go to breakfast. Showered and dressed in khaki slacks and a khaki-and-black shirt, she felt better, and relieved she'd admitted the truth to Sam, and that he was still speaking to her.

"You look a lot better than you did an hour ago," Roger said, mischief in his eyes, when he opened the door. He stepped into the hall letting the door close behind him.

"Yeah, well, after the night I had, I deserve to look like death warmed over this morning."

Roger didn't want to touch that comment. He checked his watch. "Will's coming over for breakfast. He should be here by the time we get downstairs."

"Good." Jeagan walked along the hall beside Roger. "We can show him what Sophia and I found last night."

"He's not going to be happy that you stole the document."

"I didn't really have much choice, did I? Sam had his camera with him, and he wasn't with me when I found the files. I didn't have time to wait for him.

"Tell it to the judge."

"Not funny," Jeagan commented. The elevator doors opened and they stepped inside.

Suitcases and smiling travelers filled the lobby when they reached it. Jeagan looked out the front entrance. She watched as a tour bus pulled up and stopped at the hotel entrance. *Wonder where they're going?* Cruise ship tags hanging from many pieces of luggage scattered around the lobby answered her question. *Lucky them*, she thought.

"Don't see your boyfriend Sam anywhere," Roger commented while he scanned the lobby.

Jeagan chose to ignore Roger's sarcastic tone. "How's your leg this morning?"

"Not too bad. Not much pain. I just hate this cast. Can't wait to get it off."

A hostess greeted them when they entered the restaurant. "Table for two?" she asked.

"There'll be four of us," Roger said. "We're waiting for two others."

Jeagan scanned the restaurant. "They're already here, over by the windows."

"Good morning," Will said with a smile when they reached the table. He looked rested and crisp in a soft gray shirt, which complemented his thick gray hair. He and Sam stood momentarily when Jeagan and Roger reached the table.

"I was telling Will about what you found last night," Sam said. The sharp look he gave her matched the edge in his voice.

Duly chastised for lying to Sam, Jeagan sat in the chair Roger held for her next to Will. She pulled the papers out of her handbag and handed them over to Will. While he opened them, she said, "Yes, please," to the waitress who offered her coffee.

"I thought you were going to take a picture of anything you found in the house," Will commented while he read through the document.

"There really wasn't much time."

"Sam's already told me what happened. If we're lucky, no one recognized you except Sue Coleman, and no one knows you were in the basement."

"And, now Sue's dead," Jeagan said. "I can't believe someone killed her."

"Killed her?" Sam said. "I thought it was an accident. That's what they said on the news."

Will shook his head. "It wasn't an accident. Someone bashed her head in before her car went into the ravine."

"But, who and why?" Jeagan asked. She looked at Sam. "Sue was talking to me last night when you were on the front porch with Patrice. Do you think she saw us?"

Sam shrugged. "I doubt it. I didn't even see you until I got out to the sidewalk."

"We can't help Ms. Coleman now," Will said. "But, I'll let you know if I hear anything."

Jeagan settled in her chair and sipped her coffee. Strong, hot. What had Sue known that might have gotten her killed? "If Patrice finds out I took the document, what can she do? She can't call the police and have me arrested, can she? If she did, she'd be implicating her husband in buying stolen babies."

"There is that," Will agreed, nodding thoughtfully. "But would you really want her to know you found these documents in her house?"

"Will's got a point." Sam set his cup in the saucer and rested his forearms on the table. "Patrice would stop at nothing to protect her husband's and her own reputation, and her place in Seattle Society."

"Is there any legal action that can be taken against her for having the documents?" Jeagan accepted the menu offered by the waitress.

"Not unless she was involved in buying and selling babies." The waitress gave Will a startled look, but handed him a menu anyway. "My buddies at the FBI might be interested in checking out that basement." Will held up the stolen document. "I'd like to keep this."

"It's all yours," Jeagan said. "We've got what we need." She scanned the menu, deciding quickly on ham-and-cheese quiche with fresh fruit. "We checked the phone directory last night for the names of the people who adopted Alan, but we couldn't find a listing."

"I'll do some checking and see what I can find," Will offered.

Roger poured cream in his coffee. "Did you get through to Isabel?"

Jeagan felt the presence of the waitress standing beside her. "I did," she said. She placed her order and handed the menu to the woman.

"How was she doing?" Roger placed his order.

"She sounded depressed. Wants to get out of the hospital."

Roger nodded. "I understand exactly how she feels."

"So do I," Jeagan added. "The news about the letter and the people who adopted Alan seemed to cheer her up, though, even if we don't know where to find them."

Sam handed the menu to the waitress after he placed his order. "At least it gave her some real hope."

"Did you mention that Memphis attorney to her?" Roger took a long drink from his coffee cup and reached for the carafe. "Anyone else want a refill?"

Will held out his cup.

"I did mention Christopher Greer to her. Isabel said the name sounded familiar, but she can't be sure. She said she'll mention Greer to her attorney and see if he knows anything about him."

"Well, guess we're at a standstill for now," Roger commented.

"Excuse me. I'll be back in a minute." Will got up and started toward the lobby.

"Where's he going?" Sam asked.

"Probably to the restroom." Jeagan gazed out the windows at the Seattle morning with the clear blue sky, which looked like it had been freshly Windexed. "I hate that we're going to have to wait for more information when I feel like we're getting really close." She grimaced. "Every time we find one piece of the puzzle, we have to wait to find out what it means or where to go next."

Roger reached over and patted Jeagan's hand. "Welcome to the world of private investigation. It's more waiting than investigating, with a lot of frustration thrown in."

Jeagan looked at Sam. "What's that buzzing noise?"

"It's my cellphone." Sam reached into the pocket of his navy checked shirt. "Hello?" He listened briefly and frowned. "Hold on a minute," he said to the caller. He looked at Jeagan. "Excuse me. I need to take this." He left the table.

Seconds later, Roger's cellphone rang. He pulled it from his pocket to open it quickly and stop the ringing. Several people looked over in annoyance at all the ringing phones. Roger whispered, "Hello." He listened for a second and excused himself also.

" 'And then there were none,' " Jeagan quoted from Agatha Christie. Other people in the restaurant glanced at her. She shrugged as if to say, "Beats me what's going on."

A waiter approached the table with their breakfasts. He looked around puzzled to see the empty places.

Jeagan shrugged. "Must have been something I said."

The waiter smiled indulgently at her lame joke. "Shall I hold the orders until the others return to the table?"

She looked toward the entrance. Will was striding across the restaurant to the table. "Here comes one of them now. I'm sure they'll all be back in a minute, so you can go ahead and leave their plates."

Will sat down while the orders were being sorted around the table. "I think I've found our missing parents," he said casually.

Jeagan dropped her fork. It clattered against her plate and then flipped onto the floor.

"I can't take you anywhere," Roger commented, when he returned to the table and snagged the fork off the floor. He swiped a clean fork from the empty table next to them and handed it to Jeagan.

"Thanks," Jeagan ignored the remark. "Will's found Alan's parents!"

"He did?" Roger pulled out his chair and sat. "How?"

"How what?" Sam asked when he arrived back at the table.

"I said I *think* I've found the parents," Will corrected. He took a bite of his western omelette and chewed. "That's good," he commented. He looked around the table at three pairs of expectant eyes. "I've got a friend who's a realtor. I had him check for a residential listing for the Nelsons in the Seattle area. There's no listing in Seattle proper because they live on Bainbridge."

Excited, Jeagan looked over at Sam. "We were there two days ago!" She turned to Will. "Did you get their phone number?"

Will waved a slip of paper. "And address." He handed it to Jeagan.

She took it and reached for her handbag. Her cellphone was in it somewhere.

Will chuckled. "Why don't you eat your breakfast before it gets cold? You can wait ten more minutes to make your call."

Phone in hand, Jeagan got up from the table. She hung her bag over the back of the chair again. "I'll only be a minute." She hurried to the lobby, dialing the number on her way. After five rings, the answering machine came on with the soft voice of an older woman telling the caller to leave a number.

Jeagan returned to the table and dropped her phone into her handbag.

"Well?" Roger asked.

"Nobody home." She sat in her chair feeling disappointed. "I'll try again after breakfast."

"Want to take the ferry over there after we finish here?" Sam asked, looking at Jeagan.

She brightened at his suggestion. "That would be great!" She choked down her breakfast.

"I'm coming too," Roger informed both of them.

"No problem," Sam said, unable to hide his annoyance.

"Listen, pal." Roger leaned toward Sam. "This is my investigation, remember?"

Sam spread his hands in innocence. "Hey, I'm only a tour guide."

"Guys," Jeagan whispered. "Let's just do this and get along. We're getting close."

After breakfast, Will shook hands all around and left the three in the lobby to follow up on his lead. He was on his way, he informed them with a grin, to play a round of golf with some of his retired buddies, some of whom were former FBI. He held up the document Jeagan had given him. "Try to stay out of trouble," he offered in parting. "No more stealing."

"Trying to keep her out of trouble is a full-time job," Roger complained.

"Now, that is one thing we agree on," Sam chimed in and dodged a kick from Jeagan. "We better get a taxi to the ferry," he added while he watched Will cross the lobby. "My Porsche only holds two people."

"Not a problem. I have a nice expense account."

Jeagan frowned. "I need to get a sweater. Do you need a jacket, Roger?"

"No, but I'll go with you."

"I'll grab my jacket out of the car and wait for you outside," Sam said.

"Okay." Jeagan headed for the elevators. "Why don't you try to be civil to Sam?"

"What? I'm not being civil?" Roger asked in wide-eyed innocence. He followed Jeagan onto the elevator.

"Nevermind." She frowned. "Please try to be nice. He's been a big help."

"I'm sure." Roger said unenthusiastically. He stuffed his hands in his pockets.

"Who was that on the phone?" Jeagan asked, only half-interested.

"Shelley."

Jeagan threw her head back and laughed. "Shelley? That's rich. What did she want? To be your nurse?"

"Now who's being snippy?" Roger retorted.

"Oh, nevermind!" *Men!*

Roger clumped down the hall to their rooms with her. "Want me to come in with you to check your room?"

"I'll scream if I need you." She opened her door and closed it behind her.

* * *

The fresh, crisp morning air greeted them when they walked out the hotel entrance. A bellman signaled for a taxi and held the door for the three. Jeagan sat in the middle to keep the 'kids' from fighting.

"The call I got earlier was from Sophia," Sam said on the short ride.

"She didn't get in trouble for disappearing last night, did she?" Jeagan asked.

"No, but she did say she saw the man who was in the kitchen with Patrice the night after my grandfather's funeral."

"You mean when that loud scraping sound woke her up?" Jeagan asked.

"Uh-huh."

"People are popping out of the woodwork now, aren't they?" Roger interjected.

Jeagan gave him a cold look. "Do you think that's a problem for us?" she asked Sam.

"No. It shouldn't be." Sam leaned forward to tell the driver where to stop.

"What do you mean 'shouldn't be'?"

"Sophia said she saw him talking to Sue Coleman and Uncle Chuck, and they were all three staring at you."

Jeagan shivered.

Chapter Twenty-one

"I knew I shouldn't have let you go off to that party without me," Roger said.

"I can take care of myself," she assured him, but nevertheless felt tense.

"There shouldn't be anything to worry about unless he knew who you were and what you were doing there," Sam said.

"Do you think Sue or Chuck told him who I was?"

The taxi pulled up at the ferry terminal. Sam shrugged and reached for the door handle. "Don't know, but Sue could have, considering how much your visit upset her."

Roger opened his door, got out, and held the door for Jeagan. "I'm not letting you out of my sight until we return to Denver," he whispered to her. He pulled out his wallet to pay the driver and walked over to buy the tickets at a kiosk.

The wooden dock clattered under their feet when the three strode along it to the ferry for Bainbridge Island. Jeagan pulled her black pullover sweater on while they walked. The sun was bright and warm, but she knew the wind would be brisk out on the water, and she spotted gray clouds moving in from the west. When they were on board, she and Roger followed Sam to the front of the ferry.

They joined forty or so other passengers, mostly in jeans and windbreakers, standing along the railing to wait for the ferry to depart.

"We may be in for a rough ride," Sam shouted above the noise when the ferry bumped away from the dock. "Want to go inside?"

"In a minute," Jeagan called back, wanting to enjoy the view along the harbor and feel the cool spray on her face a little longer. What would they find on Bainbridge? If they were lucky enough to find Alan's parents, would they be willing to help them reunite their son with his birth mother?

The wind gusted as the Seattle skyline grew smaller. She glanced over at Roger standing beside her. His ears and cheeks were red, but she was sure he was too macho to admit he was cold.

"I'm going inside," she called out to him over the roar of the engines. He nodded agreement. When she turned to tell Sam, he was gone. She scanned the deck for him when she started toward the lounge, but he was nowhere in sight.

"Where's your sidekick?" Roger asked when they were inside out of the wind.

"Don't know. I'm going to get some hot chocolate. Do you want some?"

"Sure," Roger said. "Order one for me. I'll be there in a minute to pay for them."

"I'll get them."

"Whatever." Roger ambled over to the sweatshirt display. By the time the hot chocolates were ready, he returned with a windbreaker. Jeagan hid her smile. Not so macho after all, was he?

They settled in seats by the windows with their drinks. Jeagan wrapped her hands around her Styrofoam cup to warm her fingers while Roger pushed his arms into the sleeves of his jacket. The swaying of the ferry made her a little dizzy, so she tried staring outside at the spot of land across the Sound that was Bainbridge, growing larger by the minute.

"Is that your buddy back there?" Roger asked.

Jeagan followed his eyes and saw Sam standing in front of the windows at the other end of the lounge. Again, he was in deep conversation on his cellphone.

"Probably talking to a producer about his script for a new TV show."

"TV?" Roger's eyebrows rose in surprise.

"I thought you knew he's a screenwriter." Jeagan sipped her chocolate.

"Nope. I thought he was independently wealthy with all his free time to wine and dine you and drive you around in his Porsche."

Jeagan could see that Roger was baiting her again. "Could it be you're a little bit jealous?"

"Ha! Hardly."

"Look, Roger, we're here to do a job. After it's done, we'll both return to Denver and pick up our lives where we left off. Sam will go back to his writing. But, give the guy credit. He's got free time right now, and he could be spending it on vacation somewhere, but instead he's offered his time and help to us."

"Help you, you mean," Roger added.

Jeagan cut her eyes at him.

"Okay. Okay." Roger held out his hands. "I'll keep my mouth shut about him. I don't trust him though, and I'll be watching him. Fair enough?"

"Fair enough." Jeagan leaned back in her seat.

A few minutes passed, then Sam appeared beside her with a steaming cup of coffee in his hands.

"Sorry about that."

"Not a problem," she said.

He sat in the chair next to her. "We should be there in about fifteen minutes."

Jeagan finished her hot chocolate and got up to toss her cup. "Guess we'll need to get a taxi when we get there."

"Yeah." Sam smiled at her. "No scooter today." He gazed out the window. "Those are storm clouds out there. Wouldn't be a good day for a scooter ride anyway."

* * *

The three bent into the wind when they walked across the ramp at the Bainbridge dock. "Wait here. I'll find a taxi." Sam left Jeagan and Roger at the terminal entrance.

Roger's mouth twisted into a "who died and left him in charge" kind of look.

Before long, the three were on their way up Highway 305 to the address on Northeast Manitou Beach Road. Again sitting between the two men, Jeagan prayed one of the Nelsons would be home.

"Storm coming in," the taxi driver commented. "Very soon now."

All three were silent, deep in their own thoughts. Jeagan watched the lush green landscape out the front window, amazed at the brilliant shade of spring green in the trees that lined the highway. Soon, the driver turned off the highway onto Madison and then onto Manitou. The road took them past large homes on spacious lots that bordered the Sound. A short time later, the driver slowed. He turned up a driveway that ended at a redwood and glass home, very similar, Jeagan thought, to the home they used in the *Stake Out* movie. Could this be the same one?

Sam opened his door and got out. He held out his hand to help Jeagan.

"Can you wait for us?" she asked the driver. "We won't be long."

"Sure. No problem." The driver reached for a book on the seat next to him. She saw that it was a novel by J.D. Hylton, one of her favorite authors.

They climbed three levels of flagstone steps to the front porch, which was also flagstone. The men stood back and let Jeagan ring the bell. She pressed the button with a trembling hand.

Immediately, they heard a dog barking and soon a chocolate lab stared out one of the side lights at them. "Hush, Suraya!" she heard the muffled voice of a woman call out. Then, the door opened.

"May I help you?" a pudgy, young woman with long brown braids asked. Dressed in jeans and a white sweatshirt with a University of Washington logo, she wore yellow rubber gloves and carried a bucket in her hands. Strands of hair, which had pulled free from her braids, hung in her eyes.

"We're looking for the Nelsons. Is either of them at home?" Jeagan asked.

"No. They're not here. They're visiting their daughter over in Seattle," the girl said. "Can I give them a message?"

Sam spoke up. "We're really trying to find their son."

"You mean Alex?" the girl asked.

Jeagan's heart lurched. "How old is Alex?"

Unfazed by the strange question, the girl thought for a moment. "Probably in his late forties or early fifties, I'd say."

Heart racing, Jeagan said "I know this is a strange question, but do you know if he's—"

Roger stepped in front of her. "Can you ask the Nelsons to give us a call when they return?"

The girl looked from Jeagan to Roger. "Is there a problem? Is Alex in some kind of trouble? I already talked to one man today who was looking for him."

Jeagan choked.

"Oh, that must have been our associate," Roger said hurriedly. "We didn't know he'd already been here."

"What did he look like?" Sam asked.

"He was about your height," she said, looking at Sam. "Big shoulders. His face was kind of splotchy, and his hair was sort of orange."

The man who was talking to Sophia in the sunroom last night! Jeagan realized.

"Did he give you his name?" Roger asked.

"Yes," the girl said and pulled a white business card out of her pocket. "Wayne Drake. Said he worked for Reilly Security?"

"Can I see the card?" Roger asked.

The girl handed it over, somewhat confused.

"Oh, this is one of our old business cards." Roger stuffed it in his pocket and pulled out his billfold.

The girl's started to object. "But—"

"Here's a newer card." Roger showed the girl one of his business cards. "It has the new name for our company." He held his thumb over the address in Denver.

"Did our friend say where he was going from here?" Sam asked.

"No, but when I told him Alex lived in Victoria, he thanked me and left."

"Well, thank you for your time," Roger said. "If you'll ask the Nelsons to give me a call at the number on that card."

"Okay." The girl read the card. "But, the card says Denver, Colorado," she said confused.

"That's our home office. The number on the card is my cellphone."

"Oh." The answer seemed to satisfy her. "Okay."

"Thank you," Jeagan said.

They retraced their steps to the taxi.

"He's the man who was in the sunroom with Sophia last night, isn't he?" Jeagan asked Sam.

"I think we can assume he was, and if so," Sam said, frowning, "his name isn't Wayne Drake. It's Anthony Eden. He's the guy Sophia said was staring at you when he was with Sue."

A chill ran up Jeagan's spine. "So Sue had to have told him who I was and what I was doing in Seattle."

"Most likely," Sam agreed, "and it can't be good if he's trying to find Alan, I mean Alex."

"You're right," Roger agreed. "We've got to get in touch with Alex and warn him." He pulled out his cellphone and punched in a number.

"Who're you calling?" Jeagan asked.

"Information." Roger held up his hand for quiet. "Yes," he said into the phone, "for an Alex Nelson in Victoria." He listened for a minute. "Can you repeat that?" He listened for a second. "Thank you." He disconnected.

"Write this down," he said to Jeagan. He repeated the number while she searched her purse for a pen and her notepad, her hands shaking. She jotted down the number and tore off the page.

When she handed it to Roger, he punched the number into his phone. He listened for a second. "It's an answering machine." He started to disconnect, but instead put the phone back to his ear.

Jeagan's chest tightened.

Roger returned the slip of paper to Jeagan. "He's giving his cellphone number." He repeated it to Jeagan, who wrote it under the other number.

Her heart in her throat, Jeagan watched Roger punch in the new number.

"Got him," he said a second later. "Alex Nelson?" Roger asked. He listened for a second and gave a 'thumbs up' sign to Jeagan, who clamped her hands over her mouth to keep from screaming in delight.

"Alex, you don't know me, but I'm a private investigator," Roger said, his face shining.

Jeagan moved over to put her ear next to the phone, trying hard to listen.

"Sorry, I can't hear you over the roar of the engine," Alex said. "Who did you say you were?"

Roger talked louder. "My name is Roger Sanderlin. I'm a private investigator. Listen, I need to talk to you right away."

"I can't talk now. We're about to take off."

"Take off for where?" Roger asked.

"I'm in Seattle and we're flying to Victoria. Can you call me in about an hour and a half?"

"Okay. I'll call you then." Roger disconnected.

"What did he say?" Sam asked.

Roger looked at Sam. "He said he's on a flight that's about to take off for Victoria out of Seattle. Sounded like cockpit noise. Must be a pilot. He told me to call him in an hour and a half." Pausing briefly, he added. "We probably need to get over to Victoria in case Eden's on his way there ahead of us."

"Good idea!" Sam leaned forward. "Have you got a ferry schedule?" he asked the driver.

"No," the driver said over his shoulder. He pointed to the clock on the dash. "The Wenatchee ferry leaves at 2:05. We'll make it in plenty of time."

"Nothing we can do now but wait." Then, Jeagan's eyes brightened. "But, you could call Alex and leave a message on his voice mail considering he's probably shut off his cell by now."

"Good idea!" Roger pulled out his cellphone again and entered Alex's number. Sure enough, the phone went to straight to voice mail.

Roger listened to the recorded message. "Alex, this is Roger Sanderlin again. I need to talk to you as soon as possible.

"I'm calling from Bainbridge. My friends and I came over here trying to find your parents, and you. We found out that someone else was here looking for you before us. His name is Anthony Eden. He could be dangerous, so please be careful.

"We're taking the two o'clock ferry to Seattle. We'll get the first plane we can over to Victoria to talk to you in person. I'll call you as soon as our plane arrives.

"I realize you probably think I'm some kind of a nut, so here's the number of the Seattle Police Department. Ask for Captain Will Thompson. He's retired, but I'll call to make sure you'll be put in touch with him when you call."

Jeagan settled back against the seat. "Thank you. I feel better now. We're doing all we can to protect him."

"Maybe not all." Sam leaned forward to talk to Roger. "Think your buddy Will has connections in Victoria? Someone who could meet Alex's plane and keep an eye on him until we get there?"

"That might be overkill," Roger said, "but what the heck. We've come this far, and I'd hate to see Eden get to Alex before we do."

"Maybe have him check out Anthony Eden also," Jeagan added.

Roger nodded and dialed again.

Jeagan smiled inwardly. It sure was great to see the guys working together.

Roger briefly talked to Will.

Jeagan heard most of the conversation, but not all of it. "What did he say?" she asked after Roger disconnected.

"Everything's cool except he doesn't have any real connections in Victoria, but he said he'd make some calls."

* * *

The return ferry ride was rougher than it had been earlier. A gray mass of roiling clouds blanketed the sky. Then, huge raindrops spattered against the windows.

"Here it comes," Sam commented.

Within minutes, sheets of rain slashed against the windows and deck.

Jeagan sat on one of the chairs not near a window. She tried taking deep breaths while she searched her handbag for a roll of Tums.

"Want me to get you a Gingerale?" Roger asked. "Might help to settle your stomach."

"That would be great," Jeagan said. "The ride is short," she kept repeating to herself like a mantra. She found the Tums and popped a couple into her mouth and chewed. *What I need is Dramamine*, she realized.

Roger returned shortly with her drink. "Where's Sam?"

"Thanks." Jeagan took the offered can. "He's probably talking on his cellphone again." Maybe he had a girlfriend somewhere that he kept calling? But, if he did, why wouldn't he be spending his time with her instead of Jeagan? "He spends more time on the phone than any other two people I know."

"Isn't that kind of strange?" Roger asked.

"Don't know. He says he's talking to people connected with the new pilot project. Probably is, but I don't guess it really matters who he's talking to."

"Probably not, but it *is* interesting," Roger said thoughtfully.

Sure enough, Sam, at that moment, rounded a corner from the rear of the lounge, phone glued to his ear. This time he was smiling instead of in a heated argument.

What's he smiling about? Jeagan wondered.

Sam scanned the lounge. Jeagan lifted her hand to signal him. He made his way across the swaying ferry to them. "We've got reservations on a four-thirty flight out of Sea-Tac over to Victoria. And, to please you," he grinned at Jeagan, "I've made reservations at the Victoria Regent Hotel. It's a beautiful old hotel that's right on the harbor."

"That's fine. Thanks, Sam." Jeagan sipped her Gingerale and put her hand on her stomach to keep it from rumbling. "I've never been to Victoria, but I've heard it's beautiful and filled with flowers."

Sam sat beside her. "You are an amazing shade of—"

"Don't say it or you'll be sorry!" She jumped up and ran to the restroom.

A while later, when she returned to the lounge, she felt somewhat better. She held onto the chairs while she made her way across the swaying floor. The noise of the engines and the slashing of the rain across the decks were almost deafening.

"Well, you're a little less green," Sam said loudly when she returned.

She held a wet paper towel against her throat and sat down. "How much longer?" she shouted

"Not long," Sam reassured her.

Roger picked up her drink and handed it to her. "Sip some of this."

"We're almost there," Sam commented. He patted Jeagan's hand. "Try to hold on a little longer."

With a nod of her head, she said, "I'm trying."

* * *

The cold, wet air on her face revived her after she got off the ferry. She inhaled deeply and followed Sam out of the terminal. Roger walked beside her and opened the door for her while Sam went out to the edge of the sidewalk to hail a taxi. Within minutes, the taxi stopped in front of the Marriot.

"Grab whatever you need as fast as you can," Sam said when they walked into the lobby. "I'll wait for you here. I don't have time to go home. I'll just pick up whatever I need for the night when we get to Victoria."

"Okay." Jeagan walked with Roger across the lobby. When they were near the elevator, she heard someone call her name. She turned around to see Ron Ferrari, head of Hotel Security, walking toward them.

"Can I talk to you for a minute?" Ron had an anxious expression on his face.

"Is something wrong?" Roger asked before Jeagan could.

Ron glanced around to make sure no one was close enough to hear him. He looked directly at Jeagan. "I wanted to tell you someone was here asking about you today. He looked familiar so he may have been in the hotel before."

"Did he say what he wanted?" Jeagan asked.

"He said he was a friend of yours who used to live in Denver."

"Did he give his name?"

Ron shook his head. "No. I tried to get a name, but when I told him you weren't registered here, I couldn't really press him for his name."

"What did he look like?" Roger asked. "Tall, broad shoulders, reddish hair, middle-aged?"

A surprised expression on his face, Ron said, "Yes. How'd you know?"

Jeagan's breath caught in her throat.

Chapter Twenty-two

Roger motioned Ron away from the group, which was gathering around the elevators. "Please keep a lookout for that man. His name is Anthony Eden, and he may come here again. Maybe next time he'll wait in the lobby hoping to spot Jeagan. We're leaving in a few minutes to go over to Victoria for a day or so, but call me at this number if you see him hanging around." Roger fished a business card out of his wallet and handed it to Rob. "If he gives you any trouble, call the police."

"No problem there," Ron said. "Now that I know you don't want to see him, I'll deal with him if he shows up again."

Roger placed a hand on Rob's shoulder. "Thanks."

"I'm sorry for the trouble I've caused while I've been here, but I really appreciate the way you guys have tried to protect me," Jeagan said. "We'll be leaving to return to Denver soon and be out of your hair."

"Stay as long as you want. I'm here to make sure you're protected as long as you're in my hotel."

"Thanks." Jeagan said. The man nodded and walked away.

"Eden again!" Roger said when they were alone in the elevator.

"He knows I found the document, doesn't he?"

Roger nodded. "Sounds like it if he's been here to find you also. I only hope we can get to Alex before he does."

"Who's he trying to protect? If Patrice isn't involved in any of the adoptions, why is Eden—"

"If he's connected to Patrice or Chuck, the McFarland name is probably what he's trying to protect. But, if he's connected to Isabel's family, he might want to make sure there's no heir to her estate."

"How could he be connected to Isabel's family?"

"I don't know." Roger rubbed his eyes. "He probably isn't. I'm just trying to think of all possibilities." Roger thought for a moment. "Is your name off Isabel's will yet?"

"I'm not sure. I told Isabel to have it taken off, but being in the hospital, I'm not sure if she remembered to have her attorney take care of it."

Roger saw the fear in Jeagan's eyes. He drew her in for a hug. "I should've made you stay in Denver with your father until this investigation was over. You're not used to this kind of life."

Jeagan pulled away and stood up to her full five-foot-seven. "Yes, I *am* scared, but I'm here, and I'm in this investigation and don't plan on going home until we find Alan for his mother."

"Fine." Roger dropped his hands. "Don't get all huffy on me. We're getting close, and we'll see this through together. Then, maybe you'll be a little easier to get along with when we get back to Denver."

Jeagan relaxed and allowed a slight smile. "We'll see."

Before ten minutes passed, they were back in the lobby, Roger with a bag slung over his shoulder and Jeagan pulling her rollboard behind her.

"We're only going over for one night," Sam teased.

"Don't give me any grief," Jeagan scowled. "I only put in what I needed."

"Whatever. Women!" Sam muttered under his breath.

"I second that," Roger added with a grin while they walked out the entrance.

Jeagan brought up the rear. She scanned the lobby, hoping she wouldn't see anyone who might be Anthony Eden. Not realizing she was holding her breath, she let it out when she didn't see him. But, she stopped short when she saw a woman with curly red hair, who looked like the woman she had seen several times before in the last few days. The woman stepped onto the elevator.

Jeagan ran to catch up with the guys. "Hey, I saw—"

"Taxi?" the doorman asked when they were outside on the sidewalk.

"Yes. To Sea-Tac," Sam said.

"You saw what?" Roger asked.

"Nevermind." Jeagan realized she couldn't do anything about the woman now. And, chances were the woman wasn't the same person who had been following her. *I'm getting suspicious of everybody.*

The rain stopped, and the gray clouds began to shred with the sun shining through on the twenty minute drive to Sea-Tac Airport. Jeagan listened to Sam describe Victoria, British Columbia, with its

European and Victorian architecture, the grand Empress Hotel, which was sinking inch by inch every year, the fabulous Butchart Gardens that Jeagan really wanted to see, and his favorite place for breakfast, The Blue Fox.

Sam's running tour guide dialogue painted a lovely picture in her mind and helped Jeagan to forget for a few minutes what might confront them in Victoria. Surely Anthony Eden wouldn't try to physically hurt Alex or her, would he? Then images flashed through her mind of how Isabel's sister and butler had bound her, knocked her out, and tried to drown her and Isabel. And, could Eden have been involved in Sue's death?

They arrived at Sea-Tac with time to spare before they were to board their Alaska Airlines flight. Jeagan admired the Indian art on the walls in the sunny terminal, now that the rain clouds were moving off to the east. Once they boarded the plane, she settled in her seat for the short flight over the San Juan Islands between Seattle and Victoria. Soon they were in the air and floating over the tiny islands, which appeared lush even from the air. Sailing on one of the clipper ships—which she spotted from the air—through the islands might be fun to try the next time she was in Seattle. Some day, she promised herself, she would do that.

Before she knew it, she nodded off and was awakened by the flight attendant when the plane landed on the runway.

"Nice nap?" Roger asked from across the aisle after she opened her eyes and stretched.

Jeagan yawned. "As a matter of fact, it was. The flight was a lot smoother than the ferry crossing from Bainbridge."

She watched the landscape, spring green and similar to Seattle's, from her window while the plane taxied to the Victoria Airport terminal. It took them only minutes to file off the commuter plane and retrieve her bag sitting on the tarmac at the bottom of the stairs.

While they walked through the terminal to the front entrance to find a taxi, Roger's phone beeped. He pulled it out of his pocket and dialed into his voice mail. "That was Alex," he said to Sam and Jeagan, who were watching him expectantly. "He said he's at Hyack Air."

"That's the seaplane terminal," Sam explained.

Roger nodded. "He said he'll stay there until he hears from me."

Sam flagged down a taxi and they piled in.

"Where do you want to meet him?" Sam asked.

"How about we meet him in a public place for dinner after we check in at the hotel?"

Sam agreed. He turned to Jeagan. "Do you want Italian, Oriental, Greek?"

"I don't care," Jeagan said. "You choose."

Now that they were so close to finding Alan, she should be excited, but she was nervous and worried about how Alan, or rather Alex, would feel finding out about his birth mother. Did he know that he was adopted? She hoped he did. Would he want to see his birth mother? What if he didn't? Maybe they should have contacted his parents before contacting him directly? No, she realized, there really wasn't any time to lose, not when Anthony Eden could be on his way to Victoria to find Alex before they did.

"Okay," Sam said to Roger. "Tell him to meet us at Café Brio, say in an hour?"

Roger dialed and listened. "There's no answer."

Sam frowned. "That's not good!"

"No," Roger agreed. "Maybe I should dial the terminal and have him paged. It can't be that big."

"Good idea." Sam looked at Jeagan. "Jump in here any time if you have an idea."

"What?" Jeagan said, still lost in thought.

"Snap out of it!" Roger said.

Jeagan shook her head to clear it. "You guys are doing fine without my input right now. I have no complaints."

"That's got to be a first," Roger commented.

"Yeah," Sam agreed with a smile.

"You guys are real comedians."

"That's more like our Jeagan." Roger rang information and got the phone number for the Hyack Terminal. He punched in the number and asked that Alex Nelson be paged. All three held their breath while they waited. Soon, Roger gave a victory sign.

"Alex," he said into the phone. "Man, am I glad to hear your voice. Is everything okay there?" He listened briefly. "Hmm. How about we come by there and get you?" He listened again and finally said, "Okay, if you're sure. Meet us at Café Brio in an hour. And, yes, we'll give you all the details when we see you."

Roger answered the question in both pairs of eyes that stared at him. "Eden was at the Hyack Terminal a few hours ago asking questions about Alex. No one gave him any information, and he apparently left, but he's probably somewhere waiting to confront Alex."

"Wouldn't Alan…I mean Alex…be safer if we picked him up from there?" Jeagan asked.

"Probably, but he insisted that he would meet us at the restaurant."

"Did he tell you what he looks like?"

"Yeah. He said he's close to six feet tall, average build. He's got gray eyes and short black hair, with some gray. He'll be wearing dark brown slacks, a white shirt, and a brown bomber jacket."

"That helps," Sam commented.

The taxi soon passed along the busy harbor area where Jeagan watched a seaplane skim across the water and lift into the air. She marveled at the European feel of the city with flowers everywhere, the Legislative Buildings that looked more like they belonged in Italy or France, and the huge, stone Fairmont Empress Hotel, partially covered in ivy.

When the taxi pulled up in front of the Victoria Regent, she looked up to see a beautiful brick-and-stone, mid-rise hotel, with stone planters bursting with spring flowers and lining the walkway to the hotel. The three passed through the airy lobby to the reception desk where they checked in and took the elevator to the fifth floor. Again, when Jeagan entered her lovely room with a Victorian decor, she felt a wave of loneliness for someone special in her life to share it with.

She deposited her suitcase on a stand and pulled out her navy wool pants suit and a white sweater for the cool evening ahead. She was fast running out of clean clothes.

In short order, she was in the hall knocking on Roger's door. They went together and met Sam, who was waiting for them in the lobby.

"Ready?" he asked needlessly.

"Ready as I'll ever be," Jeagan responded. "I'm a nervous wreck though. I hope Alex is okay and makes it to the restaurant without any problems."

"I haven't heard from him so I'm assuming everything's okay," Roger followed Jeagan and Sam out the front entrance. "Will called a few minutes ago to see if we'd talked to Alex. He said he has friends over here but didn't know anyone who could meet Alex's plane."

"He should be fine," Sam commented, "especially now that he knows Eden's looking for him. You guys want to get a taxi or walk? The restaurant is only a few blocks away."

"Let's walk," Jeagan said. She looked at Roger. "If you're okay to walk a few blocks with that cast."

"I'm fine," Roger said. "Anyway, I know you're both probably tired of sitting."

"Walk it is." Sam took Jeagan's arm. Roger grabbed the other arm. She laughed when they lifted her off the sidewalk. Laughing felt good. It eased the tightness in her chest. And, she felt protected between the two men.

"I tried to call Isabel earlier to tell her we'd found Alan, but she was asleep, according to Mark Edwards," Jeagan said when they set her on her feet.

"What did he say?" Sam asked.

"He said he knew she'd be pleased and would have her call me."

"Have you talked to your dad?" Roger asked.

"I did, right after I called Isabel. He told me to tell you two to.... . Well, I won't tell you what he said. He still treats me like I'm four years old."

"And well he should," Roger teased. "Since that's how you act about half the time."

"That's right," Sam agreed nodding.

"Oh, yeah!" She shook both their hands off her arms. "And I guess neither one of you acts like....like a cross between an overprotective big brother and a jealous boyfriend when I'm around."

"Never," Roger said innocently.

"Me neither," Sam agreed.

All three were laughing when they entered the restaurant. When they didn't see Alex waiting for them in the crowded front area, Roger went to check in with the hostess while Sam looked in the bar. Jeagan scanned the restaurant to see if Alex was already there and seated. The warm terra-cotta tones and soft lighting gave the restaurant a Tuscan feel, but didn't help Jeagan search for Alex.

"Are you Jeagan Christensen?" a male voice asked behind her. So, he was here. Her heart beat faster as she turned around. The search for Alan was over. Startled, she came face to face with a tall, broad, ruddy-faced man wearing a baseball cap. A cry escaped her as she scanned the crowd frantically for Roger or Sam.

"If you'll come this way," the man said softly. He grabbed her arm. "We don't want to alarm anyone, and I don't want to have to use the gun that's in my pocket."

"Sam! Roger!" Jeagan yelled at the top of her lungs and tried to jerk her arm away from the man.

Roger turned and ran/clumped toward her, pushing his way through the crowded lobby. Sam charged in from the bar.

Before either man could reach her, Jeagan felt herself being pulled out of the restaurant and shoved into the back seat of a car that sped off, tires squealing.

Chapter Twenty-three

Jeagan pulled herself upright and looked helplessly out the rear window. *Please, God, help me!* She saw Sam racing after the car. Terrified, she realized he had no chance of catching it. Roger had his cellphone out yelling into it.

"Meet your new best friend." Tony Eden indicated the man on the other side of Jeagan. She turned her head.

"Alan!" She recognized him at once. His head lay back against the seat and a nasty gash on his forehead oozed blood.

Before she could say or do anything else, her world went black.

* * *

Jeagan felt chilled to the bone. Her head ached. Her whole body ached. Slowly, she opened her eyes. Was it the middle of the night? She rolled over and tried to reach for the clock on the nightstand, but she couldn't move her arms. They were tied behind her. Panic seized her. *Please God! No! Not again!* She tried to scream, but only a moan came out.

"Are you all right?" a male voice said close to her.

Her whole body jerked in terror. She strained to see who was talking to her, but she couldn't make anything out in the darkness.

"Who's there?" she demanded, her heart pounding in her ears.

"Alex," the man said calmly from somewhere nearby.

Reality crashed over her. "Oh, Alex, I'm so sorry." Tears of fear and pain choked her.

"Just calm down. We've got to keep a clear head and think, if we're going to get out of here before they come back."

Jeagan gulped and tried to swallow her fear and stop the tears. "I'm sorry. I know you're right. Do you have any idea where we are?"

"I'm working on that."

She jumped at a scraping sound against the hard, cold floor. "What's that?"

"It's me." Alex let out a strained breath. "I'm rolling over to move closer to you. Roll over with your back toward me. I need you to get something out of my belt. "

"Your belt?"

"Yeah. I keep a couple of small tools in a pocket in my belt."

"You must be a boy scout," Jeagan said in an effort to keep her fear at bay. She rolled over on her side.

"Eagle Scout," Alex huffed as he moved closer.

"I'm impressed." Jeagan tried to sound brave. She could feel Alex next to her.

"Can you reach my belt?"

Jeagan moved her hands down Alex's stomach to his belt. "Got it. Where's the pocket?"

"It's on the left side. I'll roll over."

Jeagan felt along the belt with cold, stiff fingers that were close to losing all feeling. "I've got it."

"Pull the flap open," Alex said. "There's a small screwdriver inside. See if you can reach it."

After several tries, Jeagan opened the small snap of the pocket and felt the cold metal of the tiny screwdriver. She clasped it between two fingers and wedged it out. "Okay, now what."

"Hold onto it, and I'll roll over and take it from you and get you loose."

"Okay." Jeagan held onto the screwdriver while Alex shifted and rolled over. He took the screwdriver from her and began to work on the duct tape that bound her hands. After being bound with it twice in less than two weeks, she'd never buy another roll of duct tape, she vowed, if she ever got out of this place alive. "Ow!" she cried when the screwdriver dug into her wrist.

"Sorry," Alex said, grunting. "I'm trying to be careful."

"I know. It's okay. Keep trying."

"What's that?" Jeagan jumped. She heard a car driving slowly over what sounded like gravel. Fear, like ice water, crept through her veins. *Please God! Help us!*

Alex stopped. They both listened. After what seemed like hours, he said, "They're not stopping."

Within minutes, Jeagan felt the duct tape break. "Thank you," she whispered hoarsely. Relief flooded through her. She choked back the tears. She had to get Alex free, and they had to get out of there. She fumbled with the tape while her hands burned from the returning circulation. When her hands were free, she pulled them in front of her and rubbed them until the stinging stopped. Then, she began working on the tape that bound Alex. Soon both their hands and feet were free.

"Now, we need to find a way out of here."

"Do you have any idea what this place is?" Jeagan rubbed her ankles while the circulation returned.

"Not exactly. I think we're in a warehouse considering the floor is concrete."

She heard Alex standing. "Stay there until I've moved around to see what's here."

"Okay." Jeagan strained to hear Alex's movements. Metal scraped against the concrete.

"There's a table and some chairs here." He moved again, making a shuffling sound against the floor. "I've found some stairs." Jeagan heard footsteps ringing on metal stairs. "There's a door up here…and a window. Must be an office." Alex's voice echoed against the walls of the large warehouse.

"Can you get inside?" Jeagan called out, allowing herself a spark of hope.

"Door's locked," he called back, while he jiggled the handle. "I'm going to break the window." Then, the sound of shattering glass filled the air.

"Are you okay?" Jeagan said in the darkness. "You didn't cut yourself, did you?"

"No." Alex grunted as he kicked more glass out of the window. "I'm going in to see what's inside."

Jeagan heard more scraping and shuffling sounds and the creak of the office door as it opened. Within seconds, blissful light came from the window and door. She got up from the floor and followed Alex. When she reached the office, she saw that he had raised a shade, which let light in through a dirty window.

"There's a phone!" She reached over to grab it. Putting the receiver close to her ear, she prayed she would hear a dial tone. "It's dead."

"You didn't really expect it to be working, did you?"

"No," she admitted and looked over at Alex. This was the first time she'd really seen him. The gash on his head now had dirt mixed with dried blood. Dirt smudges covered both his face and clothes. His brow was knitted in concentration, but she could tell in the dusty light that he was a handsome man, starting to gray at the temples. "I'm glad to finally meet you, Alex, but I'm really sorry I've gotten you into this mess."

Alex's brow relaxed to show intelligent gray eyes, the same color as his mother's. "Jeagan, right?" She nodded. "We'll talk after we get out of here."

The window was stuck when Alex tried to open it. He searched through the desk for a letter opener, which he used to pry the window loose. When it was finally raised, he looked down. "There's quite a drop, but we don't really have a choice."

A glance out the window confirmed what Alex had said. All Jeagan could think of was to drop and roll.

"Are you up to it?" Alex asked.

"I'll jump if I have to." What was the worst that could happen? A broken leg, especially since she was wearing pumps? Better than being dead.

"I'll go first and see if I can find anything to use for a ladder." Alex unlocked and raised the window. He sat on the ledge, threw his legs over, and lowered himself out the window, holding onto the ledge. Then, he silently dropped to the ground.

Jeagan leaned out the window. "Are you all right?"

Alex picked himself up from the ground and dusted off his pants. "Yeah, I'm okay." He limped away to his left. "Be back in a minute." He disappeared around the side of the building.

The seconds and minutes passed. Where was he? "Alex!" she called. No answer. What had happened to him? She had to find out. She sat on the window sill ready to throw her legs over when she heard metal scraping again. Then, from inside the warehouse she heard a voice.

"Down here!" Alex called.

Jeagan hopped up and ran out of the office and down the stairs. "Thank you!" she said with tears smarting in her eyes when she was outside. "I wasn't too thrilled about jumping out of that window."

"Don't thank me yet. We're still out in the middle of nowhere." He glanced at the sky. "It'll be dark soon."

"But at least you got us out of that warehouse. Are you hurt from the fall?"

"No. I'm okay." He rubbed his knee absently.

"How did you get the door open?"

"Fortunate for us, the padlock on the door was rusty, and I was able to break it with that rock." Jeagan looked over at the huge chunk of granite beside the door. She didn't think she would be able to lift it much less break a padlock with it.

"Up for some walking?" he asked.

"The sooner the better."

"Let's go west." He looked toward Jeagan. "How's your head?"

She touched her forehead and felt matted hair. She winced when her fingers hit a tender spot on her temple. "Probably not as bad as yours. You've got quite a gash there."

"I've had worse." Alex scanned the grassy field around them. "Not sure where we are, but we should run into civilization before too long."

Jeagan walked beside him trying to keep up, wishing she had on sneakers instead of heels. "Alex, I'm really sorry that we pulled you right into the middle of this."

He stopped and looked at her, his brows knitted in anger. "What exactly is going on? What possible reason did those guys have for kidnapping us?"

Stopping also, she said, "Would it be a shock to know you were adopted?"

Alex stared at her for a moment and then started walking again. "Of course not. I've known I was adopted since I was ten years old."

Jeagan hurried to catch up. "Do you know anything about your birth parents?"

"No. Not really. I asked many times, but my parents really didn't know anything to tell me. All they knew was that my mother didn't want to give me up, but she couldn't take care of me."

"That's not exactly true, Alex," Jeagan said.

"Then, why on earth did she give me up?"

"She didn't, Alex. You were taken from her. Her father, your grandfather, used his position and influence to take you away from your mother and sell you to a Seattle attorney. Your mother was told you were stillborn."

Alex stopped again. Eyes misty with hurt, he said, "I find that hard to believe. Why would my...my grandfather sell me like...like an animal?"

"From what your mother's told me, he was a rich, ruthless, and powerful man." Alex started walking again. "When Isabel, your mother, refused to quit seeing your father, your grandfather killed him, and dumped his body in the Mississippi River."

Alex grimaced. "What kind of monster could do something like that?"

"Someone interested in protecting his powerful name and reputation no matter whom he hurt. He couldn't accept that your mother was in love with the son of an Arkansas farmer. Even though he planned to go to law school after the war, he would never be good enough for your mother."

"Let's go this way." Alex pointed to a ravine with trees lining the far side. "Maybe we'll find a road or houses through those trees."

Alex held onto Jeagan while she picked her way down the sandy slope and over the slippery rocks of the shallow creek. He guided her across the creek bed and up the other side. Her heels were toast.

"Okay?" Alex asked when they were on level ground again.

"Yes," Jeagan huffed and puffed. "I just need a second."

Alex stood patiently while Jeagan bent over and caught her breath. "If my mother thought I was stillborn, how did she find out I was alive?"

Jeagan lifted her head. "It's a long story."

Pushing tree branches out of their way, Alex started through a stand of trees. "We've got nothing but time right now."

Jeagan related how she'd bought the antique desk in Denver and how, when she sat at it, she had flashes of events that happened fifty years earlier in Memphis. She described how each of the different flashes had ultimately led to the murder of Alex's father.

"But, how did you connect that to my mother?" Alex continued to weave his way through the trees. He stopped for a second. "I hear traffic in the distance."

"Thank goodness!" Jeagan said, listening. When she started walking again, she continued. "As far as finding your mother, I was convinced what I saw was real, even when no one believed me. So, I took a chance and flew to Memphis to see if I could find out what really happened. It took some time and a lot of digging," she left out the part about almost being drowned," but I finally did get the truth for myself and your mother. She was thrilled you could be alive somewhere and wanted desperately to find you."

Alex held a large branch for Jeagan to pass under. "But how exactly did you find me?"

"We found a letter from the Seattle attorney who bought you."

"And my parents never knew where I came from. I asked them several times over the years, thinking they might know but were trying to protect me from the truth."

"I guess they really didn't know and were just thankful to have you. I'm sure they assumed your adoption was legal."

Jeagan and Alex emerged from the trees into an open field. Fifty yards away, an old pickup truck drove along blacktop. "Civilization!" Alex said.

"Think anyone will stop for us the way we look?" Jeagan brushed some of the dirt off her clothes. She couldn't do anything about her hair or the dried blood in it.

"We'll get someone to stop. Trust me."

Jeagan laughed in relief. She'd heard guys say 'trust me' many times over the years, but for once she was glad to hear it and actually believed it.

Getting someone to stop for them proved harder than they anticipated. Five cars passed them. Even when Alex stood in the middle of the road, one driver honked and swerved around him.

"I thought the people who lived here were friendly," Jeagan commented while they walked south along the road. Trees were all they could see on either side. Surely they would come across some kind of civilization soon. She heard another car approaching and turned around. A black-and-white police car!

"Look!" She grabbed Alex's arm.

"See, I told you to trust me," Alex said with a wry grin. They both waved until the patrol car slowed and pulled to the side of the road. They hurried over to the driver's window and waited until the officer finished his short radio conversation.

The young, muscular constable, with wavy brown hair sticking out from under his cap, opened the door and stepped out of the car. "Having a spot of trouble, are we?"

"You might say that!" Alex responded.

Chapter Twenty-four

An hour and a half later, Jeagan and Alex, steaming cups of coffee in their hands, sat in the office of Staff Sergeant Timothy Sutherland. A portly, Santa Claus-looking man with a white rim of hair around his shining pate, Jeagan could tell by his penetrating brown eyes that his appearance was deceiving.

Looking to her right when she heard the office door open, she watched Constable Andrews come in and sit down. "Glad to see you two are in a better state than when I collected you off the side of the road," he said with an attempt at a smile.

"Thanks to you, we feel much better." Jeagan glanced at Alex. He had a white bandage almost identical to hers on the left side of his head. Fortunately, the doctor at the Emergency Room who had cleaned and bandaged their injuries had not insisted they stay at the hospital but recommended rest and no stress for forty-eight hours. Fat chance! "If you hadn't come along, we'd probably still be walking."

"Someone would have stopped." Alex reached over and patted Jeagan's hand. "Eventually."

"Yes. Well, we'll need a description of the man who abducted you," Staff Sergeant Sutherland said. "I'll get a sketch artist in here after you tell me what happened."

"We don't need a sketch artist," Jeagan replied. "I'm almost positive I know who kidnapped us."

"And who would that be?" Sutherland asked.

"Anthony Eden. I believe he lives in the Seattle area."

The staff sergeant nodded while the stenographer recorded the information. He raised his bushy white eyebrows. "And why would this Mr. Anthony Eden want to abduct the two of you?"

"Because he's trying to protect the family name of a prominent Seattle attorney," Jeagan replied.

The staff sergeant squinted. "The name of the Seattle attorney would be?"

"Well, the truth is," Jeagan shifted in her chair, "he's no longer practicing law. The fact of the matter is he's deceased."

"I see. You think this Mr. Anthony Eden is trying to protect the name of an attorney who is no longer an attorney but deceased?"

"Actually, yes." Jeagan stammered, feeling like she was a teenager who had been sent to the principal's office.

Alex continued where she left off. "But, he still has a family name and reputation in Seattle, Staff Sergeant." He looked at Jeagan. "This young woman has been acting on my behalf. She's risked her life to find me."

Sutherland again nodded, reminding Jeagan of a bald kewpie doll. He leaned back in his leather chair and folded his arms across his prodigious stomach. "And you needed finding because?"

This is going to be a long night, Jeagan thought. She explained in painful detail what had brought Roger and her to Seattle and Victoria, with many interruptions by Sutherland. The crime business must be awfully slow in Victoria. Finally, the staff sergeant asked for details of the abduction.

"You first," Jeagan said to Alex.

He sat forward. "I parked my car in the lot behind Café Brio. I got out and started walking around the side of the building when a car came up beside me and stopped. When I turned around to see what was going on, a guy rolled down the window and asked if I knew where he could find Canoe Brewpub. Just as I started to give him directions, someone came up behind me and whacked me." He automatically touched the side of his head.

"Did you see the man who hit you?" the staff sergeant asked.

"Not then, no."

Jeagan's eyes widened in surprise. "You saw him?"

"When did you see him?" Sutherland asked.

"When they took us to the warehouse. I heard voices, although they sounded far away. I guess I was regaining consciousness. Anyway, I tried to move, but my hands and feet were bound. I opened my eyes and got a glimpse of the guys while they were taping Jeagan's hands and feet. They didn't see me move. I kept still and watched. One guy was a big red-headed guy. The other man was somewhat smaller and had on a baseball cap. I didn't see his face."

"Eden," Jeagan agreed. "He grabbed me and forced me out of Café Brio."

"In a crowded restaurant, no one tried to stop him?" Constable Andrews asked.

"I don't know." Jeagan shrugged. "Maybe everyone was too stunned to react. I was there with two men who have been helping me search for Alan, I mean Alex." The constable raised his eyebrows again.

Jeagan held out her hands trying to explain. "That's the name his mother gave him at birth, even though she was told that he was stillborn. But, his adoptive parents named him Alex." The kewpie doll nodded and squinted. "Anyway, I yelled for the guys with me when Eden grabbed me, but I guess they didn't hear me or couldn't get through the crowd in time to help me."

The staff sergeant rose from his desk, all kindness now. "I'm glad you were able to get yourselves free. We'll do our best to find the men who abducted you. You'll need to sign your statements when they're printed out." The stenographer gathered her equipment and left the room. "But first, Constable Andrews will have you look through the US Department of Motor Vehicles database for this Mr. Eden, and we'll get a picture of him out over the wire."

"Thank you." Alex shook hands with Sutherland.

Jeagan thanked the staff sergeant and got up. A sudden wave of dizziness hit her. She grabbed the back of her chair and stood still for a second.

"Are you okay?" Alex asked.

"I'm all right." She entered the hallway after Constable Andrews opened the door.

"This way," the officer said, indicating a hallway to their right.

When they turned to follow the officer, Jeagan spotted two familiar faces. Coming along the hall toward them were Sam and Roger.

"That was quick!" Jeagan had never been happier to see two guys in her life. "How'd you get here so fast?"

"We grabbed a cab as soon as you called. Thank God, you're all right!" Roger pulled her into a bearhug.

"Ditto," Sam said while he looked on, the color rising in his face.

"Ow!" Jeagan pulled away from Roger and touched her head.

"Oh, sorry." Roger bent to study Jeagan's bandage. "I can't let you out of my sight, can I?" he said with a lopsided grin.

"Ditto," Sam said again, trying to appear light-hearted, but failing miserably.

"Hmph!" Jeagan said. "Lot of help you two were."

"I know, I know. We promised we wouldn't let anything else happen to you, and…," Roger said looking embarrassed.

"We let you down," Sam finished the sentence. Amazed, Jeagan saw tears in his eyes.

She felt her heart swell. These guys actually cared about her. "Not much you two could have done actually. It all happened so fast." She noticed a dark handbag slung over Sam's shoulder. "Is that mine?"

"Oh, yeah." Sam pulled the bag off his shoulder. "We found it on the floor of the restaurant."

"Thank goodness you found it before somebody grabbed it." Jeagan rummaged through the bag until she found her billfold. She opened it and examined the contents. "Everything's here."

"Is this Alex?" Roger asked.

"Yes, sorry." Jeagan placed her hand on Alex's arm. "At long last, this is Alex!"

Alex held out his hand. "You're the guy who called me. I recognize your voice."

"Yes. Roger Sanderlin," he said with a huge grin. "You can't imagine how glad I am to finally meet you!" Roger pumped his hand. "And, this is Sam McFarland."

"And, I'm Constable Andrews," the officer said impatiently. "This happy reunion is all well and good, but we need to get descriptions of the abductors."

"It was Eden, wasn't it?" Roger asked.

"Yes," Jeagan confirmed. "I'm almost one hundred percent positive."

"What was he thinking grabbing you out of a crowded restaurant?" Sam said.

"Not too smart," Roger added walking beside Jeagan to the squad room. "You'd think he'd realize he'd have a dozen witnesses."

"Witnesses can be very unreliable," Andrews commented. "Generally speaking, no two people give the same description."

"Well, I know exactly what he looks like," Jeagan said, ending the matter.

"By the way, I called your dad," Roger interjected. "He said he was catching the first plane he could get and dragging you home, even if you were kicking and screaming."

Jeagan touched her head again, "I'm ready and willing. I'm tired of being whacked on the head and trussed up like a turkey."

Sam put his arm around her shoulders and squeezed gently. "You gave us quite a scare."

The tender expression in his eyes caught Jeagan by surprise. She didn't know how to respond.

"But, this time," Roger added quickly, "we really will keep a close watch on you and make sure nothing else happens to you."

"Famous last words," Jeagan mumbled.

"Have you been to the ER?" Sam asked.

"Yes," Alex said.

"You have matching bandages," Roger added, "except yours has bunnies on it."

"It does not!" Jeagan said and thumped him with her handbag.

When they were seated at Constable Andrews's desk and waiting for the US Department of Motor Vehicles database files to load, Roger said, "I tried to call Isabel this evening, but the nurse told me she was asleep, and I didn't want to wake her."

Sam checked the time. "Probably getting late in Tennessee, isn't it?"

Jeagan looked her watch. The crystal on it was scratched, but she could still read the time. It was ten o'clock in Denver, which meant it was eleven in Memphis. "Guess I'll wait until morning."

"Is this the man who abducted you?" Constable Andrews turned the computer screen toward Jeagan.

"Yes!" came the reply from Jeagan and Alex.

* * *

The taxi ride to the hotel lulled Jeagan to sleep in spite of the lump on her head. She didn't open her eyes again until the taxi stopped in front of the hotel.

"I'm going to get a room here for the night if they have one," Alex said when they exited the taxi.

"I've got two double beds in my room," Sam offered. "You can stay with me tonight."

"Thanks! I appreciate that. I'll go pick up my car tomorrow."

The four rode the elevator to the fifth floor in silence, each too tired for further conversation.

"Good night," Sam said at his door. Alex echoed his words.

Jeagan and Roger continued along the hall to their adjoining rooms. "I'll see you in the morning." Jeagan unlocked her door.

"No way." Roger pushed his way past her. "You're not going in until I've checked out your room."

"Fine, but make it quick," Jeagan said. "I'm absolutely ex—" Her half-closed eyes flew open when Roger flipped on the lights. "Oh, my God!"

Chapter Twenty-five

"Not again!" Hot tears stung Jeagan's raw cheeks when she saw the disaster that was her room—again. Clothes and shoes and her suitcase were scattered everywhere. The bedspread and blankets were torn off the bed. The mattress had been pulled up and dropped after someone obviously checked under it.

Roger mumbled unintelligible profanities while he hurried over to grab the phone. He ran his finger down the list of numbers for Hotel Security, while Jeagan stumbled over to the couch, which miraculously was fairly straight. She lay down on it like a tree being felled in the forest. "Let me know when they get here." That was the last thing she remembered until she awoke the next morning with a pillow under her head and a blanket covering her.

Friday, March 25th

"What!" Jeagan bolted upright on the couch. Who was pounding on what in the middle of the night? Where was she? She scanned the dark room and could see light edging around drawn drapes. Slowly, realization returned. The pounding, she realized, was in her head. Automatically, she touched it. Aspirin! She threw off the blanket and fumbled in the darkness toward the bathroom.

The light, when she pressed the switch, momentarily blinded her. She blinked until she could stand it and found her aspirin bottle in her cosmetics bag. After two aspirin with a full glass of tap water, she leaned on the vanity and stared at herself in the mirror. Dark circles under her swollen eyes, purple shadings around the bandage on her temple, patches of dried blood in her hair.

"Ravishing!" she declared. Back to bed or a hot shower? Which would it be? Her brain rationalized that if she got in the shower, maybe she would feel better and could get some hot coffee and breakfast somewhere. When did she last eat? She couldn't remember.

Steam quickly filled the bathroom after she turned on the shower. Just before she stepped into it, she remembered the bandage on the side of her head. She would have to take a bath instead and try to keep the butterfly stitches dry.

Thirty minutes passed before she emerged from the bathroom in a white terry hotel robe. She walked over and pulled the drapes. It was a beautiful morning, with fluffy white clouds drifting in a crystal blue sky. The city was wide awake with cars and people and water taxis—small tugboat-type boats, which were ferrying people around the harbor. When she turned back to her room, she remembered the disaster of the night before but found that everything was in its place. Who had straightened her room? And, why was it destroyed in the first place? A quick search told her nothing was missing.

The ringing of the phone startled her. "Hello?" she said when she crossed the room to answer it.

"Jeagan? Are you all right, honey?"

She recognized her dad's voice. "Yes. I'm okay, Dad."

"Thank God! I'm leaving for the airport to get a flight to Seattle."

"No, Dad. Don't do that." She sat on the bed. It might take some 'splainin,' but her Dad needed to be convinced he didn't have to come and rescue her. "We found Alan, I mean Alex, and the constable said we could leave today. So, there's no need to come."

"But—"

"No 'buts.' Roger and I want to take Alex to Memphis to meet his mother. Then, I'm coming home and hanging up my gumshoes." She chuckled at her own joke.

An exasperated sigh came across the phone line. "You keep saying you're all right, honey, and the next thing I know, I get a call from Roger to tell me what else has happened." He paused and then added. "I don't know what to think."

"Just know I love you and appreciate your worrying about me. Hopefully, after we reunite Alex with his mother, life will return to some kind of normal." *What is normal?* She wondered. "By the way, have you ever been to Victoria?"

"No," he admitted. "Your mother wanted to go there, but somehow we never made it."

"Well, you need to see it. It's beautiful. With all that's happened, I haven't seen much of it. That is, I haven't seen Butchart Gardens or Craigdarroch Castle, but maybe when my life settles down, I'll come back and be a tourist."

A light knock sounded on the connecting door to Roger's room.

"Got to go, Dad. I'll call you when we get to Memphis and let you know when I'll be home."

"Okay," Geoff Christensen said, concern ringing in his voice. "Promise me you'll do that."

"I promise. Thanks, Dad."

Jeagan disconnected and walked over to open the door.

"Well," Roger said with a cheery grin. "You look better than you did last night."

"How many times have I heard you say those exact words in the last couple of weeks?" Jeagan asked with a smirk.

"I don't know." Roger leaned against the door frame and folded his arms across his chest. He opened his mouth to speak, but the phone ringing in his room interrupted his retort. He crossed the room to answer it, listened for a minute, and then looked back to Jeagan. "Are you up for the Blue Fox for breakfast?"

As soon as Jeagan got ready, still somewhat shaky, she, Roger, Sam, and Alex took a taxi and joined the line in the breezeway next to the Blue Fox. "A popular place," Jeagan commented as a cool gust of wind made her shiver in her blue-striped shirt and jeans. She should have brought a jacket.

"Worth the wait," a man in front of them said. "Food's great."

It wasn't long before Jeagan agreed with him. They were soon seated at a small table with a bright green tablecloth. Whimsical pictures of blue foxes and other forest creatures hung at angles above the cobalt-blue fireplace and around the brick walls, while blue planter boxes separated the tables. The atmosphere was a lively and happy one with everyone leaving their problems at the door. Jeagan ordered the famous French toast. When she tasted it, she thought she'd died and gone to heaven. She could feel her strength returning.

"How's your head?" Sam asked between mouthfuls of Belgian waffle.

"Better," Jeagan and Alex answered at the same time.

"Who straightened my room last night?" Jeagan sipped her coffee, hot and delicious.

"I did," Sam said. Concern, guilt, and something else Jeagan couldn't quite put her finger on registered on his face. "Roger called our room and told us what happened. I didn't want you to have to see that mess first thing in the morning, especially after what you'd been through."

"Thanks. I really appreciate that." She took a bite of her toast.

"I tucked you in," Roger chimed in.

Jeagan laughed. "And, thank *you* for the pillow and blanket, Roger."

"Did you find anything missing?" Alex asked.

"No," Jeagan replied, "but I'll bet whoever it was was trying to find the letter and that contract that I got at Patrice's."

"Had to be," Roger commented.

"And, that could be why they grabbed you and dumped you at the warehouse. A diversion," Sam added.

"Maybe, hopefully, they had no intention of returning for us." Jeagan shivered, unsure of whether it was because she was relieved that maybe Eden hadn't intended to kill them or maybe he had intended to leave them there to die of exposure and starvation.

"Looks like they wanted you out of the way while they searched for the document." Sam poured more coffee from a carafe. "So you wouldn't have any proof of Alex being kidnapped and sold fifty years ago."

"No document, no proof. Glad I gave the document to Will," Jeagan said. "But, that makes no sense. We recognized Eden when he kidnapped us yesterday. Why would he leave himself open to that kind of charge?" She turned to Alex.

"Can't answer that one." Alex shrugged. "But, then not much of what's happened makes sense to me."

Jeagan noticed Alex's bloodshot eyes and pale face, almost as white as the bandage on his head. He needed a break. They all needed a break!

"Eden probably thought he could grab you two without anyone being able to identify him," Sam said. "Then, if no one found you... ." His voice drifted off.

Roger finished his eggs and pushed his plate away. "If Eden's smart, he'll disappear for a while."

"Does the hotel have a security camera?" Jeagan asked. "Maybe we could look at some of the tapes to see if Eden was in the hotel last night."

"We already asked the security guard that," Sam said.

"Yeah," Roger added. "The system's being updated and hasn't been working for the last week."

"Naturally," Jeagan added with a sigh.

Roger's cellphone rang. "Sorry, I meant to turn it off." He pulled it out of his pocket and answered it in a soft voice. After he recognized the caller, he excused himself.

Jeagan watched him walk out of the restaurant. "I'll call Isabel after we finish breakfast," she said to Alex. "I'd like for you to go with us to Memphis to meet her as soon as you can."

"The sooner the better," Alex said. In spite of what they had been through the previous day, his gray eyes looked excited, expectant, possibly looking forward to answers to questions he must have had all his life about his birth parents. "I can take the time off. I only fly two weeks out of the month."

"So, you've always been a pilot?" Sam asked. He finished off his waffle.

Alex nodded. "Flew for Continental. Retired last year."

"Have you talked to your family? Do they know what's going on?" Jeagan asked between bites.

"I called my wife and my parents this morning. Told them what had happened, that is about my birth mother. I didn't tell them what happened to us yesterday. It might be easier to tell them face-to-face after I get home."

"Probably a good idea," Jeagan agreed, not wanting Alex's family to blame her for what happened, although she did feel responsible. "Does your wife want to go to Memphis with you?"

Alex shook his head. "No. Gaylann can't get away right now. Our daughter just had twin boys." He smiled like a proud grandfather. "Gaylann's helping out for a few weeks."

"Congratulations!" Sam said.

Jeagan offered her congratulations also. She studied Alex's face for a minute. *This is what the visions were all about. For some reason,* she marveled, *after I bought that antique desk, I was 'chosen' to have flashes of fifty-year-old events that led to the murder of Alex's father. Then those eerie, upsetting flashes of the past pushed me to find Alex's mother and solve the mystery of what happened to her fiancé. Little did I know then that I would also find out that she had a son who wasn't stillborn, as she'd been told, but alive and well and living in the Pacific Northwest.* Again, she wondered, *Why me?*

Roger returned to the table. Curious, Jeagan waited for him to mention who the caller was, but he didn't.

"Alex and I were talking about going to Memphis," she said. "I haven't heard from Isabel, but I'm going to call her as soon as I get to the hotel."

"Good." Roger picked up the check and pulled out his wallet.

"Let me get this," Alex and Sam offered at the same time.

* * *

Isabel answered on the second ring when Jeagan called her later from her hotel room.

"Isabel, it's Jeagan. How're you feeling?"

"Much better, honey. Stronger today." Jeagan thankfully noted that her voice sounded stronger. "In fact, they're letting me out of here. A friend from my church is on her way to pick me up now."

"That's great news! And, I have even greater news for you. We've found Alan."

Isabel's exclamation of delight vibrated over the phone lines. "My son! You've found Alan?"

"Yes, we have, but his name is Alex, and he's anxious to meet you. We want to come to Memphis right away."

"Alex, Alan. I don't care what his adoptive parents call him. He'll always be Alan to me. And, yes, please come as quickly as you can. I'll call my housekeeper and tell her to get rooms ready for you. How many rooms will you need?"

"No, Isabel." Jeagan understood Isabel's excitement and call to action. "Slow down. We'll get rooms at The Peabody. You don't need to have house guests while you're trying to get your strength back."

"But, I want my son close."

"Don't worry. I'm sure he'll spend as much time with you as you want him to. You two have a lot of catching up to do."

"Fifty years worth," Isabel said slowly, thoughtfully. Then, excitement returned to her voice. "What time does your flight arrive?"

"It may be late. We're still in Victoria, British Columbia."

"British Columbia?"

Jeagan laughed. "Yes. Alex lives in Victoria. He flies seaplanes between British Columbia and the mainland."

"A pilot," Isabel mused.

"Would you like for me to have him call you, so you can at least talk to him before we get there?"

"No." Isabel sounded reluctant or shy. "I wouldn't really know what to say to him. I just want to see him and wrap my arms around him."

After she disconnected, with a smile of accomplishment on her face and a glow of satisfaction in her heart, Jeagan walked over to the door to Roger's room. She knocked.

"Come in," Roger called out. He held his hand over the receiver when Jeagan entered the room and whispered, "It's Will."

"I'll be in my room." While she waited for Roger to get off the phone, she packed her clothes and cosmetics and walked over to look at the view from her window. Nearly noon, the harbor was alive with brightly dressed tourists. She watched water taxis chug around the shoreline, while seaplanes lifted off from the dark blue water and cruise ships steamed past on the horizon. "God's in His heaven and all's right with the world," she quoted Robert Browning. *Well, at least that's how I feel in this one moment in time,* she realized. It was a feeling to be savored after the last few days.

What would the next few days be like? She wondered. After Alex was reunited with his mother, would her life as a technical writer seem ordinary and dull? Would she ever see Roger or Sam or Alex or Isabel again? Would they all forget her? Would Roger want her help in further investigations? Probably not. She smiled, realizing she was probably more of a pain in the rear than an actual help to him. What about Sam?

Her reverie was cut short when Roger knocked on the door and pushed it open. "That was Will. Someone broke into his house last night while he was out to dinner."

Chapter Twenty-six

Jeagan's mouth flew open. "The document?"

"Gone," Roger confirmed.

Jeagan sank onto the couch. "Now, there's no proof...except for the letter Isabel found in her father's personal things." She thought for a moment. "What about the other letters in the file cabinet? Is there a legal way we can get to those?"

Roger shrugged. "Will said he had an appointment at the FBI this morning. He was going to show them the document."

"I thought he played golf the other day with guys from the FBI."

"FBI retired," Roger corrected.

"But the fact that Will probably showed them the document, wouldn't that count?"

"Will's checking on that. Said he'd call me when he's got something." Roger was silent for a moment. "An interesting thing Will said."

"What?"

"His neighbor told him he saw a young woman sitting in a car for about an hour yesterday. She was parked two doors away from Will's house." Roger walked into the room and looked out the window. "The neighbor said he didn't think anything about it at the time, but after the break-in last night, he tried to recall the type of car and license number."

"Could he?" Jeagan asked.

"No. All he remembered was that the car was white, but he did remember the woman. He said she had curly red hair."

"You're not serious!"

"Afraid so," Roger admitted.

"Do you think it's the same woman and she's somehow connected with Eden?"

"It's possible," Roger said, "but if she's the same person who sent you those roses in Denver and followed you to Seattle, my question is still why?"

"How and why she would be working with Eden?"

Roger nodded.

"Do you think they're both trying to protect the McFarland name or stop us from finding Alan?" Jeagan asked.

"Don't know. Could be a little of both, I suppose."

"So, it's not over yet, even if the Victoria police can prove Eden kidnapped Alex and me."

Roger's eyes flashed. "Eden? I need to talk to Constable Sutherland before we leave." He started to his room.

A knock sounded on Jeagan's door.

Jeagan stood to answer it. "Probably Alex and Sam."

Roger held up his hand. "Stay put. I'll get it." Sure enough, it was Alex and Sam. Roger let them in. "Back in a flash."

"Are you packed?" Sam asked Jeagan.

"Yep. I'm ready to go anytime you guys are." Alex, she noticed, looked fresh and pressed. He'd obviously retrieved his car and suitcase, maybe gone home to get clean clothes. "I just got off the phone with your mother, I mean, your birth mother," she told him. "She's very excited about meeting you."

"How's she doing?" he asked. Jeagan watched as several emotions crossed his face—a mixture of apprehension, expectation, excitement, concern. "Is she well enough for the shock of seeing her long-lost son?" he asked with a nervous smile.

"She said she's feeling much better, getting out of the hospital today." Jeagan grinned. "And, yes, she's beside herself she's so excited about seeing you."

"That's good news. My mom…well, my other mom… sounded a little anxious about my meeting my birth mother, but I assured her she'd always be my mom." He face colored slightly. "You know what I mean."

Jeagan nodded, smiling.

"You'll find a way to adjust and settle in to having two moms," Sam assured him. "They'll each have their own special place in your life."

Jeagan looked at Sam, marveling at his insight and kindness.

"Well," Roger said, when he returned from his room. "They found Eden."

"Where?" Jeagan's face brightened.

Roger frowned. "In Seattle. Claims he's been there all week."

"But, I'm almost positive he's the man who grabbed me."

Roger sighed, frustrated. "He's got witnesses to corroborate his story."

"Of course he does," Sam interjected.

"Unfortunately," Roger continued, "not much the police can do if Eden can prove he never left Seattle."

"I can't believe this! He's going to get away with kidnapping Alex and me because he's got friends who'll lie for him!"

"Calm down," Roger said. "The police are still checking. If he was here—" Jeagan cut her eyes at him. "I believe you. Okay? Let the police do their jobs."

"You sure it's okay for us to leave?" Alex asked.

"Staff Sergeant Sutherland told me he'll keep in touch," Roger said. "I gave him our cellphone numbers."

"Speaking of leaving." Sam looked at Jeagan. "We're flying to Seattle in style."

"In style?"

"Yep. We're getting a free ride on a seaplane. Alex here has worked it out. He's driving us to Hyack."

"Cool!" Roger said.

Jeagan's stomach rolled over.

* * *

After checking in at the Hyack terminal, Jeagan sat with the guys in the waiting area. She watched the small planes taking off and landing on the harbor. Part of her was excited at the new experience of riding in a seaplane, yet a larger part of her was scared of the unknown.

Sitting next to her, Sam reached over and patted her arm. "Don't worry. You'll love it," he whispered so that only she could hear.

"I'll hold you to that," she said, half serious. And, she soon found out that Sam was right. Although the takeoff was somewhat bumpy, after the small plane soared into the air, Jeagan lost herself in scanning the small pieces of land, the lavish homes and resorts located on the different islands, and the changing colors of the water below ranging from deep blues to lighter blues and greens, depending on the depth. Again, she promised herself that one day she would explore the islands by sailboat.

Before she knew it, the plane slowed and made its descent into Seattle, landing on Lake Union, and finally powering into the Kenmore Air Terminal. "You were right," she told Sam with a smile after she pulled her handbag from under the seat in front of her. "It was wonderful!"

Sam got up from his seat. "I wouldn't steer you wrong." His eyes held hers for a moment. What did she read there?

Roger said from behind her. "Let's go. We've got barely enough time to get to the hotel, pack our stuff, and grab a taxi to Sea-Tac."

Jeagan deplaned with everyone else and retrieved her suitcase.

The taxi ride to the hotel seemed quiet to Jeagan after the noisy seaplane. Roger and Sam, sitting on either side of her, and Alex, sitting in the front with the driver, said little. She spent the ride thinking about what had happened over the last few days and looking forward to what was ahead.

* * *

Will rose from his chair in the Marriott Hotel lobby when the four entered. Surprised to see him, Roger greeted him and asked, "Has anything else happened?"

"No," Will assured them. Jeagan let out a sigh of relief. "I thought I'd drive you to the airport," he said, "and fill you in on what I've found out."

"Great!" Roger said. "Jeagan and I'll be down in a few minutes. Won't take long to pack the rest of our stuff."

"What's with you and Sam?" Roger asked when he and Jeagan were alone on the elevator.

Surprised, Jeagan looked over at him. "What're you talking about?"

Roger smirked. "I've seen the way he looks at you."

"You're imagining things," Jeagan said defensively.

While she added the clothes she'd left in her room to her suitcase, Jeagan wondered about Sam. They hadn't had any time alone since they left Seattle, but did she want time alone with him? After she was gone, he'd probably return to his regular routine, whatever that was.

Again, she wondered about Roger. How did she feel about him? She'd been drawn to him after he'd saved her life in Memphis, and she'd felt he had the beginnings of feelings toward her. But, during the past week, he'd been more like a big brother to her. And, his comment about the way Sam looked at her.... Was he asking out of curiosity or because he was interested in her?

She closed her suitcase. Maybe she should forget about both men. In a few days, she'd be back at Caldwell & Ottonello Engineering working on the latest proposal with little time for a social life after putting in ten-to-twelve hour days.

"Ready?" Roger called out from the open doorway.

"Ready," Jeagan called back. She lowered her suitcase onto its wheels and pulled up the handle.

Roger walked into the room pulling his rollaboard and walked toward the door.

"Do we need to check out at the front desk?"

"All done," Roger said. "Leave your key card on the nightstand."

Jeagan did as Roger instructed. They walked along the hall and boarded the elevator, neither speaking while the elevator descended. When the doors opened, she spotted Sam, Alex, and Will in the lobby area. Will stood in front of the windows facing the marina. Roger strode toward him.

Sam sat in a club chair in deep conversation on his cellphone, using his free hand for emphasis. Jeagan smiled at his now-familiar gestures. When he saw her, he quickly ended the call, rose from his chair, and strode toward her. He stopped when Roger intercepted him. They exchanged a few words and shook hands.

Sam wore his clothes well, Jeagan observed while he walked toward her, his stride long and smooth. In his case, she thought, the man made the clothes, not the other way around. Even in jeans and a gray sweater, he looked sharp. He reached her and held out his hand. When she gave him hers, he held it with both of his. "I won't be coming to the airport with you, Jeagan, so I wanted to say good-bye." An unsure look in his eyes, he continued. "I've enjoyed being with you and getting to know you. I—"

"Let's go!" Roger called from the front entrance.

"I have to go." Jeagan felt rushed and torn. "There are no words to thank you for all you've done for me. You've been wonderful. Maybe you can come to Denver sometime."

Sam's phone rang. He pulled it out of his pocket and checked the display. He looked at Jeagan. "I need to take this call."

"It's okay, Sam." She reached over and kissed him on the cheek. "Take care of yourself."

A look of what appeared to be relief crossed his face. Did he seem to be glad nothing was mentioned about seeing each other again? Was he glad to be in Seattle again and off the crazy merry-go-round they'd been on since she arrived in Seattle four days earlier?

One last glance back before she walked out the front entrance told her Sam was still on the phone, now standing at the wall of windows facing the marina where Will had been a few minutes earlier. *Good-bye, Sam,* she thought. The glass door closed behind her.

Chapter Twenty-seven

"Will was updating me." Roger turned to look at her from the front seat when they were on their way to the airport.

Jeagan sat forward. "What's happened?"

"The filing cabinet and the files are gone from the McFarland's."

"How do you know that?" Jeagan asked, disappointed. "So you were able to get a search warrant?"

"Yes. My two retired FBI golf buddies were able to convince a retired judge friend of theirs to make a case to a sitting judge friend of his that the document they saw was proof enough that illegal adoptions had taken place."

"That's pretty roundabout, but I get the point. You mean the judge signed a search warrant without seeing the document?"

Will nodded.

"You must have some powerful friends."

"Former head of the Washington Bureau," Will said.

"Well, what if I can remember the names of some of the other attorneys involved in the kidnappings?" Jeagan asked, grasping for something that would open an investigation and possibly find other children who might have been stolen from their parents.

Will shook his head. "No evidence, no official investigation."

"What about the document Isabel found?"

"We know it was real. Alex is living proof of that, but the two attorneys involved in the adoption and Isabel's father are all dead. There's nowhere to go with an investigation."

"So you checked on the Memphis attorney, Christopher Mark Greer?"

"Yeah. He passed away several years ago," Will confirmed.

Jeagan heard the sound of another door closing. But, she should be happy. They had found Alex, which was all she had originally hoped to accomplish.

* * *

"Thanks for all your help, Will. I can't tell you how much I appreciate what you've done for us," Jeagan said as he pulled up to Sea-Tac.

"Wish I could do more, but I think we've gone as far as we can with the evidence we have." Will got out and opened the door for her while Roger and Alex pulled the luggage out of the trunk. "Take care of yourself."

"You too." Jeagan hugged him. She watched while Roger and Alex thanked Will and said good-bye.

Soon, Jeagan, Roger, and Alex walked through the busy, sunny terminal, noisy with hurrying passengers and announcements over the PA system. On their way to the gate and with a few minutes to spare, Jeagan stopped in a gift shop.

"I'll meet you guys at the gate." Who knew when, if ever, she would return to Seattle. She wanted something to remember the city...and Sam. When she had searched through tee shirts, sweatshirts, postcards, and stuffed Seattle Seahawks, she chose a tiny crystal seaplane. She could set it on her desk at work. Happy with that, she searched for something for her dad. Something he would use. Didn't take long. She left the store with a silver picture frame, knowing the exact picture she would put in it. One of her dad and her with his labs, Bob and Hope, taken at Chatfield Reservoir the previous summer. Smiling to herself, she checked her watch and left the shop.

Roger, it seemed, had not gone on to the gate. He stood outside the shop leaning against the wall waiting for her.

"What're you doing?" Jeagan asked.

"Waiting for you." He placed an arm around her shoulders. "Now that your boyfriend, Sam, is out of the picture, guess I'll have to look out for you by myself."

Jeagan narrowed her eyes at him and ducked away from his arm. "He's not my boyfriend."

"Right." Roger laughed.

They walked to the gate where the last of the passengers were boarding. Alex sat waiting for them. He rose from his seat and joined them in line.

"What happened to you two?" he asked.

"She was dawdling in a gift shop," Roger commented.

"I wasn't *dawdling*. I was shopping." She felt like she was leaving part of herself in Seattle, but at least she was taking a little of it home with her.

Their seats were in an exit row, which gave her plenty of leg room. She settled in her seat and watched the ramp activity before the plane backed away from the gate, turned, and proceeded to the runway. Within minutes, the plane lifted off, leaving Seattle behind. Jeagan watched the green city grow smaller until it was finally swallowed up in puffy white clouds. When she could no longer see it, she leaned back and closed her eyes. Her part in the investigation was over.

Well, it was except for the red-headed woman and Anthony Eden. But, what, if anything, could she do about them? Nothing. Leave it to the police. Alan/Alex was found. Soon, he would be reunited with his real mother, and she could go home to Colorado.

She glanced over at Roger and smiled. He was asleep with his legs stretched out using the extra room of the exit row. Jeagan noticed the sandy hair that fell across his forehead. She was tempted to reach over and push it off his face, but that might awaken him. Instead, she gazed out the window.

The clouds parted briefly to reveal small towns and green fields that grew smaller until only the snowy peak of Mount Rainier was visible. Soon, the landscape blurred and Jeagan's eyes closed.

Ring! "What?" Jeagan opened her eyes to see passengers standing in the aisle, pulling their bags from the overhead bins. *Why do I always fall asleep on airplanes?*

Roger, she noticed, stood in the aisle talking on his cellphone. What was it with Roger and Sam and their cellphones?

He disconnected and placed the phone in his pocket. "Rise and shine." He looked down at Jeagan with a grin. "We're back in the sunny South."

His grin was as annoying as his cellphone forever ringing. She chose to ignore him while she stretched and glanced out the window. The sky was a mass of pale gray clouds. What sunny South? She reached under the seat in front of her for her handbag and waited her turn to exit her row.

Walking through the Memphis terminal toward Baggage Claim, she smelled the tangy aroma of Corky's BBQ. Alex had a treat in store.

She looked over at him, talking to Roger while each pulled his bag behind him. Being an airline pilot, she realized that Alex had probably been to Memphis many times and probably knew all about their famous barbecue: Corky's and the Rendezvous. Seemed strange to think he'd been so close to his birth mother without knowing who she was.

Her bag showed up on the carousel a short time later. Roger grabbed it off when she pointed it out. He pulled up the handle for her, and the three walked out to find the shuttle to The Peabody Hotel. How many days had passed since she had done the same exact thing? Now, she was returning to the scene of the crime, in a manner of speaking, and bringing the mystery full circle.

When they were seated in the van, she watched Alex's face. She couldn't fathom his feelings since she'd always known and been loved by her real parents. But, Alex had also experienced love and nurturing over the years by parents who loved him no less than his birth mother would have. Now, he was going to be able to fit all the pieces of his life into place and give great happiness to Isabel.

Memphis, Jeagan realized on the van ride, was even greener and more lush than it had been a week ago. Had it only been a week—six days actually—since she'd left Memphis to search for Alan? *Pretty good for an amateur gumshoe.* She looked over at Roger, across the aisle, facing her. He was probably used to closing a case quickly. Might not mean much to him.

Roger caught her eye and smiled knowingly at her. She'd miss him, even his annoying ways, which truthfully made him more fun to be around. Part big brother, part potential boyfriend, part pain in the rear.

The van soon exited the expressway onto Riverside Drive. The pear trees that lined the drive, she noticed, were even more loaded with white blossoms than they had been a week earlier. Minutes later, the driver turned east onto Union Avenue. He drove a few more blocks and then pulled up in front of The Peabody Hotel. She had returned to the scene of the crime that had taken place fifty years earlier.

The driver unloaded their luggage and the three entered the grand hotel to stroll across the elegant lobby. Tourists and businessmen and women sat around the softly lit lobby drinking cocktails, chatting, and watching the famous ducks while listening to the tuxedoed man at the grand piano playing show tunes. Maybe she could enjoy being in Memphis on this trip.

"Your rooms are on the seventh floor," the desk clerk told them when he handed over their key cards.

"Beautiful hotel," Alex commented. They crossed the lobby to the polished brass elevator doors.

"You haven't been here before?" Jeagan asked.

"No, Continental always booked us at a hotel near the airport. Nothing this nice."

"This hotel has quite a past," Roger said. "There's a history room on the mezzanine if you're interested."

Alex craned his neck around checking out the lobby and upscale shops off the lobby area. "I'll check it out if I have time."

"You've probably seen lots of beautiful hotels during your travels with the airlines, haven't you?" Jeagan asked as they stepped onto the elevator.

"Lots," Alex said. "I love the lavish newer hotels, but I prefer the older, elegant ones with all their individual stories and secrets."

Jeagan smiled to herself. *Yes, this hotel has its secrets.*

"Let's meet in my room in a few minutes," Roger said when they arrived on the seventh floor and followed the corridor to their rooms. "We can call Isabel and see if she's ready to have company."

"Are you kidding?" Jeagan said. "I'm sure she's sitting by the phone right now waiting for our call." She opened the door to her room. Again, it was decorated in subtle elegance. She set her suitcase on a stand and walked over to look out the windows to the west. The Mississippi River and the few remaining clouds blazed with orange light from the late afternoon sun.

She unpacked her cosmetic bag and freshened up before going next door to Roger's room. This time they didn't have adjoining rooms, but surely that was no longer necessary. Alex was already there sitting in an armchair by the window, looking nervous, when she knocked on the door and Roger opened it.

Roger lifted the phone receiver and held it out to Jeagan. "Ready to call her?"

A fizz of excitement shot through her when she pulled the address book out of her handbag to check for Isabel's number. They had really done it! Alan-Alex was home. She accepted the receiver and dialed.

Isabel answered on the first ring. "Isabel, it's Jeagan. We're in Memphis!"

"Oh, Jeagan! I'm so thrilled, I can't tell you! Please hurry. I don't think I can wait another minute to see my son."

"We're on our way," Jeagan assured her.

"Oh, I wanted to tell you," Isabel added, her breathing somewhat labored, "I've had my housekeeper bring in dinner. I remember your mentioning something about barbecue, so she's brought in barbecue from Corky's. I hope that's okay."

"Better than okay! My mouth is watering already. We'll see you soon."

"Please hurry!"

Jeagan turned around to the guys. "What's better than okay?" Roger asked.

"She had Corky's barbecue brought in for us." The grins on both men's faces told Jeagan what she needed to know. "Ready to go?"

The three passed through the lobby on their way to the street. Jeagan stopped for a moment to watch the famous Peabody ducks ceremony. The ducks waddled along their red carpet from the round marble fountain in the middle of the lobby to the elevator, which would take them to their quarters on the Skyway for the night. The red-uniformed Duck Master gently herded them along with his staff amid applause from spectators, who lined the red carpet to watch the daily ritual. The ducks, Jeagan remembered from her previous visit, would return to the lobby at eleven A.M. the next morning and march along the carpet to the fountain where they would spend the day.

To Jeagan, the taxi ride seemed to take forever. But, in reality, it was only fifteen minutes before the driver turned left off commercial Union Avenue onto the Parkway with its old, elegant residences. She watched Alex's face while he gazed along the street lined with hundred-year-old oaks and maples that stood proudly in front of mansions of the same vintage. What was going through his mind? Was he thinking about what it would have been like growing up here?

Suddenly, it dawned on Jeagan that she had forgotten to tell Alex that his mother was confined to a wheelchair. That was something he needed to know, but she would leave out the part about Madison running her off the road a few years earlier. Isabel could tell him that at some point if she chose to.

"There's something I need to prepare you for before you see your mother," Jeagan said. "With all that's happened, I forgot to tell you that Isabel had an accident a few years ago and can't walk. But, she does get around rather well in her electric wheelchair."

Alex looked bewildered. "That poor woman. She's certainly been through a lot in her life. I hope I can help to make her last years happy ones."

Jeagan reached over and squeezed Alex's hand. "I'm sure you can."

Soon, the driver turned into Isabel's circular driveway and parked in front of the house, an imposing three-story white stucco with a New Orleans style wrought-iron balcony over the front door.

Roger paid the driver and the three mounted the few steps to the front door. Jeagan felt a twinge. She remembered when she had been here before, when Thomas, the butler, had opened the door and tried to send her away.

"Are you okay?" Jeagan asked Alex as she pressed the doorbell. He nodded, but looked a shade paler than he had earlier. *I can't even imagine how nervous he feels.*

The door was almost immediately opened by Isabel's housekeeper, a tall, big-boned woman, dressed in a light-weight gray suit, who greeted them with a friendly smile.

Before anyone could say anything, the middle-aged woman said, "Please, come in." She opened the door wider. "Isabel's expecting you. She's in the living room."

"Thank you." Jeagan reached for Alex's hand as they entered into the wide, marble foyer. Apprehensive, he had the look of a little boy on his first day of school. She walked with him into the elegant, yet warm and alive, living room with the celery-colored sofa and green-and-blue striped overstuffed armchairs.

Isabel sat in one of the chairs. Small but still regal in spite of her illness and post-hospital pallor, her silvery hair appeared professionally coiffed and her peach-colored pantsuit looked smart and stylish. She offered no verbal greeting but her gray eyes were bright with tears of joy. Unable to stand, Isabel held out her arms to Alex. "My son," she said simply. "My precious son."

Chapter Twenty-eight

Jeagan felt like her heart would burst. Her body shook. Tears streamed down her face. She watched Alex, not hesitating, move toward his mother. He knelt in front of her and dwarfed her as he enveloped her in a hug.

Roger, standing beside Jeagan, placed his arm around her shoulder and squeezed. He handed her several tissues he'd pulled from a box on an end table. "You did it," he whispered and kissed her cheek.

"No, *we* did it." Tears, she saw, also glistened in his eyes.

In a few moments, Alex released his mother and stood up. The housekeeper brought a cherrywood chair from the dining room and placed it beside Isabel's chair so Alex could sit beside his mother.

Isabel blotted her eyes and beamed at her son. "I am the happiest woman in the world!" She reached over and held onto Alex's hand. "What happened to your head?" She frowned and looked over at Jeagan. "You have a bandage too."

"We're okay," Alex said. "We'll tell you about it later."

"Well, I'm just glad you're finally here and all right…and safe, both of you." She smiled. "All three of you." She looked over at Jeagan and Roger, who were now sitting on the sofa. "How can I ever thank you two for what you've done for me?" Her eyes filled with tears again. "All those wasted years."

Thrilled to see the happiness on Isabel's face, Jeagan said, "We're just happy we were able to find Alex."

"I second that," Roger added, looking over at Jeagan. "And, I must admit she was a pretty good partner, although at times she was as a real pain."

Jeagan punched his arm.

"Behave yourself!" Roger rubbed his arm.

Isabel laughed. "It's good to have young people in the house again."

Alex squeezed his mother's hand. "We've got a lot of time to make up for. I've got hundreds of questions about you and my southern family."

"You may not like everything you learn about your southern roots, but, all in all, most of us have been good, solid people," Isabel said with a smile. We'll talk and catch up on the last fifty years." She studied his face. "You have my eyes."

"Yes, I do, and so do our two daughters. I want you to come to Seattle to meet them and my wife."

"Grandchildren." She slowly savored the word and the idea.

"Yes, three of them and great-grandchildren. Our daughter just had twin boys."

"Looks like you're going to be busy," Jeagan said with a grin.

Roger sniffed. "Something smells awful good."

Everyone laughed, breaking the emotional spell.

"Do you like barbecue?" Isabel asked her son.

"Love it!" Alex said.

"Good. Then you'll love this." Isabel moved forward in her chair and pushed herself up. Alex moved to pull her wheelchair around so she could get into it.

"Thank you, son," Isabel said as if it were the most natural thing in the world. She colored slightly and then laughed. "Minnie has set dinner on the patio. Should be pleasant outside. It's a warm evening and the humidity is still low."

Lovely is the word Jeagan would have chosen. The tiled terrace, which is what she would have called the patio, stretched across the rear of the house. Several white wrought-iron tables were scattered across the area along with gaily cushioned lounge chairs. She followed wide tiled steps that led down to the manicured lawn, which was graced with towering magnolia, oak, and maple trees. A flagstone path wound through an English garden, starting to come in for the spring season with dogwood and pear trees displaying their white blooms, tulip poplars with pale pink blossoms, and flowering crabapple trees tiny pink flowers. Jeagan identified purple wisteria, pink lilacs, red tulips, yellow jonquils, and bright pink azaleas, among others she couldn't name. A lily pond lay at the heart of the garden, with stone benches set nearby for reflection. Time permitting, she'd love to return and spend some time there.

"It is a lovely garden," Jeagan commented on her way back to the terrace. "It's so beautiful and peaceful here, and the flowers smell wonderful."

"Gaylann will love your garden." Alex seated his mother at the glass-topped table, which was set with pale-green linen for four.

"Bring her here soon to see all the spring flowers." Isabel squeezed her son's hand.

"Speaking of smells…," Roger said.

Jeagan watched as Minnie brought out the barbecue ribs and pulled pork. "Can I help you?"

"If you'd like," Minnie replied. "You can help with drink orders."

Soon everyone was seated with glasses of wine in hand, except for Isabel, who had a glass of sweet tea. Roger rose from his chair. "I'd like to propose a toast. First, to Isabel, southern belle extraordinaire. You are one special, strong, lovely lady. May you live long and happy with your new-found son and family."

"To Isabel!" Everyone drank.

Isabel glowed with pleasure. "Thank you all so much."

"Next," Roger continued, "to Alex. May your life be richer now that you have two mothers who love you, a southern heritage to be proud of, and three new friends: Jeagan, Sam, and me!"

Alex laughed. "Here, here! And, my heart-felt thanks to you two also!"

Roger raised his glass toward Jeagan. "And last, but certainly not least, to the gal whose stubbornness and tenacity made all this possible and reunited mother and son."

"To Jeagan!" everyone said.

"Thank you, my blessed dear." Isabel squeezed Jeagan's hand.

Jeagan smiled, her heart too full to say anything but, "Thank you."

"And, now," Roger continued, in an effort to lighten the mood, "Let's eat." He sat down in his chair while the others laughed.

"Ever had barbecue better than this?" Roger asked Alex a few minutes later.

"No." Alex shook his head. "And I've eaten barbecue all over the country."

"Maybe you can visit the Rendezvous before you leave," Jeagan commented.

"Name sounds familiar, but I can't place it." Alex wiped red barbecue sauce off his face.

"It's a fun restaurant off an alley downtown," Jeagan explained. "Great barbecue also, but different. The restaurant is decorated with memorabilia from the early days of Memphis when cotton was king."

"I haven't been there in years," Isabel said. "But, I'd like to take you and your— Oh, hello, Mark."

Jeagan looked around to see a shortish man, well past middle age with thinning gray hair.

"I'm sorry, Isabel," he said. "Minnie didn't say you were eating dinner."

"That's fine," she responded. "There's plenty here if you'd care to join us."

"No. No, thanks. I only wanted to drop off your new will for you to look over."

"Thank you." Isabel took the large envelope and laid it on the table. "Everyone, this is Mark Edwards, my attorney for many years." The men stood. Isabel turned to Alex. "Mark, I'd like you to meet my son, Alan, I mean, Alex," Isabel said proudly. Alex shook Mark's hand.

Pleased, Jeagan realized Isabel was going to use the name Alex had been given by the people who adopted him.

"And," Isabel continued, "I'd also like you to meet Jeagan Christensen and Roger Sanderlin."

Jeagan and Roger also shook hands with Mark.

"Nice to meet you all, especially you, Alex," Mark said. "I've never seen your mother look happier than she does at this moment." Mark patted Isabel on the shoulder. "Well, I won't interrupt your dinner any longer. When you're able, come to my office, and we'll have the will signed and notarized."

"Thank you, Mark," Isabel said. "I think I'll feel well enough to take care of it right away."

After Mark left and the meal was finished, everyone moved inside to the living room. Isabel stayed in her wheelchair. "Now, I want you to tell me what has happened since you left here last week."

Jeagan and Roger again sat on the sofa and Alex took an armchair. Between the three of them, they filled Isabel in on what had happened over the course of six days.

"So all the documents that could prove John McFarland and my father conspired to steal my son from me have been destroyed?"

"All except the letter McFarland sent to your father," Jeagan said. "At least you still have that."

Isabel pressed the power button on her chair and wheeled over to her cherrywood secretary. She turned the key in the lock and lowered the top. Then, she pulled a drawer open and reached inside. "It's gone!"

"What's gone?" Jeagan asked.

"The letter. The one from Mr. McFarland to my father."

"You're kidding?" Jeagan got up and walked over to Isabel's desk.

"I left it right here in this drawer. I know I did." She pulled out all the drawers in the secretary and searched the contents. Jeagan watched over her shoulder.

"I can't believe that!" Jeagan said. "How could someone get to all the files and letters about the adoptions and steal every one of them?"

"Several people working together," Roger offered with a frown.

"And desperate, it seems," Alex commented.

"Minnie," Isabel said, when the housekeeper came into the room moments later carrying a coffee tray, "Do you have any idea what happened to a document I had in my desk? Has anyone else been in the house?"

"No," Minnie answered, a look of concern on her face. "I don't have any idea what happened to your papers. Were they important?"

"Yes, very," Isabel said.

"I'm sorry, but I haven't had any reason to be in your desk, and no one has been here except for the cleaning ladies. They're the same ones who've been cleaning for you for years."

"And, no one else was here?" Jeagan asked.

Minnie thought for a moment, and then the color drained from her face.

"What's wrong?" Isabel asked.

"Well, it's just that I found the kitchen door unlocked this morning when I got back from the grocery store," Minnie said. "I always lock it when I leave, and I realized I must have forgotten."

Roger got up from the sofa and strode toward the kitchen. "Let me have a look at that lock." Everyone followed. When he reached the kitchen, he opened the door, squatted, and inspected the lock. "Looks like it's been picked. There are scratches on it."

"So someone broke into my house?" Isabel asked, incredulous.

"Sorry, Isabel, but, yes, it looks that way," Roger said.

"I'm sorry, Miss Isabel," Minnie said, tears forming in her eyes. "Would you like for me to call the police?"

"Not your fault, Minnie," Isabel said, nevertheless upset. "Yes, I guess we should call the police."

"Might want to wait to call the police until after you've check to see if anything else is missing," Alex suggested.

"Probably wouldn't do much good to call the police," Roger commented. "I'll bet there are no fingerprints, and my guess is nothing else was taken."

Jeagan nodded. "That would be my guess also."

Isabel sighed heavily. "Well, at least you saw the letter and it helped you find my son. That's the most important thing to me."

"That's true," Jeagan agreed. "But, I'd hoped we'd be able to turn all the letters we found over to the FBI and maybe help some other children find their birth families."

"Guess we need to be thankful for what we *have* accomplished," Roger said.

* * *

Jeagan, Roger, and Alex said their good nights to Isabel when their taxi arrived half an hour later.

"I plan to read through my new will tonight. And, if it doesn't need any changes, I'll go in to see Mark in the morning and sign it. I'd like for you three to go with me."

"I'd be happy to," Alex said.

"On a Saturday?" Roger asked.

"Mark's office is open 'til noon one Saturday each month, and I believe tomorrow is his half-day."

"If you feel up to it, we'd be happy to go with you. Our plane doesn't leave until late afternoon," Jeagan said. She looked to Roger for confirmation.

"Absolutely," Roger agreed.

That settled, the three rode to The Peabody in silence, each deep in his own thoughts.

* * *

"Want to have a nightcap?" Roger asked Jeagan and Alex when they walked in the hotel entrance and on into the softly lit lobby. Small groups of people sat around at tables or conversation areas talking, most with drinks or coffee in their hands.

"Sounds good," Jeagan said. "I'd love to have a mint julep, just to see what it tastes like."

"Mint julep?" Roger asked.

"Sure," Alex said. "It's supposed to be an authentic southern ladies' drink."

"Yep," Jeagan continued. "Southern belles are supposed to sit in their hooped skirts on their white-columned verandas sipping mint juleps."

"With all their beaux dancing their attendance?" Roger asked with a wry face.

"Works for me."

The three settled into comfortable armchairs in a conversation area and placed their drink orders when a waitress appeared.

"What are your plans now?" Jeagan asked Alex.

"I'm going to stay for a few more days to spend time with... ." Alex hesitated and then grinned. "With my mother."

"She'll like that," Jeagan said. "I'm glad to see you're happy."

Alex leaned forward. "It's great to finally really know who I am, and I want to learn more about my family—the good and the bad."

"That's what every family is made of," Roger commented. "If you shook my family tree, train robbers, horse thieves, and con artists would probably fall out."

"Now, that I can believe," Jeagan said with a smirk.

"I'd like to see what would fall out of your family tree, Miss Smartypants," Roger shot back.

Jeagan gazed off into the distance. "Oh, probably rocket scientists, Nobel Prize winners, or New York Times bestselling authors."

"Yeah, right!" Roger's cellphone rang. He pulled it out of his pocket. When he recognized the number on the display, he got up. "Sorry. Won't take a minute." He clumped off toward the front entrance to answer it.

"Roger and his cellphone." Jeagan shook her head. "Those two are joined at the hip."

Alex laughed. "Maybe he's got some other work going on in Denver."

"Maybe," Jeagan said, thinking. "If so, I wonder what it is?"

"Why?" Alex asked. "Do you want to become his full-time partner?"

Jeagan chuckled. "No way! I'm going home my tech writing job. It's safer. I've had enough of being beat over the head." Involuntarily, she reached up and touched her head. The soreness was nearly gone.

Their drinks arrived just as Roger returned. "Sorry about that." He averted his eyes. "That was Will. He was checking to see how things went with Isabel."

"That was nice of him," Jeagan commented. "Did he say anything else?"

Roger continued to look down. He picked up his drink and sipped.

"Roger?" Jeagan said, expectant.

Roger looked up at Jeagan, his face ashen. "He said Anthony Eden is dead. Someone shot him in the head."

A small cry escaped from Jeagan. "You've got to be kidding!"

Chapter Twenty-nine

"Did he say who shot him?" Alex asked.

Roger drank from his brandy snifter. "No. Will doesn't have the complete details. He got a call from one of his retired FBI buddies. All he knows is that early-morning runners found Eden on a deserted beach near Kenmore Air Terminal." Silent for a moment, he continued, "Could be someone's tying up loose ends."

"Sounds like it," Alex said.

"But *who*?" Jeagan asked.

Roger shrugged. "I don't know. It's tragic, but I don't plan to lose any sleep over Eden's death—especially after what he did to you two."

"And maybe Sue Coleman," Jeagan added. "Maybe he killed Sue, like I said before, because Patrice knew Sue had talked to me and was afraid of what she might tell me. Maybe after Eden flubbed getting rid of Alex and me, Patrice got rid of Eden."

"Neat, clean, no one left to point to her?" Alex offered.

"Could be."

Roger disagreed. "Not likely."

"You didn't meet Patrice," Jeagan countered. "So you've no idea what she's capable of."

"True," Roger admitted. He set his empty glass on the coffee table between them. "Well, I'm going to bed. I've had enough excitement for one day."

"Good idea." Alex stifled a yawn.

"I think I'll stay a few minutes longer and wind down," Jeagan said.

A look of alarm registered on Roger's face. "But, you don't need to be here by yourself."

"I think I'm probably safe now that we're in Memphis. We've already found Alex and now that he's found, my name on Isabel's will makes no difference."

"So I'm the only target left, aren't I?" Alex frowned.

"It's possible," Roger said truthfully. "Just need to be careful. We'll watch your back while we're here."

"Thanks, but I'm not going to let some unnamed threat stop me from spending time with," he hesitated, "with Mom, but I *will* be careful."

"Only threat I can see now is from Isabel's sister," Roger commented. "I assume she'd be the beneficiary of Isabel's estate if something happened to you."

"And you said she's in jail waiting to stand trial?"

"No. She's out on bond."

"Oh," Alex said. Jeagan watched his eyes while he evaluated his situation. "Okay. Give me her description so I'll know her if I run into her."

"Her name's Agnes Harraway. She's around sixty or so, tall and angular. Dark hair with lots of gray. Hard looking."

"Don't forget about your buddy Darrell Hannah," Roger added.

"You mean Madison? I didn't forget him, although I wish I could," Jeagan said. "He's a thirtyish black man with light skin, medium height, trim, a former attorney."

A few minutes later, after Roger and Alex had gone upstairs, Jeagan picked up her mint julep, which she found sweet and refreshing, and wandered up the marble stairs to the mezzanine. She walked along the carpeted hallway to the history room and roamed around the quiet, stately room, again feeling like she was stepping back into another century. She sat at the rectangular table and studied the items in the mahogany glass-fronted cabinets. What were the people like who had used the china and silverware on display? The people who wrote the letters and sent the embossed invitations? The musicians who played big band music on the Skyway?

She got up a few minutes later, feeling peaceful inside, and wandered back out into the hall to continue her stroll around the mezzanine, where she peered through glass doors into long meeting rooms. Before she reached the stairway, which led to the lobby, she glanced over the marble handrail and did a double take. Madison! Madison was standing in the lobby!

Chapter Thirty

She set her glass on a nearby table and ran down the stairs. When she reached the lobby, she looked around for Madison, but he was gone. Where could he have disappeared to so quickly? She hurried along the hallway toward the upscale shops. He wasn't there. Retracing her steps, she searched the restaurant areas at the west end of the hotel. Not there either. Maybe he was outside. She ran out the front entrance to the sidewalk and looked around. All she saw were a few cars along Union Avenue and an empty white carriage with only the horse and driver.

Maybe she'd been mistaken. Madison couldn't possibly know she was in Memphis, or could he? And, why would he be looking for her? *When will I feel safe again?* She realized she wouldn't feel safe until after the trial when Agnes, Williams, and Madison were locked up.

Feeling rattled, she opened the brass doors and re-entered the hotel. It was time to go to bed. The elevators were on her left. It only took a few strides to reach them. She passed one of the hotel shops on the way. In the morning, she promised herself, she'd look for a new outfit in one of the shops. The clothes she'd brought with her needed to be either laundered or dry cleaned.

* * *

In her room again, she sat on the vanity bench and creamed the makeup off her face while jumbled thoughts ran through her head.

Madison: Was that really him in the lobby of the hotel? If it was, had he followed her? *If he had followed her, then who had told him she would be in Memphis?* She had no idea.

Sam: Thinking of him gave her heart a tug. She remembered his kiss that made her insides quiver. The image of his face with his sky-blue eyes. The way he had teased her and helped her with the investigation, acted as tour guide, and straightened her hotel room so she wouldn't have to face the destruction the next morning. He had said nothing about any feelings he might have for her, but his eyes, they had told her a lot. He did care, but obviously not enough to say anything about seeing her again.

Roger: He was a great partner, even if too bossy at times. They did make a good team, but she had no desire to continue the 'partners in crime' relationship. Writing and editing were a much safer profession for her. Did she have feelings for Roger? She honestly had no idea. Under all the banter and bossiness, was he ready for another relationship after what happened to his fiancée? And, who were all those phone calls from? It seemed like he and Sam spent half their lives on their cellphones.

Que sera sera, she thought, what will be will be. She got up and brushed her teeth. Soon afterward, she slipped into bed, thanking God for the day and the privilege of seeing mother and son reunited. A smile on her face, she fell into a deep, restful sleep.

Saturday, March 26th

The phone woke Jeagan the next morning. She reached to grab it. "Hullo."

"Good morning, Jeagan," Isabel said cheerily. "I hope I didn't wake you."

Jeagan pulled herself up against the headboard. "No, I was almost awake and thinking about getting up." She covered the mouthpiece while she yawned. "You sound much better this morning."

"I feel wonderful, like I did twenty years ago. Anyway, I called to tell you Mark said I could come in and sign the new will about mid-morning. My driver is taking me, and I'll have him swing by the hotel to pick y'all up if you like. I talked to Alan, I mean, Alex a few minutes ago, and he said he'd be ready." She stopped to take a breath. "I really do have to start calling him Alex instead of Alan, but I guess that will come in time. Anyway, do you and Roger still want to go with us?"

Jeagan laughed. "You don't know how good it is to hear excitement in your voice. Of course, we want to go with you. What time?"

"Wonderful! We'll pick you up around eleven. We can have lunch afterwards in the Crescent Club. Wonderful food and a beautiful view of the city."

"Sounds great!" Jeagan threw back the covers and sat up on the side of the bed. "We'll be ready."

After Jeagan hung up, she hopped up and got a bath, carefully washing her hair around the stitches. When she was dressed in the only clean pair of jeans she had and a white shirt, she went next door to knock on Roger's door. He didn't answer. *That's strange*, she thought. She turned back to her room, and started to unlock the door but stopped when she found a note taped to it.

It read, "Didn't want to wake you. We've gone to Café Expresso, L&K, Roger and Alex." Jeagan chuckled and grabbed the note.

She stuffed it in her jeans pocket and strode toward the elevator to join the guys for breakfast. While she waited for the elevator, she checked her watch. Ten after nine. They had plenty of time to have a light breakfast after which she would have time to shop before Isabel arrived.

The restaurant was busy on a Saturday morning. Reminded her of when she'd first met Madison, and he'd offered her a seat at his table in the crowded restaurant. She looked around, soon spotting Roger and Alex, and told the hostess she would join them.

"Mornin' guys," Jeagan said when she reached the table.

"Sleeping Beauty has awakened," Roger said grandly. He got up to pull out a chair for her.

"Morning." Alex raised his coffee cup to her.

"Thanks," she said to Roger when she sat down. Alex's gray eyes were clear and he looked rested and happy this morning. *Good*, she thought. *He deserves it.* He had replaced the bandage on his temple with a bandaid as she had done. They were on the mend.

"Coffee?" asked a waitress at her side.

"Yes, please," Jeagan replied. Roger and Alex were already eating. "And I'll have a croissant."

"Have you talked to my mom?" Alex asked with a slight flush. It was going to take a while for him to get used to the idea of Isabel being his 'first' mom.

"I did." Jeagan watched while the waitress poured coffee into her cup and thanked her. Then she emptied a packet of Sweet 'N Low in her coffee and added a little cream. "Isabel said she'd stop by for us around eleven. She's also invited us to have lunch with her at the Crescent Club after she signs her new will."

Roger wiped syrup off his mouth. "Are you going like that?"

He certainly knew how to rile her. "No, Mr. Smart Aleck, I'm not going like this. This is about all I have left to wear that's clean. I'm going to do some shopping after I finish breakfast."

"Thank goodness," Roger teased. "Guess we ought to take our bags with us when we go. That way Isabel can drop us off at the airport after lunch."

"Good idea." Jeagan sipped the strong, hot coffee. Chickory, she guessed. The waitress walked up to set a large croissant with butter and raspberry preserves in front of her, the same breakfast she'd had two and a half weeks earlier in the hotel. She broke apart the roll and added preserves, glad she didn't have to repeat the last time she was here.

"I may not get another chance to talk to you two alone." Alex set his coffee cup on the table. "What you've done for me has changed my life and my mom's. There are no words I can think of to tell you how much that means to me."

Roger smiled. "The look on your face is thanks enough."

Jeagan reached over and squeezed Alex's hand. "And, the look on Isabel's face when she saw you last night. We couldn't ask for more than that." She looked over at Roger for confirmation.

"Absolutely."

"If I can ever do anything for you, please let me know." He fished business cards out of his wallet and handed one each to Jeagan and Roger.

When they were finished eating, Alex insisted on paying the bill. After he paid, the three strolled along the corridor lined with the hotel shops. Jeagan passed a jewelry store, men's store, and finally came to a ladies' shop. She stopped.

"I'll see you guys later."

"Let's all meet here in the lobby a few minutes before eleven," Roger said.

"Fine." Jeagan entered the shop. A friendly sales clerk greeted her and helped her pick out an outfit that would be perfect for the day ahead, a light-weight pants suit with a small black-and-white herringbone design. She left the shop with a spring in her step, which buying a new outfit always gave her.

* * *

At ten-fifty, Roger knocked on Jeagan's door. "Nice outfit," he commented when she let him in.

Pleased, she said, "You look pretty sharp yourself in a sports coat."

"Can't do much dressing up until this blasted cast is off, but I try."

"Well, maybe you won't have to have it much longer after we get back to Denver." Jeagan checked the room one last time to make sure she hadn't left anything. She pulled up the handle of her suitcase, left her key card on the nightstand, and closed the door behind her.

While she walked with Roger toward the elevators, she wondered if she would ever return to this beautiful hotel.

Alex was waiting for them when they reached the lobby. He rose from his chair when they walked up and stuck out a hand toward Jeagan. "This is for you."

Surprised, Jeagan took the black velvet box. She opened it to find a small, gold, exquisitely detailed Peabody duck on a slender chain. "It's beautiful!"

Alex grinned almost shyly. "Just a small thank-you."

Jeagan threw her arms around Alex's neck and kissed his cheek. "It's beautiful. Thank you."

Jeagan released Alex and took the necklace out of the box and handed it to him to fasten around her neck. "How does that look?" she asked when he was done.

"Great!" both men said.

"And this is for you with my thanks." Alex held out a chunky, square box to Roger.

Roger's face lit up when he opened the box to find a gold golf ball marker—with a duck on it. He laughed. "Shouldn't have trouble identifying my golf balls now. Not many guys use ducks as markers." He shook Alex's hand. He and Jeagan tucked the boxes into their luggage, and all three strode toward the hotel entrance.

Just then, Roger's phone rang. "I'll be out in a minute." He fished in his pocket for the phone.

Jeagan shrugged and walked toward the entrance.

"Can I get a taxi for you?" the doorman asked when he opened the door for them.

"No, thanks," Alex replied. "We're waiting for someone."

Soon, Roger joined them.

"Everything okay?"

"Uh, sure." Roger turned his head away.

"Why are you being secretive?" Jeagan asked.

"I'm not being secretive." He looked directly at Jeagan. "That was Shelley. She wanted to know if I needed a ride home from the airport."

Jeagan laughed heartily. "And you had the nerve to give me grief about Sam being my boyfriend."

Before Roger could come up with a retort, a black Lincoln Towncar drove up and parked at the curb. The chauffeur got out as the back window lowered. "Good morning," Isabel said.

All three greeted her and got into the car after the chauffeur opened the doors. Jeagan and Alex got on either side of Isabel while Roger went around to the front passenger side.

"You look very elegant this morning," Jeagan commented.

Isabel spread her hands. "Thank you. I feel wonderful." She reached over the seat and tapped the driver on the shoulder. "Austin, go along to the Parkway and over to Poplar. I want them to see springtime in the South firsthand."

Young and shaggy-haired, but dressed in a neat dark suit, Austin said, "You got it, Ms. Isabel."

"Austin is a part-time chauffer while he attends Rhodes College," Isabel explained. "He's a sophomore with a 4.0 GPA."

"Wow!" Alex said. "Impressive."

"What're you majoring in?" Roger asked.

"Law. I hope to get into Harvard Pre-Law."

Surprised, Jeagan would never in a million years have thought this teen-ager, who looked more like a rock star, would be interested in law school. For the umpteenth time in her life, she realized that you really can't judge someone by their looks.

Austin drove sedately along Union Avenue and turned left. To Jeagan, it seemed like every stately home along Parkway was an artist's rendition of what spring should look like. Azalea bushes with bright pink blooms lined the front of the houses and surrounded huge oak trees. Flowering dogwood, Bradford pear, tulip poplar, and redbud trees graced the front lawns along with bright yellow tulips and buttercups and purple pansies. She drank her fill of the scene before Austin turned east into a more commercial part of town.

Twenty minutes later, the chauffeur ended his circuitous route to Poplar Avenue and turned right into the Crescent Center parking lot. He hopped out and opened the door for Jeagan. Then, he popped the trunk and pulled out Isabel's wheelchair. Roger opened the opposite door for Isabel and Alex. While the men helped Isabel into her wheelchair, Jeagan looked up to see that the building looked like its name. It was crescent-shaped with almost a solid frontage of windows, which reflected the blue sky and scattering of white clouds.

"Can we sit for a minute before we go upstairs?" Isabel asked after they entered the lobby.

"Of course," Jeagan said, thinking Isabel was feeling weak. They found a conversation area in the lobby with black leather chairs. When everyone was seated, Isabel opened her handbag and pulled out two envelopes. She handed one each to Roger and Jeagan.

"I know there's no way to place a dollar value on what you two have done for me, but I hope these will show my appreciation."

Surprised, Jeagan opened her envelope. She choked. "Isabel, I can't accept this. I volunteered to help Roger."

"This is too much," Roger chimed in. "I haven't had time to add up my expenses and daily rate, but it's not anywhere near this much."

Isabel smiled. "Now, children, don't argue with me. What you've done is worth every penny." She snapped her handbag shut, ending the discussion, and looked at her watch. "Now, let's go upstairs and get my new will finalized."

"Yes, ma'am." Roger saluted her.

Still in shock, Jeagan stuffed the envelope into her handbag and hugged Isabel. "Thank you," she whispered.

"You're more than welcome," Isabel replied and kissed her cheek.

They followed the others to the elevator.

The short ride took them to the seventh floor and the law offices of Mark Edwards. A smartly dressed young woman, with pale blonde hair that brushed her shoulders, greeted them with a smile when Roger opened the tall oak doors.

Jeagan looked around at the warm, rich tones of pale gold, russet, and chocolate brown in the reception area, wondering if it had been professionally decorated.

"Good morning, Ms. Lloyd. Mr. Edwards is expecting you," the young woman said. "If you'd like to have a seat, I'll tell him you're here."

"Thank you, Missy. I'd like you to meet my son, Alex Nelson," Isabel said proudly. She turned to look up at Jeagan and Roger and introduced them. "And, she continued, this is Missy Scruggs. She's been Mark's secretary for a number of years."

Everyone said hello.

Isabel powered her chair over to the sofa, where Alex sat down. Jeagan watched Isabel reach over and squeeze her son's hand.

Within minutes, Mark Edwards came along the carpeted hallway with the receptionist. The smile on his face faded and he stopped when he saw the four people in the reception area. "Oh, I didn't expect anyone to be with you."

"Good morning, Mark." Isabel said. "I wanted Jeagan and Roger to witness my new will, considering they're responsible for making it possible."

"Yes, okay," Mark readjusted his glasses on his nose. He turned to Missy. "Would you take them into the conference room? I'll be along in a minute."

"Of course. Missy looked over at Isabel. "If y'all will come this way."

The four followed the receptionist along the hallway to the left where they were ushered into a carpeted conference room with a polished mahogany table surrounded by brown leather chairs.

"Can I get y'all something to drink?" Missy asked. She took orders and served coffee around the table while they waited for Mark to return.

"I wonder what's keeping him?" Isabel commented after five minutes. She looked at her watch. "Our lunch reservations are for eleven-thirty."

Jeagan noticed movement behind her. She turned expecting to see Mr. Edwards. Instead, she saw someone walking through the reception area toward the front doors. It was a young woman with curly red hair!

Chapter Thirty-one

No, Jeagan thought, *it's not possible she's the same woman. Don't let your imagination run away with you.*

"Sorry about that." Mark entered the room moments later followed by Missy. He appeared less tense now. "This shouldn't take long unless you have more changes you want to make to your will."

"No," Isabel replied. "It's perfect the way it is."

When the will was signed, witnessed, and notarized by the receptionist. Jeagan felt a wave of relief. Her name was completely off the new will.

"We're going up to the Crescent Club for lunch, Mark. We'd love for you to join us." Isabel tucked a copy of the new will into her handbag.

"Thank you, but I've got another appointment in a few minutes." He checked his watch. "I'll talk to you next week, to make sure you don't need anything else." He escorted Isabel to the reception area. After he gave her a brief hug, he shook hands all around and turned again to Isabel. "Call me if you need anything."

"I will, and thank you, Mark."

Mark nodded and strode along the hallway to his office.

"I'd like to visit your ladies' room before we go, if you don't mind," Jeagan said to Missy.

"Of course. It's down the hall on your right."

Jeagan looked toward Isabel. "I'll meet you in the restaurant."

"That's fine, dear. Just take the elevator to the top floor. We'll see you there in a few minutes."

Jeagan walked along the hall to the restroom. She went inside and stared at herself in the mirror. The more she thought about it, the more she realized the red-headed woman she'd seen was indeed the same person she'd seen many times over the last week. But, how could she find out for sure? She opened the door a crack and looked out, but quickly closed it again. Mark was coming toward her, briefcase in hand, and hurrying toward the reception area. She waited until he was past before she opened the door and listened.

"See you on Monday." Mark said to the receptionist.

"Have a good weekend, Mr. Edwards."

Jeagan heard the sound of the front door closing. She slipped out of the restroom and walked toward what she thought was Mark's office. Silently she opened the door. Inside she saw a polished mahogany desk and bookcases set into the wall. Degrees and certifications and honorary awards covered the paneled walls along with oil landscapes. Jeagan saw what looked like family photos set on the bookcases. She moved over to look at them. Maybe, just maybe. She studied the pictures. It looked like Mark had five children and several grandchildren, but none of them were red-headed. Frustrated, Jeagan turned to leave.

But, she stopped in mid-stride when she spotted an eight-by-ten photo of what looked like a graduating class. It was. Princeton. Beneath it was a framed picture of a thirtieth class reunion, according to the imprint on the bottom of the picture. The date was August 1992. She quickly picked out Mark, but her eyes darted back to another face in the picture. He looked familiar. It couldn't be, but she was almost positive it was. Bob McFarland, Sam's father! Now that was curious.

"Can I help you?" someone said behind Jeagan.

Startled, Jeagan jumped. She grabbed her chest and turned around. "Oh! You scared me."

"Sorry. I didn't mean to. I was getting ready to lock up and realized you were still here. Did you need something?"

"No. I'm just looking around. These offices are beautiful and the view is spectacular." She turned to the windows behind her.

Missy walked over to stand beside Jeagan. "The view *is* wonderful. Very calming when things get busy and tense in the office."

Jeagan started walking toward the door and making polite conversation. "Do things get tense around here often?"

"Sometimes." Missy closed and locked Mark's office door. "The last few weeks have been a little tough. Mr. Edwards has been on edge, which is unusual for him."

"Any particular reason?" Jeagan followed Missy to the front of the office and waited while she retrieved her handbag. They walked out into the hallway.

Missy closed and locked the front door. "None that I know of, except he's been worried about Ms. Lloyd."

"We all have been." They were now at the elevators. This was Jeagan's chance to ask one more question before Missy was gone. "I saw someone in the office earlier. She looked familiar, had red hair. Do you know who she is?"

"Sure." Missy pushed the down button. "She's Trisha Jorgensen."

Jeagan pushed the up button. "Is she a client of Mr. Edwards?"

"No, she's—"

The elevator dinged and the doors opened. Mark Edwards stepped out. "Oh, excuse me." He nearly ran into Jeagan. "I forgot something in my office."

"Do you need me to do anything before I go?" Missy asked.

"No, thanks Missy. I need to grab something. You go on."

"Okay. See you on Monday." Missy stepped on the elevator and pressed the lobby button. "Bye. It was nice meeting you." The doors closed behind her at the same time another ding sounded for the up elevator.

"Well, good-bye again." Mark started along the hall.

Not hesitating, Jeagan decided to grab her chance. "Who's Trisha Jorgensen, Mr. Edwards? Does she work for you?"

Mark stopped in his tracks, waiting a second too long before he turned around. "Who?"

"The red-headed woman who was in your office earlier today."

Red splotches appeared on Mark's face. "I don't think I know who you're talking about. I don't remember anyone like that in the office this morning."

"You must've seen her," Jeagan said. "I saw her coming down the hall from your office."

Mark's eyes narrowed. "I'm sorry, but I saw no such person. Now, if you'll excuse me, I have to get something from my office." He turned and headed up the hall.

An elevator dinged again. Jeagan looked at the arrow. It pointed down. Good! Two people stepped out. She hopped on after they were out and jammed the lobby button. Maybe she could catch Missy. Fortunately, the elevator didn't stop again until the lobby. Jeagan bolted when the doors opened and ran toward the entrance and out the door. She quickly scanned the parking area. *Yes!* Missy was sitting in her car applying lipstick. Jeagan raced over to the car and reached it as Missy started to back out.

"Wait!"

Missy put on the brakes and looked out the open window, alarmed. "What's wrong?"

"Nothing, but I need to ask you again about Trisha Jorgensen. Who is she?"

"She works for Mr. Edwards. She's an investigator."

Jeagan felt her heart stop in mid-beat. She patted the girl on the shoulder. "Thanks, Missy." She ran back toward the building and into the lobby. An elevator dinged. Mark might be on the elevator.

Where could she hide? Frantically, she looked around the deserted lobby and spotted the ladies' room. She dashed toward it and jumped inside as the elevator doors opened. Out of breath, her heart racing, she leaned against the wall for a second before she peeked out the door. Sure enough, Mark Edwards was leaving the building. Jeagan opened the door and watched Mark, talking on his cellphone, walk toward his car. He pressed a key fob and opened the door to a silver Mercedes. Fortunately, Missy's white Corolla was at that moment turning right onto Poplar Avenue.

* * *

Jeagan emerged a few minutes later from an elevator into the quiet, elegant Crescent Club. Soothing music, exquisite floral arrangements on polished tables, soft lighting, and a smiling hostess greeted her. After giving her name, the hostess escorted her to a round table set next to windows overlooking the city. Padded cornice boards covered in tapestry fabric with creamy swag curtains softened the windows. Cream-colored draperies were set at intervals along the wall of windows.

"There you are," Roger said when she reached the table. He stood and held out a chair for her.

"Are you all right?" Isabel asked.

"I'm fine." Jeagan felt flushed and winded. She picked up a glass of ice water from the table and drank half of it. "I saw the red-headed woman in your attorney's office," she said while trying to catch her breath.

"You're kidding!" Roger said, his eyes wide. "You sure she's the same red-headed gal you've been seeing all over the country."

"I'm sure." Jeagan finished off the water in her glass. A waiter appeared to refill it. "And, I talked to Missy. The woman's name is Trisha Jorgensen. She works for Mark Edwards!"

"Curiouser and curiouser," Roger commented. "Why would Edwards have someone follow us and warn us off?"

Jeagan shrugged. "You think that's curious? I went in his office after he left, thinking maybe the red-headed woman was a daughter or something and that I might see a picture of her. I didn't, but I did see a class reunion picture from his Princeton Law class."

"And?" Roger made circling motions with his hand.

"Mark Edwards went to law school with Sam's father," she announced.

Jeagan watched the wheels turn in Roger's mind. She let him think while Alex explained to Isabel who Sam was. At that point, a waitress appeared to take their orders.

"But, why," Isabel asked when the waitress was gone, "would Mark have someone follow you around?"

"And send blood-red roses with threatening messages," Jeagan added.

A puzzled look on her face, Isabel said, "That makes no sense."

"No, it doesn't make sense, unless—" Roger added.

Jeagan finished his sentence. "Unless Mark had a real reason for not wanting us to find Alex."

Isabel sipped iced tea and set the glass on the white linen tablecloth. "What reason could he possibly have?"

"I don't know." Jeagan shrugged. "But, I think we need to find out. And, I'd like to find out if he's been in contact with Bob McFarland lately." She thought back to when Sam had introduced her to his father at Patrice's fundraiser. The unfriendly look in Bob's eyes and the way he'd crushed her hand when he shook it. He disliked her intensely, for what reason she didn't know.

And, another unhappy thought occurred to her, had Sam really been trying to help her or was he only keeping an eye on her for his father? *No,* she thought. *Surely not.* But she couldn't shake the tiny doubt in the back of her mind.

A waitress approached the table with bowls of lobster bisque and served them to everyone. Jeagan thanked the waitress and sipped a spoonful. "Umm. This is heavenly."

"The food here's excellent," Isabel commented.

"It *is* good," Roger agreed. "So, now what?" He looked at Jeagan.

"I for one don't care what Mark's doing." Isabel reached over to pat Alex's hand.

"You don't care that your attorney may have had someone follow Jeagan and try to keep her from finding Alex?" Roger asked.

Isabel stopped with her spoon in midair. "I can't believe Mark would do something like that."

"Hard to believe or not, it looks like he did," Jeagan said, "and I'd like to find out why."

"So would I." Roger echoed.

"Well, let's enjoy our lunch," Isabel said. "I'm so happy. I don't want to think about anything unpleasant right now."

"I'm sorry," Jeagan said, understanding. "We can talk about it after lunch." She finished her cup of soup. "I'd love to have the recipe for this. My dad would really like this."

Isabel eyes twinkled. "I'm friends with the chef. I'll get it for you."

The club manager came over to the table when the soup was cleared. "Good afternoon, Ms. Lloyd. It's nice to see you again."

Isabel turned to talk to the friendly manager. She introduced everyone to him. When she came to Alex, she started telling the man about her long-lost son who had returned home.

Jeagan took the opportunity to speak to Roger. "We need to change our reservations."

Roger agreed. "I'll go out to the lobby and call the airline." He slipped from the table while Isabel was occupied, still talking animatedly with the manager.

Alex observed him leaving and gave Jeagan a questioning look. She put her finger to her lips and shook her head. Alex nodded understanding.

Isabel turned back in her seat when the manager walked off to greet other club members. "Where's Roger?"

"Isabel, how nice to see you!" a smartly dressed silver-haired woman approached the table. "I heard you were in the hospital."

Again, Isabel turned to talk to a friend and introduced the other people seated at the table. When she looked at Roger's empty chair, she said he had most likely gone to the men's room. Before she finished her conversation, Roger returned.

He gave a quick nod to Jeagan. "All set."

"And the hotel?"

"Yes."

After lunch, when they were all on the elevator going to the lobby, Isabel asked, "What time does your flight leave?"

"Oh." Jeagan looked at Roger, "Didn't we tell you? We've decided we're going to stay another day, so we need to get our bags." *And, I need to call my dad,* she thought.

"I see," Isabel said, a suspicious look in her eyes. "I'm glad you're staying, but if it's because of something you think Mark has done, I'm sure you're mistaken."

"Look, Isabel. I think we owe it to ourselves, and to you, to find out why your attorney had that woman follow me. And, she might have been responsible for breaking into my hotel room and Roger's friend's home in Seattle. Maybe even your house."

The elevator stopped and they got off in the lobby.

"You might be right, and I guess you have to do what you think is best." Isabel's happy look reappeared. "Since you're not leaving today, why don't you come out for dinner tonight? I'm having several friends over to meet Alex. Mark will be there. Maybe you can talk to him and resolve this misunderstanding."

Jeagan and Roger looked at each other. "Sounds like a good idea," Jeagan said. Roger nodded agreement.

"Wonderful! Be there at seven." Isabel looked outside. "I called Austin. He should be here any minute. Oh, there he is."

Alex pushed the outside door open for her. When they reached the limousine, Isabel said, "Why don't we take you to the hotel so you can drop your bags?"

"Thanks," Jeagan replied, "but we thought we'd roam around this area for a while. Looks like there are some interesting shops across the street on Shady Grove."

"Mom will be dropping me at The Peabody. I'll take your bags," Alex offered.

"Thanks," Roger said. "We were able to keep our same rooms. If you don't mind, have the bellman take them up for us."

Jeagan hugged Isabel and told her she would see her that evening. She and Roger watched the limo drive out of the parking lot.

"Now." Roger looked at Jeagan. "Are you ready for a little B&E?"

"Why not? Turn about's fair play."

On the elevator ride to the seventh floor, Jeagan phoned her Dad to tell him she was staying in Memphis for another day or so.

"Well, at least you appear to be safe in Memphis, this time." He chuckled. "So, how was the reunion of Isabel and her son?"

"It was a wonderful, emotional reunion. Isabel's on cloud nine. She looks *so* happy. In fact, she's having a dinner party tonight to introduce Alex to her friends."

"Didn't she just get out of the hospital?"

Jeagan laughed. "Yes, she did, but I don't think reminding her of that would do any good. She wants to show Alex off to all her friends."

"Well, that's good news, honey. I'm very proud of you...and your mother would be, too."

Jeagan felt tears sting her eyes. "Thanks, Dad. I love you."

"Love you, too, little girl. Call me and let me know your plans."

Roger ended his call to Shelley about the same time Jeagan ended her call to her dad.

"Is the— What did you call her? A vampiress? Is she okay with your not coming home today?" Jeagan asked.

"Ow! Your claws are showing." Roger grinned. "She's fine. Actually, she's doing some investigating, for me. Well, for *us* really."

"Really?" Jeagan commented more than asked when they got off the elevator.

"She's following up with the police on the truck that hit us."

"Oh," Jeagan said, somewhat deflated. Now, she couldn't really rib him about Shelley. "Well, that's good thinking on your part. Have they found out anything about the truck or driver?"

Roger scanned the hall to make sure it was empty when they reached the law office. He reached into his pocket and pulled out a small black case. "It was her idea, not mine. And no, the police don't have a clue who hit us. Or, if they do, they're not sharing their information." Within seconds, the door was unlocked and they were inside.

"I know we're breaking the law," Jeagan said in a subdued voice, "but I don't feel in the least guilty about what we're doing after Mark sent his investigator after me. Do you think she's the person who drove that truck into your car?"

"No. I think we're dealing with at least two people here." Roger looked around the area. "Where's Edwards's office?"

"It's this way," Jeagan pointed and started along the hallway to the right. "So, the hit-and-run could have been just that?"

"Maybe," Roger said, his voice lowered, "or it could have been your ex-fiancé."

"I still find that hard to believe," Jeagan said.

Roger tried the door to Mark Edwards's office. He frowned and pulled out his small black case again. When they were inside, he said, "You start on the desk. I'll look through the credenza."

"Okay." Jeagan heard Roger picking the lock on the credenza while she moved across to the desk. She pulled out the file drawer and flipped through the hanging folders quickly. Looked like clients, mostly estates and corporations. The smaller drawers didn't have anything useful in them.

"I've got something." Roger pulled a folder from the bottom drawer.

"I'll take that if you don't mind," a low, menacing voice said from the doorway.

Chapter Thirty-two

Startled, Jeagan and Roger whirled around to see Mark Edwards standing in the doorway pointing a black handgun at them. The benign mask of the attorney was gone. Edwards walked toward Roger and stretched out his hand. "Like I said, I'll take that!"

Roger, recovering from his first shock, laid the folder on the desk. "That's very interesting reading, Edwards."

"I'm glad you think so," the attorney said mockingly. "You've made this awfully easy for me. Two intruders in my office. Shoot you in self-defense. No questions asked."

"But, as you can see, I don't have a gun." Roger held out his hands.

"You do now." Edwards pulled another handgun from his briefcase. "After I take care of you two, I'll see what can be done about Isabel and her newly found son."

Jeagan choked. "Are you crazy?"

"He is." Roger moved toward Jeagan to stand in front of her. "Agnes Harraway is still trying to get her hands on their father's estate, isn't she?"

Eyes widening in fear, Jeagan said, "She's still trying to kill her sister, while she's out on bail?"

"Yes," Edwards confirmed. "No witnesses. No charge. No heir."

"The money goes to the next of kin," Roger finished the thought. "And, no doubt, a hefty chunk for you."

"So, now you have to get rid of us?" Jeagan ventured.

Edwards let out an exasperated breath, as if tired of explaining the obvious.

"You hired Eden to kill us while we were in Seattle, didn't you?" Jeagan asked.

Edwards offered no comment.

"And Denver, I'll bet," Roger added.

Edwards looked at Roger's cast. "If he'd done what he was supposed to do in Denver, we wouldn't be having this conversation."

Jeagan shivered remembering the accident. She had to keep Edwards talking. "But, how did you know Anthony Eden?" Then, she remembered the class reunion picture. "Bob McFarland."

Edwards's eyes lit with a dark intensity. "Congratulations, Miss Christensen. You're right. I met Eden when I visited Bob a few years ago."

"So, what happened to Eden? Did you kill him?" Roger asked.

"No. But, I would have been happy to if someone else hadn't saved me the trouble. Enough talk. Let's go." Mark motioned his gun toward the door.

They needed to stall as long as possible. She held onto Roger. *Think of something*, her mind cried. "Did you hire Eden to kill Sue Coleman?"

Edwards shrugged.

"How could she possibly know anything that could hurt you?" Jeagan asked. Suddenly, the pieces started to fall into place. "You not only wanted us out of the way so you could get your hands on a share of Isabel's money—"

"He's Christopher Mark Greer's son," someone said from the doorway.

Chapter Thirty-three

Edwards jerked around to see who had come into the room.

Roger lunged forward, landed a blow to Edwards's arm, which sent the handguns flying across the room. The second blow caught Edwards's jaw. He stumbled and fell sideways, struck his head on the corner of the desk, and crumpled in a heap on the carpet.

"Is he dead?" Jeagan asked, moving across the room.

Roger knelt beside Edwards and felt for a pulse in his neck. "No. He's alive." He stood and grabbed the phone to dial 9-1-1.

Jeagan turned toward the person who stood in the doorway. It was Madison. Wanting to run and hug his neck, she restrained herself. "What're you doing here?"

"Looking out for you." He walked into the office.

"Never thought I'd be glad to see you," Roger said with a wry smile. He crossed the room and picked up the handguns.

"But, why would you be watching out for me?" Although neatly dressed, she could tell he had lost weight, and he looked much older.

"Agnes told me what was going on with Mark. She still wanted to get rid of Isabel before you found her son, and Mark was helping her. But, they couldn't devise a way with Isabel in the hospital and all her friends visiting. So, Agnes decided she'd have to wait until Isabel was released, but by that time, you were back in Memphis with Alex."

"So, the plan changed," Roger said.

"Yes," Madison looked down at Edwards. "Agnes knew she also needed to get rid of you two. That way she could have the money and not go to prison because all the witnesses to the attempted murder would be gone."

"Does she think the police are stupid?" Jeagan asked. "They'd figure that out in an instant."

244

"They might figure it out, but if the plan was carried out the way Agnes intended, nothing could be proved against them, and supposition doesn't carry much weight in a court of law."

"But what about Edwards?" Roger asked. "Why was he involved in all this?"

"His family name was at stake," Jeagan answered. "His father was the Memphis attorney who arranged the adoption of Isabel's child." She looked to Madison for confirmation.

"Yes. Greedy though he was…is," Madison glanced down to see Edwards stirring, "Mark didn't want to be tied to the name of Greer in the event anyone ever found out his father bought and sold stolen babies. That would ruin his law practice."

"So, he kept the name Mark, I assume after his father?" Madison nodded. "But where did the name Edwards come from?"

"I think he took his mother's maiden name when he turned twenty-one. At least that's what I've been told."

"Is Bob McFarland involved in any of this?" Jeagan asked, hoping he wasn't and Sam wasn't.

Madison shrugged. "Not as far as I know. The only thing I ever heard Agnes say about him was that he didn't want his son helping you destroy their family's name."

Relieved, Jeagan let out her breath. "So, who removed the files from Patrice McFarland's basement?"

"Edwards and McFarland had Tony Eden remove and destroy the files."

"Was Patrice McFarland involved in any of this?" Jeagan asked.

"Only in agreeing to allow the files to be destroyed, as far as I know," Madison said.

"There are still more files in here." Roger pulled another file out of the bottom drawer and opened it.

Sirens sounded in the distance.

Jeagan picked up the file Roger had dropped on Edwards's desk. Inside on top was the faded letter addressed to Isabel's father from John McFarland. "Edwards stole this letter about Alan's adoption from Isabel."

"Either he did or Trisha Jorgensen did," Madison said.

Roger shuffled through the papers in the file he held. "There are a lot of letters here about other children to be adopted."

"Why would he keep these files?" Jeagan looked over at Roger. "If he wanted to protect his family's name, you'd think he would've destroyed these files years ago."

Roger shrugged. "Who knows? Maybe he forgot about them or felt safe with his name changed."

"Or, he might have tried his hand at a little blackmail?"

"Could be." Roger stuffed the file into the drawer. "The police will have a field day with all these files."

"The information in those files could cause a lot of heartache," Madison commented.

"Yes," Jeagan agreed, "but it could also answer a lot of questions for a lot of people."

"Well, we don't have to make that decision," Roger commented. "We'll leave these for the police and FBI to deal with."

The front door of the office suite burst open. Voices sounded in the reception area.

Jeagan looked at Madison. "How did you know all this?"

"Agnes has been talking to me and trying to persuade me to help save her...and me."

"But, you didn't." Jeagan watched his sad eyes.

"No." He shrugged. "After what I did to you, I had no intention of hurting anyone else."

Three police officers stormed into the office. The next hour was spent explaining what had happened.

* * *

When Jeagan and Roger arrived at The Peabody later, they stopped in the lobby bar for a drink. She sank onto a cushy sofa after they placed their drink orders. She wanted to kick off her shoes and prop her feet on the coffee table, but she restrained herself.

"I'm ready to go home," she said, tired to the bone.

"Me too," Roger agreed, settling in an overstuffed chair. "I'll call and get our reservations set for tomorrow mid-morning."

"Sounds great to me. I'd like to skip dinner at Isabel's tonight and go downstairs for a massage."

Roger checked the time. "It's only three-thirty. You've got plenty of time. We really need to go to Isabel's tonight, so we can be the ones to tell her what happened today."

"Okay. I know you're right. I'm just beat and ready to get home to Colorado."

The waitress brought their drinks. Another refreshing mint julep for Jeagan. She was beginning to acquire a taste for them. And, a scotch and water for Roger.

She sipped her drink. Finally, it was truly over. Nobody would be stalking her. The police were on their way to arrest Trisha Jorgensen and Agnes Harraway, again, and Madison had accompanied them to the police station to tell the police what he knew. Hopefully, the information he provided would help with his sentencing. If it were Jeagan's decision to make, he would be placed on probation and released. If his case went to trial, she would do everything in her power to make that happen.

Roger's phone rang. He pulled it out of his pocket and answered it. "It's Shelley."

Jeagan smirked. "Bye-bye, y'all." She grabbed her handbag and drink and started toward the elevator. Mentally, she reviewed what she had to wear tonight. Nothing appropriate, she decided. She ought to make one more trip to the ladies' store. So, she did.

* * *

At six-forty-five, Roger knocked on Jeagan's door. "You look great!" he said when she opened the door.

"Thanks. The massage sure helped to relieve some of the knots in my shoulders."

"That outfit looks good, too."

"Thank you, again," Jeagan said smiling. She walked into the bathroom to get her handbag. She checked her makeup and hair, liking her reflection in the vanity mirror. The pink silk top and pants made her lightly tanned skin glow. She felt she looked almost as good as she had when she'd dressed for the party at Patrice's. But, that was a lifetime ago, she realized, and she didn't have the same sparkle she'd had that night. What had caused the sparkle then? The investigation or being with Sam?

"Ready," she said when she walked back into the room.

She hooked the Do Not Disturb sign to the outside of her door before she closed it and walked to the elevator with Roger.

"Our flight reservations are for eleven in the morning," he said.

"Hope we finally make it." She pulled out her cellphone and punched in the number for her dad. "Hi, Dad," she said when he answered. "I'm coming home tomorrow."

"Famous last words," Geoff Christensen said.

Jeagan laughed. "This time it's for real. And, you don't need to meet me at the airport. Roger will be with me." She didn't tell her dad Shelley was meeting Roger. He probably would have insisted on meeting her to follow her home, and she didn't want him to do that.

"Okay, come out for dinner tomorrow night."

"I'll be there."

Within minutes, they crossed the lobby to the hotel entrance. While they waited for a taxi, Jeagan watched a white horse-drawn carriage pass the hotel carrying a young couple who were smiling and talking. *When will it be my turn to feel love?*

Roger held the door for her when the taxi stopped at the curb. He gave the address to the driver. Fifteen minutes afterward, the driver turned up Isabel's driveway. Several cars were already there and parked around the crescent of the driveway. Cadillacs, a Lincoln, BMWs, and a Mercedes. Isabel had wealthy friends.

Minnie answered the door after they rang the bell. "Good evening." She ushered them into the living room, where guests stood around with wine glasses in their hands, the men wearing dark suits while the women wore floral dresses or light spring colors.

"Hello, you two." Isabel powered her chair toward them with Alex walking beside her.

Jeagan and Roger both reached down and hugged her.

"When did you get here?" Roger asked Alex. "I called your room to see if you wanted to ride over with us."

"I came a little early to help out."

"We need to talk," Roger said to Alex and pulled him across the hall to the music room.

Isabel looked up at Jeagan. "What's going on?"

"I'll tell you later," Jeagan said quietly.

"Well, come on," Isabel said. "I'd like you to meet some of my friends."

Jeagan smiled and followed Isabel into the living room. She looked around at the guests, and then her eyes stopped.

"Who's that woman in the champagne-colored outfit?" she whispered to Isabel.

"She's the mother of a young friend of mine from the church. She's visiting from Colorado, I believe."

Jeagan's face eased into a smile. "Candice Franklin. She's the woman I met on the plane when I came to Memphis to look for you."

"What a coincidence," Isabel commented.

Synchronicity, Jeagan thought. They 'worked the room.' When they came to Candice and her daughter, along with her husband, Jeagan said, "Hi, Candice. Do you remember me?

Candice frowned for a moment trying to remember. Then, recognition registered in her eyes. "Oh, you're the girl I met on the plane."

Jeagan grinned. "That's me."

"Did you finish your research?"

"I'm sorry?"

"You said you were coming to Memphis to do some research," Candice reminded her.

"Oh...yes." Jeagan looked at Isabel. "This lady is my research. I came to Memphis to find Isabel."

"And give me a new life," Isabel added.

A question registered in Candice's eyes, but she didn't ask what Isabel meant. Instead, she introduced her daughter and son-in-law.

After the introductions, Jeagan asked Candice when she was returning to Denver.

"The day after tomorrow," Candice said. "Although I hate to go, I've got clients waiting for me."

"I need to talk to you before you leave tonight," Jeagan whispered before she completed the circuit of the room with Isabel.

* * *

After dinner, Candice approached Jeagan, who was talking to Alex. "You wanted to talk to me?"

"I sure do." Jeagan took her arm. "Let's go outside. Have you seen Isabel's garden?"

The ladies walked out onto the patio and down the tiled steps. "It's beautiful!" Candice commented.

"It is," Jeagan agreed. They crossed the lawn to the lighted garden path where they strolled along admiring the fragrant flowers. When they came to one of the stone benches, Jeagan said. "Let's sit down for a minute."

"Okay. So, what did you want to talk to me about?"

"Well," Jeagan started, feeling tongue-tied and embarrassed, "I'm not good at this, but what I wanted to ask you is, would you be interested in meeting my dad?"

Candice's eyes widened. "Your dad? You want to fix me up, I think that's the right term, with your dad?"

"Yes," Jeagan said with a nervous smile. "My mom died two years ago, and I think it's time he started dating again. I believe you told me your husband passed away a few years ago also."

"Three years," Candice said, a slight sadness in her voice. "I haven't even thought of dating again. I've stayed busy with my real estate, and I do play some golf."

"Golf?" Jeagan said enthusiastically. "That's perfect! I know you two would hit it off. Dad's a banker but plays golf every chance he gets."

"Well." Candice hesitated. "I don't know."

"Will you have lunch with us one day and just meet him?"

Candice laughed, a light musical sound. "Okay. Yes, I'd like that."

"Wonderful! With all the great restaurants in Denver, I'm sure we can find a place that's convenient for both of you."

Candice reached over and placed her arm around Jeagan's shoulders. She squeezed lightly. "If he's half as special as his daughter, I'm sure I'll like him."

* * *

Isabel, Alex, Jeagan, and Roger settled in the living room with cups of coffee after the other guests were gone. "Will you tell me now what's going on?" Isabel asked.

Roger explained what had happened in Mark Edwards's office earlier in the day.

Isabel gasped and her hand flew to her mouth. "I can't believe Mark would betray me like that! How could he have kept it from me all these years that his father helped to take my son away from me?"

"I wish we could answer that question." Jeagan watched as Alex reached over to hold his mother's hand.

"All that's over now," Alex said. "Don't let what your attorney or your dad did ruin any more of your life. I want you to come to Seattle as soon as you're a little stronger to spend some time with Gaylann and the rest of your family."

Her eyes misty, Isabel smiled. "You're right. I have a whole new life now, and family." She reached into her pocket and pulled out a handkerchief. "I can't wait to meet them."

Roger's cellphone rang, startling everyone. He answered it and listened for a moment. "Okay. We'll be right there." He disconnected and looked at Jeagan. "They want us to come to the police station."

"Why?" Jeagan asked.

"They've got Trisha Jorgensen in custody."

Chapter Thirty-four

After good-bye hugs and promises to keep in touch, Jeagan and Roger took a taxi to the Memphis Police Department, Union Avenue location—the same one where she had reported Roger for stalking her! She wondered if Lieutenant Freshour would be on duty tonight. When she'd finally convinced him that she wasn't a nut case two weeks earlier, he had helped Roger save her life.

Fifteen minutes later, when Jeagan and Roger entered the reception area and explained who they were, the desk sergeant called Detective Lynette Mulert.

The detective appeared within a few minutes. At six feet tall, Jeagan had to look up at her. She was what her dad would call a 'long drink of water.' Who did she remind Jeagan of? Ah! Susan Anton: Fortyish, tall, blonde, and gorgeous.

"I'm Detective Mulert." She extended her hand. "Sorry to ask y'all to come down here so late, but I understand you're returning to Denver tomorrow. So, if we could get you to sign your statements and give us your contact information, you'll be through here for now."

Jeagan and Roger followed the detective to a small interview room with windows all around. They sat at a rectangular table that had seen better days. "There's coffee over there, if you'd like some."

"Thanks, but I think we're coffee'd out," Jeagan said.

Detective Mulert gave a dry laugh. "Probably a good thing. Excuse me a minute."

Jeagan got up and idly looked out into the hall. Across from them and to their right, she saw a similar room. In it was a red-headed woman sitting at a table facing a uniformed officer. Jeagan recognized the woman immediately. Trisha Jorgensen!

Sensing someone looking at her, the woman looked up and locked eyes with Jeagan. Several emotions crossed the woman's face simultaneously: shock, malevolence, and a look that read, "I'll get you for this."

The officer in the room with Jorgensen followed her eyes. He spotted Jeagan across the hall, after which he got up and closed the blinds.

Detective Mulert re-entered the room.

"That's Trisha Jorgensen," Jeagan said, as much a question as a statement.

"Yes," the Detective confirmed.

"By the look she gave me, I think she'd like to kill me."

"It's not your fault. It's because of me." Madison entered the room behind the detective.

"Madison! You're still here?"

"He's helping us with our investigation." The detective pulled out a chair and sat down. She opened a folder, paged through the contents until she found what she wanted, and slid two statements across the table. "If you'll both just look these over and sign them if they're okay."

Jeagan still stared at Madison, once again surprised to see him. "You were in The Peabody the other night, weren't you?"

A look of surprise crossed Madison's face. "I was."

"Were you looking for me?"

He shook his head. "Not really. I knew you were there, but I was following Trisha to make sure she didn't try to," he looked away, "to do anything stupid."

"You mean like you did?" Jeagan couldn't hide the bitterness in her voice.

"Yes," Madison admitted.

"Did Edwards send her after me?" She looked at Roger. "I mean, us?"

"Either him or Agnes. Plus, she had a more personal reason for wanting to get rid of you."

"What personal reason could she possibly have?" Jeagan pulled out a chair and sat down.

Madison sat also. "We were sort of dating before you came to Memphis a few weeks ago. When I met you and we became friends, I stopped seeing her."

"She was jealous of you." Roger looked at Jeagan.

"Jealous of me?" Jeagan was dumbfounded.

Madison didn't say anything.

"If you'll please look over your statements and sign them," Detective Mulert said.

Jeagan reached for the statement and pulled it toward her. Madison, she realized, had had feelings for her, more than just friendship, before he betrayed her.

"So, Jeagan here upset Jorgensen's plans to snag an up-and-coming Memphis attorney. I'm sure she had visions of a fancy house somewhere near Shady Grove with all the trimmings," Detective Mulert explained.

Jeagan looked at Madison.

"I'm sorry for what I did to you," he said.

"I'm sorry too," Jeagan replied. "All I wanted was—"

Madison held up his hand. "I know. All you wanted was friendship. I couldn't even manage to get that right, so how could I expect anything else."

The door opened and a petite, blonde uniformed officer walked into the room. "Excuse me, Detective, but you told me to let you know when we had Jorgensen's statement." She walked over to hand the document to Detective Mulert.

"Thank you, Melody." Mulert took the document from the officer. "If you'll go ahead and look over your statements and sign them, we'll call it a night."

Jeagan and Roger did as they were instructed while the detective scanned the statement she'd been given. She whistled. "That gal's got a colorful vocabulary."

Jeagan signed her statement and slid it across the table. "Did she admit to following me and sending the roses?"

The detective nodded. "Sure did. Says here she sent you flowers in Denver to try to stop you from looking for Alex Nelson after Tony Eden crashed into a Range Rover." She looked at Roger. "Yours?"

Roger nodded.

"Nice. Wish I could afford one."

"I'll sell you a used one, cheap," Roger said with wry grin.

"Uh. No thanks." The detective continued. "Then when y'all didn't take the hint, Jorgensen followed you to Seattle," she said glancing at Jeagan. Jeagan nodded.

"Looks like Jorgensen tried again with the flowers in Seattle." The detective read further. "She blames everything on Agnes Harraway and Mark Edwards. Says they planned the whole thing. Oh, and Tony Eden. Eden got her to search your room in Seattle."

Jeagan looked over at Madison. "Speaking of Eden. How did she get hooked up with him?"

"Through Mark Edwards," Madison replied. "Mark sent her to Denver to work with Eden. When their threats didn't work there, they followed you to Seattle."

A sudden chill shook Jeagan. "Was she with him when he kidnapped Alex and me? Was she the one driving the car?"

Madison shrugged. "I don't know. Nobody mentioned that to me."

"Says here Eden planned the kidnapping, and she was in Seattle about that time, breaking into a Will Thompson's house." Mulert looked up from the document. "Who's Thompson?"

"A friend of mine in Seattle," Roger replied. He also slid his signed statement across the table to the detective. "Will had a copy of the first letter about the stolen baby."

"So, who drove the car when Eden kidnapped us?" Jeagan asked. "I'd sure like to find out."

"We may never know now that Eden's gone," Roger said.

"But," Jeagan said remembering, "Alex saw the guy. Well, not his face, but he saw him when he regained consciousness while Eden and whoever were taping my wrists and ankles." She again felt the terror of awakening in a dark warehouse with her hands and feet bound. "I'm going to call him and see if he can remember anything about the guy."

Roger checked his watch. "Why don't you wait until tomorrow?"

"It's not that late. He may still be at Isabel's." Jeagan looked at the detective. "Okay if I use the phone?"

"Sure." The detective pushed the phone across the table.

Jeagan picked up the receiver and then stopped. "I don't know his cellphone number."

"I have it." Roger pulled a small notebook from his pocket.

When she got the number from Roger, she dialed. Alex answered on the second ring. "Hey Alex. I didn't wake you, did I?" Jeagan listened for a moment. "Good. We're still at the police station, and I need to ask you something. You said you didn't get a look at the guy's face, the guy who helped Eden kidnap us, right?"

She listened for a minute. "Well, is there anything you can tell us about him? Anything at all?" Again, Jeagan listened. Then, a slow smile spread across her face. "You're sure?" After she hung up, Jeagan turned to Roger. "Alex said the man who helped Eden had a British accent."

"So?" Roger shrugged. "Lots of people in British Columbia have a British accent."

"But," Jeagan paused for emphasis, "how many people in British Columbia would make a comment like, 'They didn't train me in the fine art of duct taping at Oxford.' "

Blank stares all around, Jeagan continued. "Charles McFarland went to Oxford."

Chapter Thirty-five

"Our plane arrives at two-fifteen, Dad, but you don't need to meet me at the airport." Jeagan shifted in her vinyl seat in the Northwest Airlines gate area and listened to her dad's argument for meeting her at Stapleton International. "I'll make a deal with you. As soon as I go home and unpack, I'll be out there. Okay?"

Again Jeagan listened. She smiled. "Good. I'll fill you in on everything when I see you tonight." A moment later, she said, "I love you, too. See you around six."

Roger walked up and sat beside her. "I just talked to Will. He said the police brought Charles McFarland in for questioning this morning."

"That's good," Jeagan commented. "But, I'm sorry it was him. I kind of liked him, and I can't imagine why he would get involved with somebody like Tony Eden."

"The same old thing, protecting the family name and his business and reputation."

"But," Jeagan looked thoughtful, "we still don't know who killed Eden."

"But, we do," Roger said. "McFarland killed him. He says it was accidental. Something about extortion and blackmail and Eden pointing a gun at him. He says they struggled, and the gun went off."

"It was Eden's gun?" Jeagan asked.

"Yeah. I think Will said it was."

"That's good." Jeagan stood and shouldered her handbag when first class boarding was called. Somehow that might work in good ol' Chuck's favor if the gun belonged to Eden. Why she cared, she didn't know, after Chuck had helped Eden kidnap her and leave her for dead.

* * *

257

Monday morning, Jeagan pulled out her chair and sat at her desk. It felt good to be back at work: safe, dull technical writing. She focused on her in basket. It overflowed onto her desk and partially covered the picture of Brandon. She frowned and reached for the picture. With a *thunk*, it hit the wastebasket, frame and all. But, thinking better of discarding a perfectly good frame, she pulled it out again and removed the picture. "So long, Brandon." She ripped the picture in half and dropped it back into the can. That felt good.

She smiled remembering dinner last night with her dad. He'd finally settled down when she explained to him that everyone connected to the kidnappings and coverups was in custody. And, he'd reluctantly agreed to meet Candice for lunch. In the next day or so, she'd work on setting a date for their lunch.

Her thoughts drifted to Roger. Shelley, the vampiress, had indeed met him at the airport and had even graciously given Jeagan a ride to the economy lot to get her car. Roger, she had to admit, looked a little overwhelmed by Shelley's strong personality but didn't seem to be struggling to free himself from her. Well, good for him, if that's what he wanted. Maybe, working together, they could find the person who ran down her sister.

Jeagan felt a small stab of regret. Now, she was alone. She had broken her engagement to Brandon. No second thoughts there. Roger had met his match in Shelley. She hoped he knew what he was in for. Isabel was reunited with Alex. She touched the pendant Alex had given her and smiled. Her dad was going to meet Candice soon. And, Sam had returned to writing scripts and dealing with his agent.

The thought of Sam sent an unexpected jolt through her heart. She reached for her handbag under the desk. In it lay the box with the crystal seaplane. Carefully, she pulled the top off the white box and pealed away the tissue. The little plane sparkled in the fluorescent lighting. Without thinking, she kissed the piece of crystal and set it next to her computer. Then, her phone rang.

"This is Jeagan." After listening a moment, she said, "Okay. I'll be right there."

Hmmm, she thought while she strode toward the reception area. *Who's sending me flowers?* Then, she stopped in her tracks. Surely, the flowers wouldn't be blood-red roses! Not now! She reluctantly rounded the corner to the reception area. There they were. A dozen red roses!

Jeagan's breath caught in her throat. "Where did those come from?" she stammered after she crossed the lobby.

The receptionist gave her a blank look. "A guy from a florist just delivered them."

Jeagan searched for the card. She recognized the florist's name. Hands trembling, she pulled the card from the envelope and read it. "Wanted to again say how sorry I am for all I put you through. Madison."

Tears of relief filled Jeagan's eyes. She picked up the glass vase. "I'm sorry I yelled at you, Jen. It's just that the last time somebody sent me red roses, they were threatening me."

Plump with curly gray hair, Jen said in her motherly tone, "That's all right, sweetie. Keri told me all about what happened. I'm just glad you're back here safe and sound."

"Not for long, she's not." Jeagan whipped around. *Sam!* Speechless, she just stared at him. "You forgot this." Sam held up a bottle of wine and grinned like the Cheshire cat.

"What?" A smile eased across her face. "You came all the way to Colorado to bring me a bottle of wine?"

Sam stood there with his dark wavy hair and sky-blue eyes, wearing jeans and a white shirt with a pseudo-hurt look on his face. "Not just any bottle of wine. It's the bottle I bought for you on Bainbridge, which you carelessly left in your hotel room. You never even opened it," he said feigning hurt.

Sure enough, Sam held the Lake Country White he'd bought for her. She couldn't remember what she'd done with it after she'd taken it to her hotel room. Must have been misplaced and forgotten after all that had happened.

"Oh, there you are," Jeagan heard someone say behind her. She turned to see who was talking to her. It was Lorin Ottonello and Dave Caldwell, her bosses. "We've been looking for you," Lorin said. He looked from Jeagan to Sam, a question in his eyes. "Need you in the conference room in ten minutes. We're going over a schedule for this Department of Energy proposal that's due in two weeks.

"Ten minutes is all I need." Sam grabbed Jeagan's hand and pulled her along with him out the front entrance.

Jeagan laughed. "Where are you taking me?"

He led her across the parking lot and down wooden steps to a small lake with benches scattered around it. "Have a seat. I have something to say."

Jeagan, her heart thudding loudly in her chest, obeyed.

"I haven't been able to stop thinking about you since you left Seattle."

"But, I—" She interrupted.

Sam placed two fingers on her mouth. "Let me finish. I thought you and Roger had something going, and then—"

"But, we don't. Roger is—"

He held up his hand again. "I know. I talked to Roger this morning. He told me he thought something might develop between you two until he saw us together. Much as he didn't like what he saw, he said he could tell we…we were attracted to each other."

"But, I thought you—" Jeagan started again.

"You thought I didn't care and let you leave without saying anything?"

Jeagan nodded. "Yes."

He took her hands. "I didn't want to let you go, but I also didn't want to interfere if there was something between you and Roger." He grinned. "You're a magnet for trouble and can be really obstinate."

Jeagan matched his grin. "And, you're a cellphone addict. I swear, I'm surprised your cellphone hasn't grown to your ear. I thought some of those calls were probably to a…a girlfriend."

Sam pulled her into his arms. "No. Besides calls to my agent, some of those calls were from my dad. He tried to talk me into staying away from you, but I couldn't, even if you were stirring up a lot of trouble for the good ol' family name. So, how about we call a truce? You quit getting into trouble, and I'll spend less time on my cellphone."

A wave of relief and happiness washed over Jeagan. "I'll try if you will."

Sam kissed her cheek, her hair, and then her mouth. Jeagan felt a tingle all the way to her toes.

He held her away from him to look at her. "Will you come back to Seattle with me? You're my lucky weather girl. It was sunny almost the whole time you were there, and it's been raining constantly since you left."

"Maybe after I finish the DOE proposal, but Lorin's not going to like it if I ask for more time off." Jeagan brushed away tears of happiness that sparkled in her eyes.

"Who said anything about time off? I'm talking about coming back to Seattle with me—to stay." He looked at her tentatively. "I'd like to give *us* a try."

Jeagan threw her arms around Sam's neck. "Me too!"

Made in the USA
Charleston, SC
22 October 2010